In the year since Simon's death, Alinor had been too tired and worried to think of herself as a woman. Now, without warning, she became aware of her long starvation. The blood rushed from her face to her loins. She put a hand on the tub to steady herself, and she thanked God that Ian, naked and ready for the bath she had prepared, was staring past her into nothing.

Then, as she stepped back, the full impact of his dark beauty hit her. There was violence and passion lurking behind those hot brown eyes, and although Alinor had loved Simon and been content with him, she had never denied that Ian was a magnificent male animal who could be very attractive to her.

I am not only 'Simon's wife,' she thought. *I am Alinor.*

is the second book of a magnificent four-volume saga, THE ROSELYNDE CHRON-ICLES. A richly detailed and panoramic story set in medieval England, the novel continues the tempestuous adventures and romantic passions of its beautiful and vibrant heroine, *Alinor.*

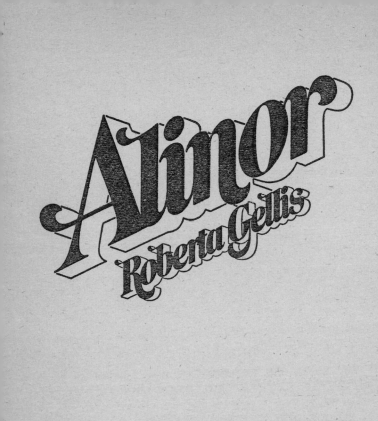

Alinor

Roberta Gellis

PLAYBOY PRESS
PAPERBACKS

ALINOR

PRODUCED BY LYLE KENYON ENGEL.

Copyright © 1978 by Roberta Gellis and Lyle Kenyon Engel.

Cover illustration by San Julian: Copyright © 1978 by Playboy.

Published simultaneously in the United States and Canada by Playboy Press, Chicago, Illinois. Printed in the United States of America. Library of Congress Catalog Card Number: 78-51278. First edition.

This book is available at quantity discounts for promotional and industrial use. For further information, write our sales-promotion agency: Ventura Associates, 40 East 49th Street, New York, New York 10017.

ISBN: 0-872-16468-3

Other books by the author:

BOND OF BLOOD
KNIGHT'S HONOR
THE DRAGON AND THE ROSE
THE SWORD AND THE SWAN
ROSELYNDE

CHAPTER ONE

A lone knight in full armor spurred a tired, lathered horse up the winding road toward Roselynde Keep. That sight was so unusual in this year of our Lord 1206, the seventh year of the reign of King John—the accursed, as some called him—that the guard in the tower rubbed his eyes as if to clear his vision. Times had been bad periodically during the reign of King Richard because Richard did not love England, and the officers he appointed to rule and tax the land were often harsh. However, there was little lawlessness, and old Queen Alinor had been alive and had moderated any dangerous extremity in Richard's demands.

In 1199 Richard had been fatally wounded by an arrow at a siege he was conducting in one of the innumerable wars he waged. John, his youngest brother, the last of Henry Plantagenet's wild brood, had come to the throne. Although John actually loved England the best of all his possessions, he was driven by political necessity to even greater harshness than Richard and, to make all worse, he was a vicious man. Then, in 1204, the old queen died, and a strong force for balancing necessity against unreasonable taxation disappeared. The spite and exactions of the king then fell so heavily on so many that marauders prowled the land, and the roads were unsafe. In these days, men who had stitch or stick about them rode in armed groups.

Within the bounds of Roselynde's demesne, this was less true. Sir Simon Lemagne and his wife Lady Alinor had kept the peace on their own lands for a time, but Sir Simon had been stricken with a violent disorder of pains in the chest and arms more than a year past, and in late June he had died. Sir Giles had come from Iford when Sir Simon first fell sick, but his wife was not of the stuff of which Lady Alinor was made, and he had had to return to his own lands lest they fall into total disorder. Lord Ian had come also, but the king had summoned him away to the wars in Normandy. Beorn, Lady Alinor's master-at-arms, did what he could. There was still peace, although not what it had been in Sir Simon's time. Nonetheless, the guard knew that this knight did not come from the lands around Roselynde. It was plain from the state of his horse and his garments that he had ridden far and hard.

At the edge of the drawbridge, the knight pulled up his horse and shouted out his name. The guard's face lightened, and he called an order down the tower. The portcullis was raised as swiftly as possible; this was a welcome guest. The guard's surprise diminished when the knight said his troop followed and they should be passed when they arrived, but he still wondered what had brought his late lord's friend so far and in such haste that he outstripped his men. It was, however, no business of his to ask questions. He turned back to his duty of watching as the knight rode through the outer bailey, across the smaller drawbridge, and under the inner portcullis into the inner bailey.

Here a groom ran forward to take his horse, and a grizzled man-at-arms rose to his feet from a cask on which he had been sitting and watching two children, a girl of nine and a boy of seven, at play. The children looked up and tensed when they saw the true mail of a knight instead of the leather of a man-at-arms. Then they shrieked with joy and ran forward.

"Ian!" the boy cried.

The knight dismounted in one smooth movement, pushed off his helmet and shield, and bent to gather them to him, one in each arm. He kissed them both, then suddenly buried his face in the boy's hair and began to sob. The children, who had been wriggling with delight, quieted at once.

"Are you weeping because Papa is dead, Ian, or is there more bad news?" the girl, who was the elder, asked gravely.

Simon's daughter, Ian de Vipont thought, struggling to control himself. She is as like him as if she had no mother.

"Did you only just hear of it?" the boy asked. "It was in June. It is a shame you could not come to the funeral feast. Everyone enjoyed it greatly."

The boy stood quietly, his arms around Ian's neck, one small hand patting the knight's shoulder consolingly. His voice, however, was cheerful, irrepressible. In the midst of his tears, Ian choked on laughter. Alinor's son. Kind enough to wish to offer comfort but with a spirit that could not be quenched. He squeezed the children to him tightly once more, then stood upright and wiped his face with the leather inside of his steel-sewn gauntlet.

"No, no more bad news," he said to Joanna, and then, smiling on Adam, "I heard in July, but I was with the king in France besieging Montauban, and I could not get leave to come."

"Tell about the siege—tell!" the boy cried.

"Oh, yes, Ian, please tell," the girl begged.

The sun came out from behind a cloud, lighting green and gold flecks in the boy's hazel eyes and turning the girl's hair to flame. They were totally unlike in appearance, as if the mother's and father's strains were each so strong they could not be mixed; but that was only in coloring. Adam's hair was straight and black, his skin startlingly white, like his mother Alinor's, but his frame was sturdy and already very large for his age. That was his heritage from Simon, and a good heritage it was. It might be needful, Ian thought sadly, in the bitter times that loomed ahead, if King John did not mend his ways.

Ian had not known Simon when his hair was as red as

Joanna's, but her eyes, a misty gray sometimes touched with blue, had cleared and brightened just as Simon's did when he was angry, eager, or happy. She was slighter than her brother but still sturdily made, no frail flower. No frail spirit either. The eager expression on Joanna's face mirrored that on Adam's.

"Did you scale the walls?" she asked.

"Did you burst through the gates?" Adam echoed.

"Master Adam! Lady Joanna!" the grizzled man-at-arms protested, "can you not see Lord Ian is dirty and tired? You shame our hospitality. A guest is bidden to wash and take his ease before being battered with questions."

"*Beoth hal,* Beorn," Ian said in English.

"*Beoth hal, eaorling,*" Beorn responded, "*wilcume, wilcume. Cumeth thu withinne.*"

Adam's eyes grew large. Beorn was an important man in his life. He taught the boy the fundamentals of sword and mace fighting. Adam could dimly remember that his father had started his lessons, but in the last year Simon had barely been able to come down to the bailey to watch and offer breathless and halting advice. Adam knew Beorn spoke a special language of his own. Adam could even understand some words, but Beorn would never address him in that tongue and would never permit him to speak it.

"Ian, Beorn answered you," the boy said.

The man-at-arms flushed slightly, and a faint frown appeared on Ian's brow. He made no comment, however, merely saying that it was time he went in and greeted their mother. After refusing the children's offer to accompany him and assuring them he would see them later, he strode into the forebuilding and mounted the stairs to the great hall, unlacing his mail hood and stripping off his gauntlets as he went. He looked up at the stair that led to the women's quarters, but he did not pause. Lady Alinor was as likely to be anywhere else in the keep as there, and he was sure someone had run ahead to announce his arrival.

In that supposition he was quite correct. Before he had crossed the hall to the great hearth, Lady Alinor came running from a wall chamber. She seized the hands he held out toward her and gripped them hard.

"Ian, Ian, I am glad at heart to see you."

"I could not come when I first heard. I begged the king to let me go, but he would not."

"You do not need to tell me that."

Suddenly her eyes were full of tears. She stepped forward and laid her head against his breast. Ian's hands came up to embrace her and then dropped. He fought another upsurge of his own grief. Alinor uttered a deep sigh and stepped back to look up at him.

"It is good to have you here," she said, only a trifle unsteadily. "How long can you stay?"

"I do not know," he replied, not meeting her eyes. "It depends on——"

"At least the night," she cried.

"Yes, of course, but——"

"Never mind the buts now. Oh, Ian, you look so tired."

"Our ship was blown off course. I meant to land at Roselynde, but we were blown all the way to Dover. We were attacked three times on the road. I could not believe it. In the worst days of Longchamp, things had not come to such a pass. I rode through the night. I had to——"

"You have bad news?" But Alinor did not pause for him to answer. "Do not tell me now," she said, half laughing but with a tremor in her voice. "Have you eaten?" He nodded. "Come, let me unarm you and bathe you." It was customary for the lady of the manor to bathe her guests, although Alinor had not usually done so for Ian.

"My squires are with the troop," he protested. "I rode ahead."

At that Alinor laughed more naturally. "I have not yet grown so feeble that I cannot lift a hauberk. Come." She drew him toward the wall chamber from which she had emerged. "The bath is ready. It will grow cold."

For one instant it seemed as if Ian would resist, and Alinor stopped to look at him questioningly. However, there was no particular expression on his face, and he was already following, so she said nothing. Something was wrong, Alinor knew. Ian had been her husband's squire before they were married. After their return from the Crusade, Simon had so successfully advanced his protégé's interests that Ian had been granted a defunct baronage that went with the estates Ian had inherited from his mother. He had been a close friend all through the years and a frequent visitor, particularly attached to the children. His fondness for them, coupled with his resistance to marriage had once made Alinor ask her husband whether Ian was tainted with King Richard's perversion. Simon had assured her that it was not so, that Ian was a fine young stallion, and he had warned her seriously not to tease the young man.

Alinor had been careful, because, despite being 30 years her senior—or, perhaps, because of it—Simon was no jealous husband. Indeed, until his illness, he had no cause to be jealous; he had kept Alinor fully occupied. Thus, when Simon warned her against flirting playfully with Ian, it was for Ian's sake. Alinor acknowledged the justice of that. It would be dreadful to attach Ian to her, dangerous, too. There was violence lurking behind the young man's hot brown eyes and, although Alinor had loved Simon and been content with him, she had never denied that Ian was a magnificent male animal who could be very attractive to her. Ian had been careful too, seldom touching Alinor, even to kiss her hand in courtesy.

Nonetheless, they had been good friends. Alinor knew when Ian was carrying a burden of trouble. Ordinarily, she would have pressed him with questions

until he opened the evil package for her inspection.
Alinor had never feared trouble. Simon had said sourly
more than once that she ran with eager feet to meet it.
That was because she had never found a trouble for
which she or Simon or both of them together could not
discover a solution. Trouble had been a challenge to be
met head on, trampled over, or slyly circumvented—
until Simon died. Now, all at once, there were too many
troubles. Alinor could not, for the moment, muster the
courage to ask for another.

The afternoon light flooded the antechamber with
brightness, but the inner wall chamber was dim. Ian
hesitated, and Alinor tugged at his hand, leading him
safely around the large wooden tub that sat before the
hearth. To the side was a low stool. Alinor pushed Ian
toward it, grasping the tails of his hauberk as he passed
her and lifting them so he would not sit on them. She
unbelted his sword before he had even reached toward
it, slipped off his surcoat, and laid it carefully on a chest
at the side of the room. Ian gave up trying to be helpful
and abandoned himself to Alinor's practiced ministra-
tions, docilely doing as he was told and no more.

In a single skillful motion, Alinor pulled the hauberk
over his head, turned it this way and that to see whether
it needed the attention of the castle armorer, and laid
it on the chest with the sword. Then she came around
in front of him and unlaced his tunic and shirt. These
were stiff with sweat and dirt, and she threw them on
the floor. Next, she knelt to unfasten his shoes and cross
garters, drew them off, untied his chausses, and bid him
stand. Again Ian hesitated. Alinor thought how tired he
was and was about to assure him he would feel better
after he had bathed, but he stood before she could
speak. Still kneeling, she pulled the chausses down and
slipped them off his feet. When she raised her eyes to
tell him to step into the tub, she saw the reason for his
hesitation.

There could be no doubt now that Simon had been

right. Ian was a fine young stallion, and he was displaying the fact with startling effect. Alinor's first impulse
was to laugh and make a bawdy jest. A flickering glance
at Ian's face checked her. He was certainly well aware
of the condition he was in, but he did not think it was
funny. Briefly, Alinor was hurt. During the many years
she had bathed high-born visitors to her keep, the reaction Ian was having occurred with other men once in a
while. Sometimes it was deliberately produced by men
who thought Alinor had to be dissatisfied with her husband because he was so much older than she. They had
underestimated Simon, and from Alinor had received
such icy courtesy that the deliberate provocation did not
occur a second time. With those in whom it was an
innocent accident engendered by too long a period of
continence or an inadvertent physical contact, it was
best to make a jest, laugh, and forget.

It was usually best, but Alinor somehow knew she
must not laugh at Ian's stony-faced refusal to acknowledge his condition. She rose from her knees and stepped
back, and for the first time the full impact of his beauty
hit her. The black curls that usually tumbled silkily over
his forehead were lank and flattened, but that did
nothing to reduce the luminous quality of his large, dark
eyes. The nose was fine, the lips both sensitive and
sensuous. He was very tall for a man, head and shoulders both topped Alinor, and he was surprisingly hair-
less—just a shadow of dark down at the end of his
breastbone and a narrow line from the navel to the
pubic bush. His skin was very dark, very smooth, where
it was not bleached and knotted by scars of battle.

In the year that Simon had been ill, Alinor was too
tired and too worried to think of herself as a woman.
After his death, the fatigue and worry had only intensified. Now, without warning, she became aware of her
long starvation. The blood rushed from her face to her
loins. She put a hand on the tub to steady herself, and
thanked God that Ian was staring past her into nothing.

"Get in."

Had Ian been in any condition to notice, Alinor's voice would have given her away. However, he was having his own problems and was grateful that they would be hidden if not solved so easily. He stepped into the tub and eased himself slowly into the water, which was rather hot. Alinor moved quickly to stand behind him. She wondered whether she could bear to touch him, and decided it would be simpler and safer to run away and send a maid to wash him. She could always say she had remembered something overlooked in the excitement of his arrival. Even as Alinor tried to steady her voice to excuse herself, her eyes were drawn back to Ian. They rested briefly on the strong column of his neck, dropped to his broad shoulders.

"Ian! Holy Mother Mary, what befell you?"

Right across the shoulder blades, a large section of skin looked as if patches had been torn away. The wounds were not deadly, but they were horridly ugly, and gave evidence of having been reopened and rubbed raw more than once. Ian twisted his head, saw where her eyes were fixed, and laughed.

"Oh, that. A barrel of burning pitch blew apart. I was like to be a torch. My men doused me with water, but when it came to taking off my clothes, some of me went with them." His voice was normal, light, laughing at a stupid mishap. "I was ill enough pleased at it because we had taken the keep the day before, and I had not a mark on me from all the fighting. No one noticed that the barrel was afire, I suppose."

"But that was in August," Alinor exclaimed, also completely back to normal. "You idiot! Did you not have anyone look to you?"

"There were no physicians. The leeches treated me— for all the good they did. To whom should I have gone?" Ian snapped irritably. "To Queen Isabella?"

Alinor made a contemptuous noise. "At least she is not so bad as the first queen. Isabella might refuse to soil her hands on such a common slave as a mere baron, but Isobel of Gloucester would have rubbed poison into your hurts. Oh, never mind, I will attend to that later. A warm soaking will do the sores good. First I want to wash your hair. Wait, you fool, do not lean back yet. Let me get a cushion to ease you. You will scrape your back against the tub."

"You will ruin the cushion if you put it in the bath."

"It can be dried. The maids are too idle anyway."

She went out. Ian closed his eyes and sighed. An expression of indecision so intense as to amount to fear crossed his face, changed to a rather grim determination. Alinor returned with a maid at her heels. She slipped the cushion behind Ian, and he slid down against it and tipped his head back. He could hear the maid laying out fresh clothing and gathering up his soiled garments. Alinor reached over him to scoop up a ladleful of water, poured it over his head, and began to soap his hair.

"Tell me something pleasant," she said.

"Well, we took Montauban," Ian responded a little doubtfully, but at a loss for anything to say that Alinor would consider pleasant. "And a truce between Philip and John is being arranged."

"What is pleasant about that?" Alinor asked disgustedly. "It means the king will return here. Oh, curse all the Angevins. Richard loved England too little, and John——" She gave Ian's hair a rough toweling so it would not drip in his face. "Sit up and lean forward."

"Yes, Alinor, but John *does* love England." Ian elevated his knees, crossed his arms on them, and rested his forehead on his arms.

"Most assuredly. Like a wolf loves little children. He could eat three a day."

Alinor began to wash Ian's back very gently. She felt him wince under her hands, but his voice was steady.

"That is his nature. Like a wolf, he is dangerous only when running loose."

"And who will cage him?"

There was a long pause. Ian jerked as Alinor touched a particularly painful spot and then said, a trifle breathlessly, "I have much to say about that, but not here and now. To speak the truth, Alinor, I am tired and sore, and that is no condition for me to match words with you."

"With me? What have I— No, never mind. I see you are about to engage in some harebrained enterprise, but I will not fret you when you are so tired. There, I have done with you for the moment. Sit up. Do you wash the rest while I go and get my salves."

Alinor handed Ian the cloth and soap. She could, of course, have told the maid to bring the medicinal salves she needed, but she was afraid to wash the rest of Ian's body. There was too much chance of arousing him and herself again. By the time she returned, he was out of the tub and had drawn on a pair of Simon's chausses. Alinor was surprised they fitted so well. She knew Ian and her late husband were much of a height, but Simon had always seemed to be a much heavier man. Perhaps it is the coloring, she thought, and the lack of body hair.

"Sit," Alinor directed, and then, "no, go lie on the bed on your face. This will be a long piece of work, and there is no need for my knees to be sore from kneeling."

"Do comfort me," Ian laughed. "Torturer."

"You will feel much better when I am done," Alinor remarked without the slightest sympathy. "Now, what other news is there?"

"None I care to tell—oh, yes, one thing. There is a rumor that the queen is at last with child."

"Poor thing," Alinor commented. "With such a father and mother, I wonder what it will be."

Ian laughed. "Do you expect horns and a tail? Do not be so harsh. There is good blood on both sides. The child need not be exactly like to the parents, although God knows yours are like enough. And now I think on it, there was something I wanted to ask about. Did you forbid Beorn to teach Adam English?"

"Forbid it? No."

"Did Simon?"

It was the first time Ian had said his name. It had slipped out quite naturally, but he tensed, fearing Alinor's reaction. There was none.

"I cannot imagine why he should. Why do you ask?"

"Because I think—ouch! Alinor, leave me what little skin I have. Give over a minute. Let me rest." He turned to the side so he could see her. "I think Adam wishes to learn, and it is no bad thing to understand what those beneath you say."

"Of course not. It is most necessary. I understand English myself, although I cannot speak it. Thank you for telling me. I will speak to Beorn. Sometimes he is overcareful."

"There is something else. Beorn is a good man, but—" Ian's voice checked as the sound of childish laughter came in the doorway.

"Oh, you are here, are you?" Alinor called. "Come in then. You might as well be of some use. Ian, lie flat again. Adam, hold this pot so I do not need to bend for it each time. Joanna, look you here. See how I clean this. It is not proudflesh, which must be cut away, as I showed you aforetime. When the wound is of the skin, rather than of the flesh, wide and not deep, it must close all at once rather than from the inside. It is needful to be most gentle or the new, tender growth will be torn. See, here, where the shield strap rubbed? There is no mending this. It will heal hard and shiny—and belike tear again."

"Were you wounded in the siege?" Adam asked excitedly. "Tell, Ian. You promised to tell."

"Mother, look here. What is this?" Joanna asked.

"Pox take it! That is an old scar torn open. That will need to be cleaned deeper."

"Ian, you promised," Adam insisted louder.

"Yes, in a moment," Ian gasped, stiffening as Alinor directèd Joanna to spread the lips of a pus-filled sore so she could clean it thoroughly.

"Adam, be still!" Alinor snapped.

"But Mother— Oh, Mother, may we sit at the high table for dinner? May we?" the irrepressible Adam demanded, jiggling up and down.

"May we, Mother?" Joanna echoed, unwisely looking up from her task so that a finger slipped and Ian jerked and groaned.

"Joanna, you careless girl! Adam, stand still! Sooner than reward you both, I will send you dinnerless to bed."

"Alinor," Ian said sharply, "do not punish them the first day I am here. They are excited. If you will be quiet, Adam, I will tell you at dinner."

"I am sorry, Ian," Joanna whispered.

"Never mind, love," he soothed, "it is nothing. Just do as your mother tells you. Do not be frightened. I will not die for a prick."

"One more sound from either of you and all Ian's pleading on your behalf will be naught. If I must speak to either of you again, I will make good my first threat and add a whipping to your dinnerless state," Alinor warned.

With her helpers properly subdued, Alinor finished her work quickly. Over the medicinal creams she spread a thin layer of grease to prevent the bandages from sticking to the sores, told Adam to pack the pots carefully and take them away, and instructed Joanna in wrapping Ian firmly but not tightly in soft, old linen. Then she sent the girl away also. Ian started to get out of the bed.

"For Mary's sake," Alinor exclaimed irritably, "lie down and sleep until dinner. If you show your face, those little devils will be at you."

"I do not mind," Ian said pacifically, then smiled. "It pleases me that they love me."

Alinor opened her mouth, shut it firmly for a moment, and then said, "Oh, go to sleep! If you do not, *I* will be at you, and you are too tired now to be of the least help to me."

"Alinor—" He reached for her hand.

"No, Ian. Let me be. Let me go."

He watched her run from the room and, after staring some time at the empty doorway, lay down again. The task he had set himself grew harder and harder. Somehow he had expected Alinor to be less affected, more like Adam. He had never known her to carry a burden of woe for long. Even when she lost children— You fool, he told himself, she would not make a parade of her grief for you. There was Simon to comfort her.

"It is too soon," he muttered, but there was no way around that part of the problem.

Although Ian had craved leave to attend Simon's funeral, when that had been refused he had not, as he implied to Alinor, come as soon as he could. In fact, he had delayed as long as he thought it safe, until the terms of the truce between John and Philip were fixed and it was apparent that the king intended to sign and return to England. Simon had told Ian, not long before he died, that King John had some long-standing grudge against Alinor, which for Alinor's sake he could not explain further. The years of John's reign had been too troubled, even from the first, to permit him to vent his spite on so powerful a vassal as Simon, but now Simon was dead. Until now, the king had had more important things to think about, but if he returned to England and someone drew Alinor's defenseless state to his attention, he would work off that grudge in the most vicious way. John never forgot a grudge, and he was a vicious man.

One could not kill a woman outright or challenge her to mortal combat with a proven champion, but imprisonment and death by starvation was one of John's favorite methods of dealing with helpless prey. Ian would not give a pin for Adam's life either, and Joanna would be sold to the highest and vilest bidder, probably after the king had used her himself.

Ian groaned softly. It was hell to serve such a man, yet his faith was given. Even if he had been willing to besmirch his honor by violating his oath of fealty—and John had driven many otherwise honorable men to that pass—who else was there? Arthur of Brittany was dead. John had disposed of him, some said with his own hands. Alinor of Brittany, Arthur's sister, was kept tighter in the king's hand than his own wife, and in any case she was not like her grandmother, not a woman men would obey. The male line of Plantagenets was finished, unless John's wife bore a son. There was no one else except French Philip and his son Louis. Ian sighed. Not again. Not ever again a king who loved France better than England. There had been enough of that in Richard's day. Whatever John was as a man, he was king of England and his interest lay first with that realm.

There was no one else and Ian could not rebel, but he could keep Simon's wife and Simon's children safe from John's vengeance. He started to turn onto his back, and hissed softly with pain. Alinor was right. The sores troubled him so little now that he had forgotten them. Alinor— Would she hate him when he told her what he had planned and had arranged? That would be unendurable, yet he must endure it for Simon's sake.

Simon was not Ian's father in the flesh, but in a more essential way he was the author of his being. Ian could remember his real father only dimly, and even that was too much. Simon had saved him from the hell of that dimly remembered existence, had taught him honor and pride and gentleness. It was a debt that could never be repaid, until now.

If only debt and desire were not so intermingled. Ian's trouble was that he wanted Alinor for herself. He had worshiped her from the day he had first seen her, almost 20 years ago, kneeling in the road to greet King

Richard's mother. But one could not worship Alinor for long. She was far too real, far too much of the earth and the flesh, too kind and gentle, too hot-tempered and bawdy, to be seated on a pedestal. A man could only love or hate Alinor. Ian stirred restlessly, wondering again whether he was really paying his debt to Simon or reaching to snatch something he had always wanted.

It was no use worrying that bone again. He had been at it as soon as his initial shock of grief at Simon's death was over. His first rational thought had been that he could now have Alinor. Sickened by the exposure of that long-repressed desire, Ian had recoiled from the idea, but it returned again and again. Each time the notion seemed more reasonable. The children loved him, and he loved them. He would not steal their heritage or harm them as another might to gain absolute control of Alinor's vast estates. And as for Alinor— there was nothing Alinor could not have from him just for the asking.

In the privacy of her own chamber, a place she seldom sought now because it was redolent of happy memories, Alinor took herself to task. Of all the men in the world to lust after, Ian was the last. If she had such a need, there were a dozen men she could ask outright to service her. It would be a pleasure to them both and mean nothing to either. But not Ian. Simon had molded Ian into a mirror of his own uprightness. Not that Simon was a prude—far from it—nor that Ian would object in the least to mating casually with this woman or that. Considering what he looked like, there must have been plenty of women, particularly in John's lascivious court. The king was openly a lecher and preferred that his gentlemen and his queen's ladies should not be overly virtuous. Ian would not be horrified at bedding any lady of the court; he would only be horrified that Simon's wife could feel such a need so soon after his death.

Simon would not have been horrified, Alinor thought, chuckling while tears ran down her face. He would have bewailed her lack of morality aloud while his eyes laughed at her. Who would have believed that Ian was not old enough to accept that the flesh had its own laws, and they had little to do with the heart or mind? Yet look at his reaction to a most natural accident. Unless they were willing to use the common whores, men engaged in military actions were deprived of women. Alinor was fairly certain that Ian had little need to use a whore under ordinary circumstances; there would be plenty of willing fine ladies. She was also sure that he would recoil from using the filthy creatures that serviced the men-at-arms in a military camp. She understood that when a strong young man had been continent for months, the slightest thing, the lightest touch, would wake his body. She would have laughed and forgotten it had Ian himself not been so appalled at his reaction to "Simon's wife."

"I am not only Simon's wife," Alinor sobbed softly. "I am Alinor."

Some hours later and many miles away, across the narrow sea, a sweet, rich voice suddenly developed an ugly snarl, interrupting itself in the midst of a sentence to ask, "What did you say about Pembroke?"

The man addressed did not blanch, even though King John seemed angry; he laughed. "I said, my lord, that we did not miss him in the taking of Montauban or in our other ventures. We did not miss him nor that mighty and sanctimonious man of his hands, Simon Lemagne, whom your brother leaned upon so heavily."

William, Earl of Salisbury, the king's bastard half brother, straightened from his bored slouch and shook his head. He was a little the worse for wine, a condition not uncommon with him when the king and his cronies gathered. It was easier, Salisbury had discovered, not to hear too clearly when he was a little befuddled. Normally this was an ideal situation; it saved him from needing to reply and from the danger of losing his temper at what he heard. Moreover, nine times out of ten, nothing of any importance was said, the talk consisting of gross flattery of the king and gross conversation in general. Unfortunately, tonight was the tenth time. Salisbury knew there was something dangerous about the name Simon Lemagne, but at the moment he could not marshal his wits into remembering what.

"Lemagne is dead. Let him rest in peace," Philip Marc said idly.

"Dead?"

The purring tone of the king's voice pierced the vague haze engendered by the rich Burgundy wine Salisbury had been drinking. He was still not sure where the danger lay, but when the king used that tone, someone soon suffered for it.

"There was a letter," Salisbury said thickly. "I remember, because it came the day de Vipont and I were planning the assault—"

His voice died. The mention of Ian's name suddenly brought the danger clearly to Salisbury's mind. He remembered the younger man's stricken face, his own anxious questions. Now he remembered the answers to those questions, and he was made dumb by remorse. He had said the worst possible thing in his drunken effort to divert John.

"You mean you were putting some small touches to the king's plan," Fulk de Cantelu growled aggressively. "The king told me the whole thing before ever you thought of it."

Salisbury lifted his bleary eyes from the stained table where he had been seeking a way of mending his drunken slip. In general, William of Salisbury was not a man given to hate. He tended, in fact, to blame himself for another's fault and to see the best in all men. However, he had learned over the years of his brother's reign to hate Fulk de Cantelu and the man who sat some places down from Fulk on the other side, Henry of Cornhill. It was not only that these cronies of the king were low-born, cruel, and greedy in themselves; they seemed to bring out the very worst in John.

It was not fair, Salisbury thought. There was much good in John. He was clever, he could be warm and loving and generous. That he did not often show that side of his nature was the fault of circumstances. John had been the youngest of a large and violent brood, un-wanted by his powerful and magnetic mother, whom he adored, and spoiled by his father, who had already di-vided his vast possessions before John's birth. Thus, he had been called John Lackland, had been made the butt of jests, had been blamed for all the dissensions in the family. Salisbury knew that John felt that deep in his father's mind he had even been blamed for the re-bellions and, finally, the death of his eldest brother. Al-though old King Henry had buried that thought deep and had been even more insistent about finding a suit-able heritage for his youngest son, he could not com-pletely conceal the canker in his heart.

Then Henry's frantic efforts to carve a kingdom for John out of Richard's domain brought about the rebel-lion of his second son. John was near demented. If Richard died, he would have the whole, because Geof-frey, the third brother, was dead of disease. He would also have the undying hatred of his mother, already im-prisoned for her efforts in Richard's cause, and the no-less-bitter grief and hatred of his father, no matter how concealed. How much John wanted that kingdom no man, not even Salisbury, knew. At first he threw himself into the war on his father's side, but Richard was more than a match for the aging, guilt- and grief-ridden Henry.

John was clever. He saw there was more than one way to skin a cat. The kingdom could be inherited from Richard more easily than it could be wrested from him by war. John knew his brother Richard was not likely either to reign long or to breed up an heir to the throne. Richard was a lover of men; to prove himself no woman, or perhaps in some deep and concealed desire for a heroic death that would glorify his name and bring him peace, Richard fought constantly—in tournaments, if a war was temporarily lacking. What was more, Richard had taken the Cross and would go on Crusade. It was very likely that the diseases of the Holy Land would kill him if the warriors of Saladin did not.

John withdrew himself from his father's war. When the time was ripe, he went to Richard, received his indulgent brother's kiss of peace, wrested from Richard the promise of vast territories, and turned on his father. He turned on his brother, too. When it transpired that neither disease nor war had destroyed Richard, John had conspired with the ancient enemy of his family, King Philip of France, to murder Richard or, failing that, keep him imprisoned for life. That, too, failed. John's mighty mother was still alive, and she so bedeviled the Pope and the Emperor of Germany, who held Richard prisoner, that they set a ransom for him. Then, by draining the lifeblood from England and her own territories in France, she had paid that ransom and procured her son's freedom.

Now, Salisbury thought, John is being blamed for that also. Perhaps John's actions were not all that they should have been with respect to his father and his brother, but the taxes and fines that had brought such misery to England were not John's fault. Richard's Crusade and Richard's ransom had impoverished England. Richard's wars against Philip after he was freed had also cost money, and those wars were more often started by Richard than by Philip. On the other hand, it was Philip who had attacked John. John did not go looking for war, and it was not his fault if he had to pay for a war that was thrust upon him.

It was the need to pay that brought the like of Fulk de Cantelu and Henry of Cornhill into John's favor.

There was no mercy in them, and they did not fear God. They would take a cross from an altar or wrest the last farthing from a starving widow with equal indifference. That was what made them valuable to John, who could do neither. From a distance, he could order the widow's property confiscated or the cross to be torn down, but he could not put his hand to such work.

The drink-muddled train of thought had brought Salisbury back to the danger of mentioning Simon Lemagne's death. It was Ian de Vipont who had told Salisbury that Simon's marriage had displeased John, who had planned to give the woman Simon married to another man. Ian wished to marry her himself now that Simon was dead, largely, Salibury thought, to protect her children, who were the heirs to a very large property. Ian loved those children as if they were his own; he was never done talking of them, and he feared that another man might be tempted to deprive them of their rights or even, to enrich himself or his own children, do away with them. The letter Salisbury mentioned had been from the widow. It was a stupid thing to bring her into John's mind. Salisbury giggled drunkenly. For once he had reason to be grateful for Fulk's jealous spite, which would leave Salisbury no credit for anything in his brother's eyes. In Fulk's desire to deprive Salisbury of the honor of planning a successful assault, he had said what was most likely to divert the king's mind from Simon's widow.

While Salisbury's mind was in the past, however, the fulsome praise of the king had come to an end, and the end, unfortunately, brought Simon's name back into the conversation.

"He is no loss," John agreed, and he smiled.

It was a pleasant smile, if one did not look into John's eyes. The king was not an unhandsome man. He was growing stout, but that was characteristic of the body shape he had inherited from his father: short and very broad, with enormous strength. His coloring was his mother's: crisp, dark hair, graying very slightly now, cut evenly a few inches below the ears and growing from a decided peak on the forehead. His mouth was small and well-shaped, but the thin upper lip betrayed his cruelty, and the full lower one his lust. His nose was good and straight; the wide-springing nostrils would have warned of choler, but no man needed that warning.

All the Angevins had fierce tempers. John's, in fact, was less apparent than Henry's or Richard's. The former had been driven into such rages that he rolled the floors and tore at carpets and pillows with his teeth; the latter had more often broken furniture or heads. John was seldom violent. His temper seethed within him, gnawing at his vitals. Thus, it was not well to look into his large, dark eyes, which otherwise would have been his best and most beautiful feature.

A chorus of sycophantic laughter greeted the king's dismissal of a vassal who, if he had not loved John, had yet been faithful and had answered every call for military service until illness had made it impossible. Salisbury was saddened by his half brother's long-lived rancor, but he accepted it as he accepted John's other weaknesses, making what excuses he could for the baby brother he had protected and shielded all his life.

"He is dead, so forget him," Salisbury urged. "Tell me, brother——"

"But his lovely and wealthy widow is not dead," John interrupted, forestalling Salisbury's attempt to lead him to some other topic.

The purr was back in John's voice, and Salisbury shuddered inwardly, but he could not drive his wine-sodden brain to conceive a subject that would be more interesting. Suddenly John laughed.

"Poor woman, likely she was as glad to be rid of him as I. He must have been a useless hulk to her these many years. It comes to my mind that I would do the lady a favor by cutting short her mourning and providing her with a husband who would know how to use her abed and abroad. She is a little hot at hand—er—I have been told. Perhaps she would need a little taming. How would that sit with you, Fulk? Or you, Henry? Are either of you man enough to take such a task in hand?"

"You would do better," Salisbury said desperately, "to take a rich fine from her and leave her to her own devices. Every pound you gain will lessen the toll you must ask for from the kingdom at large. Any husband you choose will very soon bethink him that the lady's gold would go into his purse if it did not go into yours."

John looked at his brother, and for a moment the cruel mouth softened, and the hungry eyes grew milder. "You always see the best way for me, William. That was a shrewd reminder. Yes, indeed." He laughed uproariously. "I will offer the lady her choice, and when she has made it, she shall pay richly for the privilege. And you," his eyes swept the table, "my dear and loving friends, will be able to place no blame upon me. It will be the lady's choice, not mine, that makes one man master of her estates."

That was not what Salisbury meant, but it was better than having John commit himself to any one man. Several would doubtless offer some bribe to get their names into the letter to Alinor. Doubtless John would wait a day or two to be sure that the bidding had ended. Then the letter must be written and sent. If John should fall into one of his periodic bouts of lethargy, and that was rather likely because he had been showing the signs Salisbury recognized of the onset of such a period, it might be weeks before he moved in the matter.

The fluctuations between periods of great energy and periods of total indolence that John suffered had been a puzzle to Salisbury—and to anyone else who knew the king—for many years. For weeks or months at a time, John would be busy every moment, riding from castle to castle, paying strict attention to the affairs of the kingdom, sitting in justice himself, and prosecuting every duty and pleasure to the fullest. It was not unknown in those periods for the king to come from the queen's bed to that of one of his current mistresses and even to go on to, or summon to his bed, still another. Then the intensity would begin to fade. John would show less interest in the details of governing; more of his time would be spent in sport or pleasure, in drinking bouts carried far on into the night. At last, even an active seeking of pleasure would end. John would fall asleep in his wife's bed after he serviced her, would lie abed late into the morning and spend much of the day in Isabella's company, hardly speaking, simply staring at her beautiful face and form.

In the depths of these periods of lethargy, nothing could rouse the king. Such a period had cost him Normandy. Even when he had been badgered and cajoled into moving toward the fighting, he could not be driven to take an active part in it. Then, for no apparent reason, John would become a little restless; sometimes he would withdraw from the court for a night or a few days. When he reappeared, he was bursting with energy again.

Salisbury had no hope that during his lethargy the king would forget what he had said about Alinor. There had been hate in his purring mention of Lemagne's widow. Salisbury did not understand that, but he knew his brother never forgot a planned revenge on anyone marked by his hatred. Salisbury would never hurt John, but if he could shield the woman without doing his brother any harm, he was willing to do so for Ian de Vipont's friend.

CHAPTER TWO

Ian's real trouble was not diminished when Alinor sent Joanna to wake him and help him dress instead of coming herself. The child told him gravely that his troop and squires had arrived, but that her mother had sent them to rest and she hoped he would be content with her poor services. Naturally, Ian found no fault with that arrangement. He was touched and amused by the serious way Joanna took her responsibilities. Wisely, he made not the slightest attempt to help her—except for surreptitiously steadying the stool she climbed upon to pull his shirt over his head and lace it up. He raised his arms, lowered them, and turned as she directed with a completely solemn face. She hopped off to fetch his gown, hopped on again—that time Ian had to catch her to keep her from overbalancing with the unwieldy garment in her arms, but he bit his tongue and did not laugh.

It was a delightfully refreshing interlude. He had caught Joanna in his arms when she had finally fastened his belt, kissed her, squeezed her tight, and told her what a fine woman she was growing to be. If he had not also thought how kind and clever Alinor was to use Joanna to relieve the tension, he could almost have forgotten what lay before him. Fortunately, there was no immediate need for him to face the problem. Adam seized upon him the moment he came to the table, and whenever his mouth was not full of food, Ian was busy describing the siege of Montauban in the most minute detail. Joanna and Alinor were almost as eager listeners as Adam, so that dinner passed easily.

31

When the meal was over, Adam had to show Ian his new skills in arms. Joanna wished to display her ability to read and write and cipher. Both insisted that he measure their progress in horsemanship. Alinor said tentatively that Ian had had enough of them, but she was obviously well pleased when he denied it and went with them. They came in from their ride just as dusk was falling, laughing and disheveled. Alinor said it was time for bed; they pleaded for a little longer, for Ian to tell them a story he had learned from the bards in the Welsh strongholds when he stayed with his clan brother Llewelyn.

Ian was not Welsh, but he had captured Llewelyn, the grandson of the most important chieftain of North Wales, in a punitive war when he was still Simon's squire. It was Ian who had conducted Llewelyn to a brief, honorable and most luxurious captivity at John's hands, and the two young men had ended by becoming fast friends. In later years, when Llewelyn had inherited his grandfather's power, he had not only given Ian several estates in Wales but had gone through the elaborate ceremony that inducted Ian into his clan and made them "brothers in blood."

Ian spent a fair amount of time in Wales and had grown to love the people and their traditions. He was well pleased to tell the story of the hunting of the great boar Twrch Trwyth. It was full dark when he finished. Torches blazed in the hall, and candles glowed golden in the area before the great hearth that was reserved to Alinor's family and guests.

"And now to bed," Alinor said very definitely.

More pleas, eyes raised adoringly to their champion. Ian glanced at Alinor, almost as pleadingly. She laughed but shook her head. He sighed.

"You must obey your mother. I will be here tomorrow."

"Only tomorrow?" A double shriek that made Ian clap his hands to his ears.

"I do not know."

"Only one day!" "You have barely come!" "It is not enough!" "Please, Ian, please." The chorus was ear-splitting.

"If I can—" Ian said uncertainly.

"Enough!" Alinor ordered very sharply. "You shame me. One does not plead with a man to turn aside from his duty. Begone!"

"Let me kiss them good night."

"As you will. But they do not deserve it."

He embraced both, one in each arm, as usual. They walked slowly away, drooping dejectedly. Ian started to rise. "Sit!" Alinor hissed, fighting the twitching of her lips. Eventually, feet dragging, they disappeared into the stairwell.

"Let me go up," Ian said. "They are so sad."

Alinor laughed softly. "Ian, they play you like a fish. You are too indulgent. You will spoil them."

"Am I? Will I? But they are such good children, so clever, so beautiful."

"Clever and beautiful, perhaps, but good? They are little hellions." She was laughing fondly. "All that sorrow was for your benefit. Doubtless they are already pummeling each other, throwing the pillows about, and creating general havoc."

Ian smiled. "I hope so. I cannot bear to see them sad." He hesitated.

Before he could bring himself to say what was obviously next, Alinor shook her head. "You do not look much rested," she remarked. "Did you sleep at all?"

"Yes."

"I am about to commit the sin I just scolded my children for," Alinor sighed. "I wish you had a little time to spare us. I am worried about Adam, about Joanna, too, but that is a lesser problem."

"About Adam? But he is the happiest child, and clever, and strong in arms, too."

Alinor turned her head so that she faced the flames. "He has no man to look up to," she said. "He has had no one but Beorn for more than a year. Simon tried, but he was too sick. Adam is still too young to send for fostering. I cannot send him to William and Lady Isobel. The king is so bitter against William. I suppose I must get a tutor for him, but who, Ian? I cannot take a young man in. Do you know of a married man, perhaps with children, who would do fealty and be loyal to me?"

Surreptitiously, Alinor raised a hand and wiped tears from her cheeks. Ian clenched his fists, and then carefully and deliberately opened his hands. Had Alinor turned to look at him, she would have seen he was unnaturally flushed. It was all she could do, however, to keep from wailing aloud. There were far worse troubles than Adam's burdening her, but it was not fair to worry Ian when it was plain he had problems of his own and could not help. If Ian could suggest some man to tutor Adam, Alinor felt that even so small a lessening of her burden would be like a foretaste of heaven.

"Set aside Adam's needs for the moment," Ian said. His voice was very harsh.

Alinor bit her lips together. She had no claim on Ian. She had no claim on any man living, except her vassals, and the best of those, the men most closely bound to her in love and loyalty, were dead. Their sons had obeyed Simon gladly, but whether they would accept Alinor's rule docilely she did not know. In any case, it was not Ian's responsibility. She lifted her head defiantly.

"Of course. If you can help, I will be grateful. If not, there is no reason why you should trouble yourself. Let me get you some more wine, and tell what brings you back to England, and——"

"No reason why I should help! Do you know what Simon was to me?"

"I know you were his squire and he loved you dearly, but I have no claim——"

"Simon made me a man. He never told you? No, I

suppose he would not. My father was—I do not know what to say. He killed my mother—beat her to death. He tortured and murdered for amusement. Do you know I have no memory of my childhood—no, I have two. I remember my father killing my old pony with a mace because it was beyond work and because I, he said, was too soft to useless animals. And I remember my mother dying. The rest is blank. What he did on his lands I learned not so many years ago by reading the records of the king's court. It was not that I was too young to remember. I was fourteen when Simon came to bring order to our lands."

"Oh, Ian———" That was why, Alinor thought. That was why Ian could never deny the children anything, never bear to see tears in their eyes, or even sad faces. He had known suffering—too much of it—and he had known gentleness, and he had gone too far in his desire for the latter.

"There is nothing I would not have done for Simon. There was nothing I ever could do for him. He would never permit me to repay that debt."

"Because there was none. To Simon's mind, there was no debt. He loved you for yourself, I know that, but what he did for you was because he felt it was the right thing to do. He did not do it for *you*. Thus, you owe him nothing."

"My father's lands were forfeit, but Simon outfaced the king to secure my mother's lands to me—and they were the greater part."

"Because it was right," Alinor insisted. "Because whatever ill your father did, you were innocent."

Ian made an impatient gesture. "I do not care why Simon did for me. It was done. Whatever I have, whatever I am, is his."

"Simon is dead, Ian. You are free."

"That is a stupid thing to say, Alinor," he said angrily. "Stupid and unkind. Simon lives in you and in his children. There is nothing I will not do for Simon's children and for Simon's wife."

"It is you who are stupid," she flared back, her color mounting and her eyes bright with gold and green lights. "I cannot collect a debt my husband did not acknowledge. You idiot! I would choke now to ask a favor of you."

"*I* am an idiot?" he roared, and suddenly began to laugh. "No. I will not quarrel with you. Not if I die for it. Not if I burst." He paused, took a deep breath, and said in a pleasant, indifferent tone of voice, "Tell me what worries you about Joanna."

"I would not tell you my own name," Alinor hissed.

"Come, Alinor," Ian wheedled, "there is no favor in talking of Joanna. What could I do for her? That is woman's business."

She cast a fulminating glance at him, and he put his hands together prayerfully and said, "Please?" with so spurious and wistful an expression that Alinor began to laugh and put out a hand to him. He rose to take it.

"Forgive me. I spoke with more passion than sense. I never felt a weight of obligation. Simon and I could not have been friends as we were if I did. But you know I love Adam and Joanna."

Alinor's quick glance took in the tension under the pretense of calm. Something was eating Ian. It was no part of a friend to refuse to follow his lead.

"The problem is that we are very rich," she said slowly. "Simon was Sheriff of Sussex for many years, and we are not expensive people. Money poured in and we bought land. We could do it because Richard trusted Simon. Then there was even more money and——"

"For God's sake, Alinor——" Ian protested.

"No, no. I know you do not care for that, but that is where the problem with Joanna lies. I am not and never was a great lady."

He started to protest again, and Alinor held up a hand to quell him.

"I mean that I see to my own maids and keep my own accounts and suchlike. I do not know how to pass the days in idleness, sewing and singing. Yet Joanna's position, by virtue of her dower, will place her in just such an estate. If I keep her here, she will only learn my ways."

"They are best," Ian said definitely.

"I think so, too," Alinor agreed. "When you do your own accounts, no one cheats you. But I remember that when I went to court I almost died of boredom from having nothing to do."

"You will not send Joanna to court!" Ian exclaimed.

"No, of course not, but I think I will send her to Isobel. She has the fine art of doing nothing and enjoying it."

"Not yet."

"Not yet?" Alinor echoed, bristling a little. She thought he was concerned for the shadow that lay upon William, the Earl of Pembroke, and that he thought she had not sufficiently considered her daughter's safety.

"I have a great value for Lady Isobel. She is kind, gentle, and loving; clever, too, but if God had not given her William Marshal—oh, I mean Pembroke—for a husband, she would be nothing."

"There is more in Isobel than you see."

"Perhaps. You know her better than I, but that does not change my feeling. Joanna is very like Simon. She has a seriousness and a deep desire to do right. Young as Joanna is now, Lady Isobel might implant too deeply the conviction that obedience is always right."

"Ian!" Alinor smiled archly. "You! You who have loud and long bewailed my headstrong nature, right to my face. Do I hear aright? Do I hear you advising me against teaching Joanna obedience?"

"Hellcat!" Ian laughed, but then he sobered and shook his head. "If Joanna were Adam and Adam Joanna, I would agree with all my heart. Nothing will make Adam believe obedience is a virtue, and even if he did believe it, it would make no difference. Adam is kind, but he does not care a pin to be virtuous—and neither do you! Joanna is different."

Alinor, too, had become serious. She turned her eyes, dark with worry, up to Ian's face. "I know. But—" Alinor checked herself suddenly and looked away. She was supposed to be inducing Ian to speak of his troubles, not really pouring out her own. Ian covered the hand he was holding and pressed it gently.

"But you wish to send her away into safekeeping before the king returns. Alinor, what grudge does King John have against you? Simon told me once that you had displeased him."

"Displeased the king?" Alinor echoed, completely at a loss for a moment. "Why I hardly ever set eyes— Oh, good, merciful God!" Remembrance narrowed her eyes. "I had quite forgot!" Her lips firmed, and her jaw came forward stubbornly. "Sir Giles it will have to be. Sir Giles and Sir Henry I can trust. Men can be drawn from Ealand, and young Sir John will likely honor his vows—at least, if he does not, I know where to look next. Men will be no problem altogether. It is easy enough to hire men in these times. Yes, and Joanna will have to go, because I cannot leave her here in the charge of maidservants. Adam too—oh, dear. Well, it cannot be helped. The danger that might come to him from being in William's care——"

"Alinor, what are you talking about?"

Her glance at Ian was brief and abstracted. She was so deep in planning that she hardly remembered who he was and answered the question without thinking.

"I must remove and replace three of Simon's castellans. They——"

"You plan to go yourself, bearing arms?" Ian's voice was hushed. He did not know whether to marvel or curse, laugh or weep.

Irritation flickered across Alinor's face. "Well, not bearing arms, of course. Do not be a fool or think me one. Nonetheless, I must indeed go. Sir Giles is honest and strong and not stupid, but he is no leader of men. Sir Henry can lead, provided there is someone to point him in the right direction. Sir John is too young, and I am not sufficiently sure of his loyalty. Naturally, since there is no other leader, I must go to keep them to their purpose and perhaps to prevent them from some utter stupidity."

Alinor looked up at Ian again and gently withdrew her hand from his clasp. "I must thank you for reminding me about that old trouble. I would have walked unsuspecting into the king's maw—well, perhaps not, since I have heard enough of his doings—but now I will be doubly on guard."

"You think well of me, do you not?" Ian remarked bitterly. "Where am I classed? Too stupid? Too weak? Or too disloyal to be of help?"

"But Ian," Alinor exclaimed, "how could I ask you when——"

"For sweet Mary's sake, do not rub salt into my wounds!"

"No, I was not thinking of that foolish argument," Alinor assured him. "The heat being gone from my head, I would ask you to serve me for love quickly enough, but I have seen that you have some great matter in hand that is weighing on your spirit. Forgive me that I did not ask you to unburden your heart. I knew you wished to tell me, but——"

"You have seen clearly enough, but not all there is to see." Ian's voice was gratingly harsh again. "Will you tell me how you offended the king—I mean, are you willing to tell me?"

"Of course I am willing, but I do not see that it will be of any use to you. However, it was thus. You know that Simon and I were wed in the Holy Land and that when we came back to England none knew of it. Simon hastened to tell the queen. I remained to make straight all that had gone awry on my lands. By a ruse I was

brought to Kingsclere and fell into Lord John's hands—
it was before he was king, of course. He wished to
marry me to a man of his own choosing and use my
lands as he saw fit. I told him he was too late, that
Simon had me already. Then he said," suddenly Alinor
began to giggle like a little girl, "he said that he would
not have picked the bud—in deference to the man he
had chosen for me—but that since the flower was open,
he would sup some of its nectar."

Ian had looked away, seeing where the tale was leading and not wishing to embarrass Alinor. His nostrils
spread and then pinched with distaste. "Filth," he
muttered. "Did he force you?"

"Would he hate me if he had?" Alinor laughed mer-
rily, and Ian looked at her, realizing that the little
choked squeaks he had heard were not tears. "He called
me a frightened little bird," she sputtered, "and—and
he chucked me under the chin."

"But how did you preserve your virtue?"

"Virtue?" Alinor spat. "Virtue had nothing to do
with it! Stupid clod! He made me lose my temper,
calling me a little bird and chucking me under the chin
as if I were a maidservant. I rammed him in the belly
with an embroidery frame." Alinor began to laugh
again. "I think I may have caught his upstanding member, and when he ceased writhing with pain, I drove him
from the room with a lighted torch and my knife."

Ian stared down at her with open mouth and glazed
eyes.

"If only he had not made me angry," Alinor sighed,
shaking her head remorsefully. "It would have been
more politic to yield, but he did not give me time to
think!"

"Alinor," Ian gasped, "have you no morals?"

First she laughed, which did not really surprise Ian,
but then she burst into tears. He bent over her, cursing
himself for forgetting that she could be overly sensitive
to everything just now.

"That is just what Simon said," Alinor sobbed, "those very words. And then we laughed because Simon knew the act itself, without the love that bound us, was worthless. A little more pleasure than pissing, Simon said."

A flash of rage flicked Ian. Simon said, Simon said. Was he doomed to a life of what Simon had said? "Just a few minutes since you told me Simon was dead. Now I tell it you," he snarled. "It is time to stop weeping for him."

Surprised, Alinor looked up. "I am not weeping for Simon. Not even I could have wished him to live longer. He hated himself for his illness. I did not try to keep him. That is my comfort. Not once, not once did I bid him rest, or not to climb the stairs, or not to do whatever he wished. I let him go. But—but I am so lonely. I weep for me, for me, not for Simon."

"You will not be lonely long."

Ian stood before her like a statue, his eyes as blank, his face as set. Shock silenced Alinor. She stared at the expressionless face, trying to make sense of what he had said. Was Ian trying to warn her of a threat to her life, implying she would soon join Simon? The notion that he might threaten her himself did not even flicker through her mind. Alinor did not even think that no one would dare threaten her here at Roselynde, where every man was devoted to her. She simply knew that, no matter how he looked, Ian would never harm a hair of her head.

Then what? Her mind leaped to the talk about King John. Not lonely— King John— Of course, a marriage that would punish her for the way she had humiliated him. Alinor's face became as blank as Ian's as she considered the alternatives. Her first impulse was outright defiance. She put the idea aside, to be used as a last resort. With her hold on Simon's property insecure and doubts about her own younger vassals, she was not strong enough. That left acceptance.

Well, why not? Had she not just said that mating was a meaningless act without love? It was a cheap price to pay for time to gather her forces, and it might not come to that. A fatal accident could easily befall the man before marriage actually took place. No, not fatal, and not before. A glow woke in the depths of Alinor's eyes. She had a worse fate prepared for any henchman of King John's who wished to take her in marriage. She would indeed marry him, and she would be a tender and loving wife to the crippled, speechless, sightless hulk that would remain when her men were finished with him. That would be of multiple benefit. She would have her husband's property to administer, and she would be protected from still another marriage.

At this point a frown crinkled Alinor's brow. Would Ian bring such news? It seemed most unlikely, unless the man chosen was respectable. The first supporter John had chosen for Alinor had been a decent man. If that were so— Little, bright sparkles came into Alinor's eyes to brighten their glow further. If that were so, Alinor thought, I will soon have a willing slave to do my bidding. But that would be too easy. A decent man was not likely, because Ian had asked what grudge John had against her. Unless the king had mentioned the matter, what could have recalled that old, old incident to Ian's mind? Simon could not have spoken of it recently.

The idea, which slipped so quickly in and out of Alinor's mind and which she accepted without examination, led her astray. In fact, the last thing Simon had ever spoken to Ian about was King John's grudge. Two months before Simon died, Ian had been summoned to serve in the king's expeditionary force to France. He had offered to buy release from that service so that he could continue to act as Simon's deputy. The dying man had considered and then refused. It was more important, he said, for Ian to see how King John reacted to news of his death and to be where he could counter any plans to harm Alinor.

"I do not worry about the men and the lands. They may be safely left to her management." A wan smile had touched Simon's lips. "What is 'hers to her' is more a part of Alinor than her soul. The king's spite is another matter. He has a cause to hate her, and he is not the kind that forgets. If you love me, Ian, shield her from the king."

There had been no mention of marriage. Had Ian permitted himself to consider it, he would have suspected that Simon could not bear to think of Alinor in another man's arms. However, Ian himself had not thought of marriage then. Simon had lingered near a year already. Less generous than Alinor, Ian could not bear to let the suffering soul depart. He would rather have Simon alive, no matter how tormented, than let him die and face his own grief and insecurity. Alinor had known nothing about what was said at that last meeting. If she had, she might have been better prepared.

"Did you hear me?" Ian's voice grated into the long silence.

"I hear you," Alinor assured him calmly, "but I do not understand."

"It is clear enough. The solution to all your troubles is to marry again."

"To whom?" Alinor asked dulcetly.

Ian's rigid stance broke. He clasped his hands and pushed at a bright flower on the carpet with his toe. His eyes no longer met Alinor's blankly. They were watching the operation of his tone with enormous interest.

"Me."

Surprise rendered Alinor speechless. She was still caught up in her own baseless reasonings, and Ian's statement was at one and the same time so much part of those reasonings and so far outside them that she could not reorient herself.

"Do you mean the king has ordered that you marry me?" Alinor faltered.

Ian lifted his eyes from the rug. He had not been sure what to expect, but an explosive and perhaps revolted refusal had been a strong possibility. He knew Alinor was practical enough to realize that another husband was an eventual necessity, even if only to protect her from overinsistent suitors. Three months was a rather short time, although great heiresses were often remarried within weeks of their previous mates' deaths. On the other hand, few marriages were blessed with the single-minded devotion Alinor and Simon felt for each other.

In terms of Alinor's immediate reaction, however, that had worried Ian less than the fear that she might recoil from marriage to him as from incest. He had never dared probe how Alinor felt about him, and all these months that he had been arguing the question in his mind had brought no clarification. One gesture he brought to memory would seem to betray in Alinor a fear similar to his own—a fear that too great intimacy would lead to attraction. Another, just as clear, pointed to the sexless friendship a healthy man had for another. Still another bespoke the tenderness of a sister to a brother. The last was the most dangerous. There was no sign of revulsion in Alinor's face, however, merely confusion.

"Ordered?" Ian repeated. "No. My purpose, in truth, is to have you safe from him before he remembers you are alive. We were fortunate that the news about Simon came just at the height of the siege. The king had no time to think about it. Since then, I have taken good care that no one should bring it to his mind."

Alinor's thoughts were beginning to come straight. "This was something you decided upon yourself?" she asked.

"Yes," he replied shortly.

Alinor put out her hand to him again. "How kind you are, Ian. How very kind."

To her surprise he did not take her hand, and the blood rose into his face so that even in the candlelight she could see his swarthy skin was a dark red.

"I do not know whether it is kind or not. It is simply the best thing to do. I hope you think I am a suitable man to train Adam. I can whip Simon's castellans into line. And when you summon your vassals to our wedding, they can do homage to you again, which will clear their thinking on the subject of fealty."

Alinor looked steadily into the beautiful face. The deep flush made Ian's eyes more luminous. "I believe you are right," she said softly; "for me it would be a wise thing." Then she shook her head. "I do not think it is the best thing for you, Ian."

"I am old enough to know what is best for me."

So firm a statement of an obvious untruth made Alinor laugh. Her grandfather, who had been over 80 when he died, had only known what was right, never what was best for him. The 60-odd years of Simon's life had not been long enough to teach him the difference between what was right in principle and what was best for him. Alinor was strongly of the opinion that Ian was another of the same type. Experience had made her wise. She did not attempt to explain the difference between "right" and "best" to Ian. Long ago she had talked herself hoarse on that subject.

"I do not see what is funny," Ian snapped, his voice tight with anger. "If I am no match for you in wealth, I am no pauper either. I am sufficiently a man of my hands to be well respected in tourney and battle. I am not contemptible——"

"Ian! Ian!" Alinor rose and went to him, gripping his upper arms. "You are all that any woman in her right mind could desire."

"Any woman except you!"

A faint color came into Alinor's pale face. "My dear, I cannot allow you to make such a sacrifice, nor to endanger yourself by gaining the king's hatred for my sake."

The flush receded from Ian's complexion, leaving it gray and tired; his eyes went blank and hard again. She had avoided answering him with skill and kindness, but there was no doubt of what Alinor meant in Ian's mind. "You do not understand," he said quietly. "I am not asking you to marry me. I am telling you that you must do so. I will take no naysay from you. There is no sense in raging. I do not mind if you do, if the raging will make your heart lighter, but I tell you there is no sense in it. Whatever you do, I will have you to wife."

"You are mad!" There was sufficient color in Alinor's face now, and her eyes were brilliant. She backed off, tensed as if to attack or resist attack. "Do you think I am some delicate court flower, some powerless, poor puppet——"

"You are powerless against me." He did not move toward her, and there was no triumph in his expression. "Oh, I have heard you say a dissatisfied wife should search for love in her husband's heart with a knife, and I believe you would do it—but not to me, not when you know I desire only your good and your children's good. You can even call your men and have me thrust out of your keep—you can, but you will not. What would Adam and Joanna think when they saw the gates locked against me? What will you tell them? That I wished them ill? Even if you could bring yourself to lie to them, to destroy the love that has always been between us, you cannot stay pent in Roselynde. You must visit your other lands, especially in these times. You have delayed too long already in that duty. The moment you are out, I will have you. Will you order your men to kill me, Alinor?"

"Do you think I will love you for this?" she blazed.

"You may well hate me." His voice was very low. "I

cannot help that. I can only do what I know is best for the children and for you."

The flat despair beat down her anger. "I will never hate you," Alinor soothed. "I desire only to save you from hurting yourself. There must be some other way. I have thought already——"

"You have thought for an hour. I have thought for three long months. I did not come to this decision quickly or lightly, Alinor. It will solve all your problems, and suit my needs also. It is time for me to marry. I need an heir for my lands."

"But I am no fecund mare," Alinor protested. "In all the many years Simon and I were married, I conceived only four children. Of those, one I did not carry long, and one died."

Her plain, unembarrassed earnestness made Ian smile. "Simon was not a young man," he suggested. He shook his head at the indignant rejection he saw rising to her lips. "I did not mean that he was no ardent lover, but it is known that fewer colts are vouchsafed to older stallions, no matter how willing or eager they are. In any case, it will be of less account to me in that Adam will be mine. If I get no brother for him on you, he may have it all with my love and good will."

That was too practical and reasonable a solution for Alinor to argue against. "The king's hate is not so lightly put aside. It seems to me it were better to allow him to foist whatever man he wishes upon me. I will settle with any unwelcome husband."

"I have no doubt you could," Ian agreed, torn between anxiety and laughter. "But whatever is said of the king, he is no fool. Do you think he would not notice if husband after husband fell off cliffs, or was accidentally drowned while sailing, or shot while hunting?"

"I am no fool either," Alinor snapped. "What would that get me except another husband? I assure you that the man chosen for me by the king would not die. I would care for what was left of him most tenderly, and most assiduously would I pursue those who harmed him." She paused and added with a half smile, "I can think of a number of men I would be well pleased to be rid of."

Ian swallowed. She was not jesting. She would not only have the king's henchman maimed, which he would probably deserve, but would put the blame upon some person who had nothing whatsoever to do with it but had happened to incur her dislike. Alinor certainly needed a firm, guiding hand. It was quite useless to reason with her about right and wrong. He knew Alinor. However, she was never impervious to practicalities in a situation.

"It will not do," he said more calmly than he felt. "Who knows what rights or lands of yours the man might swear away in order to have you for a wife? Whatever he promised would be forfeit to the king."

Alinor thought about that with narrowed eyes, but it was the horrible truth and one thing that she had not considered. Alinor did not mind parting with money, but she would not willingly give up a stick or a stone of her property nor a tittle of her right to administer it as she thought best. Ian was right. It would be best to marry him. No one knew what was in the strong rooms of Alinor's castles except Alinor, but she was confident that whatever fine the king set she could pay. Her vassals would contribute, too. She had a right to an aide for being married.

Having added up the benefits, Alinor raised her eyes to Ian's face. God help her, what was she thinking of? This was Ian, not a book of accounts. This was a man with whom she had quarreled, with whom she had laughed, a friend who had wept for her when her baby died.

"Ian," she exclaimed with real distress, "I would repay you for your help and care with false coin."

He did not misunderstand her. With those dear to

her, Alinor was always honest. She was telling him she could not love him. Ian shrugged. "There is nothing to repay." He looked away into the fire. "This will suit my needs as well as yours."

For the first time in years, Alinor again wondered why Ian had not married. Certainly he was not afflicted with a love for men. Equally as certain he was not indifferent to love altogether. If he had been, he could have married greatly to his profit many years ago. Between the deaths on Crusade and the deaths in the wars Richard had waged, there were suitable heiresses in plenty. There were also well-dowered daughters of mighty houses that would have been glad of a blood bond with Ian de Vipont. Thus, either he still sought a woman he could love or, more likely, there was already a woman he loved but could not have. As I love and cannot have, Alinor thought. She was moved by sympathy for him who might also suffer the hopeless longing she endured.

Only doubtless his woman was still alive. Alinor was shocked to feel a prick of jealousy. I will be no dog in the manger, she admonished herself. I will be blind and deaf. I cannot demand from Ian what I cannot offer to him. If he loves, I will look aside. So much I can do for him, who does so much for me. Perhaps that is what he desires, a woman who cannot offer a heart-whole love and thus would not be hurt because he cannot offer that either.

"Since you say you *will* have me, and I can see it will be greatly to my benefit that it should be so, let us consider what fine the king will lay upon us."

Ian turned sharply from his contemplation of the fire, his face a comical mixture of incredulity, relief and wariness. It was not like Alinor to yield so readily. On the other hand, she was essentially reasonable and clear headed, and the solution he had offered was practical. Watching her, he said, "None. I have paid already for the right to marry 'whomsoever I will.' It is common enough to gain such permission when a man does not know from whom he will obtain the best offer."

"The king was not suspicious?"

"He was so delighted by the success of the siege and his attack on Montmarillon and Clisson, he had no room in his heart for anything else. Besides, I had a strong advocate. I had a piece of really good fortune at Montauban. I did not wish to tell the children, because I would not have it spoken about, and they are heedless. I was so fortunate as to save William of Salisbury's life."

More concern than delight was apparent on Alinor's face. "Is that fortunate?" she asked. "I never thought it a comfortable thing when one of the Angevin blood owed a debt."

"Not Salisbury. I suppose his nature must come from his mother. I cannot deny that I was not easy at first, and I sought to avoid him. He came to me." Ian's lips twitched with remembered amusement. "He said, 'Thank you.' I said, 'It was nothing.' Then he began to laugh and said his life might be nothing to me but it was rather valuable to him. I replied that that was how it should be. From that we came to talk, and later we were close battle companions for some months. He is a good man."

"Perhaps," Alinor agreed, but doubtfully.

She was not willing to condemn out of hand a man to whom she had never spoken more than indifferent courtesy. On the other side, she did not trust Ian's judgment of men the way she had trusted Simon's. Simon might have dreamed of the long future, but his near vision was keen, and he was not given to enthusiasms. Ian was more warm-hearted than Simon, more easily moved to sympathy, and, of course, he had not Simon's years of experience. That, naturally, would make him less tolerant of doubts of his judgment.

"I fear, however," she added hesitantly, "that the old saw is true, and birds of a feather flock together."

"But he is not," Ian insisted. "He is as unlike King John as it is possible to be."

"Salisbury loves the king, or at least pretends to do so."

"There is no pretends with Salisbury. He is very open, and he does, indeed, love John."

Alinor's silence was eloquent. Ian frowned, trying to find a way to say what he meant. "Look, I think it comes from their being children together. Salisbury is some two or three years the elder. John, being what he is, was always in trouble, even as a child. Salisbury, as elder brother, always protected him. It has grown into a habit. Often he disapproves of what John does——"

"You did not listen to him say that?" Alinor asked, horrified.

"Yes I did," Ian snapped, "and I spoke my mind on the subject also, and neither of us spoke treason! You need not look like that, Alinor. I am not a child."

"That remains to be seen," Alinor flared back, "but I have no desire that my husband be summoned for conspiracy or whatever other fancy name the king wishes to use to destroy you. Do you doubt that every word you said was poured into the king's ears?"

Several impulses hit Ian at once. There was the normal male reaction—a desire to tell Alinor to mind her needle and keep her mouth shut. Unlike Simon, Ian had not been raised in a court where the queen wielded almost as much power as the king. Long as he had known Alinor, he was still often surprised by her masterful manner, more now because she had been so soft and yielding to Simon in the last year of his life. Then, there was his desire to defend Salisbury from the accusation of deceit and, incidentally, himself from the implied accusation of being a fool. Overriding all was the conviction that Alinor really had accepted his offer. The possessive way she had said "my husband" left no doubt in his mind. He moved closer.

"You will take me, then?"

"I have said so. This business———"

"We will come back to that anon. To me there is something more important." It still seemed unnatural to Ian that Alinor should yield so quickly and easily. He had said she was powerless against him, but that was not true. There were a number of expedients she could use. She had not even tried very hard to reason him out of the marriage. "Upon what terms will you take me?"

"Terms?" She was impatient, feeling that he was trying to draw her away from a more important issue. "I suppose the same terms upon which I took Simon. Yours to you, mine to me, during life. Your lands to be left in male tail—unless you wish to set something aside for a daughter, but that is not necessary. I have enough to dower any girls. There would have to be a special clause if you wish to leave your lands to Adam, failing male issue of your own blood. It is for you to say. He will be well enough to do with what he has from Simon. Ian, this can wait until we summon the clerks to write the marriage contract. You will not find me unreasonable. It is more important to consider what Salisbury means and what he may do."

Certainly the catch was not there. She did not mean to set impossible conditions so that he would withdraw his offer. For some reason of her own, which doubtless he would know only in her own sweet time, Alinor had decided after the most token protest to marry him. Tension oozed out of Ian so that his limbs felt weak. He was suddenly aware that he had not slept at all in three days and little enough before that. His eyes were burning with tiredness. He yawned jaw-crackingly, and then grinned.

"I can tell you one thing he will do very soon. If you will deign to invite him, he will dance at your wedding."

That was interesting. More than that, fascinating. Since Ian knew of the king's grudge, he would be un-

likely to invite anyone to the wedding beyond those
obliged to come; particularly, he would not invite a
confidant of the king. That meant that Salisbury had
offered his company. Was this the result of simple
gratitude and friendship, as Ian thought, or was Salisbury planting some secret seed? He was the youngest
royal bastard that Henry II had fathered, but strong
bastards had sat on thrones before. Color rose in Alinor's face; she raised eyes sparkling with interest to
Ian. He was so tired he was swaying on his feet.

"Good God," she exclaimed, "what a fool you are.
Why did you tell me you had slept? Why did you not
go to bed right after dinner?"

"Because I had to know—" His voice was thick with
the sudden overwhelming fatigue that followed relief.

"There is nothing more you are going to know. Go
to bed!"

The answer Ian began was interrupted by another
jaw-cracking yawn. That defeated him. He laughed,
stepped still closer to take and kiss Alinor's hand.

"Yes, madam," he agreed meekly.

She watched him turn away. Even staggering slightly
with sleepiness, he was as graceful as a big cat. "Ian."
He stopped abruptly, stiffening a little, turned his head.
"Do not you dare dress in the morning before I have
seen to that back again."

The stiffness melted. He offered a last, sleepy smile.
"Yes, madam."

CHAPTER THREE

The year and a half since Simon had fallen ill had seemed like a thousand, thousand years to Alinor. Each day had passed on leaden feet filled with terror, with an ear always cocked for Simon's laboring breath. And when that breath was stilled, time seemed to stop altogether. There were periods of light and dark that Alinor knew were days and nights; there were sounds that she knew were her voice; sometimes there was even a sound that she recognized as laughter. None of it had any particular meaning. Then time began to move again, but it had gone all wrong. Each day was endless, and yet the things that needed doing never seemed to be done.

Ian's arrival broke the dull round of "I should"—"I cannot." Somehow his physical presence brought urgency and reality to problems, and somehow Alinor found herself able to cope with them. This was not because Ian himself was of any particular help. In a reaction to three months of grief, indecision and anxiety, coupled with enormous physical effort, Ian quietly collapsed. He slept the day through, waking only long enough to eat enormously, have his sore back dressed, and go meekly back to bed when he was told to do so. He was so sodden with exhaustion that he did not see the terror in the children's eyes. So had their father been for a time, and then he had never played with them again. Alinor herself would have been worried except for the fact that Ian was eating for three men. She was able to comfort Adam and Joanna with the assurance that he was only tired; in two days or three he would be well and strong.

Meanwhile, life seemed to come into focus. There was a reason to drive the children out to play; if she did not, they would wake Ian. There was a reason to talk to the cooks about meals, to be sure the laundresses were attending properly to the linens and Ian's soiled clothing. Alinor picked through his baggage, discarding things that were damaged and soiled beyond repair by neglect while on the field. Some could be replaced from Simon's clothing—shirts and chausses and the rough, homespun tunics worn under mail. The outer garments, however— Life blurred a little again as Alinor folded away the gray gowns and surcoats. Simon had always worn gray. No one would ever wear those garments again. It was not sentiment. Merely, no shade would fit Ian worse. His coloring was designed for the jewel tints—ruby, emerald, sapphire would make his dark beauty glow.

Chests long unused were sought for and turned out. Alinor cut the wine-red velvet, the soft, thick, green-woolen cloth. Her maids were wakened at first dawn and harried through the day. With half an ear she noted, as she bent over her embroidery, that the maids were chattering and singing and laughing again. The sounds were strange to her; she had not realized how long it had been since there were other than hushed whispers in the women's quarters.

On the fourth day Ian woke of himself at dawn. A boy was sent running, and Alinor came sleepily down in a hastily donned bedrobe to clean and bandage Ian's back.

"Where do you go?" she asked as she worked over him.

The question gave him pleasure and reassurance. It was no polite inquiry of a departing guest but a demand that bespoke the right to such information.

"Where I am needed first. When I came, I had the

feeling that Beorn wished to speak to me, but I gave him no opportunity. There were more important matters to settle."

"You have the time to give him?"

Ian twisted his neck to look at her. "Why not?"

Alinor's lips tightened, and she made a gesture that sent maids and squires scurrying out of the chamber. "I had the impression that you had stopped only for a brief visit, that you were on your way somewhere."

Annoyed for the moment by Alinor's casual assumption of authority over his servants, Ian was now grateful. "Oh, well—" He replaced his head on his folded arms. "I was not sure how angry you would be when I proposed we should be married. That excuse was for the children, in case you should order me to leave."

There was a silence that soon struck Ian as unnatural. He lifted his head again and was shocked to see hurt and real anger in Alinor's face. He curled around, sat up, and seized her hands. "Alinor, what have I said?"

"Ask instead what you have not said."

A weird mixture of hope and disappointment gripped Ian. The only thing he knew he had not said was that he loved her. The need that grew larger in him as he grew surer Alinor would marry him was the need to be loved by her. He had thought it was the last thing Alinor wanted to hear. If she could love him, that would be heaven. If she had loved Simon, could she change so soon? So soon wipe out so many years of love? How long would her love for him last? Did it matter? If she would look at him once with the eyes that had dwelt on Simon, it would be enough. The warring emotions made him hesitate.

"Did you think I had forgotten your talk of caging the wolf?" Alinor asked coldly.

"What wolf?" Ian got out, totally confused, except

for the conviction that his initial instinct had been right. Alinor wanted no talk of love from him.

"The wolf that loves England."

That could only be John, Ian realized, but what had he said? All his memories of that first day in Roselynde were blurred by fatigue, and completely unimportant compared with Alinor's acceptance of him.

"You may remember, Alinor, but I do not. I was half dead on my feet."

"You said you had much to say to me on the subject of caging the wolf but pleaded tiredness not to match words with me. You had better match them now or reconsider your offer to take me to wife. I am no meek and obedient slave. Where my lands and my people are concerned, I will see where I go before I set a foot forward. I will not be dragged, will I nill I, into treason. If I saw a reason for it—or rather, some hope of success, because the reason is self-evident——"

"Alinor," Ian snapped. "There is *no* treason in my heart or my mind. John is King of England, and I will do my uttermost to preserve him in that state with my mouth or with my body."

The sincerity of that statement could not be mistaken. Alinor was annoyed with herself. She knew Ian had done fealty to John. Honorable idiot that he was, he would not break that oath. She had gone the wrong way about finding out what she wished to know.

"I know you do not wish to supplant the king," she said pacifically, "but are there not other forms of treason?"

"In my mind, no."

That was flat and clear. As far as Ian was concerned, it ended the discussion. He began to loosen his grip on Alinor's hands, but she turned them and gripped his. Ian thought he knew Alinor; he had been her friend for many years. He had argued with her before, but her argument had always been maintained for his good. He had yet to learn what Alinor was like when she felt her own good was at stake. He had yet to learn that when she agreed to marry him, he had become "hers, to her." That meant not only that his good and hers were inextricably bound together in her mind, but also that no part of his mind or soul would be left in peace until Alinor had picked it apart and understood it thoroughly.

"Ian," she said softly but insistently, "what of the king's mind?"

His lips twisted bitterly. "What of it? To his mind there is no word or act, except "yea," that is *not* treason. Has he not deprived Pembroke of every honor he could strip from him for giving him good advice? That, too, is treason in King John's mind. If it is not by his order, it is treason. And what was by his order yesterday may be treason tomorrow."

Alinor folded Ian's hands together and held them between hers. "And yet you will follow him and obey him?"

"There is no one else!" Ian cried. "Do you not understand? Since Normandy was lost to Philip three years ago, England is all there is for the English lords. We must have a king who understands that."

"You believe John understands that? His whole mind is fixed upon making his provinces in France safe and winning back Normandy," Alinor remarked caustically.

Ian's lean cheeks showed bunches of muscle as his jaw clamped. "It is true and yet not true. John would not see his patrimony eaten—well, Alinor, what of you? Would you sit and see someone take what was yours? Would I?"

It was an honest and reasonable point. Alinor nodded.

"But for all of that, John knows England is most important," Ian continued. "It is England that is his home and the place he best loves. Here he comes to rest and take his pleasures——"

"And to collect the taxes to pay for them and to pay for his wars in France," replied Alinor.

"What of that? To whom would you prefer to pay? To Philip's son Louis?" Ian asked coldly. Frustration made Alinor stamp her foot, and Ian laughed. "Well?" he insisted. "Who else is there? The sons of Stephen of Blois' daughters?"

"There is Salisbury," Alinor said softly.

To her surprise, Ian did not roar a protest or tell her to hold her tongue. He shrugged and sighed. "Who has not thought of it? It is hopeless. Salisbury would not agree. He has been sounded. Old King Henry did his work well on Salisbury. The idea that he cannot be king is bred deep into the bone. Do not shake your head at me, I know him, and you do not. More important even than that—once you open that door, on whom can you close it? Do not the bastards of the first Henry have even better claim? Do you not see that a dozen 'kings' would spring up? John may be a running sore, but to overset him would bring on a plague."

He was right, and Alinor knew it. "Then what will you do to cage the wolf?" she asked tartly, reverting to her original question.

"You know that the trouble has become much worse since Hubert Walter died last year. Thus, the first step is a man as great as Walter to be Archbishop of Canterbury, a man who can stand against John if need be."

Alinor had been prepared for some vague generality or some hopeful, illusory nonsense. This flat, practical statement woke an instant response in her. "I thought the king had already chosen that ass-licker Gray to be archbishop. How can another be appointed? Who?" she asked eagerly.

Ian freed his hands gently and lay down again. "Finish with me, Alinor," he suggested, "while I tell

you. There are matters closer to us that I must see to
also."

"Of course. Turn a little this way." She swabbed
another spot and then sighed. "It is an excellent
thought, but I do not see——"

"You have been taken up with another matter," Ian
reminded her. "You must call to mind that the monks
of Canterbury had long been dissatisfied with Walter,
who, they felt, gave more thought to the kingdom than
to their church or to God. Thus, as soon as Walter
was dead, they elected their subprior, one called
Reginald, to be archbishop and sent him off secretly
to Rome. Fortunately for us, the man was as foolish
as proud, and no sooner out of England than he put
on airs and announced his election to the world."

"You are right, I had forgotten," Alinor agreed.

"Well, as you can guess, that did not suit John. He
needs the weight of the Church behind him, since the
barons are not overwilling servants. And, to speak the
truth, many bishops do not love the king any better
than do the barons. Peter des Roches——"

"The bishop of Winchester. He is John's creature."

"Not so much a creature. Peter of Winchester is no
man's creature. Like me, he is John's man. The king
advanced him, and he is decently grateful, but he also
sees that to allow the king free rein is to drive the
barons into rebellion. John does not see it. He believes if he has the Archbishop of Canterbury to back
him, he will be able to control both barons and
bishops."

"Doubtless. Sit up, Ian, and let me bandage you."

He came upright and lifted his arms as instructed,
but his mind remained with what he was saying. "The
king made haste to Canterbury and so terrorized the
monks that they repudiated Reginald and elected Gray
as John demanded. Another delegation was sent posthaste to Rome with this new election."

"That I did remember. So where is your hope?"

"Wait, wait, that is not all. The bishops subordinate to Canterbury also sent a protest that they, who are most nearly concerned in the appointment, were not consulted, as is their right. That muddied the waters so thoroughly that the Pope has called all parties to Rome and has put off judgment until December. Now, Innocent III is no Celestine. He is a learned and scholarly man, but strong and ambitious——"

"That sounds more dangerous to me——"

An eager assent cut her off. "Oh yes, we are playing with fire, but Winchester says—and the bishops of Bath and London, too, and they are not John's creatures— all say that Innocent is intelligent as well as ambitious. He will try, of course, to tighten his grip upon the country, but in order to do so he must needs offer us an archbishop who is really acceptable to all and a worthy man."

Alinor shook her head. "He might be a saint and yet be worse than useless. If Innocent should appoint one of his Italians——" Then she drew breath sharply. "Think, Ian, what would be if he should appoint a Frenchman."

"I said he was not an idiot. Do you think the Pope does not know how things are between the English and the French? An Italian would be unfortunate, but not a disaster. Certainly for our purposes he would be better than Gray. He would owe nothing to John and be more inclined to listen to the advice of the bishops. I do not think that will happen, and neither do Winchester, London, and Bath. I am not sure, but I think there have been letters offering a compromise. The bishops do not really have a right to participate in the election of Canterbury, but they have done so in the past and could continue to complain and appeal and hold up Peter's pence. Winchester hinted to me that the subordinate bishops implied they would make no protest over the Pope's decision to exclude them from the election if Stephen Langton were preferred."

"Who?"

"Stephen Langton, an Englishman. He is now cardinal priest of Saint Chrysogonus in Rome. You do not know him, but my lands are in the north and I met him twice, oh, many years ago when he was a prebendary in York. It was just after I came out of Wales. I was, perhaps, eighteen or nineteen years old. I have never forgotten him. No one who has ever met him has ever forgotten him. He will serve our purpose if any man alive can. He is the stuff of which martyrs are made."

Alinor fastened the bandage and reached out absently to hand Ian his shirt. He smiled as he began to struggle into it. She was looking at him with a frown on her brow but obviously not seeing him at all. Her thoughts were all for the political matter under discussion. Again Ian was aware of pleasure oddly mixed with pain. Obviously, he was no longer an honored guest, one who must be waited upon hand and foot. Husbands might do for themselves when wives were otherwise occupied. The abandonment of formal courtesy was reassuring, but Ian was not a husband of long standing. He was a young lover. He wanted his lady's eyes to dwell upon him with desire.

The shirt was Ian's own and thus too tight over the bulky bandage. Simon's chausses had fitted well because both men were long of leg and narrow of hip, but Simon had been bulkier of shoulder and chest than Ian. In a moment Alinor's attention was recalled by his contortions. She "tchk'd" with irritation, snatched the shirt off over his head again, and went to fetch another.

"I can see that it will help to fix John's attention on a contest with the church, although that is a chancy thing and may bring grief in its train; but it is not enough," Alinor said as she maneuvered the larger shirt over Ian's body.

Now started, she continued to dress him with automatic efficiency, dropping to her knees to pull the chausses over his feet and up over his legs. Ian's hand twitched toward her glossy hair, as black as his own, but thick and straight as a horse's tail, so long that it swept the floor around her as she knelt. He had only seen her hair twice before in his life. Once, when he had first known her and she still wore the old-style headdress of a veil under a chaplet, he had seen her hair under the veil in braids. Once, when she had miscarried of a child, Simon had brought Ian to their bedchamber to talk to Alinor and lighten her heart. Then her hair had been loose as now. Ian drew his hand away.

"Not enough," he agreed. The effort he made was successful. His voice was steady. "What more must be done remains to be seen." He paused for a moment and then went on somewhat hesitantly, "Weddings are a good reason for men to meet without seeming to have any suspicious purpose."

"Excellently thought upon," Alinor agreed heartily.

There was no quiver of disappointment in her voice. She knew this marriage was an arrangement of political and personal convenience for Ian. It was quite reasonable that he should think of the wedding in terms of its political usefulness. In fact, she could not understand why she felt differently. There was no change in her love for Simon. Nonetheless, when she thought of being married to Ian, her breath came a little shorter and warmth suffused her. It would be necessary to be very careful to hide such things from him. It would be unfair to display an interest and eagerness he was unable to match.

"Stand up." Alinor tied the chausses, dropped to her knees again, and tapped his right foot. He lifted it enough for her to slip the cross garter under. "Tighten that leg."

Ian seized the cloth at his thigh and drew it upward while Alinor expertly twisted the cross garter round his leg and tied it under the knee. The left leg was similarly treated. Then Alinor looked up. She held out her hands quite naturally so that Ian could assist her to her feet. She could only pray that the dim light would hide the hot color she felt in her cheeks. Alinor lowered her eyes again.

"When shall the wedding be?"

The grip on her hands tightened suddenly. "Soon."

There was so much eagerness in Ian's reply that Alinor raised a startled gaze to him. He had surprised himself almost as much as her, however. By the time her eyes found his face, he was looking past her, and his mouth was hard. He released her hands.

"It must be very soon," Ian went on. "I know the king intends to hold Christmas in England. And it would be well to assume he will come here a week or two earlier. Thus——"

"The beginning of December or, to be safe, the end of November." Alinor put a hand to her cheek. "For how many must I make ready?"

"On my part about twenty noble lords. Five, at least, will have large retinues."

"You are asking Llewelyn?"

"Yes. I am not sure he will come, but I hope he does. There is some chance of it because he will want to see his son Owain, who is with me, and if John is not yet in the country, it would be safe enough."

"Safe enough? Is Llewelyn not married to John's daughter Joan? And surely that was only a few years ago. This Owain——"

Ian laughed. "I have a fine crop of bastards among my squires—but they are good boys. Owain is Llewelyn's eldest natural son. Geoffrey is William of Salisbury's boy." He nodded at her expression of satisfaction, but returned to the subject that worried him. "If Llewelyn does not come, I will have to ride into Wales. I fear he is brewing up trouble there and I must speak to him. You understand, Alinor, that if the king ceases to split himself between the French lands and these islands, his strength will be greatly increased here.

Moreover, the barons who would not go with him to France will eagerly flock to his standard to subdue Wales or Scotland or Ireland."

"I see that clearly enough. What I do not see is what success may be looked for if John leads the army."

"Hush," Ian said, grinning at her. "After his great victories in France to be so untrusting." He laughed again. "Most of the time Salisbury leads. That is all to the good. If John were not a cursed fool, William of Pembroke would lead—and that would be still better. However, John is learning. He will never be a great battle leader because—because he thinks too much, although he is not so totally useless about war as he once was."

Alinor was listening with only half an ear. Most of her attention was devoted to adding and multiplying in her head, and her eyes were growing larger. "Oh, Ian, with those I must ask it will be nigh on forty lords with their ladies and near—near a thousand servants."

"Yes." Ian wrinkled his brow over her calculation. "That sounds right to me. Of course, some men we must have counted twice. The number will doubtless be less by a few."

"It will strip a year's supplies from Roselynde."

"To be sure," Ian agreed. "That cannot matter. You have spent far too much time here."

"But——"

He turned away a little. "You need not excuse yourself to me. I know why it was done. Nonetheless, now it is time to correct your necessary neglect. You must go on progress, and it will be natural to stay awhile at each keep and set all to rights."

Being far more used to hearing that she gave too close attention to the doings of her vassals and castellans, Alinor was temporarily reduced to silence.

"We have wasted too much time on this already," Ian continued, his eyes on the brightening light of morning coming into the antechamber. "When the children are abed after dinner, we can list those who should be asked." His quick smile and the next words took the sting from the remark. "I am starving."

Alinor chuckled. "If you do nothing but eat and sleep, you will get fat."

"Not I. I have been trying to put on some flesh for years. It would do wonders for my jousting." But his thoughts had already left the jest. "Alinor, do you know what Beorn's trouble is? I mean, is it somewhat to do with his duties or is it some personal matter?"

"I am sure it has to do with the outlaws that infest the roads. A private matter he would have brought to me. They have been eluding him more and more easily, and he does not know why or how to lay them by the heels. He is not accustomed to watching what men do and judging from that what next they will do. All his life he followed orders—my grandfather's, Sir Andre's, Simon's. They planned; he obeyed. He does not know how to change, and I cannot explain."

"That was what I feared. I saw a burned village, and I saw the serfs hide when they heard my horse. I will go out with him today and see what I can discover. *Peste!*" he exclaimed, "you will have to take those bandages off. My hauberk will not go over them."

"I will not, nor will you. Those sores are healing at last. I will not have my work undone. You can wear Simon's." There was a momentary tight silence. This was far different from giving Ian Simon's clothing. It was customary for clothing to be lent to any noble visitor to a castle, but not a precious chain-mail hauberk. Then Alinor went on smoothly, "And do not dare wear your shield and rub that whole side raw again. Let one of the squires carry it."

Ian shook his head and then suddenly smiled. "Let me take Adam. He is strong enough to wear it, I think. I will tell Beorn to bring along an extra ten men who can guard him, and anyway, I doubt we will meet any resistance."

Alinor smiled quick permission. "How kind you are. He will be in heaven. Are you sure he will be no trouble to you, Ian?"

That made him laugh aloud. "Of course he will be a trouble. If Adam was no trouble, I would call a physician to see to him at once." Then he said soberly, "Do not worry. I will not permit any harm to come to him, and it is time for him to ride out and to learn that in the field orders must be obeyed."

There was a faint tone of question under the statement. Ian knew Alinor to be a very sensible woman, not one who ordinarily would wish to keep her son under her tutelage. However, her situation had not been normal. With her husband dying by inches under her eyes, it was possible she could not bear the thought of any danger, no matter how remote, threatening her only son.

"You do not need to tell me. It is more than time. Beorn would not take him. I spoke of it, but Beorn was so distressed that I did not press the point. Too much responsibility has been thrust upon him. I could not add more."

"I should have come sooner," Ian said guiltily, "but—" He cut that off. It would never do to say why he had delayed.

"I understand," Alinor soothed.

Ian did not contradict her mistaken impression. She assumed the king had kept him out of spite or capriciousness. If this once John was innocent, Ian was not troubled at heaping the blame upon him. He was guilty often enough, and in this case a thread more or less would not overburden the ass.

"Oh, heavens!" Alinor exclaimed as a bar of sunlight touched the doorframe of Ian's bedchamber. "Look at the hour. We have both missed first Mass. I must run and dress. I will send your squires in to you."

"Wait, Alinor. Have you told Adam and Joanna? How— How do you desire that I address them? That they address me?"

She did not come back nor even turn around to face him. "I have told them nothing."

"Do you want me to tell them? What would you have me say? Will they be distressed? Angry?"

Alinor turned slowly, leaning back against the doorframe so that Ian would not see she was clutching it. "To every question I can only say, I do not know."

"For Jesus' sake, Alinor, you must believe I do not wish to wrest Simon's children from him."

"You cannot help it," she whispered. "In a very little while Adam will not remember him at all—except as a name in your mouth or mine. He was only a little more than five when Simon fell ill. He will wish to forget a father who could not climb a stair or lift a sword."

"You need not worry about that. I will build memories for him."

It was useless to tell Ian that the memories would have Simon's name but Ian's face. In fact, Alinor knew it was better so. Her son would never be wrenched apart by any feeling of disloyalty. For him, Simon and Ian would be one composite father. It would not be so easy with Joanna. Alinor nodded acceptance of Ian's offer and then spoke her last thought aloud.

"Do not be hurt if Joanna seems angry at first."

"What is the use of telling me not to be hurt?" Ian rejoined irritably. "It must hurt me if Joanna, who has always loved me, should hate me instead."

"She will not hate you," Alinor soothed. "Only be patient. Give her a little time."

In the event, the telling came easier than Ian or Alinor expected. When Ian appeared at the table set with the bread and wine customary for the breaking of a night's fast, he was full armed except for his helmet and gauntlets. A double shriek of protest rose.

"You promised to stay a day!"

"You were asleep all the time. It is not fair!"

"Quiet!" Ian thundered.

A breathless, wide-eyed silence fell. The men-servants in the hall stiffened apprehensively. Even Alinor caught her breath. Ian never shouted at the children.

"I am not going away," he said, grinning at them, "but how can I make myself heard if you both shout at me at once."

Adam slipped from the bench, crawled under the table and embraced Ian passionately around the thighs. Alinor laughed softly. The servants, free of the startling fear that their well-known guest had suddenly become a threat, went about their business. Ian's squires stood a trifle awkwardly behind him. They knew the formal moves the squire of a guest should make, but in this intimate family situation they were at a loss. The elder, Owain, son of Llewelyn, simply waited. His acquaintance with his master gave him assurance that he would be told without rancor or unreasonable punishment what to do. The younger, Geoffrey FitzWilliam, had come to Ian from being a page in the queen's court. A month of good usage had not been sufficient to wipe out the terrors that had been bred into him in three years of Isabella's service. He stood frozen, masking his fear.

"How long? How long?" Adam begged.

The opportunity was too good to miss and Ian too good a tactician to overlook it. He dropped his hand to the boy's head, but his eyes sought Alinor.

"I am not going away at all, not ever again, except if I must answer the king's summoning or see to some necessary business where it might be dangerous to take you." He could have stopped there, but Alinor's eyes approved and he continued. "I have asked your mother to marry me, and she has consented. From this time forward, I will be your warden."

"Mother?" Joanna breathed.

"Lord Ian has done me the honor of asking me to be his wife, and I have accepted his offer," Alinor confirmed formally. "In the future, you must obey him as you would obey me or your father."

"Will you teach me to joust?" Adam asked eagerly.

"When you are old enough."

"I am old enough now. I am big and strong. You said yourself——"

Alinor watched Ian's face, where a most interesting struggle was taking place as Adam pleaded with him. Long habit and strong affection urged Ian to yield to the child. A new sense of responsibility checked him. In the past he had been the children's advocate against their parents, secure in the knowledge that Alinor or Simon would not yield on any point that was really important or might be harmful. Now, particularly in Adam's training, he himself was the final judge. Reluctantly he shook his head.

"You are not old enough. There are many things to prove before the question of jousting arises."

"But Ian——"

"Do you have anything new to say? If not, hold your tongue, or I will take it as a proof that you are not old enough to be reasonable and obedient. If you are not reasonable and obedient, then you cannot be trusted to come out with Beorn and myself to search for the outlaws who have been attacking the serfs. If you are, you can carry my shield for me."

Eyes and mouth rounded into ecstatic Os. With an effort, Adam swallowed his further protests. To go out with Ian was a present much too marvelous to endanger for any future benefit. Besides, after the hunt for the reavers was over, there was nothing to stop him from asking about the jousting again. Adam had discovered that if one asked for a thing often enough one usually got it. There might be a sharp slap or two in between the asking and the getting, but if a thing was not worth a slap or two, it was not worth asking for either. He followed Ian around the table and began to squeeze himself between his mother and his idol.

"Go to your mother's left hand, Adam," Ian ordered.

"But Ian, I want to sit next to you. I want to know——"

"Gentlemen do not sit together when ladies are present," Ian reproved, "nor do they speak of subjects that would not interest their companions."

So clear an expression of horror appeared on Adam's face that Alinor had to bite her lips, and Ian's mouth twitched uncontrollably. The child frowned. "You are not near so much fun as my warden as you were when you were my friend," he complained.

"That is true, because it is now my duty to see that you grow into a man worthy of your breeding and station. And the doing of one's duty is more important than any other thing, even the pleasure it would give me to sit beside you or the joy it would give me to give you pleasure."

That was sufficiently complex a statement to send Adam, silent as he thought it over, to the seat indicated. Meanwhile, Ian stepped over the bench and sat down between Alinor and Joanna. The squires, who had been waiting, came from the sides of the table to pour wine. Ian watched their handling of the flagons, noting that Geoffrey's hand shook so much that some wine was spilled. Alinor remarked politely that she had ordered cheese and a cold pasty to be served, since the "men" were riding out. Ian thanked her formally. Then she turned to Adam and he to Joanna. He heard Alinor murmur softly to her son that the proper thing was to offer her some of the pasty and the cheese the squires were slicing. Again that peculiar joy-pain tore Ian: the intense pleasure of being in the bosom of this family, of knowing he was truly a part of it as he had never been before; the equally intense fear that he was snatching at something that was not rightfully his.

"May I serve you with cheese, Lady Joanna?"

The gray eyes, suspiciously liquid, turned up to him. "Why are you trying to take Papa's place, Ian?"

In spite of Alinor's warning, the question hit him like a blow. "I am not," he snapped, "nor could I, nor would your mother permit it. Moreover, such remarks are not for public places like a table in hall while we are being served by— Good God, Geoffrey, what are you doing to that cheese? Do I have to teach you to carve at this late time of your service?" His eyes lifted from the mangled cheese to the white, stricken face. "How now, child," he said more softly, "are you ill?"

"No, lord."

The boy was slight and on the fair side, with straight, lustrous, medium-brown hair and light-brown eyes of a peculiarly changeable hue. Just now the eyes were nearly black with misery, and the young skin had turned from white to crimson with either shame or fever. Ian could see that not only the boy's hands but his whole body was trembling. Joanna, distracted from her shock, looked at the young squire with pity. Alinor turned her head from Adam's halting effort at polite conversation, cast a single glance at Geoffrey, and touched Ian's arm. Their eyes met. Ian sighed with relief.

"Very well. Owain, Geoffrey, we have sufficient to our needs. You may go and break your own fasts now."

The relief Ian felt had a sound cause. Without words Alinor had offered to see to the boy—a natural duty for a wife toward her husband's squires, but a form of assistance Ian had naturally not had before. He knew little or nothing about medicine, beyond a rough treatment for wounds until the leeches could take care of them. It was the women who treated and cared for the sick, and they were often more skilled than the learned physicians who discoursed gravely of humors while their patients died.

Both of Ian's squires were a heavy responsibility. Owain was the eldest and most dearly loved of Lord Llewelyn's natural children. Since Llewelyn had married the natural daughter of King John and might be expected to have legitimate children, Owain was excluded from succession in Wales—at least for the time being. Llewelyn had no intention of keeping this son in the shade or allowing him to grow up a rustic, and Owain had been entrusted to Ian to be given an elegant Norman polish. Owain had never given Ian any cause to worry or to fear Lord Llewelyn would be disappointed. He was quick to learn, merry of heart, strong and supple as well-tanned, well-braided hide, and solidly determined to make the most of every advantage and opportunity offered to him. Ian had already had two advantageous offers of marriage for Owain.

Geoffrey FitzWilliam was another matter entirely. One day Salisbury had commented favorably upon Ian's relationship with Owain. Naturally, Ian could not help expatiating on his own development under Simon's care and on his conviction that the best could only be drawn from a squire who loved and trusted as well as obeyed his lord. It was so innocent a discussion that Ian was surprised to hear Salisbury clear his throat awkwardly and to see, when his eyes were drawn by the sound, that Salisbury's color was considerably heightened.

"You do not think that bastardy stains the child?" he asked.

Ian looked at him in amazement. "How can it stain the child? The mother, yes; the father—I think, yes, although God knows I am scarcely lily-white in continence myself, but I do not think any can claim me as father. But how the child? God knows the fruit of the union is innocent of all except the original sin of man, and that he bears whether born in or out of wedlock.

Who can blame a child for the weakness of his parents?"

"Isabella can!" Salisbury spat bitterly.

Before Ian could remark soothingly that Queen Isabella was capable of any idiocy and should not be used as an example of what others thought, Salisbury was launched on an ugly tale. He had a son born out of wedlock. The mother, a lady, had died in bearing. The child had been raised in his grandfather's household, but the old man had died when the boy was ten. Since he was well old enough for fostering, Salisbury had entrusted him to the queen.

"He is a good boy, quiet and obedient. He did not seek me out nor complain. I saw he was unhappy in the beginning, but I believed it could not be otherwise in a strange place. I thought he would grow accustomed. Then you know what befell. When John came to cuffs with the barons and then lost Normandy, I had no time to think of Geoffrey. When matters became more quiet, and I saw what had become of him——"

Ian had a premonition of where this was leading, but he could think of nothing to say.

Salisbury ground his teeth in a rage. "The other pages and even the older squires made him their butt, and Isabella encouraged them. She sought him out to punish for anything and everything—for having brown eyes, for his hair hanging straight. I suppose it is because she is jealous of the love her husband bears me, but to torment a child— And she said to his face and to mine that he was a lesser thing, a bastard, and his mother was a whore—which I swear she was not."

"You must take him out of there at once," Ian said intensely. The black, blank years of his own childhood rose in a wave behind the wall Simon had built to hold them back. "Even if the king should be angered and Isabella hate you more, you must——"

"I know. Will you take him? I have watched Owain

to some purpose. He has a kind heart. Moreover, he is in the same case himself. You I trust."

"I? But I have no household. I cannot train him up to fit his station."

"What is his station? The bastard of a bastard—poor boy. Oh, I have something for him, and his grandfather left him something. He will not be penniless. It would do no good to move him from one great household to another. He must be close, and he must be used gently. Ian, he will die, mayhap by his own hand, if something is not soon done for him. Do not fear, I will not blame you if you cannot save him. I am to blame. Only I."

Thus Geoffrey had come into Ian's care. He had more toughness, Ian discovered, than his anxious father believed. Ian did not think, after coming to know Geoffrey, that he would ever have succumbed to the cruelty practiced upon him. He had blossomed very rapidly under Ian's and Owain's kindness, putting on flesh, developing a ready tongue, and even getting into serious enough mischief once to merit a whipping. This Ian had administered and Geoffrey had withstood without flinching, apparently indifferent, until Ian caught the boy roughly into his arms to growl, "You little fool! You could have been hurt or killed!" Then came tears and remorse and promises of amendment. The boy had good spirit. He could be led by love but not cowed by pain.

It was therefore a worrisome thing to see Geoffrey suddenly reduced to the condition he had been in when he had first been removed from Isabella's household. There had been nothing Ian could discover to account for it. He could not believe that anyone in Roselynde Keep would have insulted his squire and, anyway, Owain would have put that to rights or have reported it. Ian could only believe that Geoffrey was sick—and that was best left to Alinor. He would bid Geoffrey remain in the keep today, and Alinor could put him to bed and dose him if necessary. Ian put that concern aside and turned again to Joanna.

"I am sorry I spoke so sharply to you, love," he said gently. "It hurt me that you should think I would do anything that would displease your father."

A horrid qualm passed through Ian. He did not really believe that it would please Simon that Alinor should lie under him in the marriage bed. Yet there is no other way, he told himself; there is no other way to be *sure* she will be safe.

"I must keep you safe," he said aloud to Joanna. "I owed your father a deep debt of love, and I can best repay it by keeping you and your mother and Adam under my protection. When she has time, your mother will explain to you why this is needful. A little you must know already in that you heard me say I must go with Beorn to search for the reavers. But, Joanna, you are old enough to know better than to speak of such things while the squires are in attendance."

"I am sorry. I was so—" She stopped and struggled to find a safe word, "—surprised." She seemed almost reconciled. She had always adored Ian, but he seemed so different when he spoke to Adam. And there was something else that troubled her. She needed time to think. "Is Geoffrey ill?" she asked.

"I hope not," Ian replied, as glad as Joanna to leave the subject of his new relationship with Simon's wife and daughter, "but even if he is, your mother will make him well, I am sure. I hope Geoffrey and Owain have been pleasant guests?"

"Oh, yes, but Owain said I am 'just a girl.' That is neither nice nor true. Some day I will be the Lady of Roselynde. *That* is not 'just a girl.' "

"No, indeed," Ian said in a slightly constricted voice. "I will speak to Owain. He will not be so discourteous again."

"You need not," Joanna replied loftily. "*I* have spoken to him—and Geoffrey did, too."

"Geoffrey?" Ian asked faintly. Geoffrey admired Owain with all the hero worship a younger boy feels for a kind elder. Ian knew that to Geoffrey he was still a slightly unapproachable god; Owain was on the order of a kindly and helpful saint.

"Geoffrey said that nobody is 'just' an anything. They are all persons, and each must be judged on his own."

"Geoffrey is very wise for his age," Ian remarked approvingly.

Then his attention was drawn to Alinor, who had just given Adam permission to leave the table. She glanced across Ian at her daughter's untouched bread and cheese and watered wine.

"Do you not wish to eat anything, Joanna?" Alinor asked.

"It is my fault," Ian said quickly. "I kept her talking."

"Then eat now," Alinor urged. "Lessons in courtesy are over. If you do not hurry, you will be late for your lessons in ciphering—not that that would grieve you, but it will grieve me."

Actually Joanna rather enjoyed her lessons, which was more than could be said for Adam. He went protesting and groaning that reading and writing were for clerks and he would not be a clerk. Why should he learn? Why should he waste time that would be better spent practicing with his sword, or riding. Joanna, on the other hand, found reading, writing and ciphering much more interesting than spinning, weaving and embroidery. Her mind diverted to the lesson Father Francis would probably give, Joanna bit hungrily into her bread and cheese.

"I will tell Geoffrey that I will not take him," Ian said, turning to Alinor. Then, low-voiced, he explained something of the boy's background and trouble.

"That Isabella," Alinor hissed. "Only she could hurt

a child because she was jealous of the father. And what sort of uncle is the king——"

"Indifferent, belike, or truly unaware. John loves Salisbury and would not, I think, allow his boy to come to harm—unless— No. It must be that the households are so large that he did not see what Isabella was doing. I hope the boy is not seriously ill."

"I doubt he is ill at all. He has been perfectly well these four days and even this morning."

"Then what happened to set him first pale, then blushing and trembling—" Ian's voice faded.

A horrible notion had just occurred to him. Geoffrey had been carving the cheese, which was standing in front of Joanna, and Joanna—Ian cast a glance at her —Joanna bid fair to be a beauty to make men mad. But not now! She was nine years old! Yes, and the boy was not quite 14. Only 14? Ian had another memory of his youth that he had not mentioned to Alinor—that one was quite pleasant. He had not been much more than 12 when he had had his first woman. Fortunately, at that moment Joanna bolted her last bit of bread and asked permission to go. Alinor nodded, and the girl ran off. Ian's eyes followed her.

"Do not leave Geoffrey and Joanna alone together," Ian said sharply to Alinor.

She looked at him in surprise, then raised her brows. "I had not thought of that, but you are right. It is possible. Is he forward in that manner?"

"I do not know, but in John's court he would have sufficient opportunity to learn. Take care. He who is safe is not later sorry."

CHAPTER FOUR

It was late in the morning before Alinor was free to go to Geoffrey, who had been ordered to lie down on his pallet in Ian's bedchamber and rest until she had time for him. He had begged to go with Ian, assuring him over and over that he was not ill. By then he was so flushed with distress and with struggling to restrain his tears that he felt very feverish to Ian's touch, and Ian remained adamant. It could not hurt the child to rest abed for a day, even if he was well, and if he was beginning some illness, the rest might check it.

Alinor found Geoffrey with his face turned to the wall. She wondered whether he was asleep, because he could not have failed to hear her coming. Then a glimmer of an idea came to her. Joanna might not be the only child to be distressed by her marriage to Ian. She drew over a low stool, settled on it, and put a hand under the boy's hair on the back of his neck. He was not asleep. She could feel the tension of the muscles, but he had no fever.

"Turn round, Geoffrey."

Rigidly, reluctantly, the boy turned. His face was as blank as a mask, his eyes nearly black, fixed on nothing and as much as possible hidden under lowered lids. Alinor loosened the laces of his shirt and found the pulse in his throat. It pounded hard and fast, not weakness or fever.

"I do not believe you are ill, Geoffrey," Alinor said quietly.

"I said I was not, madam."

"Sit up, then. It is easier to talk." She waited until

he had settled with crossed legs and his back against the wall. "You are fond of Lord Ian, are you not, Geoffrey?"

"Yes, madam."

Alinor smiled. "And not overpleased that he should take a wife?"

The young face was still expressionless, but the eyes flicked to her swiftly, once. "I must be glad of anything that makes my lord glad. Of course I am pleased."

Restraining her impulse to laugh aloud, which would surely offend the delicate sensibilities of youth, Alinor patted Geoffrey's tightly clasped hands. "That is very generous of you, since you must fear that Lord Ian's time will be spent in different ways and that he will not be able to give so much attention to your training and advancement. But it will not be so. First, Lord Ian would never forget his responsibilities in that way. Second, I could not wish it nor permit it. It will be very important to me that you be strong and skilled in your duties. Many times Lord Ian's safety will depend upon you, so I must urge him to teach you all he can as quick as he can."

Something was stirring behind the fixed young mask. Alinor waited, her hand resting gently on Geoffrey's. The boy stared at her, taking in the white skin, the full, generous mouth, the short, slightly tip-tilted nose, the large green-brown eyes shaded by black, black lashes. Geoffrey was young, but not too young to recognize that the way the features were put together produced beauty. It was a beauty different from the queen's, but it was still hateful and suspicious. In his grandfather's house, the women had been kind to him. None of them looked like the queen or like Lady Alinor.

"But you are so beautiful," he burst out.

"Why, thank you, Geoffrey," Alinor replied. She was considerably startled. The exclamation was no compliment. There had been a ring of fear in the boy's voice.

"I assure you Lord Ian will not be ensorcelled and lose his reason. He has known me for a very long time, longer than your whole life. He is quite accustomed to my appearance."

For the first time Geoffrey's eyes came up and stared defiantly into hers. Their color was lighter and brighter, a golden brown. "Do you know I am a bastard, madam?"

Alinor laughed aloud. "Yes, indeed. What of that? So was my great grandfather and my great-great grandfather, too. My grandfather was not; but that was only because the priest hurried the service in accordance with my great grandmother's need. I understand that it was a very near thing."

"You think it is funny?" Geoffrey's eyes were darker again and the corners showed the sheen of tears.

"I think it is of no importance," Alinor said seriously, contrite at her carelessness. The young were so easily hurt. "A man is what he makes of himself. He can be a filthy thing, although born of high estate, or he can be like my Simon, born to little but greater than the kings he served." Alinor bit her lip. How quickly Simon's name came to her. To Geoffrey she should have spoken of Ian or of his father. "Perhaps," she continued, "your mother and father should have been wiser, but sometimes it is very hard to be wise. Geoffrey, my love, you will hear no word of blame from me, even of your parents, and for you, my child, you are innocent of any wrong. Did you think I would care what you were born?"

"But you are so beautiful!"

The reiteration, coupled with what Ian had told Alinor, suddenly clarified at least part of Geoffrey's trouble. Queen Isabella was one of the most beautiful women alive. Alinor slipped off the stool onto her knees and drew Geoffrey into her arms.

"Child, child," she murmured, "not every beautiful woman is cruel—at least not to children." She uttered a shaken laugh. "You have a few years before you need to worry about the other form of cruelty, I think." She released him, leaned back onto her heels, and took his hand into hers. "You must not blame the lovely ladies overmuch. You must try to remember that they are poor, weak things and their beauty is the only power they have. Thus they have no choice but to use it—sometimes unwisely."

"A—a queen has power," Geoffrey faltered.

"Not as much as appears, and Queen Isabella has many private sorrows that—that make her impatient and—and jealous where, really, she should not be. Never mind her anymore, Geoffrey. You now belong to Lord Ian and, a little, only as much as you yourself desire, to me. Lord Ian will not allow anyone, even the queen, to harm you. And if you will permit it, I, too, will love you. There is no need to answer that. Just keep it in your mind. Now, since you are not ill, perhaps you would run some errands for me?"

"At once, madam."

"Good." Alinor thought the best thing for him was to be kept well occupied until calm was restored to him. "I want my chief huntsman and my head falconer. They are somewhere around the castle grounds, but I do not know where. Do not worry if it takes you time to find them. Just tell them to be sure to dine in hall today. Oh, yes, the chief groom also, but I am not sure he is in the keep. Do not ride out after him if he is not in the grounds."

"I am not likely to fall off my horse, madam," Geoffrey said indignantly, and then drew in his breath sharply as he realized he had been insolent.

Alinor laughed. "Of course not, but Lord Ian would be justly angered if, after leaving you with me because he feared you were not well, I allowed you to go careening off all over the countryside and paid no attention to you."

She wondered whether she should make some reference to Joanna. That she had found one seat of trouble did not mean that another did not exist. Better not. Better let the children meet in hall before dinner under her eye and see what there was to see. Alinor rose easily to her feet, and Geoffrey jumped up and started out. Alinor had to call him back to take his cloak, noting that he would need more gentling. He had stiffened apprehensively when she called out peremptorily. Nonetheless, she had made a beginning. The order to take his cloak had won a shy smile. Now, another trial, a harder one. Alinor straightened the pallet automatically, glanced around the chamber. It might not be so easy to deal with Joanna.

She found her daughter with Father Francis reading a simple saint's tale with little enthusiasm. Ian might be right about Joanna's desire to be good, Alinor thought, but if so, that desire certainly did not take the form of ardent religion—which was just as well. She called her daughter away and started up toward the women's quarters, ignoring Joanna's heavy sighs. Joanna was even less enthusiastic about sewing, weaving, and spinning than about saints' tales. There is more of me in her than that red hair and blue eyes show, Alinor reminded herself.

But Alinor had no intention of setting her daughter to some distasteful task that would leave her mind free to brood on this day. For the next week or two, Joanna would be occupied only with those aspects of the coming wedding that would excite and interest her. The whole affair, Alinor hoped, would take on an aura of pleasure while Joanna grew accustomed to the idea. Before Alinor could start her campaign with an order to turn out the chests of fine brocades and velvets to choose suitable cloth for the dresses to be worn, Joanna spoke.

"Why is it so important to be chaste, Mother?"

"Oh, heavens, today is my day for being proved by hard questions," Alinor exclaimed. She gestured her daughter to a seat. "What put this into your head?"

"Saint Agatha," Joanna said succinctly.

"Oh." Alinor wondered why she was always cursed with chaplains who were as good and kind and virtuous as they were unworldly, unwise and impractical. One could not explain to Father Francis that this was the wrong time to give a nine-year-old stories to read about martyrdom to preserve purity. First of all, it was unlikely that Father Francis' mind had grasped the fact that Alinor was planning to marry again five months after her husband's death. Even if it had, he would see no connection. Chastity was, of course, the holiest state, but as Paul said, "It is better to marry than to burn." Marriage, for those who were not strong enough for total continence, was not an unchaste state.

"Well," Alinor temporized, "Saint Agatha had dedicated her body to God. She wished to keep it unspotted for Him."

"But would it not be better to use it to some good purpose, such as converting the man who desired her, than to die?"

Alinor struggled with herself and, as usual, lost. She chuckled. "My love, I am afraid I think as you do, but that is because I am a coarse and worldly creature. For the holy, purity is more important than life. The question is not likely to arise for you. The future Lady of Roselynde will not need to take the veil. You will need to marry and breed up heirs."

"Were you chaste, Mother?"

"Yes, Joanna. I knew no man until I married your father, and I never touched another man in all the years that we were man and wife—touched in the way of love, I mean." Alinor said nothing of how willing she had been to take Simon, in or out of wedlock. Alinor did not lie to her children, but it was not a lie to omit a fact she considered beyond the comprehension of a nine-year-old girl.

"Why? Because it was a sin to be unchaste?"

"No, I fear not," Alinor replied, still honestly, although her voice was not quite as steady as it had been. "I fear I did not think much of sin when I was a girl. Before I met your father I had never seen a man I valued high enough to give my body or my heart—which was more important. After I married I was chaste because I loved your father and it would have hurt him if I gave to another what he believed belonged to him."

"You do not love Papa anymore?" Joanna whispered.

Although Alinor had known that had to be the next question, she winced. To be prepared for pain does not really diminish the pang. She drew a deep breath, and then another.

"Of course I love your father, Joanna. I will always love him, always and always." She stopped and fought the tears, but she lost that battle, too. They welled slowly over her lower lids and down her cheeks.

"Do you think Papa will not care any longer that you give to Ian what used to be his?"

Alinor brushed away the tears. Joanna had not seemed to notice them, but that was not surprising. She had seen her mother's face wet so often in the past year and a half that it was a usual thing to her.

"That is certainly true," Alinor replied. "Papa still loves us all, but he has no more use for my body, Joanna, and he was never the kind to hoard for himself what he did not want just so that someone else should *not* have it. Papa will not care about that. He will only care if we forget him, and I will never forget him and never stop loving him."

That seemed to satisfy Joanna, and she wriggled toward the front of the chair as if she was about to slide off. Then she suddenly frowned. Obviously, a new problem had occurred to her.

"But what about Ian? If you love Papa and then you marry Ian—will you be unchaste after you are married to Ian because you do not love him and do not care if you hurt him?"

"Who said I did not love Ian, Joanna?" Alinor asked gravely. "You know it is very possible to love more than one person at a time. I love you. Does that mean I may not love Adam, who is also my child? Why should I not also love Ian, even if I continue to love Papa? And if I love Ian, then I would never do anything to hurt him. I assure you, I will be as chaste a wife to Ian as I was to your father."

This time Joanna got as far as the floor before she found another question. "Is Geoffrey sick, Mama?"

Alinor did not sigh with relief, but she sent up a prayer of thanksgiving. So far she and Ian both seemed to have traveled the right path toward peace of mind for the child. "No," she began, and then a notion came to her that might accomplish several good purposes. She pulled Joanna close so that she could speak softly enough that the maids would not hear.

"You asked me why it was needful to be chaste. Geoffrey is a good reason. His mama was not chaste and was not married to his papa—I do not know why, so do not ask me that. Of course, that is not Geoffrey's fault at all, but many people who are cruel and stupid, taunt him with that and call him 'bastard,' as if he was to blame for his birth. Geoffrey was not sick. He was afraid that once he was part of our household and no longer a guest, you and Adam and I would be unkind to him. If you are not chaste, you may have a child and that child would suffer for what you had done. That is certainly wrong."

"Why do not his mama and papa protect him?" Joanna asked, dismissing the subject of chastity for one far more interesting to her.

"His mama is dead. His papa loves him very much, but he cannot protect Geoffrey against the whole world.

He cannot keep Geoffrey with him always. You know that Adam will go away to be fostered in a few years. Ian and I will do our best to find people who will love him and be kind to him, but mistakes can be made. Someone was unkind to Geoffrey before he came into Ian's care. He is wounded in a way you cannot see. Thus, just as you would not touch Ian's back, you must not use certain words to Geoffrey. You must not call him whoreson or bastard, even in anger." Alinor smiled. "Call him louse, or feeble-minded worm, or gaping oaf if you will, but not those others."

"Gentlewomen do not use such language," Joanna said sententiously.

"Well, I never said you were a gentlewoman—only that I was trying to make you into one," her mother replied tartly. "And if the argument I overheard you having with Adam, right here in this room, last week is any proof, I am not succeeding," Alinor teased. She laughed as she saw Joanna beginning to marshal arguments as to why brothers, especially younger brothers, were exceptions to the rule that a gentlewoman use gentle language. "Never mind that now," her mother cut her off. "We have idled away time enough."

Even being lectured was better than spinning. "But mother—" Joanna began.

"We must be all new dressed for the wedding," Alinor interrupted temptingly, "and the clothes must be very grand to do us honor before our guests. What would best become you, do you think? Shall we look through the cloth?"

Some time before Alinor had sought out Geoffrey, Ian watched Owain slip his shield strap over Adam. The child braced himself sturdily under the weight. He had a good seat in the saddle, too, even though he had to turn his body to allow the shield to clear the horse's side. Then Owain mounted to Adam's left and Beorn brought his horse to Ian's right.

"In the open," Ian said to Adam, "this is how we ride. You must not ride ahead or behind, so that I can take my shield when I desire it. Listen hard, Adam. You are being asked to do a duty beyond your years and experience because Geoffrey is not well today and my back is sore. You must obey orders quickly and exactly. If you do not, you will be a danger to us all, and I will not dare take you out again for a long time. Further, you must not speak to me unless you believe you see a danger I do not perceive. You may speak to Owain, but if he tells you to hold your tongue, do so at once."

"Yes, lord," Adam replied, in so fine an imitation of Owain and Geoffrey that Ian was forced to bite his lips to keep from laughing.

The reply was an excellent prognostication, however. In watching his squires and thinking back on his own experiences with Simon, Ian had come to understand how men were made. Adam was pretending to be Geoffrey—or any boy old enough to hold the position of squire. And when Adam was a squire, the thoughts continued as Ian touched his horse into movement and rode across the drawbridge, he would pretend to be the knight—as Owain was now pretending. Owain was speaking very kindly to Adam and answering his questions as he imagined he would answer such questions when he was Lord Owain and squires rode in his tail. Ian smiled and sighed at the same time. Pretending and pretending, we pretend ourselves into men, he thought. Somewhere inside him there was still a small, frightened boy, but the covering of pretend-man was so thick by now that the frightened child had no outlet, except once in a long while to cry out to God.

"Eorling, beoth heil hym to taken?" Once over the drawbridge, Beorn had moved up on Ian's right. His eyes flicked to Adam. It was clear he trusted less in the good behavior of his young master than Ian did, or

perhaps it was Ian's ability to control his charge that
was in doubt in Beorn's mind.

"Alle heil," Ian reassured him and then switched to
French, because he wanted Adam to understand what
was said. "We will not go far today. I only mean to ask
some questions. I want to discover, if I can, whether
it is one band or more, how many men, and from what
direction or directions they come."

In accordance with this purpose, the troop set off
eastward along the coastline. At each fishing village Ian
asked his questions. It was soon clear that the raiders
did not come from the sea but were based inland. They
turned north along the border of the demesne lands.
Here and there a robbery was reported, but these were
obviously single attacks by one or two individuals.
Beorn mentioned that one thief, at least, had already
been captured and hanged.

At the northern border, they turned west. Almost at
once they found trouble. A farm had been stripped of
its cattle, the bailiff badly beaten, his wife raped, two
female serfs carried off. One young male serf, limping
and with a bloody weal across his scalp, had seen the
reavers. More men than his fingers and toes, he reported, and they had come from the west. Ian promised
help and some recompense for their losses. He would
return the next day, or the day after, he said, to arrange
some kind of warning system and some suggestions for
preliminary defense measures.

They continued west, passing some untouched farms.
Two had not been troubled, but one of those bred pigs.
Few robbers, no matter how daring, would try to drive
a herd of pigs without the aid of the herdsman. And
should they harm the herdsman, those vicious and
highly intelligent animals would soon make pig food
of both men and horses. A few pigs might die, but no
man who stayed to fight them would live. Ian spoke
to the bailiff and requested information from the herds-

man. Let him pen the pigs for a day or two, Ian said, he would be by tomorrow or the next day for his answers. Another untouched farm, however, reported that tribute had been paid. The description of the taker made Ian raise his brows. Two men only, dressed like gentlemen, and speaking the gentle tongue.

"I think," Ian said to Beorn, "that these are clever villains not in any way connected to the reavers but using the fear of them to their own purpose. The reavers take money if they find it, but they are more interested in food and women."

If they came again, Ian instructed the bailiff to take them prisoner. The Lady of Roselynde would go bail if there were any losses incurred because of that, he promised. The bailiff looked doubtful. Ian said sharply that he was betrothed to the lady. Beorn confirmed his claim. The bailiff grew warm, invited them in to drink a measure and break a crust. Ian refused with thanks. They still had far to go, and the lady expected them to dinner. That stilled all argument and healed all hurt. Ian was amused by the bailiff's obvious conviction that a male master was an immediate necessity in Roselynde and equally that the male master would defer in all things, save battle, to the Lady of Roselynde.

As they neared the westernmost border of the demesne, more and more troubles were reported. One farm where stiff resistance under a determined bailiff had been made had retained its cattle, but most of the outbuildings had been burned. Northwest was the direction the reavers had come, this bailiff reported. In the next place, right on the edge of the demesne lands —a looted village—the headman also said the robbers had come from the northwest. Ian sucked his teeth with annoyance.

"You see what this means?" he said to Beorn as soon as they were riding south toward Roselynde.

"I beg pardon. No, lord, I do not."

"It means they come from outside our land, curse

them. They may be lairing on the royal demesne property in or around the Forest of Bere or mayhap on church property as far away as Bishop's Waltham. I will wager also that they do not raid the land they lair upon. We have trouble, Beorn. I had hoped they were hiding on the estate itself or coming off Rowland land."

"Where is the difference, lord?"

"The difference is that I would rather offend Rowland than the king. If I must trespass to root out this band of brigands— Well, it is not my decision to make alone. I must talk to Lady Alinor."

The expression of relief on Beorn's face almost made Ian laugh aloud. However, it was significant of more than the fact that Beorn respected and feared his mistress. Obviously, he knew that Simon consulted Alinor on such matters, or he would have been surprised by what Ian said. That was very interesting. Ian knew, of course, that Alinor had managed the fiscal and, at need, the judicial business of her estates. He had not realized how closely she was involved in the defense of her lands.

"There is little more we can do now," Ian continued. "Let us return. Tell your men to eat well and get what sleep they can. We will ride out again tonight. Think also of about ten men who would make reliable battle captains. I will see them in the great hall after dinner."

"Yes, lord."

Ian glanced sidelong at Adam. They had been out longer than Ian had expected. Beorn had made the understandable error of concentrating his patrols close in to Roselynde Keep. In a war condition, that was logical, because the raiding would be connected with spying out the castle and its defenses and the best area into which to settle an attacking force. That was the type of situation with which Beorn was familiar. During the reigns of old King Henry and even Richard, the countryside had been relatively free of landless, marauding bands. When attacks were launched, they were private wars of the nobility directed at gaining property or avenging an insult.

The troubles that were racking England now were of a different sort. Heavy taxation and poor crops had ruined many villeins, small farmers who owned a few acres of land, and even some of the lesser squirearchy. Some understanding or rich landlords, like Alinor, simply carried the burden, allowing the debt to mount and hoping that better times would permit the free smallholder to repay it in the future. Some landlords did not care, or were so pressed for money themselves that they could not carry nonpaying tenants. These put the villein off his land and found another tenant who could pay; it was a double profit, in that the new tenant had to buy the land as well as pay the rent. Unfortunately, this left the previous tenant with nowhere to go and no way to keep his family from starvation.

Some sold themselves into bondage, sinking to the level of serf to keep bread in their mouths and a roof over their heads. Some went into the growing towns, where the fortunate found employment in the new industries of trade and manufacture, and the unfortunate died of want or were flogged or hanged. Many, however, desperate and embittered, formed together into bands and preyed upon those more fortunate than themselves. Occasionally these bands would be led by a dispossessed knight or the rebellious younger son of a nobleman. These marauders, managed with discipline and intelligence, were the hardest to deal with, and Ian feared that that was what he had found here.

It seemed to Ian that they had been out too long for Adam. The boy still sat straight in the saddle, but he looked pale to his suddenly anxious stepfather. They had another two hours of riding, even if they did not skirt the borders of the estate but rode directly for the keep. Ian glanced at the sun, or, rather, at the bright area that betrayed the sun's presence in the cold, gray sky. He could not afford to stop and call a rest if he wanted the men to have time to eat and get a little sleep. And he could not simply take his shield from Adam. The child had behaved beautifully. To relieve him of his duty without any cause—to say he was tired would be the most shameful excuse of all—would be an insult.

"Adam," Ian said, "do you understand what I have done and what I have discovered?"

The boy turned his head. His eyes were heavy, and his lips looked a little blue. Consciously, he lifted the hand that held the rein from the saddle pommel, where he had allowed it to rest.

"I—I do not—I am not sure, lord."

"Very well. I am glad you are so honest. Give me my shield and come sit before me so that I can explain it to you."

"I can listen while I ride," Adam protested uncertainly.

"No doubt," Ian replied, "but you know I have lately been ill. It is tiring for me to need to raise my voice for so long. If you sit before me, I can talk softly."

"A damwein y gadei yr un y dwyn," Owain said.

For a moment Ian was surprised. It was an odd time to be quoting old fairy tales. Then he laughed. Owain had made a reference to proud men who "rarely allow anyone to be carried."

"Diamheu!" Ian replied. The one word, "undoubted," carried his meaning without exposing his lack of mastery of the incredibly complex grammar of Welsh or his inability to sing the exquisite language as it deserved.

Beorn watched as Ian lengthened his shield strap and swung it over his shoulder, took the boy into his arms, tenderly tucking his cloak around the youngster. He thanked God that he need not worry about that beloved hellion any longer. Lord Ian loved him and could control him. Owain caught the reins of Adam's horse and fastened them to a loop on the rear of his saddle so that he could ride beside his master. He knew the lecture was really for him. Adam was too young. Ian began to describe why he had taken the route he had chosen, how he had put the information he had received together, and what his conclusions were. Adam's eyes closed. Owain listened intently, interspersing questions. Someday not too far in the future he would need to ask similar questions and draw conclusions from the answers. Beorn retired into his own thoughts. Why a thing happened or must be done was the business of the lord. Thank God there was again a lord to do that part. His business was to follow orders. The lord required ten worthy battle captains. Beorn began to consider his subordinates.

When a manservant came running to tell Alinor the troop had returned, she put down her needle and went to a window that overlooked the bailey. Although she had to unhook the scraped hide that kept out a little of the cold and let in some light, she was in time to see Ian waking Adam, his head bent affectionately over the boy, who was stretching and yawning in his arms. Alinor shook her head at the sight of Ian's shield on his shoulder, but she knew she would say nothing. The explanation was apparent. They had been out too long, Adam had tired, and Ian would not injure the boy's pride by giving his shield to another bearer.

Fear touched her. A messenger waited for Ian in the castle, a messenger wearing the colors of the Earl of Salisbury. The unfolding scene below increased her anxiety. The cheerful voices and laughter of the men reflected the sense of satisfaction of their leader. When they had been out with Beorn, they had come back sullen and uncertain, frustrated by their repeated failures to accomplish anything. Even Beorn looked relaxed. There was a spring to his step, as if he had cast off an enormous weight. Owain, a far more suitable companion for a boy than the crude men-at-arms, was shepherding Adam's sleepy steps into the forebuilding.

Alinor was intensely grateful for Ian's presence. She did not wish to lose him.

He came into the hall directly behind Owain and his staggering charge, walking lightly in spite of the weight of mail. The shield was gone, Alinor noted as she turned to bid Joanna take her brother up to the women's quarters and see that he was washed. Geoffrey, who had been playing chess with Joanna, sprang to his feet. Alinor bid him fetch the Earl of Salisbury's messenger to his master.

"Did he say where he came from?" Ian asked.

"France."

"Peste! Then Salisbury has not sailed yet, and it is something to do with the king." The messenger appeared on Geoffrey's heels before there was time for more speculation. Ian took the letter he held out. "This is my betrothed wife, Lady Alinor," he said to the messenger. "Whatever you have to say may be said to her."

"There was no verbal message, my lord."

Ian looked down at the letter and groaned softly. "It is in his own hand," he said to Alinor as he gestured dismissal at the messenger.

"Then it is bad news?"

"Yes, likely," Ian replied with a wry smile, "but what is worse is that I may never find out what it says. I told you Salisbury was not like the Angevins. It must be said for them that they all take to scholarship like a bird to the air. Every one, even the daughters, writes a fine hand." He broke the seal, looked at the letter, shook his head, and handed the rolled sheet to Alinor. "Salisbury, may God bless and keep him, is the only one of Henry's sons who seems perfectly impervious to clerkly skills."

In spite of her anxiety, Alinor had to laugh as her eye scanned the page. If anything, Ian's remark seemed an understatement. Words appeared interspersed with blots and spatters of ink straggling at odd angles across the page. Sometimes it was not possible to determine whether certain words belonged to the line above or the line below. In certain areas the words did not appear to form any lines as they rose above or curled around blotches on the sheet. Alinor also wondered whether Salisbury had bothered to cut the quill, or whether he had merely plucked the feathers from some unfortunate bird and used them in their natural state. The heavy flow of ink had smeared; a's, o's, e's and c's appeared indistinguishable, as did m's, n's and w's.

Ian's brow contracted. "Yes, but it is not really funny. It will take hours and hours to decipher that, and I must go out again after dinner if we are to take the reavers. Yet I must know what he says."

"If you will trust me," Alinor suggested, "I will write you a fair copy."

"Of course," Ian said, and snapped his fingers. "It is so foolish. I know you can read and write—I have seen you at it and doing accounts, too—but it is so odd a thing for a woman that it goes out of my head. But do you think you can manage this? A tale or a letter written by a scribe is a far different thing———"

Alinor laughed. "More easily than you could, I suppose. My heart warms toward William of Salisbury. This letter is so like unto my grandfather's scrawls that I must love Salisbury for its sake. Go and unarm yourself, Ian, and I will set dinner forward and get to work on this.

A week before Salisbury's message arrived at Roselynde Keep, Salisbury had been reading a letter from his wife. When he finished, he stared into space for a time. Eventually a slow, amused, and affectionate smile softened his worried expression. He sighed and rose. He had done what he could, and failed again, and now John had slipped completely into apathy. Since he could do no good, he might as well go home. Still smiling, he carried his letter with him and craved audience with his brother.

The Lady Ela was more than usually ill, William reported. John looked at him with dull eyes. The queen was known to be with child now and John, with the legitimate excuse that he dared not touch his wife for fear he would do some harm to the long-awaited heir, was making merry with a dozen ladies at a time. He had little interest or strength for anything else. Moreover, he knew Lady Ela well and was aware that her husband's absence for three months without an occasional visit would increase her ill health markedly. He smiled lazily as he gave Salisbury permission to leave.

"I do not know why you do not strangle her, brother," he said. "I promise you, there is no man who would not call it justifiable murder. Certainly not I, and I would be your judge."

"I am accustomed," Salisbury replied, grinning. "There are worse things that can befall a man than a wife who desires his company. She is less ill when I am with her."

"Then go, by all means. Even I have been receiving letters."

"I am sorry, John. I will tell her not to do that again. You should not be troubled by Ela's megrims."

"Do not scold her," John replied indifferently. "I assure you, her letters do not trouble me at all."

No, Salisbury thought, bowing himself out, just now nothing troubles you. At another time he might have tried to rouse his brother, but at present he was pleased that John should be idle. When the king woke from this lethargy that afflicted him periodically, he would rush into feverish activity, and Salisbury was worried about what that activity would produce. For one thing, it would bring the king back to England and, flown with his French success, John had determined on a new round of taxes. Further, he would doubtless begin to press the Pope to approve the Bishop of Norwich as Archbishop of Canterbury.

A minor matter, but important to those involved,

John would certainly act in the matter of the widow
that Ian de Vipont wanted to marry as soon as he was
ready to act at all. Salisbury sighed. He could only
suppose the woman had been approached and had
refused John's advances. Salisbury deplored from his
heart his brother's habit of meddling with the wives and
daughters of the great nobles of the land. It was one
thing to take the daughter of some minor knight to
your bed. Usually in those cases the father was flat-
tered. Adequate provision could be made for the girl,
either with a small estate or a marriage to another minor
knight who would be happy to obtain the king's favor
at the small cost of his wife's maidenhead. It was something else again to try to play with the wife of a man
like Simon Lemagne.

Well, Salisbury thought, he had done what he could
—which was nothing. He was sorry for the woman, but
de Vipont could be satisfied with some other heiress.
Then suddenly he stopped stock-still. That was nonsense. Ian was not concerned with the lands of the
heiress. His talk had been all of the children, and if
John gave the woman to any of the men he had suggested— Salisbury turned cold. The boy would not
survive a week, and the fate of the girl might well be
worse. He had a sudden clear image of Ian's face when
he spoke of the children and an equally clear memory
of Ian's gentleness with Geoffrey. Ian had been a loyal
vassal to John, but his loyalty would not survive that.
Lemagne had other friends, too—Pembroke and Leicester—and Lord Llewelyn of Wales was close-bound to
de Vipont.

Salisbury nearly turned and went back to reason
with John again. Coupled with the new taxes, an affront of that kind—the forced marriage of a lady of
high estate and wide connections to a low-born favorite—might be just the ugly little spark to ignite a con-
flagration of rebellion. But Salisbury knew it was no
use reasoning with John now. John would only smile

and say it did not matter or even promise to do as Salisbury urged; however, neither the seeming indifference nor the promise would stop him from taking vengeance once he was in one of his fits of frantic energy.

CHAPTER FIVE

Salisbury's letter was not really so difficult once one settled to it and gave close attention, but Alinor's eyes darkened with worry as she rewrote the message. Guilt plucked at her also. Ian had said he would marry her, will she nill she, and he knew about the king's ill will. She had hoped, however, that they would be married before King John remembered his spite and therefore that the spite would not flow over onto Ian. It was too late for that now. Had she really resisted enough? Had she advanced the right arguments to deter him? Truly, her lust for Ian had so beclouded her mind that there was neither conviction nor honesty in her resistance. I could offer to release him, she thought. Immediately she hissed impatiently at her own dishonesty. That would merely insult Ian in order to give a sop to her conscience.

There was a great deal to discuss and little time. Alinor remembered that Ian had said he must ride out again. That meant that he probably would be out all night and they would not have time to talk after the children were abed. She thought a moment, then called to a passing maidservant and bid her set places for Ian's squires and Adam and Joanna at Beorn's table. Lessons in courtesy were all very well, but not when they interfered with more serious matters. When all was ready, and her children had been ordered in a tone with which they did not argue to sit where they were told, Alinor sent a manservant to fetch Ian. He came from his chamber looking tousled and sleepy and so very young and beautiful that Alinor's breath caught.

For all his sleepy looks, he did not miss the significance of the two places set at the high table. He gestured toward the table set just below Alinor's and said to Owain and Geoffrey, "Sit and eat. I will serve myself and Lady Alinor this day. We have no time for elegance. But mind your manners with Lady Joanna. I will have my eye upon you. And do you both mind that Master Adam comports himself like a gentleman." Then he put his hand out and Alinor laid her fingers formally on his wrist. "It is not good, I suppose," he said softly.

"No."

"Oh, well." Suddenly he laughed and shrugged. "Do you want my bad news first, or should we consider Salisbury's before we come to the reavers?"

He pulled the bench out so that Alinor could go around without lifting or catching her skirts, pushed it in behind her, and stepped over it to seat himself. The gesture was so practiced, so automatic, and Ian's mind was so plainly elsewhere that Alinor was stung by jealousy. A very polished courtier indeed, this second husband. Simon had been, too, of course, but except for one incident—which Alinor knew had existed only in her own imagination—she had never doubted for a moment that Simon loved only her. Thoroughly ashamed of the trend of her thoughts, considering the danger into which Ian was putting himself just to protect her, Alinor wrenched her mind to what he had said.

"The felons are not hidden on my land then?"

"No, nor on Rowland land either."

"That means they must lie in the Forest of Bere or in the church lands south of Bishop's Waltham. You are well-acquainted with the Bishop of Winchester. Would he not give you leave to pursue them onto his lands?"

Again Ian was surprised. His general knowledge and acceptance of women as beautiful, helpless idiots, useful only for the bearing of sons, was in constant conflict with Alinor's capability. Simon had always said Alinor could manage the property, except for the actual practice of war when that was necessary. However, Ian had never had occasion to discuss such matters with her. When Simon was well, their talk had always been of politics, not the hunting of reavers or the control of vassals. For the past year and a half, moreover, he had seen Alinor at an enormous disadvantage, absorbed as she was by Simon's illness. There were other capable women—Nicola de la Hay, for example—but their abilities seemed to have rubbed off on their persons. They were mannish of manner as well as of mind. Alinor alone, it seemed to Ian, was totally feminine—even when she was overbearing.

It did not occur to Ian that Alinor was honest with him, whereas those among the women with whom he had played at love, who had brains and ability, had had reason to conceal those attributes from him. Although Ian was unconscious of it, he encouraged their silly simpering by his acceptance and seeming approval of it. In fact, he was known not to keep company with women who talked of serious matters. This was not because Ian particularly liked gabbling nonsense but because he did not trust the women he played with. Surely a woman who betrayed her husband with her body would think little of betraying a lover with her mouth. In the past, Ian's relations with women had been totally formal or purely physical—the quicker info bed the better. The only reason he did not confine himself to professional whores was that there were so few of them that were not completely filthy and degraded both in mind and body.

Now, although he was surprised by Alinor's quick understanding and analysis, Ian was not offended by it. He was relieved that he would not need to make a long explanation for which he had little time. "I will write to Winchester, of course," he agreed, "but I am not sure where he is. I do not greatly fear his anger in any case. He is a reasonable man, and I can easily compound with him for any damage or insult."

"The king's land is something else again," Alinor commented. "Perhaps you had better look at what Salisbury says before you consider the danger of enraging John further." She pushed toward him the sheet of parchment that was lying near her on the table.

"To Ian, Lord de Vipont, greetings," Ian read. "I write in haste before I take ship for England. I have lately left my brother, King John, and at that time someone fulsomely praising him did mention Lord Pembroke, he who was William Marshal, saying neither he nor his late friend Simon Lemagne could have better fought the war. Sir Simon's death being thus called to my lord brother's mind in an idle moment, my lord began to speak of comforting the widow's lonely and unprotected state. He has not yet decided who would be most suitable, but, among others, Fulk de Cantelu and Henry of Cornhill were mentioned. As I know you had an eye to the lady and her lands yourself, and since I am much in your debt, I write to advise you that if your mind is still fixed upon her, you should move apace to gain her consent and even to wed and bed her before my lord fix upon a partner for her and make your suit impossible. If you succeed, remember that I wish to share your joy by being a guest at your nuptials. You will find me fixed for the present at my main seat in Salisbury. My lord brother will grace Winchester with his presence this Christ's Mass, so he will easily be near enough for you to make your peace with him at that time if your suit to Lady Alinor speeds well. I do suppose my lord will come into London some two weeks before his coming to Winchester, but it may be that he will sail to a port nearer Winchester. I hope this finds you as it leaves me, well. Written on the fourth day of October by William, Earl of Salisbury."

Ian raised his eyes from the letter and stared straight ahead. Fool that he was to allow Alinor to write a fair copy. He should have known what Salisbury would say. Alinor was first puzzled and then felt an uneasy flicker of contempt at the dismay that showed on his countenance. It seemed that she had misjudged Ian after all. He was not prepared to withstand the king's wrath.

"There is no need to regard your offer to me as binding," she said icily. "We have sworn no oaths——"

"For sweet Mary's sake, Alinor, I never said it! I swear," he interrupted passionately, "I swear on my soul—on Simon's soul—I never said a word about your lands. That was Salisbury's thought, not mine! I am no pauper. I have more than enough——"

Alinor began to laugh. It was by the grace of God that she, who of all women might have expected to be married for her wealth, should be the wife of two men who were morbidly anxious to avoid any stain of greed. She put her hand on his arm.

"Ian, I never thought of that. I thought, since King John has gone so far, that it might be better to think again of my plan. Let him choose——"

"No!"

They had been speaking quietly. Even Ian's anguished protest had been expressed in an undertone. His explosive bellow of negation, however, drew all eyes and silenced the eaters in the hall. Alinor patted his hand. The confident, intimate gesture reassured the startled servants. Whatever had disturbed the lord was nothing to do with the lady.

"You do not know the men Salisbury named," Ian continued in a lower voice. "I would not even dignify them with the name of beast. It would be an offense to the filthiest animal to be compared with Cantelu and Cornhill."

"Yes, of course. I guessed that. The whole letter is a warning, although he has written so cleverly that if it were taken and read, none could accuse him of more than a friendly hint to someone he owes a favor. His marking of Winchester is to say that John might send for me, being not so far off from Roselynde, and would be near enough to take me by force if I refused. Or even—note how he writes of a port nearer Winchester than London—that he might land here and come in person."

"You are very quick to see."

"Quick enough when I am the quarry of the hunt. Now, what is to be done if the king write his commands to me?"

"Ignore them. You are betrothed already."

Alinor opened her mouth, and then shut it. She had a far better idea than openly flouting the king's command, but it would be foolish to tell Ian. Doubtless he would regard the stratagem as dishonest or as a reflection on his courage. Briefly, in spite of years of experience, Alinor was washed with a feeling of irritation. She would never understand why men always wished to butt stone walls down with their heads instead of climbing over or going along until they found an opening. At the same time, she was proud that her man would not sneak or lie but would stand up bravely for his own act when he thought it right.

"Very well," she concurred mendaciously. "Probably he will not bother. To return to the question of the reavers——"

"Yes. I fear we have more here than a few outlawed men. The attacks are well organized and, except for one or two instances, are not directed against the weakest and easiest target but against the richest. The outlying serf's huts are usually left in peace. It is the main farm buildings—your property—that are the goal. Whole herds have been driven off, and large quantities of grain have been taken. This argues a large band, and a large band controlled by someone who has some knowledge of military practice."

Alinor's eyes narrowed in thought. "Then they must be encamped in the Forest of Bere. The Church lands are too well settled for any large group to be concealed thereon. How will you do, Ian? To go in after them without leave would be a grave offense against the king —yet to beg his leave just at this time——"

"Why should he know aught of it?" Ian's voice was cold. "I will not touch even one of his precious deer. And does it not seem odd to you that the foresters— who would be quick enough to report my going into the forest—have not this long while noticed whoever is there?"

"John knows!" Alinor gave an outraged gasp.

"No, no." Ian soothed. "It is more likely that the foresters are bought. John may be no prize," he continued bleakly, "but if you take a man's penny, you must give him honest service. There will be a few less foresters if I find it needful to go into the Forest of Bere. Alinor, I will give a few days or a week to trying to trap them on your land. It will put a good face on matters if the king should hear of my invasion of his forest. I can say that, in the heat of pursuit, I did not mark where I was. But to have any hope in this matter, I must strip Roselynde of men-at-arms. Thus, you too will incur the king's displeasure should he hear of it."

"How can you be so silly?" Alinor laughed. "Can his displeasure with me be any greater?"

"No, but this is a matter he can bring up openly against you. Moreover, it will mean that for some time there will be none to defend Roselynde beyond women, old men, and babes."

Alinor considered, then shrugged. "You will not be so far that you cannot come to our assistance, and even women and babes can make shift to hold these walls until you come to us. As far as I know, I have no present enemy."

Ian accepted that, but he insisted on having warning beacons set up, as well as messengers, so that word of trouble at Roselynde Keep would reach him more quickly and surely. It was less the thought of enemies that Ian feared than that someone would try to snatch his prize from him before he could enjoy it. He did not say that to Alinor, only, as he rose to speak to the group of men Beorn had chosen, he urged her to set Father Francis to work on the marriage contract.

"I will sign it as soon as I return or, if I am away longer than I think to be, you can send it to me by messenger, and I will sign."

"But what shall I say? And I need a list of your holdings. Why such haste?"

He looked at her for a long moment before replying, and a red spark flickered in his dark eyes. Alinor found her breath quickening under his stare. For that brief time, a hot avidity showed in his face that roused an instant response in her. Ian muttered something under his breath that Alinor did not ask to have repeated. Then he cleared his throat.

"Do not act the fool. Once that contract is signed, the king will need to fight the Church to get you out of my hands. And he has trouble enough with Church matters just now not to desire to add any straws to the ass's load. I will send you a list of my lands. It will give me something to do while I wait for the reavers. As to what to say—" Suddenly he looked away, and the animation died out of his face. "The contract you signed with Simon will do for me, except that you must add that if I do not get heirs of my body on you, my lands are to go to Adam. If—if aught befall Adam, which God forbid—then to Joanna—or to Adam's heirs or Joanna's in the event I and their children survive them."

Alinor wished she could say something to comfort him. What was there to say to a man who was forcing himself to marry his friend's wife to protect her? Ian kissed her hand as he was leaving the table and said he would return for a word just before he left the keep. Perhaps he could close his eyes, Alinor thought bitterly, and see a different face. All bodies were like enough in the act of love. But Ian's eyes had not been closed. It was her face he had devoured with his looks—until he remembered she had been Simon's wife. Alinor rolled her wine goblet between her hands, then sipped from it, although she knew wine would not warm the chill she felt. Was even the simple pleasure of bedding to be denied her?

How could she explain to Ian that the body was something Simon understood, that Simon would never blame them or think less of them for enjoying each other? That Ian desired her physically was plain enough. That he thought the desire wrong was equally plain. What does that mean for me? Alinor wondered. Will he be disgusted by me, hate me, if I expose my need and my satisfaction with its fulfillment? Tears burned her eyes, but she did not let them fall. I will always be "Simon's wife," she thought. In his mind there is another woman that he wishes were "Ian's wife." Thus, I must remain Simon's wife to whom he must do his duty.

The heavy thought lay on her mind and was not lightened by the formal manner with which Ian took his leave. Of necessity her farewell was equally formal. Ian said he would keep her informed, and turned away cursing himself for his unguarded display of passion. The warmth and friendship had gone out of her. It is not I, myself, she finds repugnant, Ian told himself, wishing he felt as sure as the words sounded. It is an offense to her that I could desire her so soon after Simon's death.

"Fool of a woman," he muttered under his breath, "does she think that Simon's shade casts some kind of pall on her beauty? How can I sit by her and look at her and speak to her—and yet not desire her? I am not made of stone!"

"Lord?" Owain asked. "Did you speak?"

"Only to myself," Ian said wryly. "It is a sign of aging."

Owain laughed dutifully at what he assumed was a joke as they emerged into the bailey, but the sound cut off at the sight of the fully caparisoned horse a hulking groom was holding with some difficulty.

"What is this?" Ian asked sharply in English.

"The mistress begs that you will use the old lord's destriers," the groom panted. "There is no one else who can manage them. If you will not ride them, the lady says, they must be destroyed."

"Very well," Ian snarled.

It was ridiculous that this should hurt him. The horses were superb and very valuable, with a strength and endurance few, if any, could match. It was also true that the breed of gray stallions seemed possessed of devils. They bit and lashed out at anyone unless controlled by a powerful hand. It made them invaluable as war horses. In fact, they often seemed more eager to fight than the men who rode them, and needed to be restrained from charging at anything that moved. The men-at-arms would not ride them, nor even go near them by choice.

Simon had had no trouble with them. Possibly his weight communicated some force of authority. Ian could manage them also. He had had a gift of one when he was still Simon's squire and had learned—after some painful experiences—how to deal with them, and he had ridden them when he had helped out during Simon's illness. Now he warned Owain and Geoffrey to stand well away, seized the reins from the groom, and vaulted into the saddle. The horse leapt straight up into the air, came down on its forelegs, and lashed out with its hind. Ian drew in the reins against the beast's resistance until the neck was arched into its breast. It reared, but with somewhat less enthusiasm. He kept the reins drawn tight but steady. The horse came down, danced a bit, lashed out once more with its hind legs, and settled.

"So," Ian soothed, patting its neck. "So. So. Now we are friends."

From a window above Alinor watched. He was so different from Simon in every way but his upright soul. There could be no confusion between them in her heart.

"Oh!" Adam's voice beside her drew her eyes. "Oh! Ian can ride Papa's horses," the boy marveled as he watched Ian start off toward the small drawbridge that led to the outer bailey and thence beyond to the walls. "No one else can, not even Beorn. But someday I will," he said, looking up. "I will."

"Yes, you will, and doubtless Ian will teach you— God willing," Alinor sighed. Then caution rose into her eyes. Her voice sharpened. "And even more doubtless, Ian will beat you witless if he finds you have tried to ride one of your father's horses before you are ready. Those are valuable beasts. If one should be hurt by your inexpert handling, Ian would be so angry and so disappointed that I do not know how he would get over it."

Relief flooded Alinor as she saw the sparkle die out of Adam's eyes. That little devil had been considering trying to sneak a ride on one of those monsters. Probably she had nipped the idea in the bud, but she would have a word with the head groom. Still, the thoughtful expression on Adam's face gave his mother some comfort. It would be dreadful, indeed, the boy was thinking, if one of Papa's war horses should be injured. A whole estate might be put up as a bond to buy a horse like that. It did not occur to Adam that his frail body would be far more likely to break than the leg of a horse or that his mama had never expressed concern for the mishandling of the beasts when she told Beorn to see if he could find someone, anyone, who would ride them.

"When will I be ready?" Adam asked.

"I am not perfectly sure. Your father told me once that it was a matter of weight as well as of mastery.

When the weight on them is too light, the horses are afraid. They do not understand what is astride them. They do not believe it is a man, and are too proud to carry women. Papa weighed about fifteen stone, and the horses were always quiet under him. Ian weighs about thirteen stone, I should guess. If your horsemanship continues as well as you promise now, Adam, I imagine Ian will mount you on the gray destriers when you weigh—oh, eight or ten stone."

That seemed safe. Adam weighed a little more than four stone already, and he was aware of how quickly he was gaining height and weight. Therefore, it would seem to him that putting on another four or five stone of weight would not take long. Alinor knew, of course, that Adam would not continue growing at the rate he was now, and, more important, that long before he gained another four stone he would be in some other household, well away from the temptation of her grandfather's strain of horseflesh.

Fortunately, the interlude had broken Alinor's mood. Chilling fears of her inability to live up to Ian's standards were overlaid by the pleasant concept of day-to-day life with him. Instead of turning back to her embroidery, over which she could brood and indulge in her fears and self-pity, she sent Adam off to make up the lessons he had missed. To his groans of protest that it was a stupid waste of time for a man to learn to read and write, she replied that Ian read and wrote fluently.

"You know he would not bother to reply to a letter written by a scribe," Alinor suggested, "but if you write with your own hand and ask him when you will be ready to ride, I am sure he would write a letter back to you. I will lend you a messenger to carry your letter."

To send a letter by a messenger all his own! "What seal will I use?" Adam asked with a spark of enthusiasm.

"Your father's, of course," Alinor replied gravely. "It is yours now by right. You will find it near to mine in the small brown chest on the writing table in the chamber where I do my accounts. When you have finished your letter, I will give you the key to the chest, and Father Francis will show you how to use the seal."

"Will you read my letter?"

"Not unless you show it to me and desire that I read it. It is impolite, even dishonest, to read other people's letters, except by their leave."

Adam turned and started away, then came back. "Will you—will you mind if I do not show it to you?" he asked hesitantly.

"Of course not, dear heart," Alinor said, bending and kissing him quickly. He was a good, kind child in spite of his deviltry. "I know that men have things to say to each other that women do not need to know or understand."

Ian, Alinor thought, watching Adam tear across the hall in the direction where Father Francis was most likely to be found. His name was a talisman. Everything, even convincing Adam to do his lessons, was made easy at once by it. Yes, and if I do not bestir myself, her thoughts continued, his name will be as black as mine in the eyes of the king. Alinor called a manservant and told him to summon her chief huntsman to her at once.

The man was near 20 years older than the last time Alinor had set him a task far outside his normal duties, but he did not look much different. The hair had always been very pale; now it was white. The naturally fair skin had long ago been weathered into leather that seemed near imperishable. Perhaps there were more wrinkles and seams now in his face, but it was hard to tell. What was important was that the same intelligence gleamed from the bright blue eyes in the broad countenance.

"Will the lord hunt tomorrow, lady?" he asked eagerly as he bobbed a sketchy bow. "It is long and long since my men had work."

"He hunts two-legged game for a time, huntsman,

but I have work for your men—although it is not hunting. Listen close. There will come, sometime within the next moon, I believe, a messenger. This messenger must not reach Roselynde, but he must not be harmed, either. Nor must he come to know that it is *my* people that have taken him prisoner. When he is captured, he is to be kept in some shelter in the woods, as if by outlaws."

"How will we know this man, lady?"

"That I cannot tell you. This means that you will have to take all messengers coming to Roselynde."

"One came this morning."

"Yes, he brought the news that this other messenger would soon follow—the one that must be stopped. Any man riding in haste to Roselynde should be taken and stripped. The clothes and every other thing must be brought here to me. I will then tell you whether to release or hold the man. Huntsman, watch carefully. It is a matter of great weight to me and to the new lord. If the messenger comes through, there might be war or a change of overlords in Roselynde."

"Be at ease, lady. Not even a worm will come through that you do not know of it."

"Your men will be well rewarded for their diligence, all of them, and a special prize to the man who takes the messenger. Remember, he must be held straitly, but nowise harmed."

"I hear, lady."

No one would come by land. Now to block the passage by sea. That would not be so easy. If the messenger took passage in a merchantman, she could do nothing except arrange to have him killed when he came ashore. If he came across the narrow sea in a small fishing boat hired for the occasion, as was most common, her fisherfolk might be able to take him. Alinor glanced toward the window embrasure. There would be light enough, she thought. She sent a servant to the stables to order her horse saddled and to send up whoever had been left in charge of the men-at-arms in the castle while she changed into riding dress. She found Cedric of the Southfold waiting when she came down skirted and wimpled for riding. The old man's brow wrinkled with concern.

"Lady, we have no proper guard for you. Lord Ian took all but ten cripples like me."

There was fear in his face. Had the lady been in ignorance of Lord Ian's orders? Beorn was with the lord, and no one doubted that the lady's permission had been obtained. Had it not, heads would roll.

"Yes, I know," Alinor answered calmly, quieting her henchman's alarms. "If you can spare me five men fit for riding, that will be sufficient. I only go into the town and to the fishing villages along the shore. It will be safe enough."

It should have been safe. Cedric would not have argued with Alinor in any case, but he felt as she did. Nonetheless, he chose the ablest men he had and saw that they were well-armed. There was no trouble on the short road into the town. Alinor dismounted at the harbormaster's house. The man was already at the foot of the outside stair and bowed her cringingly into the solar. Alinor's eyes swept the room, the fine rug on the floor before the hearth, the cushioned, carved chairs. After a sullen, gloomy day the sun had decided to peep out in the afternoon. Its golden light, glancing in through the gable window that faced south, gleamed on the polished wood of chests and warmed the reds and browns of the tapestried flowers on the walls.

It was time, Alinor thought, to check her harbormaster's accounts again. He held his place by her pleasure and by paying an annual fee for the right, and his wealth came from rents and fines on the merchantmen and ships that came into Roselynde harbor. This was all accepted practice, but if the fees and fines were set too high, ships would seek out other harbors. It seemed to Alinor that the harbormaster's comforts had grown apace since Simon fell ill. Either trade had increased abnormally or the man was cheating the ship-masters and her. Alinor stated what she wanted done, watching, without seeming to watch, the play of emotion on the man's face.

"You understand," she concluded, eying him coldly, "that if the messenger reaches Roselynde Keep, you will die. It is within your right to examine the credences of any man who enters the harbor. Until I give permission, no man bearing the king's credence may come into Roselynde Keep. If you can find reason to imprison the man, do so. If you must kill him—well, I give justice here. None is likely to trouble you. I would prefer he be kept alive, but that is less important than that he be kept away. And if word of these orders be spread abroad, you will lose your tongue. That will make you less talkative about my business in the future."

"Lady Alinor, I will do my best, but if he come secretly——"

"There is no reason for him to do so. However, that is no business of yours. I will take measures to prevent that also. You need not concern yourself for that."

"Yes, my lady."

The next stop was an inn very close to the water-front. Here Alinor did not dismount. A man-at-arms brought the innkeeper out. He bowed low. He and the lady understood each other. She did not meddle in his business. When those who sheltered with him tres-passed too boldly, the lady passed him word. Either the malefactors were surrendered to the lady's justice or they disappeared. Alinor gave her orders. The inn-keeper bowed again.

"My people will watch. Any writings will be sent to the keep. Do you desire the man also?"

"If killing is not needful, hold him. I will send word whether he should be slain or what else should be done."

"As you will. Word comes there will be a new lord. True?"

Alinor laughed. "The birds fly swiftly with news from the keep. Yes, it is true. But I hold justice in my hands still. There is no need to concern yourself with the new lord other than to obey him if he give an order."

"As you will."

The innkeeper bowed himself back into his inn. At the door he paused a moment to watch Alinor. She did not go back up the steep road toward the keep. Her party turned instead to the west and threaded its way through the alleys. It would be well for him, the innkeeper thought, if the messenger fell into his hands. The Lady of Roselynde was very generous to those who served her well, and it was clear that this was a matter of importance. She was riding to alert the fisherfolk also.

Had he not paused to watch Alinor, the innkeeper might have noticed that two strangers were also interested in her movements. As it was, there was nothing to draw his attention to the fact that they finished their ale and left almost as he cleared the doorway. He was more intent on spreading word of the wanted man among his "people"—the beggars and petty thieves who made their livelihood off the merchants and sailors that came into Roselynde's excellent harbor.

Once out of the town, the strangers left the rough road that meandered toward the nearest fishing village and struck north. Somewhat less than a mile inland there was a small wood, actually a finger stretching down from the Forest of Bere. Here the two found the rest of their party and excitedly gave their news. The lady of the keep was out, with only five men. If they took her, the ransom would buy them all new farms and pay the taxes on them also for years ahead. There was some argument from the less bold members of the group. It seemed too dangerous an enterprise to attack a noblewoman. They had come hoping to raid a small merchant train, and that was a far different matter.

The two who had brought the word of Alinor's availability pointed out that no new ships were in and that there would be no traveling merchants for some days. The longer they remained this close to the keep, the greater their danger. Any day a hunting party might come into the woods. Besides, taking the lady would put silver and gold coin into their hands. There would not be the additional terrible danger of having to sell the goods stolen from the merchant. When they had their ransom, they could flee far, where no one would know them or question them. Gold and silver pieces were all alike; they could not be traced. They would not hurt the lady.

The argument took time, but the men were not concerned. Their position had been carefully chosen so that lookouts could command both roads leading out of Roselynde Town. To return to the keep, Alinor and her party would need to come either by the one road or across the open country just south of the little wood. By the time they had been sighted by the lookouts, the more adventurous souls had won. The lady's party was outnumbered better than two to one. They were between her and the town, where presumably the rich merchants would come to her aid. The short evening of autumn was already darkening into night. Everything was to their advantage. The outlaw band mounted on their stolen horses and set quarrels into their wound bows.

CHAPTER SIX

The marvelous gait of the great gray destrier, moving as if there were no more than a feather on its back—a feather that must not be dislodged by uneven jostling—soothed Ian. For a while, he had returned to the happy days when Alinor's gift to him carried him proudly among the hills of Wales, when his friendship with Lord Llewelyn had been first forged. Girls were for tumbling then, without love and without regret. Love was a star, so distant that to look upon it was an unalloyed joy. One does not hope to seize a star.

Deliberately Ian did not think of the later years when a more mature man suppressed a less pure longing. He thought of the gray stallion, now grown old, running loose among the mares on his northern lands. So far, the animal had not brought forth a get of his own nature. There were colts, better than the mares that bred them, but seemingly none with the thews or spirit of the sire. The flicker of regret Ian felt for that was immediately washed away by pleasure. It no longer mattered. He possessively stroked the silken gray neck. They were all his now, stallions and mares. What a fool he had been to feel hurt at Alinor's offer of the horse. She was keeping her promise. Everything she could offer him was being given freely and without grudging.

Shying away from the thought of what could not be given by her will, Ian turned his attention to the countryside. He was momentarily distracted from tactical considerations by its beauty. The sun had finally emerged, and the beeches and oaks that dotted the pasture or served as windbreaks on the crests of the knolls flamed gold and crimson. The stubble of the reaped grain, a softer gold, lay thick on the winter fields. Roselynde was very rich. Not only was the land fertile, but it had been fortunate in a succession of good masters.

The burned-out farm buildings were an offense against the good management and tranquillity. Ian flushed a trifle with anger when his eyes fell upon them, but he checked his flare of temper. It was not really senseless or wanton destruction. There was spite in it, but spite directed by intelligence. Ian had a glimmering of an idea. He could not permit himself to develop a hatred or rage against the perpetrator of this outrage until the man was in his hands and his motives—aside from the obvious ones of a need for food—had been examined.

The attacks on Alinor's land might be the result of a mistake. By and large, only the properties of King John's favorites were still as prosperous as the Roselynde estate. Those whom John did not love were taxed and fined until even good landlords were forced to squeeze their serfs and tenants. Roselynde's freedom from excessive charges was owing to several diverse causes, but not to John's love. Simon had been deeply beloved of John's mother, who had not died until 1204, and the king had remained sufficiently in awe of that mighty woman to leave her favorite in peace. After 1204 John had been too busy with incipient revolt in England and military reverses in Normandy to bother with Alinor and her husband.

All taxes and demands had risen, of course, and many who were not prepared could not meet those demands even when no special fines were added. This problem also did not touch Roselynde. Alinor kept her own books and her own secrets. There was no one who knew what Alinor's revenues were, except Alinor herself. Moreover, the land was only a small share of her income. What Alinor made from the fishing trade in Roselynde and Mersea only Alinor knew, and the ships often carried more than fish. Simon had brought back enormous loot from the Crusades and had made enormous profits from his office as sheriff of Sussex. As taxes rose, Alinor increased her demands on her people, but not enough to ruin them. She and Simon knew what John was like. They had been prepared for lean years.

If the leader of the reavers was wreaking his spite on one whom he believed to be a favorite of the king, it might be possible to turn the man from his purpose. The more Ian saw of his work, the more he respected the common sense and ability of the leader of the outlaws. Considering the situation, he kept his men under good control, Ian thought. Looting was to be expected, since that was the purpose of the raids, but wanton burning was minimal and, Ian had discovered, the women who had been carried off were either widows or whores. Very interesting. Rape, too, was minimal, largely confined to the wives and daughters of the bailiffs. Spite showed there; a special kind of spite. Ian could only hope that the iron had not bit too deep into the outlaw leader's soul.

Ian directed 20 men-at-arms from Roselynde Keep and ten of his northerners to take cover around the burned-out farmstead. Other groups had been deployed at various positions all along the boundaries of the lands, but Ian had decided to take this position in person because he did not believe the man who led the reavers would permit resistance to defeat him. He would be back for the cattle he had not previously been able to take.

In a nearby serf's hut, Ian gathered the remainder of his troop, ten wiry Welshmen with long hair bound back by leather thongs and odd, very long quivers strapped to their backs. Short swords hung from their belts, but as Ian explained what he wanted them to do in French and Owain translated swiftly into Welsh, they did not finger their swords as men preparing for action often did. Those who did not stand quietly ran their hands caressingly along the six-foot bows of ash or yew that they held.

"No killing unless it be needful," Ian snapped.

He knew what those yard-long shafts sped from the enormous bows could do. They were as effective as a crossbow and could be aimed and fired many times more swiftly. Not many men in England knew the use of the longbow, but any man who had fought the Welsh respected and feared the weapon. When he had time, Ian intended to introduce its use to Alinor's men, but skill with it came slowly. Only a few of his northern men-at-arms had mastered the art.

"I wish to know where they lair, but I do *not* want them, or anyone else, to know that my men are making free of the king's forest," Ian continued. "If you kill, hide the bodies—but mark the place, so the poor creature can have a Christian burial when we find a chance to give it to him. It is sufficient evil that any such man die unshriven."

The last was said with more hope than conviction. Welsh hillmen said they believed in Christ, but weird ceremonies still took place in the light of the full moon, and the fear of those sins that Christian teaching most deplored sat very lightly indeed on these stalwart fighters. The men were fond of him, Ian knew, and might mark their victim's bodies to please him. He doubted very much that any concern for the souls of the departed would trouble his Welsh bowmen. Yet he could not help loving them. They were as wild and free as falcons, and they did his bidding out of the same kind of combination of feral greed and affection that a trained falcon has for its master.

He went to the door of the hut to watch them, totally fascinated, as always, by the way they disappeared into the landscape when only a few tens of yards from the place where he stood. Llewelyn could do it, too, and he had tried and tried to teach Ian. The only result had been despair and a conviction that it was an art one had to learn from childhood on Ian's part and desperate attempts to conceal amusement on Llewelyn's. Ian shrugged. Each man had his own arts. Ian knew now he would never make a Welsh woodsman; on the other hand, Llewelyn would never be much of a jouster.

When the disappearing trick was complete, Ian went out to make sure his other men were suitably concealed and the lookouts placed were they could actually see something. As he went, he described what he was doing and why to Owain and Geoffrey. The younger boy's attention was dutiful rather than interested. He did not yet really perceive himself as the master of an estate that he would need to protect. When Geoffrey dreamed of his future, he saw himself as a knight of the romances with streaming pennon riding in a joust, or leading an army into battle. Hunting outlaws because they had burned out a few little farms was not romantic enough for a 13-year-old.

Ian's lecture was automatic; he had listened to so many he could say the words by rote. What he was really thinking about was what to do with Geoffrey. He had forgotten to talk to Alinor about the boy and had been so distraught when he left Roselynde that he hardly realized Geoffrey was following him. Now he had an ill-prepared 13-year-old to protect as well as his 15-year-old squire. Of course, Owain was no longer much of a burden and would soon be a great asset. He was quick and cautious and knew how to hold his place. Although Owain was not yet as strong as a mature man, he was well taught, and could guard himself and get the best out of his weapons. All that was necessary was for one of Ian's hard-bitten northerners to keep one eye on the young man to be sure he did not get carried away by his enthusiasm for fighting.

Geoffrey was something else entirely. He had been

well started and then totally neglected. Not only was he naturally slight, but he did not handle his sword and shield well, because no one had bothered to teach him. Ian had started to work with him in the few weeks of quiet after the end of the action in France and was pleased by the boy's eagerness and progress, but that progress was not enough to make an efficient fighter of Geoffrey. It would be necessary to leave him behind in the care of some men or guard the boy during fighting. Ordinarily there would have been no question; Geoffrey would have to be left in safety. However, in this case, where the opposition was not well-trained men-at-arms but runaway serfs or villeins with stolen weapons, the danger would be less and it might be well to blood Geoffrey now.

Having set his lookouts and decided that the farm showed no obvious signs of his troop, Ian returned to the serf's hut. He sent Owain to check the horses, warning him to beware of the gray destrier. True, the horse was not as vicious once his saddle was removed; he had been trained to strike out at anything that ran away when there was no rider on his back. This was a device to prevent enemy men-at-arms from seizing a fallen knight. Unfortunately the horse had no way of knowing whether his rider had fallen in battle or simply had not yet mounted, although the smell of blood always heightened the animal's fury. Nonetheless, Ian did not want Owain to take any chances; the stallions of Roselynde were never sweet-tempered.

When Owain was gone, Ian gestured Geoffrey to sit at his feet and settled himself on the hut's only stool. "Geoffrey, I need you to think like a man, for I have a choice to give you. You must try to think what will be best and safest, not for you but for me. Through no fault of your own, you are not well-skilled with weapons."

The boy flushed painfully. "I practice with Owain——"

"It is not your blame. There is great promise in you, but you are young yet. Now think. Can you swallow your pride and remain well behind me, where I and Jamie the Scot can guard you, or will you forget yourself and thrust yourself forward, thus endangering us all? If you think your spirit will overcome your sense, I can set two men to guard you out of the fighting."

Geoffrey's cheeks remained pinker, his eyes brighter than usual, but he took time to think over what Ian said. He was accustomed to weighing words, because many traps had been set for his unwary tongue in the past, and a misjudgment meant a beating. Here, however, Ian had stated the situation so cleverly that whatever choice he made was flattering. If he chose to go with the fighters, obviously there could be no question of his courage, and Ian had ordered him not to join the battle in such a way that no contemptuous implication about him could be made. If he did not wish to fight, Ian had stated the case to seem that remaining behind was the result of too-great courage.

"Please, my lord," Geoffrey said softly, "I will obey you exactly. I will not speak or move except by your order. Please let me come. I will not forget that it is you I would harm by a foolish act."

"Very well, Geoffrey, that will suit me excellently well," Ian said noncommittally.

In truth, he was delighted with the choice Geoffrey had made. However cleverly he had phrased the conditions to salve Geoffrey's pride, to Ian it would have been a sign of cowardice if the boy had decided to remain behind. Good heart, Ian thought. Good blood will tell, and if it kills me, I will undo the damage that bitch has done the child. I will save him, and he will be a fine man. Ian stretched and yawned.

"Tell Owain when he has seen the horses fed and watered to come back here and catch what sleep he can. You also. We will be watching most of the night."

With no more ado, Ian drew his sword and laid it

beside one of the stinking straw pallets on the floor, rolled himself into his furred cloak, and dropped off to sleep. His last thought was that he would have to tell Alinor to delouse him as soon as he came back to Roselynde. He had considered lying on the floor instead of on the infested pallet, but he knew from sad experience that the creatures would be attracted to him wherever he lay, so that he might as well seek what comfort he could find to compensate for the discomfort of the bites to come.

When the boys came in they shut the door, and there was little difference between day and night inside the hut. For a while a circle of light came in through the smoke hole, but it did not disturb the sleepers and soon began to fade. Ian stirred into part wakefulness a little while later, but his half-conscious mind soon identified the sounds that had disturbed him. They were the cowherds bringing the beasts in from the field to the newly repaired pens for milking. He drifted into the depths again, unaware of the steady darkening of the smoke hole or, later, the single star that peered in through it.

Before the lone star had moved out of position, Ian was as instantly and completely awake as he had been asleep a moment before. His sword was in his hand before he was upright or really aware of what had wakened him. Then he heard it.

"Eaorling! Eaorling!"

Something was wrong. The northerners would cry *"thegn,"* the Welshmen *"pendeuic,"* Alinor's men-at-arms "lord." Ian applied his foot firmly to Owain and Geoffrey to rouse them, flung open the door, and hurried out. Three shadows were converging upon him. The foremost was still gasping *"eaorling";* the other two were gabbling at each other in broken French, of which Ian caught the words "guard . . . warn," in one voice and "huntsman" in another.

"Quiet!" Ian ordered.

The men were close upon him now, and the foremost tumbled down to his knees. Ian could see his body heaving even in the dim light.

"The leuedy! The leuedy!" the kneeling man gasped.

Ian went cold. There was only one "lady" in Roselynde. Something had happened to Alinor. Had John, with that sudden unpredictability of his, arrived at Roselynde?

"Take hold of yourself, man," Ian said harshly in English. "Speak slow. Tell me what has befallen the lady."

Alinor had visited two fishing villages and was well satisfied with the result of her efforts. The headmen had assured her that if they could not arrange to remove any messenger headed for Roselynde from the boat he had hired, they would mark where the boat came ashore. Whether they would attempt to take him themselves, seek the help of the innkeeper of Roselynde Town or the help of the huntsmen would depend upon circumstances. In any case, they assured her, no messenger would reach Roselynde Keep from the sea. They would pass the word along and warn all the other fisherfolk up and down the coast.

The light was failing by the time Alinor and her men were on the road home, but she expected to reach Roselynde before full dark without trouble. Absorbed in her own thoughts and not particularly alert, because she was in the very heart of her own holding, Alinor did not notice the troop of men that emerged from the little wood. She continued to ride toward them until the group moved to block the road. Then one of her men cried a warning just as Alinor herself pulled sharply on her reins. Almost before she had completed the movement, she comprehended the trap into which she had fallen. The men coming toward her could not be her people.

"Back!" she cried.

The men-at-arms parted to make way for her and formed again behind her when she had turned her horse. All whipped their mounts into a gallop. If they could reach the village, it might be possible to hold off their attackers until help could be summoned. That hope lived for only a very few minutes. Voices cried out for them to halt, promising no harm would come to them, but little time was wasted waiting for a response. Hardly had the sound of the order died than one of Alinor's men cried out in pain. He clung to his saddle for a few moments, then fell.

Too far. The village was much too far. Even though her horses were far better than those of the men who followed, they could never outstrip the arrows. The shot that hit her man might have been an accidental accuracy, but a similar accident might strike her. There were too many in the group that followed them to chance it. Of 12 to 14 quarrels, at least one or two were bound to hit something in so compact a fleeing group. It was also useless for Alinor to tell her men to spread out in different directions. That might save the men from injury, but it would mean certain capture for her. There was no hope that the pursuers might follow a wrong lead. The light was more than strong enough for them to make out the difference between her dress and the clothing of the men-at-arms.

Alinor was not afraid of being harmed deliberately, but she cursed herself bitterly for having forgotten that Simon's death again made her a marriage prize. Ian might cry out with perfect truth that he did not desire her lands, but Ians were few and far between in this land at this time. Many men would cheerfully dishonor themselves and her to gain control of her property—and Simon's, too, because Adam was a child. An arrow passed between two of her men and missed her horse very nearly before it flew ahead of her onto the road.

"Halt," Alinor ordered.

"Lady—" Cedric protested.

"They will do me no harm," Alinor assured her man. "My unharmed person is necessary to their purpose."

She reined in her mount and came forward to face the pursuers. Whoever had taken her was going to receive a very rude surprise, she thought. There was no need, however, to give him warning. Alinor lowered her blazing eyes and set her teeth into her full lower lip while she struggled with her temper. By the time her small party was surrounded, she had won her battle.

"You have made a mistake," she said quietly. "Go your way and allow me to go mine, and I will not recount this incident to my betrothed husband, Lord Ian de Vipont."

Alinor had spoken deliberately to inform her captors that she was useless as a marriage prize. If she were already betrothed, the Church would readily annul any forced marriage. Moreover, Ian's name would give weight to the idea. Any nobleman would know that Ian de Vipont was a familiar of the king's and had long served him. Thus, it might be expected that John had approved the marriage between Ian and Alinor and would press the annulment of any other union. Alinor had a brief qualm as the thought crossed her mind that the abductor might be one of John's henchmen.

"Norman bitch," one of the captors snarled in English.

"Peace!" Alinor hissed as her men stiffened with outrage.

The remark was momentarily incomprehensible to her. Her reaction in restraining her men had been instinctive, a response to the hopelessness of their position. Slowly it dawned upon Alinor that no servant of a nobleman in England in this day and age would use "Norman" in that derogatory sense. This was no abduction to gain a marriage prize. These were the reavers—or, at least, a part of that group. What did they want? Could they be mad enough to desire to take revenge upon her for the hurts done them by others? Alinor stared down at her mare's braided mane to hide her expression. She hoped her captors were too busy disarming her men-at-arms to notice her quickened breathing and the slight tremor of her hands. Then her tension eased. Ransom! That was what they wanted—ransom.

"Cedric," Alinor said, "ask if we may go back so that I can see to my man's hurts, if he be still alive."

Cedric's guttural question sparked an argument which Alinor followed with interest, although she kept her eyes on her saddle so that the men would not guess she understood them. There were two differing parties —a bolder one, which had suggested abducting her and was now willing to go back for the wounded man-at-arms, and a more timid one, which had opposed her abduction in the first place and now only wished to retreat to the safety of the woods with all speed. The more cautious group was now in the ascendant. The whole party was put into motion and hustled toward the shelter of the wood, where they would be concealed from the eyes of any chance traveler.

Soon they stopped again at a place that gave evidence of previous habitation. At first, Alinor promised herself that she would have her huntsman's head off for overlooking a nest of thieves so close to the town and keep. In a few minutes, however, she realized that this was no camp, merely a place the group had stopped to rest and probably to wait for news of prey. It was almost full dark now. Alinor wondered whether they would stay the night, but it was quickly apparent that was not their purpose. Alinor's men were pulled from their horses, stripped of their armor and tied hand and foot to the sorriest of the beasts the outlaws had been riding.

Another argument then ensued, the cautious party desiring to leave Alinor alone and warning that laying

a hand on her, even to tie her wrists, would worsen
their situation. Any insult would make pursuit more
determined. They nearly won again, but the man who
had called her a Norman bitch burst into a passionate
tirade. Alinor could not follow all of it, but she caught
enough to realize he was recalling the men's wrongs
to them and urging them not to give even such comfort
as the smooth gait of her own horse to one of the hated
oppressors. There were murmurs of protest, but doubtful ones. Alinor was wrenched from her saddle. Her
men struggled fruitlessly with their bonds at the insult.

"Norman bitch!" the man who held her spat again.

Alinor's breath caught at the expression on his face.
Hatred was rapidly overcoming good sense. Although
she had little concern with the purity of the body,
Alinor certainly did not wish to be raped by 14 men.
It would be an act of insanity. They would be hunted
the length and breadth of England for such an act, but
the danger was that they had no acknowledged leader.
Any idea presented forcibly enough to their minds
could sway them. The grip on Alinor tightened.

"If you harm me, your own captain will kill you,"
Alinor remarked quietly.

Before the man could make any response, one of the
most nervous of the party started. "Something moved,"
he whispered tensely. "There is someone in the wood."

Quarrels were trained in one direction, then in another. Now all was silent except the hard breathing of
the men, who stared nervously this way and that.

"Let us go. For God's sake, let us go. They may
gather wood for the town here. Someone may have
gone to get help."

"If someone has gone," the "Norman bitch" man
snarled, "it is not for help. No one wishes to help these
masters of ours."

"So you say, but I had a good lord—till the king
ruined him," another replied. "I would have helped

him, if I could. I say leave the lady here and let us fly."

"That would be even worse. Do you think she would hesitate a minute to put the whole castlefolk on our tails? You should have thought of that before," the timid man spat. "Let us go farther into the woods and kill them all and bury them deep. No one will know."

"Fool! What is the profit in that?" asked the man who had proposed the abduction in the first place.

"Our lives are the profit. They will not hang us for this—they will draw and quarter us."

"They will draw and quarter us anyway," the "Norman bitch" man laughed. "Let us use her first and bury her after. Thus we will have a little profit. It will be no small pleasure to lay a Norman bitch. I wonder if their little holes are daintier than those of our women."

"That is not the kind of profit I meant, you swine."

"Fools! Fools! To stand here and argue about doing this or that. Let us go, I say. When we are safe off this land, then we will have time to talk of what to do."

Ian did not permit himself to give a single thought to Alinor. If he did, he would run mad. He concentrated instead upon each individual step of what he had to do. The cowherds had to be told to take their cattle out to pasture again and scatter them so that they could serve as bait for the reavers another time. The men had to be roused and called to arms. The huntsman was fordone. He could run no further. Wulf of the Lea must take him up to ride pillion to direct them.

Everything seemed to take a million years to accomplish, but Ian did not scream at his men or threaten them. To acknowledge the need for haste would break the blankness that he was keeping in his mind. Any crack in that blankness would somehow connect with what lay behind the black wall that covered his childhood. Something would come out through a crack in that wall that would destroy him utterly, changing him so that he, in turn, would destroy everything and every one around him. Ian's hand trembled a little on the rein of his mount. The gray destrier reared and pawed the air and neighed. Ian swallowed and tightened his grip. The horrors gnawing away at the black wall were coming closer.

Actually, the time between Ian's comprehension of what the huntsman told him and the time the troop started was between ten and fifteen minutes. It took much longer to ride across the fields and pastures that separated them from the forest, but it was a far shorter time than was safe. Ian led the troop at a full gallop, and they followed, cursing and praying under their breaths that the horses would not spill them in the dark. By God's grace, only two men were lost to the troop. More took falls, but neither they nor their mounts were badly injured, and they remounted and followed. The gray horse never missed a step.

The moon rose. To the men who had been straining their eyes in what luminosity the starlight gave, it was light. Ahead, however, blackness loomed. Ian stared at it without comprehension, aware only of the little writhing things in the corners of his mind.

"Slower, master," the huntsman hissed. "The wood is near. Those we seek must have traveled far in the time I came afoot. They might hear us, or we might pass those who watch."

Near. The word caught Ian's attention and permitted him to listen and understand. He pulled in his horse. The beast resisted, sensing his quickened breath, his quivering eagerness. Again the stallion reared, bucked, lashed out. It was a blessing. While he fought his mount, the wriggling madness retreated a little. Reined in, the party approached the woods at a walk. Suddenly, a nightjar whistled almost in Ian's ear. Some distance south, a figure detached itself from the edge of the shadow and began a steady loping run toward the oncoming horsemen. The nightjar whistled again.

"Stop," the huntsman urged.

Ian ground his teeth and tried to pray.

"They have not passed this way," a coarse voice muttered when the running shadow reached them. "Either they are farther in the wood or they have stopped. Go south of the moon for a little. Horn is in the wood."

Stopped. If they had stopped—Ian took a grip on that thought, strangled it, and buried it. He turned his head to give further instructions to Jamie the Scot about what was to be done when they came upon the group they hunted. Alinor's men pressed close behind him.

"Quiet!" Ian snapped. Their angry muttering set his own rage boiling under the tight lid he had on it.

They moved forward again, slowly now, because the trees blocked the moon except for intermittent brighter patches, and there was the constant danger of being swept from the saddle by low-hanging branches. The coarse-voiced huntsman also rode pillion, from time to time emitting the nightjar whistle. The shrill sound was doing Ian no good. Each time, something inside him shivered. At last, the birdcall woke a response other than birds; the whistle was followed almost at once by a weasel's shriek. Ian jumped, but the huntsman uttered a grunt of satisfaction and bade them stop again. Horn came slipping through the trees, nodding recognition as the nightjar whistled still again. He did not speak but, as soon as he was sure they had good sight of him, beckoned them to follow and ran south.

Ian moved his shield to his arm and unhooked the morningstar from his saddle. Owain stared at his master. He had never seen him use that weapon before and had had lectures, when he was being taught to use it himself, about the impropriety of using it except in emergencies. He could only presume they would be badly outnumbered. He thought about it as he slid his own shield from shoulder to arm. Then he heard Ian's voice, low and sing-song.

"Did you speak, lord?"

There was no reply. The morningstar swung suggestively on its barbed chain, but the continuing spate of words were too low to hear. Owain licked his lips nervously and settled his helmet firmly over his mail hood. Something bad was going to happen.

There was not much longer to wait, which was just as well, for Ian's mental balance was teetering nearer and nearer the edge of dissolution. Horn stopped and pointed ahead. Faintly there was the sound of voices; the tone indicated that men were shouting, although distance softened and made the words indistinguishable. The two huntsmen slipped from the cruppers of the horses and moved west. Ian signaled, and some of the troop, Jamie leading, followed them.

"Wait," Ian whispered to himself. "Wait. Do not spoil all. Wait."

One last time the nightjar whistled.

"Forward!" Ian snarled softly, but the men heard.

The shouting increased in volume as they moved, increased until there was one louder shriek of alarm. Then all sound cut off.

"Forward!" Ian bellowed, setting spurs to his horse.

It seemed as if a single stride took the stallion the last few yards. He burst into a small clearing where three men stood centered within a larger group, all motion arrested by surprise. Another leap took the horse into the group. One man flew from the destrier's shoulder, another shrieked as he fell beneath the iron-shod hooves. There was a sweet, wet squelch as a third was brained by the morningstar. That man did not cry out at all, but another screamed as the return stroke tore half his face away, and screamed as he fell, and went on screaming. The tableau shattered. The clearing was full of frantic motion—men-at-arms on horses swinging weapons and men running, dodging, crawling, shrieking with pain and fear.

"Kill them!" Ian screamed. "Kill them! Kill them!"

He swung the morningstar and missed as the destrier's momentum carried him past a bloodied, white-faced thing that held up unarmed hands in supplication. Cursing, Ian loosened his shield and cast it from his arm, flung himself from his horse, swung the morningstar again, and again, and again. In a single glimpse he had seen a heap of bodies at one edge of the clearing and, a little to one side, a smaller heap that, even with the colors bleached by the moonlight, was wearing the dress of a gentlewoman.

CHAPTER SEVEN

"Ian! Ian! Stop! Ian, stop!"

No man's voice could reach that pitch. No one there would call him by his name. How long had it taken him to hear her? Ian opened the hand that held the shaft of the morningstar, allowed the loop of the weapon to slide off his wrist. He lifted his eyes from what lay at his feet. There should have been a wild rush of relief when he saw Alinor, safe and well. He did feel gladness, but it was strangely muted, as if the emotion was blanketed under a heavy weight or was a thing perceived at an immense distance.

Alinor was spattered and streaked with blood, but the sight did not shock him. Although it was true that he was, at that moment, incapable of feeling shock, Ian knew the blood was not hers. Obviously, it had come from the dead things in the clearing and had sprayed from the weapon he had been wielding. Slowly and carefully, Alinor raised her hands and took his face between them. Ian stared at her with recognition but without feeling. There was a surprising absence of human voices. Horses stamped and nickered nervously, and there was a soft sound of sobbing. Ian looked more closely at Alinor, but the sound did not come from her.

"Ian?" she questioned gently.

It was very peculiar. Ian felt cold and tired and as if everyone was a stranger to him. Most peculiar. He turned his head a little to one side and then to the other. His men-at-arms were backed away as widely as the clearing would permit. On the ground were the remains of what had been men—probably, it was hard to tell now. Ian brought his eyes back to Alinor.

"I lost my temper," he said inadequately, then, distantly, remembered why. "I thought—Are you all right? Did they——"

"I am quite unharmed. Unhurt. No one touched me except to bind my hands and lift me from one horse to another."

Alinor's words were slow and distinct, her voice exaggeratedly soothing, but Ian's eyes were quite sane now, merely shadowed with a faint anxiety. Alinor let her hands slide from his face to his shoulders. He sighed, remembering terror, but as a faint, faraway thing.

"The way you were lying—I thought you were dead."

"No. The fools did not even take my eating knife from me, and they tied my wrists in front. I curled up so that they would not see me freeing my hands while they stood and argued."

"I see. Well, thank God we were in time." He glanced around again. The killing done seemed unnecessarily brutal, but what was wrong with everyone? "Do you remember how many men there were, Alinor?"

"Fourteen," she replied promptly, still watching him.

He could not understand her expression. That was most peculiar also, but he was too tired to ask. "Good," he replied. "You keep your head."

"Why not? I was not even much frightened." If she had been shaken to a jelly, Alinor would not have admitted it. The last thing she wanted was to set Ian off again. She allowed one hand to drop away from him, but she touched his cheek with the other. "You should not allow yourself to be so overset," she suggested gently. "If they had been clever, they would never have laid hands upon me. Since they were so stupid as to try to take me, you should have known I would manage somehow to keep them at bay until you could come for me."

Ian sighed again. He wondered why Alinor said he had been overset. It was surprising how tired he felt. His arm ached as if he had been fighting all day. Yet it could not have taken long to subdue 14 ill-armed and ill-trained men. He turned from Alinor and counted. Eleven. Three were missing. That was what was wrong. His eyes swept the circle of men-at-arms.

"You allowed three to escape," he said harshly.

"*Nae, thegn,*" Jamie replied. He gestured quickly, and three trembling creatures were dragged forward.

"Kill them," Ian said coldly.

"Ian," Alinor protested, laying a hand on his arm. "They did me no harm."

He looked down at her. "They dared to threaten violence to a gentlewoman. If they had only dared *think* of it, they would deserve to die." He nodded sharply to his man-at-arms, and repeated, "Kill them." To Alinor he said, "I am in a hurry, or I would have had them drawn and quartered in the town in public as an example."

The berserker was completely gone, Alinor realized, watching him. There was no hatred, no emotion at all, in his order to kill. It was a rational, considered act. As Alinor thought it over, she realized she would have been capable of giving the same order had she not been momentarily sickened by what she had already seen. There was also the fact that she could hardly believe what had happened. Alinor could hardly believe that any group of commoners would abduct a gentlewoman. Such a thing had never happened on her lands before, and she had never considered what would be a suitable penalty. Now that she did think of it, her brisk nod mirrored Ian's.

"You are right, my lord."

Suddenly the people in the clearing jerked into normalcy. A babble of voices broke out as the brief execution was arranged. Owain came forward carrying Ian's discarded shield. He proffered it to his master, who looked at it a moment in amazement before he slid it automatically over his shoulder. Alinor "tchk'd" with irritation but said nothing. Perhaps the bandaging would be sufficient to keep Ian's back from being rubbed raw again. Owain bent and picked up the morningstar, which was bloodied and clotted with pieces of flesh right up to the handgrip.

"Where is Geoffrey?" Ian asked sharply.

Owain jerked his head toward the far edge of the clearing. "Sick," he said briefly, and then swallowed convulsively himself.

Ian shrugged. "Tell him to swallow his gorge and come here." His eyes fell on the morningstar, which swung from Owain's hand. A faint frown passed over his face. "See if you can clean that a little. It will drive my horse mad."

For some reason Ian could not understand, Owain swallowed hard again. "Yes, lord," he remarked feelingly.

"Where is the horse?" Ian asked next with some concern, aware suddenly that everyone was afoot.

"There are four men battling with him back in the woods," Alinor said. "Most of that," she waved toward the mutilated corpses, "is your work, but some of it is the beast's. Any creature that rose up and tried to flee and ran by mistake in his direction he kicked and tore to pulp. Is he safe to ride, Ian?"

"Of course," he replied, rather surprised. "That is his training. He did not touch me. He knows my smell now. He will be quiet as soon as I am in the saddle."

"Then perhaps you should mount him," Alinor suggested, "before we are four men-at-arms the less."

"Let Geoffrey go tell the men to bring the horse," Ian agreed, almost smiling.

Alinor shook her head and took hold of Ian's arm. Seeing the message in her eyes, he gestured to Owain to wait and bent his head so that she could speak softly. "You had better speak to the child, Ian. He is not only sick, he is sickened. He saw what he is really too young to see, and the horse will make everything worse."

"It is his first battle, Alinor. That he should be sick is a usual thing. Every boy needs to be blooded. He must grow accustomed."

"God forbid!" Alinor exclaimed.

"God forbid!" Ian echoed in amazement. "Geoffrey must learn that battles make dead men. Thirteen is not too young to see death."

"It is too young to see his master fighting berserk."

"Berserk? I?" Ian's eyes wandered to the flesh-and-blood-caked morningstar, then down his own body. He was completely covered with blood, his hands and arms dyed with it well above the elbows, his surcoat stiffening almost as hard as untanned leather as the blood dried. "Good Lord," he said mildly, "no wonder you said I should not permit myself to be so overset." He turned from Alinor to his squire. "Owain, did I act in any way unusual?"

"Lord, I have never seen the like. Of the eleven men, you struck down eight. And the horse followed you, trampling any who rose."

"Not then," Ian said impatiently, "before the battle. Did I fail in giving any order to the men that was needful?"

"Oh no, my lord."

Ian nodded with satisfaction. "I thought I remembered dealing with the men as usual. The rest is not important. Go send Geoffrey to me. Give order also that the bodies be tied to the worst of the beasts. They can be loaded into carts when we come to the nearest farmstead."

"Ian," Alinor said softly when the squire was gone. "It is not unimportant. You threw your shield away. Those creatures were nothing, but in a real battle—"

"I do not run berserk in an ordinary battle," he replied drily. "Why should I? I do not hate or fear my opponents in battle." He put out a hand, looked at the blood on it and let it drop without touching Alinor. Suddenly feeling came back to him, and he needed to stiffen his body to keep from trembling like a leaf, to keep from clutching Alinor to him and weeping over her. "Do you not understand? It was because——"

"Lord?"

The trembling whisper checked the words on Ian's lips. A flicker of anger was swallowed in relief. Alinor was herself again, warm, concerned for him, friendly. He had almost pushed her back into coldness by speaking of love. Fool that he was, would he never learn? He turned toward Geoffrey. The boy did not cringe away, but his eyes widened apprehensively. Ian smiled at him.

"You know, Geoffrey, I was pleased when you decided to stay with the fighting group because I thought it was time for you to be blooded. I did not expect there would be—er—quite so much blood."

The strained look diminished appreciably as Ian's calm voice and practical words began to penetrate. The vision of the berserker, bludgeoning already dead men into red jelly, faded. Geoffrey watched his master remove a gauntlet and grimace distastefully at the red-stained hand. There had been so much blood that it had soaked right through the leather glove.

"You must not be distressed that you felt sick," Ian continued. "I hate to tell you how often I have emptied my belly after a battle, and Owain still does so now and again. It is a common thing. No one will say aught to you or think less of you for it."

Alinor retreated gently. The boy did not need her and would speak more easily to Ian if they were alone. He was a most excellent master to his squires. It was too bad Adam could not stay with him. But that would not be suitable anyway, Alinor thought. Even if she were not going to marry Ian, he was not the right person to be Adam's lord. He was too fond of Adam, too accustomed to thinking of Adam as a "baby" to deal with his young manhood. Either Ian would overprotect the "child of his heart" or, in trying to avoid that pitfall, would thrust him into too much danger. He could judge what to do for Geoffrey and Owain because they were not "children" to him. He had never held them in his arms or received their wet little baby kisses or steadied their first stumbling steps. Ian knew Geoffrey and Owain only as young males growing into manhood. She half turned away, as if her attention was elsewhere, but her ears were tuned to the pair she had just left.

"I was frightened, lord," Geoffrey said, very low.

A fine boy, Alinor thought. The words came as if drawn by a winch, but he had confessed what he probably believed was the ultimate sin and shame.

"But you did not run away," Ian comforted gravely. "As you grow more sure of your ableness with weapons, that feeling will grow less. Even if it does not, so long as you do your duty, it does not matter how you feel inside. For example, it is my duty to instruct my men and deploy them so that they accomplish their purpose at the same time as they suffer as few losses as possible. Usually this is easy for me out of long practice. Today I was so angry because that filth had dared—" his voice faltered. "What I mean to say, Geoffrey, is that I did not wish to bother to tell you where to ride or to tell Jamie to guard you or to tell the men to surround the clearing before they charged. I wished only to come to grips with those who had offended me. Yet had I not done my duty, had I charged and laid about me as I desired, most would have escaped."

The boy nodded stiffly, still not able to accept what he had seen. Ian smiled at him.

"Usually, of course, this trouble does not arise. In a war called by the king or even to defend my own lands, there is no reason to be angry with those who fight against me. Or, at least," Ian's lips twitched, "not so angry as that." He gestured toward the shambles in the clearing.

There was interest in Geoffrey's eyes now, and a tinge of color in his cheeks. Ian judged that whatever shock the boy had was sufficiently dissipated to allow time and the next battle, which was bound to be cleaner, to complete the process of adjustment to violent death. An unguarded crashing, to which Ian had been attending with half an ear while he soothed Geoffrey, resolved itself into the gray destrier being brought around through the woods behind the clearing because no one dared try to lead it across past the dead men. Ian looked at the horse and barely restrained a shudder.

Blood dyed the destrier's legs right to the hocks and splattered the belly and breast and even the face. Two men hung on the reins close to the bit and two others to the harness. Even with that weight restraining him, the horse persisted in trying to rear and snap. Weals on shoulder and neck showed where someone had taken a stick or the flat of a sword to the animal. Ian's mouth opened to ask who had committed that outrage, and then closed. Doubtless there had been no other way to subdue him. In essence he had committed the outrage himself by abandoning the poor dumb creature to his own devices. Trained to respond to the smell of blood with rage instead of the normal reaction of terror, the horse had run as mad as he when the controlling hand was gone.

Ian gathered the rein in his hand and rose into the saddle. As soon as his feet found the stirrups, the men sprang away from the horse's head and ran for safety. It was, as Ian had foretold, completely unnecessary. The stallion stood quietly now that authority and security had been restored with the solid weight on his back and the steady pull of the bit on his lips. Ian uttered an exclamation of irritation. In his concern for his mount, he had forgotten Alinor. He turned to apologize for not lifting her into the saddle and saw that she, too, was remounted.

How kind of her, Ian said to himself, to spare him embarrassment, but somewhere inside an uneasy feeling that she wished to avoid having him touch her woke. To a certain small degree that was true. Now that the violent action had subsided and the most necessary reactions to it had been taken care of, Alinor wanted to avoid Ian's notice. She knew he was sure to begin wondering how she had made herself vulnerable to abduction by so inefficient and ill-armed a troop. Alinor needed a little time to decide what to say to him, because she had no intention of confessing her true purpose. Ian would not be any more approving of the idea of waylaying and possibly murdering a king's messenger than Simon would have been. Thus, she not only needed an excuse for being out of Roselynde Keep so close to evening for herself, but also some explanation of what so large a number of huntsmen were doing wandering around when no hunt was planned.

The latter was easy enough to explain as soon as Alinor's fertile mind concentrated on it. The huntsmen were out marking game for killing when they should be needed for the wedding feast. The animals would be kept close by laying out fodder for them. What she herself was doing abroad was less easily explained. Alinor thought of and discarded a number of lame excuses while the troop finished gathering up the corpses, mounted, and got started back toward Roselynde.

Actually, Alinor had more time to think than she had expected, because Ian had arrangements of his own to make. Obviously it would be too late, by the time he had escorted Alinor back home, to hope to catch the outlaws that night. Nonetheless, some men had to return to the farm in case the Welshmen came back with

news of the reavers' camp. There was also the chance
that one of the other groups had come to grips with
a band of the thieves. They might need to summon other
portions of the dispersed troops to their aid, or they
might have taken prisoners who should be questioned.
Owain would have to go. He was the only shadow of
authority and, besides, the only one who could make
head or tail of what the Welsh would say.

As long as the troop rode east, the path of those who
headed for Roselynde and those headed for the farm
lay together. Ian spent that time giving Owain instructions. At the parting of the ways, he sent ten men back
with the squire. When he finally had time to turn his
attention to Alinor, she diverted him from the topic
she feared with a mention of the wounded man-at-
arms. Ian dispatched two men to search for him. Then
Alinor made an ingenuous remark as to how fortunate
her huntsmen were abroad in force. That led to mention of the wedding feast and thence to the subject of
the wedding. Alinor was delighted at how willing Ian
was to discuss that event. She could have wished that
his interest was more personal and less political—he
concentrated mainly upon the men he wished to have
invited—but she reminded herself that it was ungrateful to look a gift horse in the mouth.

In fact, it was not until Ian was getting ready to step
into the tub to wash the blood from himself that he
asked the question she feared. First he said something
about killing the lice with which he had become infested and then, as Alinor turned to tell a maid to
fetch the stavesacre salve, he said softly, "Stay, Alinor."

Alinor instructed the maid and came back, glad that
the flaring light of the torches would conceal the color
that had risen to her cheeks. The last thing Ian said,
before he mentioned the lice, had been a clarification
of a final detail in the marriage contract. Alinor thought
his mind had returned to that; perhaps he would at last
say something that was not purely business. Could the

rage and fear that turned him into a berserker when she was threatened all be his duty to "Simon's wife"? Was it possible for duty to spark such violence? Surely the fear had been—a little, at least—for Alinor.

"I have just bethought me," Ian said sharply, "that my one chance of taking the reavers completely by surprise has been ruined by this little excursion you made into the woods. What were you doing abroad at night, Alinor? And with only five men-at-arms?"

The disappointment was like a blow in the face. Alinor had all but forgotten that Ian was likely to ask that question. Driven by her own desire, she had unconsciously prepared herself to hear words of love. Ian's nakedness, the dimly lit chamber, the late hour, the quiet aftermath of the bloody rescue, had all suggested that tender words, even embraces, should follow talk of marriage. Before she could think, Alinor lashed out to avenge the hurt.

"My purpose can be nothing to you," she replied icily. "I am sorry for the disruption of your plans. I am sorry also for my carelessness, but no sign of the outlaws had ever been seen so close to the keep or to the shore. I thought it would be safe. You need give no further thought to the matter. I will not be so caught another time."

"What did you say? I have just killed fourteen men. Will you not deign to tell me why?" Ian responded furiously.

"You *said* you killed them for the threat to me." Alinor's brows went up disdainfully. "I did not realize that was a polite fiction and you needed a better reason. I am sorry if you do. I have no better to offer you. In fact, I bade you spare the last three."

"Alinor," Ian bellowed, "what were you doing outside the keep with only five men-at-arms when night was drawing on?"

"I was attending to my own business, using half the men you had left me, and I expected to be back in the keep before dark," she replied in no milder voice than his own.

"When I ask a question," Ian choked, striding toward her, "I expect to be answered."

Alinor drew her knife. She held it close to her body, tilted up wickedly like an experienced knife fighter. There was no waving the weapon at arm's length, which was typical of hysterical women.

"And when I do not choose to answer a question my husband asks, he may rest assured the answer does not affect his profit or his honor. It is a subject private to me, and I will keep it that way."

Ian stared at the knife in Alinor's hand with startling eyes. "Put that away," he said, almost whispering. "Put it away now, and do not draw upon me again or you will need to kill me to keep me from lessoning you."

"I am not one of your helpless fancy ladies, Ian," Alinor spat. "I do not choose to be beaten to soothe your bad temper."

"I will lay no hand upon you, upon my honor, if you put up that knife. If you do not——"

"Do not threaten me," Alinor shrieked. "I am no man's chattel to be used well or ill at his pleasure. I am Alinor, Lady of Roselynde."

Ian took another step toward her, raising his fisted right hand while the left, open, was ready to feint at the knife. Because his glance flickered between Alinor's face and the weapon she held, the movement brought his bloodstained hands into his line of vision. Ian suddenly uttered a gasp, dropped his hands, and backed away precipitately.

"Begone," he gasped, "get you gone from me before I do you a hurt against my will and against my honor."

The words were still threatening, but the face and the voice were not. Alinor read the fear and the pleading note aright, although she misunderstood their cause. She remembered very vividly the berserker—and she believed Ian did also. Furious as Alinor still was, she was quite sane enough not to try Ian's temper further this night. In the morning, when the heat of fighting was not so close upon him, they would have this matter out. Alinor slammed her knife back into its sheath and stalked out of the room.

For one long moment Ian remained rigid, staring at the spot where Alinor had stood. "Hellcat!" he muttered. "What did I say to make her turn on me? What did I say?" Then he uttered an explosive obscenity and looked down at himself as if he needed visual evidence of the sensation that had gripped him. So violent was the need that Alinor in her flaming rage had aroused in him that Ian's next move was to look around for a maidservant to ease his lust upon.

The chamber was empty. Not only the maids were gone, but Ian's squire as well. There was nothing for it but to master his desire as best he could. Geoffrey would come if he called, but even in his present condition Ian realized that it would be wrong to send the boy to fetch a woman for him. He would not even have sent Owain, whom he knew was not innocent. To take a maid to bed in his betrothed wife's home was bad manners and a bad example. Certainly he could not ask Geoffrey, who might well still be pure of body if not of mind, to pander for him. Cursing vilely, Ian stepped into the tub and began to wash.

Although the combatants had not noticed, the maids had sidled from the chamber as soon as they perceived the first sign of hostilities, long before Alinor had drawn her knife. Wise by long experience, they had shepherded the frightened squire before them. They were quite accustomed to marital tussles. Alinor and Simon had loved each other deeply, but their marriage had been no milk-and-water affair. Until Simon fell ill, there had been frequent explosions, most based on very similar grounds. The lady had gone her own way; the lord had asked for explanations; the lady had refused; bellows and, occasionally, although rarely, even blows had been exchanged. Invariably peace had been restored, most often in bed. In any case, it had been made plain to the servants in the household that no audience was allowed either to the arguments or to the settlements.

In her own chamber Alinor tore off her clothes, casting them blindly in the direction of a chair and not caring when they missed. She was still so furious that she did not notice the absence of her maids. She threw herself into bed muttering "Convenience! He will make a marriage of convenience, will he? Mayhap he will not find it so convenient to be married to me!"

She fully intended to lie awake and marshal the demands Ian must agree to before she went further with the marriage. He must understand that she meant to retain her independence. It was one thing to yield to a man for love. A man's pride was a delicate thing, and a loving woman would not wound that pride. A business relationship was something entirely different. Partners in business did not need to worry about each other's pride. It was sufficient to be polite and honest.

It had been a long day, far fuller of physical activity and violent excitement and emotion than Alinor had had in months. Even as a faint doubt aroused by her last thought flickered in Alinor's mind, her eyes closed. She had not been very polite, it occurred to her, as she slipped into sleep, nor very honest, either. Perhaps Ian was not completely at fault. She slept deeply for the first time since Simon's death, free of the racking pain caused by the absence of his big, warm body in the bed. Later in the night she stirred and reached out, but the eyes in her dream were not blue and tender; they were as hot and as black as the silky curls that shaded them.

The warm water was soothing. As Ian washed, his violent turmoil subsided. It could not have been what he said; it must have been how he said it. His tone had been accusatory, blaming Alinor for everything that had taken place. Some fault was hers, of course, but really very little. He himself had told her that the outlaws

were not operating near the keep and were based outside her lands. Why should she fear trouble so close to
her stronghold? She was well-beloved of her people and
certainly needed no protection when she was among
them. Ian wished now that he had not had the last three
men killed out of hand. He should have questioned them
first. Were they part of the larger band? Were they riding to rejoin the main group? Had their original purpose
been to take Alinor?

As he thought her name, an inner trembling seized
Ian. God, God, he thought, what am I to do? He had
believed that when he was assured of her willingness to
marry him, he would be free of the doubts and desires
that tormented him. Instead they grew worse. Anything
to do with Alinor pushed him right beyond reason. In
his whole life, nothing had driven him berserk before,
and he had fought some very ugly battles. How could
he have been so mad as to have overlooked the need
to question those men? Possibly with the right persua-
sion they could have led him directly to the outlaws'
camp.

Even now, Ian realized, while his brain berated him
for the lost opportunity, his blood boiled anew. If the
men had been restored to life, he knew he would kill
them again. They had looked at Alinor as if she were a
common woman. One had even suggested "using" her.
The huntsman waiting in the brush to see which way
they would go had heard and faithfully reported. Ian
looked down at his hands. He had crushed the bar of
soap he was holding to pulpy fragments. It was bad
enough to fly out at others, but he could no longer
maintain his control in Alinor's presence. It seemed as
if he could hardly exchange a word with her without
either offending her or quarreling with her. Another
scene like the one just past and she would refuse him.

Ian erupted from the tub and bellowed for Geoffrey.
"Dry me," he said when the boy came running, "gently
on the back. I am still sore. When you are done, find

me some clothes. I will wear my own armor. I see that is here on the chest. Enough! That is enough! Take that salve from the pot there and smear it over me. Gently! Now that cloth around me. I will do the rest. Give me the cloth. Go. Dress yourself. Then rouse the men and bid them in the stable to saddle the horses—another of the gray stallions for me. Hurry!"

Stumbling with fatigue, Geoffrey found shirt and surcoat in one chest, chausses in another. Tears came to his eyes when he could not discover cross garters, but at last his scrabbling hands tangled in them. Already half clothed, Ian tore them from him and shoved him toward the door. Geoffrey snatched up his cloak, thanking God that he had been expecting a summons and had not undressed completely for the night. He could return for his own armor while the horses were being saddled. By the mercy of the Mother of God, his master might be gone from the chamber by then.

Owain might have attempted to reason with Ian. Jamie the Scot might have pointed out the insanity of dragging tired men out in the middle of the night for no reason. The Welshmen might have quoted staves about triad troubles bred by hasty and inconsidered acts. No one in Ian's present train was prepared to do anything except obey him implicitly. The red ruins he had created not so many hours before were too clear in all minds. Even the guards at the portcullis and drawbridge had heard about the slaughter. Old men and crippled veterans, they raised the portcullis and lowered the drawbridge without any argument.

In the morning, Alinor lay abed somewhat later than usual. Her mind skipped from her dream of Ian to her quarrel with him and back again. The quarrel had to be mended, but how? She lay very still, battling the desire simply to run to him and beg his pardon, as she would have done with Simon. Just outside of her range of vision her maid Gertrude waited for her mistress to wake, wringing her hands in distress. She had to tell

Alinor that Ian was gone. Not to tell her would bring swift and painful retribution, but it would be an evil day for them all. If the mistress could not vent her spleen where she desired, she was not averse to venting it on anyone who happened to be near.

Although it started evilly, the day was not as bad as Gertrude had feared. Her mistress' initial reactions were violent enough, but when Alinor had questioned everyone who had seen the new lord leave and had examined the chamber, her rage had diminished. For some time she had sat by her embroidery—as she had sat for weeks after the old lord died—not working, only staring at it. This time, however, the fit had not lasted. After a while, she had picked up the needle and worked with great industry. Finally, she had abandoned her position altogether and gone to seek Father Francis. Since then, peace had reigned. Lady Alinor and the priest had remained closeted together.

After Ian had flung himself down on the filthy pallet in the serf's hut, Owain tugged at Geoffrey's sleeve and drew the younger boy outside. At first Geoffrey resisted, terrified that his master would have some desire that he would not be there to fulfill. He was so exhausted and so fearful that it took some time for him to realize that Ian had fallen asleep almost as he lay down. That seemed as incredible to Geoffrey as all the other events of this totally incredible day.

"What has befallen?" Owain whispered. "Is he still mad? I could have sworn it was past. I thought he was near to falling from his horse with tiredness when we parted."

"I do not know," Geoffrey replied, his voice trembling near tears. "He was quiet all the way to the keep—at least, he was talking to Lady Alinor very pleasantly. When we came to the town he sent the—the dead men's bodies down with instructions that they be displayed by the gates with criers to tell the tale of what they had done and what their punishment was. Then we went in, and the lady called for a bath. They spoke of the wedding guests and the marriage contract. Then he told her of this hut and the dirt and fleas and said he needed cleaning, and she sent a maid for something, and—and —I do not know! Suddenly they were screaming at each other. I do not know why, and the maids ran out of the room and drew me out with them. I——"

"By God and all the blessed saints, it is the woman!" Owain exclaimed.

"It is because she is beautiful," Geoffrey sobbed.

"That is part of it," Owain agreed, "but he has played with those more beautiful, and they have never touched him. The difference is that he loves this one—and has loved her long, I think. Yes, yes, it must be so. He has been different, very quick to anger—which was never true of him before—since he had news of Sir Simon's death. I thought he was grieving for his friend and lord, but all the time it was the woman. I suppose he desired her and feared lest there be some dishonor in taking his old lord's wife."

Geoffrey sobbed again, and Owain grimaced and shook his head.

"You had better save your tears. There will be reason enough to weep in the days coming. A man in love is a devil to serve," Owain remarked from the lofty eminence of his two-year-greater experience of the world.

CHAPTER EIGHT

Suffering is, curiously, both immediate and relative. Alinor's maids, who had long bewailed their mistress' dull quiescence because it laid a weight upon their spirits, now had cause to look back to that period with longing. After she emerged from her long conference with Father Francis, the maids found their mistress had become far too lively. Nothing, however it was done, was done aright. Sharp slaps and venomous remarks drove the women from one task to another for three interminable days.

In the field, the men serving Ian were having a very similar experience. At first they thought their lord's bad temper was owing to their inability to lay the outlaws by the heels. There had been two minor clashes, but the reavers withdrew hastily as soon as they realized the farms they had attacked were defended by trained men-at-arms rather than serfs with cudgels. Ian's men had not pursued them farther than the borders of Alinor's land, according to their instructions. The men were well content with the results of their efforts. Not a single chicken or bag of flour or any other item had been lost to the outlaws.

They were puzzled by the lord's dissatisfaction, but a few finally thought far enough ahead to point out to the others that the lord desired to destroy the band. If he did not, they would have to sit here on the border forever. Even if the reavers raided elsewhere for a time, they would return as soon as they discovered Roselynde lands were unguarded again. Having got that far, it seemed reasonable that Lord Ian should be impatient

154

until his Welshmen returned with news of the outlaws' camp.

On the second evening after Ian's return, the Welshmen slipped back into the outpost, to be greeted by caustic questions as to whether they had lost their way. Well accustomed to hasty and intemperate masters, their spokesman replied mildly that it was a large forest and they had assumed the lord would desire to know where the back trails and secondary lairs were, as well as which foresters knew of the outlaws' presence. That the reasonable refutation did nothing to calm their master's ill temper did not surprise the Welshmen; that he did not even seem pleased at their detailed report, which should make it possible for him to take the reavers by surprise any time he wanted, left them shaking their heads in bewilderment.

By midmorning of the third day, the men were slinking unobtrusively out of Ian's path whenever it was possible. Since Owain and Geoffrey had held their tongues, as befitted their station, which forbade gossip with commoners, Ian's continued black mood was inexplicable and, therefore, frightening to them. Owain was neither frightened nor puzzled, but the too-sensitive pride of early manhood made him burn with resentment when an undeserved blow or bitter jibe was aimed at him. He, too, avoided his master. Geoffrey alone, who had originally been the most fearful, was quite content to linger in Ian's company.

This was not because Ian was any more gentle with him than with the others. Twice Geoffrey, who was less quick at dodging than Owain, had been knocked right across the hut, and as many "clumsy louts," "dull asses," and "crawling worms" were launched at him as at anyone else. Geoffrey, however, did not mind a bit. Initially it was owing to his feeling of kinship with Ian's pain. It was true that the beautiful Lady Alinor was not cruel to Geoffrey himself; instead she was cruel to his lord. As the days wore on, however, Geoffrey's indifference to Ian's mood was because what his lord did troubled Geoffrey not at all. He had never minded a bruise or two, and he recognized that the insults came from Ian's spleen rather than from any lack in himself. Moreover, never did those insults touch or even approach any subject upon which Geoffrey was sensitive.

A terrified and uncertain adoration of the being who had rescued him from hell, who was always kind and just, was changing into a deep and abiding love in Geoffrey. It had been impossible to be secure in his adoration when he never saw his lord really out of temper. The flashes of anger that Owain had described as Ian's lack of good humor had seemed too superficial to give proof of his lord's true character. Besides, in France his father had been near, and Geoffrey feared that Ian's behavior to him was softened to give Salisbury a good impression. Now that he saw Ian at his worst, Geoffrey knew he could trust him. Thus, when a messenger came from Roselynde Keep, it was Geoffrey who led him to Ian.

He found his lord seated on a stool and leaning back against the hut's wall, with his eyes closed. For a moment Geoffrey hesitated. He knew Ian did not sleep well and was reluctant to wake him.

"Yes, what is it?" Ian snarled without opening his eyes.

"A messenger from Roselynde, lord."

Ian's eyes snapped open. Geoffrey watched with sympathy as the swarthy complexion grayed. "Well?" Ian snapped.

The man opened the saddlebag he had been carrying over his shoulder and removed a large packet of rolled documents. Color flooded back into Ian's face as he hurriedly unrolled one, then a second. The marriage contracts. A quick check showed that all five copies were the same. Five! Alinor was taking no chances. One for her, one for him, one for the local church, one for the bishop's archives and one for the king. Ian looked

at the four closely written sheets, and a faint smile—
the first in three days—twitched his lips. It had taken
some time to compose and no little time to make five
copies. She must have started on this very soon after he
had raged out of Roselynde.

"What said your mistress?" Ian asked.

"To ride in haste, lord, which I did, and then to do
further as you bid me."

"That was all?"

"Yes, lord."

"There was no other matter? No letter?"

"What you have was what was given to me, my lord."

It was a stupid question, Ian knew. Naturally the
messenger would have given him everything. Alinor was
still angry, then. Ian glanced down at the contracts,
reluctant to start reading. If she wanted to be rid of him,
she could have written in clauses that he could not
accept. His refusal to sign could be taken as a formal
withdrawal of his offer of marriage.

"Take what rest you can," he said to the messenger.
"You will need to ride again later."

Hellcat, Ian thought, realizing she had him in a cleft
stick. The flash of rage, the determination to beat her
at her own game and have her still, gave Ian the impetus
to begin reading. He flashed through the document,
sure that the temptation to withdraw his offer would be
displayed prominently. There was nothing of the kind.
A feeling that he had perhaps been unjust, balanced by
a fear that Alinor was willing to marry him but intended
somehow to tie his hands, set him to reading again, one
word at a time, very carefully.

The second reading completed, Ian tilted his stool
back against the wall again and pursed his lips in a
soundless whistle. Hellcat, he thought again, but this
time with fond admiration. Too proud to beg pardon,
that was why she had not written or sent a message.
The contract was all the apology he would ever get. And
I am more than content, he decided. After all, if Alinor

said she was sorry for her outburst, he would have had to say he was sorry for the provocation he had given her. That, he feared, might lead to more concessions on his part than on hers.

Ian knew he should feel ashamed of himself for misjudging Alinor. With his fears laid to rest, he recognized that she was not the type to use a mean subterfuge. She would stand up to him, knife in hand if need be, and fight him face to face for anything she wanted. However, he was too well satisfied with the outcome to feel ashamed of anything. He looked around at Geoffrey, who had not been dismissed, and stood patiently waiting for orders. Ian grinned at him.

"Never try to outguess a woman," Ian said. "She will do you in, every time. And what is worse," he added with a laugh, "you will be glad of it."

"Lord?" Geoffrey asked doubtfully.

Ian laughed again. "You have some years before you need worry about it. Go now and fetch me a quill and some ink—the bailiff must have some—and find out if there is a man here who knows the way to Winchester and the country thereabout, and—oh, yes—a sheet of parchment, and then send the messenger back to me."

Rationally Alinor knew that Ian would sign the contract. It was a fair document, following the suggestions he himself had made. There was no reason for him not to sign. Her heart, however, was not as easy as her mind. Every time she started to make preparations for the wedding, whether it was to consider the clothing that would have to be sewn or to arrange for the supplies that would be needed for the entertainment of her guests, she was shaken by nervous qualms. As a friend, she knew and trusted Ian; in a deep, personal relationship, she discovered she had no idea how he would act.

Because Simon had loved her, more than loved her, doted upon her, Alinor knew she could always get her own way with him. There was no similar assurance about her relationship with Ian. Certainly she had displayed her very worst characteristics to him and at the very worst time. It was not impossible that he would seek some kind of guarantee that she would be a more docile wife than the termagant she seemed. It was also possible that he would wish to punish her by letting her dangle. If she went ahead with inviting the guests and preparing for the feasting, he could add punitive clauses to the contract and expect she would agree to save herself the shame of a canceled wedding.

Alinor had sent her messenger off to Ian just after the prime. She watched the sun flicker in and out of the clouds, rising toward its midday high and then beginning to drop lower in the sky. She knew how long it would take to ride to the farm where Ian had settled. She knew how long it would take for a man to sign five documents. She knew how long it would take for the messenger to ride back. That time came and passed. Alinor closed herself in her bedchamber to think what next to do and to save herself from murdering someone in her impotent rage.

She felt a fool, of course, when the messenger did arrive, and she realized her careful calculations had not allowed time either for Ian to read the contract or for him to write the letter the messenger was proffering to her. Nor, she thought wryly, as she opened the letter, had she considered that he might not be at the farm. Ian's purpose, after all, had been to hunt outlaws, not to wait for the contract to be delivered to him. Her reaction to her own silliness was so strong that she did not even suffer from doubts of Ian's intentions when she realized the messenger carried nothing but the letter. It read:

"To Alinor, Lady of Roselynde, greetings. I have been well pleased with what you sent to me. Having added my name and my seal to yours, I have sent all to Peter des Roches, Bishop of Winchester, that he might sign as witness. From thence my man will go on to

Salisbury, both to bid William to the wedding and to
have his name as witness to the contract also. I have
written to him, of course, to say that he need not sign
if he doubts the king's reaction. It will thus be some
days before you will have your copy back again, but I
desired to have all made safe before the king's messenger should come, if one should come. On another matter,
I have knowledge now of where the camp of the reavers
lies. I will wait some little time before attempting it,
however, in the hope that hunger will make them desperate and they will come to me. Do not, therefore,
expect to see me soon unless, of course, you have need
of me. If so, send, and I will come. Written this ides of
October by Ian, Lord de Vipont."

Having reread the letter twice, Alinor· drew breath
sharply through her teeth. Did Lord de Vipont think he
was dealing with a child having a tantrum? Glancingly,
her mind gave credit to the fact that Ian was not mean
or petty. He had signed the contract and taken every
precaution to ensure its validity. In addition, he had
taken no nasty little revenge, such as leaving her in
doubt of what he had done or what he intended. On the
other hand, he seemed to feel that withdrawing the company of his exquisite person would bring her to heel.
Did he really think she would beg pardon and plead
with him to return? Did he think she could not manage
to prepare for the wedding without him? Dear Ian had
much to learn about his lady.

The date was settled for the first day of December,
and Alinor knew the names of the men Ian wished to
invite. There was nothing else she needed him for until
it was necessary for him to take the vows in person and
bed her. Alinor stared across the hall to the fire on the
far side. A very faint smile lifted her lips and made her
expression perfectly enchanting. She was remembering
the avidity on Ian's face when he looked down at her
some days ago.

"Lord de Vipont indeed," she whispered softly. "Mayhap you think you love another woman, but I know desire in the eyes of a man when I see it." A brow quirked upward, and the smile became more mischievous. "Desire is a fine rope with which to bind a man and lead him into new pastures."

Alinor's eyes began to sparkle as her spirit lifted and danced. She sprang to her feet with a lightness she had not felt for over a year. This was a problem she was not afraid to face. She had been a fool not to think of this solution right from the beginning. For Ian it would be far better to love his wife than to eat up his soul with hopeless longing. Alinor knew she had been a good wife to Simon; they had been happy together. Once she had enslaved Ian, she would be a good wife to him also, and he would be happy, too. It was unfortunate, Alinor thought, as she tripped lightly up the stairs, that Ian had never spoken to her about the woman he loved. It would have made her task much easier if she knew her rival.

Thinking back over the years, Alinor realized that Ian had never spoken to her about women at all, except in such a general way as to mention who was at court. There had been hints of Ian's conquests, but those had all come from Simon, who would laugh or raise a brow in a significant way when a certain name was mentioned. But it was never the same name two visits in succession. Alinor would swear none of those women was more than a vent to let out the heat of a young man's blood. It was also to Ian's credit that he was no proud seducer. He had seemed more embarrassed than pleased at Simon's knowing looks.

Well, if she did not know, she did not, Alinor thought, dismissing the problem for more practical ones. Although she had spent considerable time with Joanna choosing cloth and adornment for the child's dresses, she had scarcely given a thought to her own. Now she summoned her maids and began a turning out of chests in good earnest. For Simon she had always kept the dress characteristic of a young maiden, because that was what he liked. For Ian, she needed a new persona. No more leaf-green and white and gold. Green and gold, yes, those colors suited her, but in richer tints, more brilliant dyes. And now there were a range of other colors.

Alinor fingered a length of rich, tawny, orange velvet and a cloth-of-gold veil, thin as a whisper and glittering with gold thread. The veil had lain there since she returned from the Holy Land so many years ago. She lifted it to her cheek and went to look—really look—at herself in the polished silver sheet used to reflect images. Even with the darkening and graying effect of the imperfect mirror, the image was flattering. Now for the tunic. More chests were dragged out and opened. Somewhere, once, there had been—ah!—a piece of heavy, heavy, dark-gold silk brocaded in gold until the fabric was stiff. She unfolded the cloth and sighed. It was large enough. Alinor laid the orange on the gold, heard one of her maids gasp.

"For an undertunic, madam?" another protested breathlessly.

"Yes," Alinor said slowly, "yes, indeed. I do not need to blazon my wealth abroad. I can well afford outward modesty."

That was one. There must be at least three more. Her eyes fell upon another velvet, a red so dark it was near to brown, and with that a brilliant crimson wool as soft as a kitten. That would need embroidery to embellish it. Alinor could see the pattern in her mind's eye, not too fine in the detail, so that the maids could do the work. Open leaves winding up the arm and around the throat and matching bands seeming to start from the waist of the cotte and branching out over the skirt. A headdress? The gold would have to do; there was no other color that would suit.

Other choices were swiftly made. The trestle upon which Alinor cut cloth was set up, and she began to work on the fabrics chosen. One gown and one tunic were readied for sewing before the light began to fail. Alinor was a little irritated, but in too good a humor to let such a trifle change her mood. The women could sew by candlelight, and she would cut the others the next day. Meantime, she trotted down to the great hall again and sought out Father Francis. Together they devised the different wordings needed for the invitations to friends, to great nobles, and to vassals and castellans, who were summoned rather than invited. Originally, Alinor had planned to write the messages herself with Father Francis' assistance, but now she expected to be too busy. She instructed the priest to take the list of names and the forms to a small abbey some ten miles to the east and beg the abbot to allow the lay brothers, who served as scribes, to do the copying. Naturally Alinor would make a suitable offering to the abbey church as a thanksgiving for the help. Alinor spent the evening hours writing to William and Isobel. They were friends of the heart and deserved more than an unexplained invitation to a wedding. Not that there was much need for explanation. Even if William did not know of Alinor's contretemps with the king—and it was likely that he did, because Simon usually confided everything to William—he and Isobel would be well aware of the hard facts of life.

Well content with her day, Alinor allowed her maids to undress her and brush her shining hair while her mind ranged over the activities she planned for the next day. She was only slightly tired, physically tired with excitement and work rather than heavy with the burden on her spirit, just tired enough to be aware of the pleasure of stretching in her luxurious bed. "Ian, Lord de Vipont," she murmured and giggled softly. The bed had brought its inevitable association. "You will yet sign your letters to me in a far different fashion, or I am not the woman I think I am."

In fact, the signature that rankled Alinor had cost

Ian considerable thought. If Alinor had bothered to look, she would have seen that the area had been scratched out, smoothed over, and rewritten. Ian had tried "your lord and husband" first. That was what he had scratched out when he realized that it might well be taken as indicating that he was assuming authority over her. Of course, Ian fully intended to assume authority over Alinor, but in view of her passionate statement of independence, he had no desire to be crude or obvious about it. The next idea was "your loving husband." He had thought that over for some time, trying to convince himself that Alinor would accept it as a formal ending without taking fright. It was too dangerous, he decided finally. The simplest was just to write "Ian," there being little likelihood that Alinor could be mistaken as to who was writing to her on such a subject. By that time, however, Ian had so sensitized himself to reading obscure meanings into his signature that he decided the single name might suggest he was contemptuous. Thus, Ian, Lord de Vipont had come upon the page.

The sentences which Alinor had thought to imply conceit had cost poor Ian more pain than the signature. Once the contract was signed, his impulse had been to clean out the reavers and rush back to Roselynde to admire the prize he had won. When he considered the violence of their last interview, however, and his growing inability to maintain a decent reserve to conceal his passion, he was forced to admit that such extended and intimate proximity would be most unwise. If they were apart, they could not quarrel. Once the wedding guests began to arrive, it would be safe to return. Not only was Alinor far too well bred to make public scenes, but there would be little opportunity for privacy or conflict.

In the windowless, dark, dank, immensity of the floor below the great hall, Alinor was coming to the conclusion that there would not be room enough to stand upright, let alone lie down to sleep. Torches now lit the area and fires blazed in the hearth at each end. The stores of weapons and food had been removed, the stone floor spread thickly with rushes. Perhaps, packed together like fish, four or five hundred servants would be able to find places to lie down. Another hundred servants of the better sort would sleep on the floor above with their masters. Alinor shrugged, then shivered as the cold struck through her woolen gown and tunic. She gave instructions that the fires were to be kept going night and day. Eventually the walls would absorb some heat, and the atmosphere would become more livable.

That was fine for those who would be there, but what about the four or five hundred others? The horses would have to be moved outside the keep with the other animals. The stables were the best of the outer buildings. Properly swept, there would be room for another few hundred. Then Alinor uttered an exclamation of annoyance. The weather had been remarkably fine, but it certainly could not be trusted at this time of year. She did not want her horses exposed continually if there were to be much rain, snow, or cold. Shelters would have to be constructed not only for her animals but for the mounts of her guests. And that, she realized with a sigh of relief, would solve her other problem also. The meaner servants—the grooms, horseboys, carters, and the like—could sleep with the horses. It was good enough for them and would rid the keep of their noise and smell.

Alinor climbed the stairs to the great hall and sent a maid to fetch her furred cloak, while she warmed herself for a few minutes at the fire. When the maid returned, she went down the stairs again and out to inspect the stables, with a view to human habitation. Obviously it would not be safe to have fires here. Alinor told one of the gaggle of menservants who trailed behind her to go search out all the charcoal braziers in the keep. Of course, it was warm enough in the stable now, but once the great equine bodies were gone it would be a different story.

Since she was there, Alinor went to look at one of the gray brood mares whose colt would be due in a few months. Two stalls away, an old mare whinnied. Alinor stopped and stepped into the stall to stroke the soft muzzle that was more silver now than golden. She looked sadly at the sunken temples, the too-prominent hip bones and ribs. The mare nuzzled her breast and danced a little stiffly.

"Poor Honey," Alinor crooned, "poor Honey." Then suddenly she smiled. "Saddle her up," she said to a groom.

"Lady," one of the menservants pleaded, "lady—" He dared say no more. No one would disobey the lady, but all knew of her near abduction.

"I am not going out," Alinor assured her anxious servants. "Poor Honey could not carry me far. I will only pleasure her by riding within the palisade to decide where to place the horses."

A rough palisade of logs had been built outside the walls of the keep to confine the herds of animals that would be needed to feed the guests that would overflow the capacity of the outer bailey. Most of these animals had been driven in already and were being fattened with fodder that also came from outlying demesne farms in long trains of creaking wains. Alinor rode to and fro within the confines of the log wall, checking them and looking out the best ground. Suddenly, from the wall of the keep behind her, a shout of alarm came from a lookout. Alinor cursed, kicked Honey into a shambling canter, and was across the drawbridge before the servants could wrestle the gates of the palisade closed.

By then, the precaution was seen to be unnecessary. The troop was small, and, more to the point, Beorn's voice was calling for admittance. That meant news from Ian. Alinor had had no word since she had sent him those invitations and summonses meant for dispatching to his Welsh and northern friends and vassals. It would have been ridiculous to send her men on long journeys on which doubtless they would lose their way more than once when his men already knew both the roads and the destinations. She had written a polite little note explaining this, signed "Alinor," and had received a polite note in return, agreeing that what she had done was best, signed "Ian."

Alinor had suffered a brief flash of temper over that note, which had not offered one word of information about Ian's activities, but the anger had not dampened her spirits at all. It had merely hardened her resolve. Ian had known she would be angry, and why. After all, the lands were hers, and she had a right to know what was happening. The trouble was, nothing was happening. Ian had racked his brains for something to say, but if he did not write plain lies, he had nothing else. Could he tell Alinor he was idling the days away, most unpleasantly and in the greatest discomfort, just to avoid returning to Roselynde? There had been one or two minor clashes with the outlaws the first week. After that, they had not come again. Ian did not really expect them to become desperate and come to him. It was far safer for them to raid other lands that were not so well guarded. No doubt they hoped the Roselynde forces would tire of watching and would come to the conclusion they had left for good.

The latter had been a possibility. Aside from the Roselynde farms, there was little to be had in the area. The Forest of Bere was large and, of course, totally uncultivated. There were beasts, but they were wary, and disenfranchised villeins were inexperienced huntsmen. Most men were fearful of raiding Church lands, and Peter of Winchester, who ruled Bishop's Waltham, was no frail reed when it came to protecting his own. Ian's Welshmen watched, but the outlaws did not make preparations to move. They were attacking Rowland's

property. The pickings were slim; Rowland was not as
good a landlord as Alinor, but it would be longer than
Ian was prepared to wait before the reavers starved.

There was no need for Alinor to wait outside in the
cold to greet her master-at-arms. A groom took Honey
back to the stables from the forebuilding where Alinor
dismounted; the old mare would not last much longer,
she thought sadly as she settled herself into her chair by
the fire, but nothing could keep her anticipation of news
of Ian from the forefront of her mind. A maidservant
hurried forward with a footstool, and another took her
cloak and asked if she wanted her embroidery.

"No, I do not think— Yes, bring it," Alinor said.

Embroidery was a very fine object on which to fix
one's eyes when one wished to veil their expression. It
would not serve Alinor's present purpose to display her
pleasure at news of Ian's imminent return. Beorn would
never knowingly do anything to displease his mistress,
but he was no hand at deception. If asked, he would
blurt out the truth as he saw it. Better for him to know
nothing than to need to practice concealment.

CHAPTER NINE

The embroidery frame was just in place, and Alinor had barely picked up her needle, when Beorn arrived in the hall. To Alinor's surprise, he had not come alone. Leaning for support on his arm was a stocky, limping young man clad in rough and ragged garments. Alinor watched their slow progress down the hall with mild interest. She had had an initial qualm of fear when she saw the stranger's battered appearance that he was one of Ian's men who brought bad news. It was over almost as soon as it seized her. Beorn would not be matching the stranger's slow pace if there was bad news of Ian. He would have come ahead at full speed with that information, even if his companion was the eyewitness.

As the men advanced, Alinor realized that, despite his clothes, Beorn's companion was no commoner. She was not much surprised, therefore, when Beorn introduced the young man as Sir Guy of Hedingham.

"He is paroled to you, lady, by Lord Ian. He was the leader of the reavers."

"Has Lord Ian suffered any hurt?" Alinor asked calmly.

"No, lady."

"Excellent." Alinor turned her eyes to Sir Guy. "You seem to have suffered some damage, Sir Guy. Sit down and tell me why my lord sent you to me."

"I do not know, madam," the young man replied bitterly. "I begged his lordship to let me stay and suffer the same fate as my men. I led them. I chose the targets. I held them together when they would have taken a little and fled away. If anything, I am more guilty than they."

Alinor drew her embroidery frame forward and began to ply her needle. She was very glad she had sent for it. Otherwise she would have had considerable difficulty in concealing her amusement. It was obvious from Sir Guy's first words why Ian had sent the young man to her on parole rather than hanging him out of hand. Any gentleman who had obviously fought bravely without proper arms, who demanded to suffer the fate of his common followers, and who loudly proclaimed his responsibility for his deeds in the face of threat, was well worth saving. Alinor controlled her impulse to smile at the unhappy captive and raised her eyes from her work. It was a rather charming face her eyes met, although not at all handsome. The hair was sandy and nondescript, the eyes blue, the nose snub, the mouth wide and generous. The young man did not appear very clever, but his face should have been laughing and open. The expression of bitterness and anxiety he wore sat very ill upon it.

"Do not be so certain that your fate will be lighter than that of your men. I am the Lady of Roselynde, and it is my property you have despoiled and my servants you have oppressed. Moreover, I am of the kind who is quite expert in extracting every mil owed me."

"You will get nothing from my poor men. It was because they were starving that they turned outlaw. As for me, you will get no horse and armor ransom from this knight. My armor is long gone, my horse is a sorry nag stolen from some farmyard, and I have not a relative in the world who would admit he knows my name, much the less pay a penny for my life."

Again Alinor had to suppress the urge to smile. "Suppose you tell me, Sir Guy, how you came to this sorry state."

"Through our beloved king."

The tone was so bitter, so vicious, that Alinor was startled and Beorn moved a step closer, his hand on his sword hilt. Alinor warned her master-at-arms back with a glance and then dropped her eyes to her work. "Yes?" she said encouragingly while she lifted her needle again.

"My father was one of the warders of Lord Arthur."

"My God!" Alinor exclaimed, dropping her needle. "Holy Mother Mary, be merciful."

King Richard had had a clear claim to the throne of England, but the succession after him was not so plain. Between Richard and John there had been another brother, Geoffrey. Geoffrey had died many years past, but before he died he had married and produced two legitimate children—Arthur and Eleanor. By the strict rule of primogeniture, Arthur should have sat on the throne of England. But Arthur was only 12 years old when King Richard died, and Richard had clearly named John as his heir.

Although John was not well-loved, his treacherous character already being uncomfortably well known, the barons had nevertheless opted for him. It was better, William of Pembroke said, to deal with the devil than to have continual, unremitting civil war. No one pretended that John would have accepted Arthur as king. He would have gathered every malcontent in England and on the continent and fought for the throne. John was no great military genius, but his half-brother Salisbury was a very competent general indeed. Possibly John, even with Salisbury supporting him, would have been beaten, but that would not stop him. Like the heads of the Hydra, he would breed two more rebellions for every one that was cut off.

One of John's first acts as king was to attack the stronghold in which Arthur was lodged and take the boy prisoner. That John's attack was unprovoked did not disturb his barons. It was, they believed, a most reasonable move to ensure the peace of the kingdom. Doubtless, had John not taken him, Arthur would have fled to King Philip of France, and that would also have ended in civil war.

Had old King Henry taken Arthur prisoner, he would

have kept the child by him, cossetting him into love and obedience so that he would not wish to rebel on the one hand, and watching him very carefully so that he could not rebel on the other. King Richard would never have bothered. Certainly he would have invited Arthur to come to him—he did so several times during his life—and, unless his temper was somehow aroused, he would have treated his nephew with honor. If Arthur persisted in rebellion, however, Richard would have fought him in the field with the greatest pleasure as often and as fiercely as Arthur wished to fight until he was killed in battle or beaten into submission.

Henry's way was both kind and politically expedient, although it might have bred trouble in the future. Richard's path was courageous and honorable, although it was very unwise in the sense that it would cause great bloodshed and suffering and economic loss, and still would not guarantee the future. John had seen things differently from either his father or his brother. John secured the future, but at a rather questionable price.

After his capture, Arthur was brought before John in the presence of his barons at Falaise. There John had publicly promised his nephew his protection and kind treatment if he forswore any right to the throne and gave his oath to be an obedient subject. John was 32; Arthur was 12. It was not difficult to use such phrasing that a vainglorious and passionate child would refuse. John had Arthur removed to the great fortress of Rouen. All the nobles saw him leave in good health, if not in the best of spirits.

Thus far, all was clear and open. What followed was all mystery—except for the fact that Arthur disappeared from Rouen. There were many tales, some clearly ridiculous and vindictive—such as the one that said John had dragged Arthur into a boat, stabbed him, thrown him into the river, and rowed back to the castle. Even Alinor laughed at that. Whatever else John was, he was not such an idiot as that. One does not conceal a murder by departing two in a boat—which could not be done secretly, because boat docks to great keeps are not left unguarded—and coming back alone.

It was also said that John had gone secretly to Arthur's prison cell to talk to him, had flown into a rage, and had drawn his knife and stabbed the boy in a passion of anger. That was more possible than the boat story, but not really reasonable. First of all, Arthur, a nephew of the king, would not be kept in a cell; second, he would not be without attendants; third, the king would not go to his prisoner, but would have his nephew brought to him, if he wanted to talk. If John went to Arthur in a cell, it was deliberate murder that had taken place, not manslaughter in a fit of rage.

There had been still another set of rumors, and to these Alinor was most inclined. Arthur was said to have attempted to escape and to have been killed in the attempt. William of Salisbury believed this, and it was what he had told Ian. Alinor was willing to believe it, too, because John was not such a fool that he did not know that outright murder of his only rival for the throne, and his only heir—specially since that heir and rival was still a child—would not endear him to anyone. An attempted escape and accidental death at the hands of the guards—death by misadventure—was the obvious solution.

What Alinor could not understand was what had gone wrong. Why had these facts not been proclaimed? Why had Arthur's body not been displayed and bewailed by his grieving uncle? It was impossible to hide the fact that Arthur had disappeared. To pretend it was not so and refuse to explain merely gave rise to even more disgusting rumors—like the boat story. Perhaps very few would believe in the accident, but the arrow wound or the body broken by a fall should have been used as evidence to support the claim of an "accident."

Sir Guy's implication when he said his father had been one of Arthur's wardens could be taken several ways. Possibly the man had withstood John's attempt to murder Arthur or had refused to do it himself; perhaps he had been involved in an honest attempt to help Arthur escape; perhaps he had been told to allow Arthur to "escape," and something had gone wrong. Before Alinor could ask, Sir Guy spoke again.

"My father disappeared the night Lord Arthur—" the voice hesitated and Alinor wondered if Arthur had not been displayed because he had truly disappeared, but he went on after swallowing convulsively "—after Lord Arthur was murdered."

"How? How do you know this?"

"I do not know how the murder was done, but a servant of ours, the only one left alive of all those who accompanied my father, told me that he saw my father, carrying a boy's body, jump from the keep walls into the river. The reason he saw this was that he had been running to my father to tell him that my younger brother had fallen from the castle wall into the bailey and was dying."

There was the accident that should have taken place. Alinor covered her eyes for a moment. Had the father substituted his son for Arthur in an attempt to save the prince? Had he then found he was too late, that the prince was dead already, and realized that no man who knew that would be allowed to live? Had he seen his son's fall and known the ruse had failed doubly, that he had made a useless sacrifice? In an extremity of hatred, had he taken Arthur's body to hide so that John would be blamed at the same time as he would be vulnerable to any claimant who rose up and cried out he was Prince Arthur, saved from death, come to overthrow the evil king? It was possible; it was very possible. Moreover, an honest son often predicates an honest father.

"Where were you?" Alinor asked breathlessly. "How came you to escape? How did your servant escape?"

"I was at home. My mother was ill. I have something, at least, to be thankful for. She died before the news of

Arthur's death and my father's disappearance spread abroad. The servant had a whore who hid him and sent him forth in her garments. He sought me out and bid me fly for my life. We were to be weeded out, we Hedinghams, root, stock, and branch, so that none would cry aloud that my father was innocent." Then, suddenly, Sir Guy began to laugh bitterly, and his eyes lit. "Fool that I am, fool! I know how you can obtain restitution for the losses I have inflicted upon you. Please, Lady Alinor, bid your lord pardon my men. They are worth nothing. You can sell me to the king for any price you like to name."

"Does the king know you?" Alinor asked.

"He knows I exist."

"Does he know your face?" Alinor insisted.

"I do not think so. I cannot see how he would, having seen me only once or twice and then as part of a crowd, but I can prove who I am. I swear if you pardon my men, I will not deny my name nor will I——"

Alinor began to laugh aloud. Sir Guy was shocked by the sound as well as by the sudden brilliant, greenish glow in her eyes. Alinor laughed even more at his expression.

"No, no, I am not a monster," she said, sobering after a moment. "I do not laugh at the horrors you tell me or at your sorrows and wrongs. It merely gives me great pleasure to know that I can be the cause whereby our beloved king will sleep less easily in his bed at night."

There was a moment of silence while Sir Guy stared stonily at the floor. Then his head snapped up. "Did you say *less easily,* madam?"

"If I could strew his bed with thorns or nettles, I would do it," Alinor said grimly; "but as I cannot, at least you will be a sharp fear to prick his mind."

The blue eyes, at once hopeful and unbelieving, stared at her. "I do not understand," Sir Guy whispered.

"I have a private quarrel with the king," Alinor replied. "That is no affair of yours, except that I will tell you plain that it is not of weight or moment to match your quarrel with him. Nonetheless, though no more than an insult was offered me and a deep, abiding hurt was done to you, your revenge can be no greater than mine. I will not try to convince you of the necessity of accepting this injustice. All I will say is that sometimes a man must endure a great injury for the good of the realm at large. When Lord Ian returns, he will explain more fully to you why it is wrong and impossible to do the king any injury, no matter what kind of devil he is."

"Madam, madam," Sir Guy cried, holding his head in his hands, "I do not understand you at all."

"No, indeed, and no wonder. You are wounded and tired, and I am gabbling about political matters. Beorn, take Sir Guy to the eastern wall chamber. I will send the maids to attend to him. Let them tell me if there is any wound I must see to myself." She looked at the young man's clothes distastefully. "And throw those things he is wearing to the dog boys. I will send down some suitable garments." She paused again and cocked her head, examining Sir Guy's face with attention. It had a stubble of unshaven beard, but it was plain that in less critical moments he was clean-shaven. "Yes, and do not permit him to be shaved. We will all be safer, Sir Guy, if you pretend love for the king and ape him by growing a neat beard and mustache—just like the king's."

Sir Guy stared even more uncomprehendingly. "Madam, I beg you to tell me what will become of my men," he pleaded. "You speak as if I am a guest in your castle, and this cannot be. Had I known you were at odds with the king, I would never—I beg pardon. I do not mean to excuse myself, but do not make me hang by my fingers."

"As to your men, I can only assure you that Lord Ian is both good-tempered and just. I imagine he will sieve them and dispose of them suitably to their characters and abilities. Final justice rests with me on these lands.

If it comes to hanging or maiming, I will know of it and I will do you the courtesy to tell you what is decided, so that you can speak for the man, if you believe he deserves to be spoken for. As for yourself, I suppose you are a prisoner, not a guest, but you have given your parole not to try to escape. I cannot see why you should want to escape. I assure you I have no intention of selling you to the king. You have nowhere else to go. Thus, I can see no reason to confine you or to waste my men's time by setting a guard upon you."

"But how can I make restitution, then? I have nothing!"

"You have a strong body and, I believe, a clean nature. I have some profit already," Alinor smiled sardonically, "simply in knowing that hiding you from the king will make him uneasy. The rest, if Lord Ian agrees and if you can convince us of your sincere desire to be loyal to us, I will take out of you in service. A knight is paid a shilling a day. Adding the cost of horse and armor, which I must furnish to you since yours is gone, it will take you some few years to clear your debt, but —" Alinor broke off and began to laugh again. One would think from Sir Guy's expression that she was proposing immediate entry into heaven without the intervention of death, instead of many years of hard service. She waved the young man away before he embarrassed her by too great gratitude or himself by bursting into tears. If he was what he seemed, she had made a good bargain in exchange for a few cows and a few loads of grain.

At almost the same time that Alinor opened the gateway to Sir Guy's notion of heaven, King John was considering her entrance into hell on earth. On the previous night, he had not summoned his current mistress among his wife's ladies to his bed. He had sent Fulk de Cantelu and Henry of Cornhill into the town to procure three whores. The gentlemen had gone about their task with considerable enthusiasm. If they were not as quick as the king's half brother at seeing the onset of one of his periods of indolence, they had at least come to know— far better than Salisbury—one of the signs of his emergence from that state.

The women they collected were neither clean nor beautiful, but that did not matter. All that was important was that no one should care whether the creatures lived or died. They might survive the night; some did, but in case they did not no questions would be asked. In fact, one did survive, being thrust out of the castle, muffled in the blood-stained shreds of the women's garments. There was no danger that she would tell any tales, however; her tongue had been cut out, even though she had already been reduced to gibbering idiocy by pain and terror.

In the course of the night, Fulk had suggested— shouting into John's ear to be heard above the screams of fear and pain—that the game they were playing might well tame Lady Alinor. He had tried any number of times during the past weeks to reawaken John's interest in giving him the heiress in marriage. Although the king had several times smiled and agreed that he thought it an excellent notion, he had done nothing at all to forward the idea. Now, however, his eyes lit.

"But it is Henry who is making the sweet music," he bellowed in reply, laughing. "Let me see you prove yourself as skilled."

Fulk had returned to his efforts to amuse his master with redoubled spirit, but Henry of Cornhill had heard both remarks and would not be outdone. Moreover, he reminded John of Salisbury's suggestion that the lady should be allowed to choose for herself. The exquisite humor of allowing Alinor to pay a heavy fine for the privilege of choosing between Fulk and Henry had appealed greatly to John. He had been so delighted with the idea and had laughed so heartily at it that the knife with which he was threatening one of the whores slipped and brought her a premature peace.

That little accident annoyed John. He would not go further with bestowing Alinor on one or the other of his companions that night. By the following afternoon, when he woke after a most pleasant and refreshing sleep, the notion had regained its appeal. He had sent for the companions of his peculiar pleasures and smiled upon both impartially.

"Now you know that I love you both well," the king began mellifluously. He was amused by the wary fearfulness that woke in both pairs of hard eyes, but he did not allow himself to be led down the pleasant byway of watching his men grovel this time. "Thus I am willing to expose myself to my barons' blame in order to gain for one of you a rich prize."

The men both bowed low. Although the fear receded from their eyes, the wariness did not. Their lord was not one to give something for nothing. He expected an equivalent benefit—in political advantage, murder, or money. Neither of them could conceive what they could offer that would be the equivalent of this prize.

"I want to be sure, very sure, that Lady Alinor is treated as she deserves," John continued with a broad smile.

"You may be sure, my lord," Fulk said passionately.

"Indeed you may," Henry assured him also, "and that if she be given to me she will live long enough to see her son die and her daughter broached."

Fulk began to elaborate on his own briefer statement, but although John nodded agreeably, he held up a restraining hand.

"I am sure you will equally do your best to make Lady Alinor's life full and complete," the king purred, "and that neither of you would be dissuaded from your purpose by the disapproval of my lily-livered great lords.

Nonetheless, I would not have it seem as if I had parted with the lady's rich estates only for the poor, mean satisfaction of revenge. Roselynde Keep, commanding as it does the port and anchorage, and its demesne lands also, must come into my hands."

"From what I have heard," Henry was quick to say, "there is plenty more. I will agree to that much if I can have her."

"Of course, my lord," Fulk agreed also.

"In addition, I would expect that the vassal who holds Iford Keep and lands, Sir Giles, will be removed —as forcibly as possible—from his estate. It would be best if he survived long enough to see his wife and daughters be given to your troops to use as they will, after you have tasted them first, of course, if they are worth tasting."

"My lord, it is always so great a pleasure to serve you that it makes your service very light." Fulk was first in with his agreement this time.

"The sons would have to be gathered up and removed also," Henry remarked thoughtfully.

"Oh, yes, certainly," John said approvingly. "You will probably have to remove all the other vassals and castellans also," he remarked slyly, again amused as consternation leaped into his men's eyes, and then added, "and William of Pembroke is not likely to be best pleased when he hears that his dearest friend's son is dead and his wife and daughter— But you will surely know how to deal with him."

But that time he had gone too far, John saw. There was real fear in his henchmen's eyes and sweat on both faces. Dealing with Pembroke would be a challenge neither wanted. John did not want them to back out, so he said soothingly, "Perhaps Pembroke will be too busy about his own affairs to bother, however. And I do not have any bone to pick with any of Lady Alinor's vassals, except Sir Giles, other than that their loyalty has been unwisely given. I warn you against them only because I doubt that they will accept your overlordship easily. They will all believe themselves more fit either to have the lady's hand or to bestow it where they think best— all, even the meanest, being better born than you."

That had saved the situation. Rage and hate had temporarily driven out fear. John paused to enjoy the bitten lips, clenched jaws and flushed faces that betrayed the leashed-in emotions his remarks had generated. He pricked the clods of filth that served his baser purposes quite deliberately. Because they did not dare revenge themselves upon him, the hate he bred spilled out all around. It made his "dear" Fulk and Henry more able at the work he chose for them. Moreover, the reminder of the hatred and contempt in which they were held by the great noblemen of John's court increased their loyalty even as it increased their responsive hatred. There was no one to whom they could turn for help and support. If anything happened to King John, they would be torn apart by the nobles whom his power now held in check.

"Now," he went on, "as I said when you first came in, I love you both and I love you equally and you are equally fit for this piece of work. Therefore, I find it impossible to choose between you."

"I will add whatever else you desire of the lady's lands," Fulk suggested persuasively.

"And I, of course," Henry hastened to agree, but a faint frown was beginning to grow between his shrewd eyes.

If the king was right and Alinor's vassals resisted, it would take much money and many men to subdue them. If a great part of the estate were promised away to the king, what would be left of the great prize besides debts? To Henry's relief, John shook his head.

"Roselynde and Iford I desire. The rest may remain with the lady and go to her heir when she goes, happily I trust, to her final rest. I do not mean to breed conflict between you by allowing you to strive for this prize.

Neither do I wish to have one feel I prefer the other over him. Thus we will follow my brother Salisbury's counsel —which you were clever enough to remind me of, Henry—and we will allow the lady to choose for herself."

"How can she choose?"

"That is for her to decide. To the best of my knowledge, she has never set eyes on either of you and, even if she should find someone who has and who can tell her of you, it will not matter. My love for you, I say, is equal because you are so equal in every respect." Again the two men flushed and winced under the king's tone, but he went on smoothly. "I will offer a consolation prize to the loser. With him, I will divide the fine the lady will pay for the right to pick her own husband."

Both men bowed again, their eyes lighting with greed and satisfaction. John smiled on them, well pleased with himself because he knew he had handled this situation perfectly. He would achieve his purpose concerning Alinor's person; he would have two great strongholds, both in important positions, under his own personal control; it would cost him nothing to obtain the castles; and neither of his tools would have cause for resentment. The one who achieved the lady would have considerable wealth, but only after great effort had been expended; the loser would have a rich reward for nothing at all. Neither probably knew which prize to desire most.

John had read his henchmen's feelings quite accurately, except for one thing. No matter which man gained which reward, he *would* feel cheated. He would be sure the other had benefited more than himself. Such was the nature of Fulk and Henry, that of ungrateful beasts. Nonetheless, at the moment that canker had not yet had time to take root. The only concern Fulk and Henry felt was that the king would slip back into his lethargy before setting the choice of delicacies before Lady Alinor. That had been known to happen. In this case, however, it did not. The king's men had the pleasure of seeing John call for one of his scribes, dictate the letter to Alinor, and finally, without any waste of time, summon a messenger to carry it to Roselynde Keep, or wherever else the lady should be.

CHAPTER TEN

In the next two weeks, Alinor became convinced she had made a good investment in Sir Guy. One reason was that Ian did not come as she had expected, and this fact occupied her mind to such a degree that she found it hard to give proper attention to the children. Joanna was not really a problem. Alinor kept her daughter so busy overseeing the wedding preparations that Joanna had no time to do anything except ask for instruction and then turn to her task. It was a happy solution for everyone. Joanna was enjoying herself in her new position of authority and was gaining invaluable experience, while the maids and menservants were somewhat shielded from Alinor's temper.

Adam would have borne the brunt of his mother's impatience if not for the advent of Sir Guy. The young knight was charged with exercising the child in arms and horsemanship. Of course, both child and tutor were discreetly watched at every moment. Alinor was almost certain of Sir Guy's integrity, but she was taking no chances with her son's safety. Properly safeguarded, Adam was out from under her feet and was learning skills that were necessary to him in company more suitable than that of the men-at-arms. Alinor realized that Sir Guy was not of Simon's or Ian's caliber, but there were years in which to polish Adam's performance. The basics he was learning from Sir Guy were sound.

On November 20th, a large troop of horsemen were reported coming from the west. Alinor was fit to be tied. The guests had started to arrive and her soon-to-be husband was still, for a purpose Alinor mistakenly believed she understood all too well, lingering in a louse-infested serf's hut on the borders of her land. Fuming, all but incoherent because he seemed to have beaten her and she was forced into sending for him, Alinor wrote to Ian. In her fury she was somewhat less than polite in her demand that he return to Roselynde. She did not dare weep with rage because she was too proud to expose a tear-marked face, which might be misunderstood, to the arriving guests. She bit her lips and dug her nails into her palms to curb herself into some semblance of welcoming propriety. Most fortunately, the first arrival was welcome for herself and no polite greeting was necessary.

"Isobel!" Alinor shrieked, when her guest had entered the hall. She flew across, cast herself into her friend's arms, and burst into tears.

"Beloved, beloved," Isobel crooned, holding Alinor tight. "Alas, I was afraid that your letter did not tell all your heart. Lord Ian is a good man, and the marriage is most suitable and necessary. Do not weep, beloved. It is that demon, that monster of a king, that has forced you with your grief all raw into this marriage. Do not blame Lord Ian."

Alinor caught her breath and shook her head. "I do not blame Ian for that, and—and I am not really sad." She lifted her face away from Isobel's and peered behind her. "Is William seeing to the men and horses? I will slay those grooms if they do not have all in readiness."

"William is not here," Isobel replied in a strained voice.

"Is he safe? Does he need help?" Alinor tensed for action, ready to call out her men-at-arms, ready to send another messenger to Ian.

"He is quite safe," Isobel replied, smiling in spite of her worries at the unsubdued nature of her friend. "He is waiting a mile or so outside of Roselynde Town. He wanted you to think again about asking him to come here. You know the king's hatred of him is growing instead of waning. In spite of William's submission and good behavior, that monster will not release our sons—"

"God in Heaven, does he mistreat them, Isobel?"

"Oh no, no. You know William would not endure that. No, as much as I hate him, I must admit the king is most kind to young William and Richard—really, they are well taught and—and I think they actually prefer to be at court. But I do not like it. That court is no place for a godly upbringing."

It occurred to Alinor that these were not the times for a godly upbringing, but she did not say so to Isobel, who was truly and deeply religious. "Isobel, no one will turn your boys away from God nor spoil their honor. You and William had them long enough to mold them. I am sure they have only contempt for the evil they see —and you visit them often, I know. But I do not understand what you said about William. What do you mean, I should think again?"

"My love," Isobel said placatingly, "William knows you have some quarrel with the king. He felt perhaps it would be unwise, possibly even unsafe, for you to seem to consort with those who are out of favor. Now, Alinor, do not fly into a rage!" she added hastily. "Think! It would not be well for Lord Ian either."

"Oh!" Alinor gasped. "Oh! I do not know whose neck I wish to wring first—yours, for bringing me such an idiotic message, or William's, for thinking up such an insanity in the first place."

"Well, do not wring mine," Isobel said with commendable calm. "I made him come as far as he did. He wished to stay in Pembroke. I told him that if he did, you would probably ride all the way out there to fetch him yourself."

"And so I would have done! Edwig," Alinor called to a passing manservant, "send a message to the new stables to have Cricket sent around at once." She turned back to Isobel. "There. I will make good your word and make William properly ashamed of himself by doing just as you said and going myself to fetch him. Meanwhile do you come and sit by the fire. It is growing cold apace, although the weather holds remarkably fine. I have put you and William in the south-tower room. You will have to walk across the garden, but it will be warmer there than in the wall chambers." She saw Isobel examining her with anxiety. "Do not be concerned for me, Isobel. I do grieve for Simon still, but I am well content with Ian. He loves the children so dearly, and he is a strong bulwark against trouble."

The manservant having returned, Alinor was spared the necessity of trying to decide how much more she should tell Isobel. She was not even sure she knew what to tell her. She did not know how to express the change Ian had produced in her. When she thought of Simon, her heart moved as it always had, but her feeling for Ian was just as strong. It would be best, she decided, as she and her tail of men rode out of the keep, to let matters rest as they were. As long as Isobel did not feel she was unhappy, she was not the kind to probe further. There was no need for Alinor to define her emotions more exactly.

She greeted William with mock rage and then, most sincerely, thanked him for his thoughtfulness. "Both Ian and I know what we do," she explained. "Simon told Ian about what I did to the king."

"Then all the more reason—" William began, frowning.

"Nonsense! If I did not know you better, William, I would say you were afraid to take further contamination from our company. To speak plain, you must come whatever you fear for us. Lord Llewelyn is coming, and I know Ian desires to have speech with you and him together. Moreover, we may all escape clean from this. William of Salisbury is coming also. He *asked* to be invited."

"Then it is true, what I heard, that he and Lord Ian had become close companions?"

"It is true in fact, but not in the implication you are making," Alinor said sharply. "Ian is not of Simon's get, but he is of his training. There is neither self-seeking nor treachery in him. For that matter, did you think that I would invite you to my home to catch you in a trap of King John's setting?"

"No," William admitted, "but I thought that from one cause or another you were not seeing too clearly. Do you see into Salisbury's purpose?"

"No, because I do not know him, and Ian is one who sees the best in all men, I fear, but I do not believe Salisbury's purpose is to spy for John. Ian insists that Salisbury is a good man. If so, it is possible that he comes out of simple affection for Ian. There is some support for that. Salisbury has given his natural son to Ian to raise."

While they were talking, the troop had mounted and started back toward Roselynde Keep. At Alinor's last remark, William shrugged his shoulders. He turned his head to stare straight in front of him and remarked that he knew nothing ill of Salisbury and that anything was possible, with God's will. Alinor refused to be drawn by that provocative and sarcastic hint. She asked a question about the politics of South Wales.

"Your interests are in the north, are they not?" William asked pointedly.

Alinor laughed. "Marriage has been of infinite benefit to you, William. There was a time when you would have followed that false scent without the slightest realization that I wished to turn the subject. Only it is not really a false scent. It is true that Ian's land is with Lord Llewelyn, but Llewelyn is looking in your direction."

"Is this a warning, Alinor?"

Bad treatment was souring William, Alinor thought, then corrected herself. It was not the treatment he minded. Offices and power had been stripped away from him before to reward some undeserving favorite or owing to a change in the power or condition of his overlord. It was the cause of the deprivation that was making William bitter. Never before in his life had any man doubted William's honor.

"A warning? Again, not in the sense you mean the word. Whatever John is, Lord Llewelyn is not a fool. As I told you, Ian desires that all of you have a chance to talk. I was merely curious about what Lord Gwenwynwyn will do."

"I should think Lord Ian would be as good a source of information as I."

"Yes, if we ever got to talk about such things. Somehow there is always something more pressing to discuss."

"I can imagine," William responded coldly.

Alinor had opened her mouth to explain about the reavers, but she shut it with a snap. Her eyes flashed, and she drew breath for a hot retort to William's ugly implication. Isobel had been so sympathetic that it had never occurred to her that William would feel otherwise. Suddenly it was clear why William was so suspicious of Ian, whom he knew quite well; why, really, he had not wanted to come to Alinor's wedding. Equally it was clear to Alinor why Ian would not come back to the keep even though his business was long finished. That thought gave Alinor such pleasure that it checked the angry words that rose to her lips.

"I have not forgotten Simon," she said softly instead.

William winced as if Alinor had caused him physical pain. "Of course not," he said hoarsely.

"Do you know what men John has proposed for my next husband?" she asked. It was very necessary that William not meet Ian with resentment and the best way was to show him the necessity of this marriage. "He put forward Fulk de Cantelu or Henry of Cornhill."

That made William's head snap back toward Alinor. "You jest," he roared.

"Do I?"

He knew, of course, that she did not. It was just the kind of revenge that John would take on a woman who spited him. The protest was an instinctive rejection of the idea of Alinor married to either of those coarse and brutal men. William was no practitioner of the higher courtesies toward women. He might, for a fault, strike his wife, but he would not beat her for amusement nor torture her for the fun of hearing her scream. Besides, there was considerable doubt that either of the creatures was even gently born. In fact, Henry of Cornhill was known to spring from a London merchant family. No one knew what Fulk's antecedents were, but it was rumored that they were even lower than Henry's.

"You think I am very quick to cast off the old and take on the new," Alinor went on, "but I must marry before the king thinks to lay his commands upon me. To deny him outright would be treason. Do you doubt he would take my lands and probably cast me into prison, too, for such an act? How long do you think Adam would survive?"

"Not long," William snarled. "Arthur did not live long. And as for you—yes, I see."

"Nor do not think that Ian is snatching at Simon's lands or, for that matter, lusting after Simon's wife. Ian is marrying for love, I admit, but for love of Simon, not for love of Alinor."

"I never thought—" William began, his face crimson. Then the color began to fade. "That is all the truth, Alinor. I never thought at all. When we had your letter, such a fury of pain seized me—as if I had heard newly again of—of Simon's death. And Ian—Ian is so different from Simon, so young, and with a face like a black angel."

Alinor could not help laughing. She was not resentful of William's assumption that she had lewd motives. It was, of course, the common opinion of women, but Alinor had seen further than that. Simon was 30 years older than she, but William was also considerably senior to his wife—nearly 20 years. It was plain unadulterated jealousy that had driven him to be unjust to Ian. He had doubtless seen himself dead and Isobel rushing into the arms of a handsome young man. Alinor would never suggest to William what she had discovered. That would hurt him terribly, since Alinor was sure he had never permitted himself to see the true cause of his dislike of her new marriage. She liked William and, besides, she was grateful to him for healing the hurt Ian's determined absence had caused her.

"Yes," she agreed, "Ian is as beautiful as a starry night, but his face is nothing new to me, you know. Nor am I new to him."

To her surprise William crimsoned again. "Perhaps," he said in a rather stifled voice, "I *should* turn around and go home again. I am guilty of truly disgusting suspicions. Did you guess? Was that why you came to fetch me instead of Lord Ian?"

Alinor knew that remark would be made sooner or later, just as she now knew that Ian was avoiding Roselynde just so that she could answer such comments with perfect truth. Nonetheless, she needed a moment to subdue her temper again. It was a disgusting idea that William was apologizing for. Ian had stayed for some months at Roselynde while Simon was ill. No doubt William, and many others, thought nothing of it at the time but, when they received invitations to Alinor's wedding to Ian, all had probably leapt to the ugly conclusion that they had planned their union under Simon's dying eyes or, even worse, that they had been lovers all along.

"Ian is not in Roselynde," Alinor said, failing to keep the coldness entirely out of her voice. "He has not spent more than a few nights in the keep since he came. He has been afield, hunting outlaws."

"I beg your pardon most humbly," William mumbled, responding to the tone rather than the words. "I do not blame you for being angry. If you cannot forgive me, I will go home. I cannot think what came over me, Alinor."

It was true. He did not understand. Priests preached so often of the lustful nature of women, who seduced men from the path of true virtue, as Eve had seduced Adam into eating the apple. The suspicion was always buried somewhere in a man's mind, even those men who thought they believed implicitly in the love and virtue of their wives. The preaching had its effect upon women, too. However sure they might be of their own honesty, they sadly accepted the general statement. Alinor acknowledged that William might even be right to be jealous of Isobel. She did not think so, but nonetheless she understood what he feared and was placated by his apology. She made a soothing remark and then introduced the subject of the replacement for the Archbishop of Canterbury, which kept them harmlessly occupied until they arrived at the keep.

To Alinor's horror, Ian did not arrive that evening nor the next day. Now that William and Isobel were there, the excuse that he wished to avoid gossip about their premarital relationship was no longer valid. Alinor was furious again. She could only believe he was spiting her because she had been rude in her command that he return at once. She could not make herself write to him again and fumed in private, making no attempt to explain his absence beyond telling the story of the band of outlaws. She left her guests to make the assumption that Ian was trying to arrange for the secure control of his prisoners, although why that should take three weeks Alinor did not mention. Robert of Leicester came on the 23rd, as did Sir John d'Alberin—who held Mersea for Alinor now that old Sir John was dead—and a number of the castellans who held Simon's strongholds. The 24th brought Lord Llewelyn and his wife Joan, who was King John's bastard daughter. She looked much like her father and had the same beautiful voice, but in spite of her heritage she seemed to be a warm and pleasant person.

By the 25th, the keep was packed. Until now there

had been enough variety for the guests in greeting those new arrivals with whom they were acquainted and making the acquaintance of those they did not know. That entertainment would not serve for more than another day or so, Alinor realized. A hunt would have to be arranged. Alinor found time to tell her huntsman that he would have to recall his men from their watch for the king's messenger and have them track and mark game. They should continue to keep watch as well as they could, Alinor urged, but preparations for a series of hunts was now more important.

William of Salisbury arrived on the 26th, bringing with him Aubery de Vere, Earl of Oxford—who had not even been invited. Alinor greeted him with effusive cordiality and protestations of joy at his condescension, while her mind spun like a top. What did he want here? What had he come for? And there were another 50 mouths to feed and, far more serious, another nobleman of such stature as could not be accommodated in the hall. To move someone already established in a chamber out into the hall would be equivalent to starting an unending blood feud. Smiling sweetly, Alinor excused herself from her guests and gave instructions for some men to clear the chamber that had been kept for Ian. Damn him and rot him, she thought, he can sleep on a pallet in the maid's portion of my apartment. The maids could lie on the antechamber floor between them, thus preserving the decencies—if anyone would care or notice at this late date.

Naturally Salisbury asked for Ian. Alinor told her story again, feeling as if she had only to open her mouth and the words would pour out over and over, preventing her from saying anything else ever again. Salisbury said nothing, but Alinor did not like the expression that came into his eyes. For the first time her rage changed into a sickening fear. She had been so intent on the contest of wills she imagined was being played out that it had never occurred to her that some harm might have actually befallen Ian. This was no time for pride. Again Alinor excused herself to her guests and went out into the bailey, where she sent a groom for her huntsman.

"It is not like him," Salisbury's voice said behind her as she waited for her man to arrive. Alinor jumped with surprise, not having realized that he had followed her, and Salisbury begged pardon for startling her. Then he returned to his theme. "Madam, I do not wish to worry you or to croak forebodings at this joyous time, but it would be well to send out to seek for him."

"That is what I am about to do, my lord," Alinor admitted. Color rose into her cheeks at the look he gave her. "It is not that I have been indifferent," Alinor protested. "It is that we—we had some sharp words and I thought Ian was sulking. But you are right. It is not like him. He is no sulker. Had I time to think, I would have realized it." Tears rose to her eyes. "Curse my pride and my temper," she whispered.

"Now, do not begin to imagine him dead in a ditch or you will be furious with him all over again when he walks in hale and hearty. It may well be he is delayed by something neither you nor I have considered. He cannot be sore hurt or dead. He was not alone. His men and his squires would have come to tell you."

To that specious piece of reasoning, the more ridiculous because of the anxiety that was mirrored on Salisbury's face when he mentioned Ian's squires, Alinor did not have to reply. The groom returned, breathless and fearful, to say the huntsman was nowhere to be found. Alinor hissed with irritation.

"Madam, be calm!" Salisbury snapped. "The man is doubtless about some business. Do not give an order you will be sorry for."

For a moment Alinor was speechless with surprise. "He has been my servant for more than twenty years," she said repressively when she regained her voice. "You need not fear for him." Then she turned to the nervously waiting groom. "Send Beorn to me."

Salisbury was almost as surprised by Alinor's tone as she had been by his. Indignation passed almost instantly into indulgence. She does care for Ian, he thought, and she is overset by worry. "Do you wish me to instruct your man?" he asked kindly.

That question nearly turned Alinor to stone, but in the next moment she could not help laughing. "He would not obey you," she said. "No servant of mine would obey that kind of order unless it came from me. A fine state I should be in if my servants would obey any lordly seeming man who gave them an order. I would not permit *you* to be insulted, my lord, but in a less anxious moment, if you will dress one of your men in fine garments, you can watch what my servants will do upon my order, even as you bid them cease. I promise you, I will call a halt before murder is done, but that they would do also, if I bid them."

"Lady?"

The full impact of Alinor's remarks had not hit Salisbury because he had been watching Beorn arrive at a dead run. He had thought, until Beorn spoke, that this must be some urgent news. Then he realized it was a normal response to a sharp order given by this woman.

"If the reavers that Lord Ian captured were to turn upon him, how many men would you need to quell them?" Alinor asked Beorn.

The master-at-arms looked startled. "Them? Lady, now that S—that their leader is gone, a rabbit with a loud squeak could put them to flight."

Alinor frowned. If Beorn was so sure, whatever danger there was, if there was any at all, did not come from the prisoners. Ian had kept only his few Welshmen and northerns with him, and she feared a rebellion of the captives could have overwhelmed them. Beorn did not suffer from the vainglory of a young knight who thought he could conquer the world, however. If anything, he was overcautious when asked for an opinion. Thus, if he said the captured reavers were no threat, they were none. If some other armed group had attacked, she would need information before she could act with intelligence.

"Take a few men, then, and seek out Lord Ian. If all is well, tell him that the Earl of Salisbury and Lord Llewelyn are asking for him. If some ill has befallen, discover if you can what force we will need to set it right. In any case, send back to me in haste whatever news you find."

"It will be late, lady."

"At any hour day or night, Beorn."

"As you will, lady."

Salisbury had listened to this exchange with a growing sense of amusement. It was apparent that the impression of Alinor he had received from Ian had been misleading, to say the least. A frown flickered across his face as he wondered if that could have been deliberate. Many men tried to take advantage of Salisbury's affectionate relationship with his brother. It was only a flicker of doubt that disappeared at once. Ian had never asked for anything. Nor, now that Salisbury thought of it, had Ian actually said anything much about Alinor to him. The talk had always been of Simon, of his strength and wisdom. It was from that Salisbury had assumed that Alinor was even more helpless and dependent than most women. In fact, Salisbury had openly warned Ian against marriage with a weak and stupid woman. He had been mildly piqued at the offhand assurance Ian had offered that he had no intention of seeking out such a one.

No, Salisbury thought, looking at Alinor's vivid, lovely face, while she watched Beorn's retreating back, she is neither weak nor stupid. "Come in, Lady Alinor," he said, touching her arm gently. "It is cold and you have no cloak. I begin to think I was a fool to raise this worry in you."

"Never that, my lord," Alinor responded with a

slightly absent smile. "It is never hurtful to discover the truth of an unusual happening."

Night had fallen, but the merrymaking was still going strong in the great hall. Alinor was well pleased with her guests. Their spirits were high and the talk and laughter were loud enough that from time to time the dancers had to shout for silence so that they could hear the musicians. Although her toes tapped to the measures, Alinor had refused all offers to dance. She would, of course, have danced with Ian, but since he was not there she did not think it fitting to give her company to any man merely for the sake of pleasure so soon after Simon's death. Unfortunately this thrust her into the orbit of the older ladies, or those who for some other reason would not dance, the most demanding of whom was the Countess of Salisbury. Whatever small irritation had remained in Alinor regarding Salisbury's tentative assumption of authority disappeared completely. Poor man! No wonder he thought all women were idiots.

"And of course I could not go to France," Ela of Salisbury continued in her high-pitched yet drawling whine. "My health would not permit it. William is so inconsiderate. He knows I have not the strength to attend to the children and the estates, yet he is forever rushing off here and there—"

"I am sure he does not do it apurpose," Alinor murmured—not at all sure.

If she had been Salisbury, Alinor thought, she would have left for the outer edge of the world—and stayed there. Either that or strangled the woman. The fact that Salisbury's wife not only bore no bruises but was obviously not afraid of her husband convinced Alinor that Ian was right about him. He was a good man. More than that, he was a saint, Alinor decided, as the countess' voice began again.

"You think he must do whatever the king orders,"

she whined, "but it is more than that. I tell him he loves his brother better than his wife or children. He is always eager to run John's errands, as if he were a nothing. Lesser men should be employed. And John knows how weak I am. If William said I was ill—but he does not believe how tortured I am."

And neither do I, Alinor thought, so annoyed by the pitch of the voice and the fluttering, repetitive gestures that she did not notice the very shrewd expression in Lady Ela's pale blue eyes. She looked only at the plump body and the very pretty, rosy face. You are as strong as an ox, you lazy bitch, Alinor thought.

"Men often do not understand such matters," Alinor remarked, concealing her contempt. "I have always found it best not to speak of my health at all."

"That is easy to say for someone who does not suffer ill health," the countess drawled.

There was a note of pride in her voice, Alinor noted, and in spite of her distaste for the woman, she felt a touch of sympathy. The ill health was her one distinction. Alinor raised her eyes and happened to catch sight of Isobel, who was dancing as lightfootedly as a girl with Robert of Leicester. If Isobel had not married William, who patiently taught her to handle such responsibility as she was capable of, Isobel would have become as much a bore about religion as this woman was about her health.

Farther down the hall a flash of red hair made Alinor smile. Joanna was in seventh heaven, romping with the other noble children. The two ideas connected in her mind. Better suffer boredom than need the distinction of ill health or excessive faith. Joanna would not be taught the pleasures of idleness. She would be taught that she was a necessary and valuable part of life and thus she would set a high value on her own worth. Alinor would enquire among the guests for a suitable middle-aged gentlewoman. With such a woman and Father Francis to guide her, Joanna could be left to manage Roselynde while Alinor and Ian went on progress.

"Lady Alinor," Lady Salisbury whined, "I asked you if you were never ill."

"I beg your pardon, madam. I was watching my daughter at play. No, I am never ill."

"You are not troubled by your flux?"

"Not at all, nor, to speak the truth, by breeding. I have found the last month tedious because it was difficult to ride, but—" her voice checked. Sidling down the room, pressed as close to the wall as he could get for fear of touching and thus contaminating the gentlefolk, was Alinor's chief huntsman. "I beg you excuse me, Lady Ela," Alinor said hastily, controlling the tremor of nervousness in her voice. "I see a servant of mine where he should not be, and I must speak to him."

Deaf to the plaintive protests that reprimanding servants was the work for higher servants, not for a lady, Alinor rose and hurried toward her man, gesturing him to go back to the stairwell.

"Lady, we have him," the huntsman said eagerly, as soon as Alinor reached him.

"Who?"

"The messenger."

Alinor had almost forgotten him in her anxiety about Ian, but she did not allow her disappointment on one subject to blind her to the importance of the other. "Come," she said briefly, and led the way upstairs. If this was the king's messenger that had been taken, no ears but hers must hear of it. The huntsman looked around curiously when they emerged into the women's quarters. He had never been above the great hall and never expected to be, but aside from instruments for weaving and spinning now pushed all together near the walls to make room for the beds of some of the guests, there was nothing to be seen. All the women were below.

The luxury of Alinor's chamber made his eyes bulge.

He stopped in the entryway, reluctant to tread upon the glowing rug and, when Alinor gestured him forward impatiently, he was so impressed with the softness and warmth beneath his feet that he almost lost his voice.

"Well?"

The sharp question galvanized the huntsman into action. He drew a scroll and a purse from his breast and passed them to Alinor. "His clothing and weapons I left in my hut with one of the men to guard them. I was afeard to bring them in among so many."

"Wisely done! Well done!"

It was the king's seal on the message. Alinor took a deep breath. As to this part of her plan, everything was working to perfection. She emptied the coins from the purse and pressed them into the huntsman's hand.

"This is the man I looked for. Do not stop any further messengers. You have him safe? Will he know any of you again?"

"He is trussed like a chicken for roasting and blindfolded. He might recognize the voice of John of the Marsh, but I do not think it. John took him by jumping from a tree. The man was stunned, and we took care to blindfold him at once."

"Has he said aught?"

"Only again and again that he is a king's messenger and threats as to what would befall us if we did not release him unharmed on the moment."

"Oh, most excellent! Listen close. One is to tell him, disguising his voice as best may be, that it is confirmed he is a king's messenger. Thus, instead of slaying him out of hand, one of your number will try to obtain a ransom for him from the Lady of Roselynde. If she will pay, tell him, he will be freed. If not, he will die. Now he will bid you take the message you reft from him to me. Then the one who speaks with him is to laugh and refuse, saying the lady would pay no ransom if she had the king's message already. Do you understand? But let that man tear off the seal and give it to a forester to bring to me."

"Yes, lady."

"Listen again. On the fifth day from now, I will be married. On the sixth day—the fingers of one hand and one more, so many days—you will tell the messenger that ransom has been paid. Say, if he asks, that two marks were paid. You will carry him, bound, to some place on the edge of the wood. There, give him back this scroll, loose his hands but not his feet, and leave him some sorry, half-dead nag—ask Beorn for one of the reaver's horses for the purpose. Do you be sure he catch no sight of any of you in your huntsmen's garb. If needful, let the man who frees him mask his face and —" Alinor laughed, "and let him wear the man's own garments. After that use they must be destroyed, and so must the trappings of the horse if they be marked by the king's badge or in any other way out of the usual. Let one of the men hide his horse. I will send one who is not known as my man to dispose of it. You have done very well, huntsman, very well, indeed. The coins are yours. When the horse is sold, I will give you its value to be distributed among your men—and I will add two shillings for the value of the clothes that must be destroyed. If the man's weapons are not marked in any way, they can go to the armory. If they are recognizable, they must go to the smithy to be suitably altered."

Alinor paused and thought over the situation. Had she covered everything? In the back of her mind she found that she was wondering where Beorn was and whether he had found Ian, instead of concentrating on the problem in hand. "Have I left aught hanging?" she asked the huntsman, too aware of her divided attention to trust herself.

"Nay, lady. Our part is clear."

"Do you know by sight the young knight who came with Beorn and has been teaching Master Adam?"

"Yea, lady."

"Find him and tell him quietly, that none may hear, to come here to me."

This was a fine opportunity to accomplish a multitude of purposes, Alinor thought, staring into the fire. What a good, obedient subject she was proving herself to be, paying a ransom of two marks for the king's messenger. And now, to add one good to another, she had a chance to test Sir Guy by offering him an enormous temptation. On the thought, the young man presented himself in the doorway.

"Come you in," Alinor said. "You have kept your parole, Sir Guy, and have done well and willingly each task I have laid upon you. Now, however, it is growing dangerous to have you here among my guests, and I have another task that may as well be done now as any other time. I have a horse that must be sold well off my lands, and secretly—at least the sale need not be secret, only the fact that I have had anything to do with the horse must be kept quiet."

"Very well, my lady."

"You may take some armor of the lesser sort, a sword, a lance, a blank shield, and the lesser brown destrier to ride. I will give you some money also. I do not care where you go or what tale you tell, so long as it be a decent distance and so long as you be returned here on the tenth day. The huntsman will tell you where to find the horse. Is all clear?"

"Yes, my lady."

It was interesting that he did not ask why she wanted to be rid of the horse; was he duller or cleverer than she thought? If she had guessed wrong, she would be the poorer by two horses and some arms and armor—a proper price to pay for overgreat trust in a guileless countenance. If she were right, however, if he did not ask because his loyalty was great enough to do anything, right or wrong, on her command, then she would have gained a really valuable servant. If Sir Guy did not run, having been given arms, armor, money and two reasonably valuable horses, he was truly a young man of honor. With a sigh, Alinor rose. It was time to go and continue her courtesies to Lady Ela. As awful as that was, it was better than to sit and wonder whether Beorn, too, had been swallowed by the mysterious silence that had enwrapped Ian.

CHAPTER ELEVEN

Although she had been some hours abed, Alinor was not asleep. Late, Beorn had said, and Alinor knew that it was slower to ride at night than in daylight. Nonetheless, some message should have come by now, even if it was only to say that no trace could be found of Ian or of his men. She told herself firmly that she was a fool. News would come no sooner if she lay awake. Resolutely she closed her eyes. A moment later a sound brought her bolt upright. Nothing, Alinor hissed at herself, it is nothing! A bed creaked. That is all. Desperately, she stuffed her fingers in her ears and lay down again.

The position could not be held long, of course. It was too uncomfortable. Alinor relaxed the pressure of her fingers, then pulled her hands away violently.

". . . you to leave me here. Do not wake Lady Alinor, I say."

The voice was so low that, had she not been awake and despite her efforts listening for every sound, it would not have disturbed her. Alinor slid out of bed and pulled on her bedrobe.

"Lord, lord," she heard Beorn pleading, "the lady is not one lightly to be disobeyed. She bade me wake her with news at any hour. She——"

Alinor lit a candle from the night light that stood by the bed and came into the antechamber. Ian was in one of the chairs, his left leg stretched stiffly in front of him, and Beorn leaned over him. They both looked up as she entered with identical, shamefaced, guilty expressions, like two little boys caught raiding the honey-pot.

Torn between overwhelming relief and exasperated rage, Alinor managed not to say a word. She quietly went and lit the candles that stood near each chair.

"My lady——"

"Alinor——"

The voices blended, again identical in their placatory tone. Alinor bit her lip.

"You may go, Beorn."

She could not castigate her man. He was caught between the upper and the nether millstone. He dared not disobey either one of them. Fortunately it was a rare occasion when the orders he received from his lady and his new lord would be as diametrically opposed as they had been this day. Alinor did not turn to Ian until Beorn's soft steps had faded completely. When she did look at him, his eyes were closed and even the golden light of the candles could lend no warmth to his gray pallor.

"Ian! What is amiss?"

"Such stupidity," he sighed. "Like a careless child, I stepped on a stone and wrenched my knee. You would not believe so little a thing could cause such pain."

"When did this happen?"

"Almost a week ago. The day your messenger came to tell me William of Pembroke was come."

"Why did you not send the messenger back? I would have come to you. Or I would have sent a litter so you could be carried home. Really, Ian——"

"Alinor, be still! I hurt. I do not wish to argue with you about what I could have or should have done. For the one thing, how could I send for you when the rest of our guests might arrive at any moment? That I should be absent was bad enough. That we should both be lacking would be too much discourtesy. For the second, to speak the truth, I could not endure the thought of being moved at first. I suppose I should have sent to tell you what had happened to me, but I felt such a fool!"

Impulsively, Alinor bent forward and kissed him.

Before he could recover from his surprise and take hold of her, she was gone. She called through the door to the room where her maids slept, sending one for bandages, another for cold water. She ordered also that two men be roused to bring more cold water every little while.

"Can you go so far as the bed?" Alinor asked while the maids threw on their clothing, "or should I tell them to send up some men to carry you?"

"What bed?" Ian asked bemusedly. Had Alinor kissed him? So swift had it been that he wondered now if he had willfully imagined it when she merely bent over him.

"My bed," Alinor replied. "Aubery de Vere is in yours."

"Oxford?" Ian exclaimed, totally mystified. "What is he doing here? Did you invite him?"

"Salisbury brought him, but I did not wish to ask why. I only thanked him for doing us such honor. Well, I could not ask an unexpected and uninvited guest why he had come, could I?"

"No, of course not. But did he not say anything? Surely——"

"He might have done so, but I was more exercised to find a place to put him and his servants than to press for explanations which I knew he would give you without asking."

"So that was why you sent so urgently. Yes, I see. Thank you."

That was not why Alinor had sent Beorn to look for Ian, but she did not bother to correct him, merely asked again about carrying him to bed.

"You cannot have a herd of servants tramping back and forth and waking everyone," he replied irritably. "Let me rest a little and I will make shift to get there, but why can I not sleep here on a pallet. Really, I am tired enough to sleep on the stone floor without the pallet."

"Because I do not wish to spend the whole night on

my knees tending you, and because you are a fool if you do not realize it will kill you to lower yourself to the floor and rise up again when it is necessary. And why did you not return as soon as you had taken that band of outlaws? This would never have happened——"

"Scold!" Ian exclaimed.

Alinor turned on him, color mantling her cheeks, but he was laughing. She put out her hand and touched his face. "Do you not deserve a scold for a wife? I was worried about you, Ian, but I did not like to keep sending messengers after you. After all, perhaps the less of my company you have, the easier your heart is. How can I know?"

"My heart? My heart is not in question. It has long been——"

He stopped abruptly as Gertrude hurried in with a flask of water in one hand and strips of cloth in the other. There was, of course, no reason why Ian should not tell his betrothed wife he loved her in her maidservant's presence, but Ian had never before been in such a situation. All the women to whom he had made love in the past had been someone else's property. To put them or himself into the power of a maidservant would be both foolish and dangerous. Long practice checked his tongue before thought could correct him.

It was impossible for Alinor to decide whether she wanted to hear the rest of the sentence or not. His heart had long been—what? Dead? Given? Would he have told her to whom? Alinor had dropped her hand from his face when he stopped speaking. With the motion, she decided she did not want to hear. Heart or no heart, there was that in Ian's eyes, even now, lurking behind the pain, which gave her more cause for amusement than despair. Poor Ian. Was he a believer in *amour courtois*? Had he professed his devotion to some great lady in a profusion of sickly verses? If so, his loins were surely at war now with his elevated sentiments. But if she allowed him to say he loved another, or could not love, that would lie between them. What was unspoken was easier to forget.

"It does not matter," she said briskly. "Now I have you safe, that is all that is of importance. I still say you were a fool to ride with a knee like that."

She went to get a pair of shears with which to slit open his chausses. The knee was awful, hugely swollen and darkly discolored. Ian looked at it ruefully.

"But it was almost down to normal this morning," he said. "I intended to ride in tomorrow. It is only that we rode too far, I think."

"Too far? Did you not come from the northwest farm?"

"No. Did I forget to tell you that there were a pair of sly weasels who, too cowardly to seize what they desired, were exacting tribute on the pretense they could keep the reavers away? I had told the bailiff of the Long Acres to seize them, and he sent word they were taken. I set out for the Long Acres before your messenger came, and he followed me—which is one reason everything was so delayed. Those two are for hanging, I think. I brought them and sent them into prison in the town. I was sure you would have no room for prisoners here. By the by, what did you do with Sir Guy?"

"Took him into service. Is that not what you expected me to do? What else could I do with such an honest fool? I have sent him into hiding. You heard his tale, did you not? I feared one of our guests might know his face."

While she was speaking, Alinor had set a basin below Ian's knee, placed a thick pad over it, and trickled the cold water onto the pad. Ian sighed with relief and closed his eyes. He had been right to trust her judgment in Sir Guy's case. This marriage would be perfect, if only— Well, she had not allowed him to finish when he started to tell her how long he had loved her, but she had not withdrawn from him either. There was something he had to ask—something— Oh, yes, the king's messenger. Wearily, he forced his lids open, but it was Gertrude who held the flask so that the coolness flowed softly over his throbbing knee. Later Ian woke with a cry of pain when the chair was lifted, but his leg was held rigid on a board, and the pang was brief. He remembered mumbling something about being full of fleas, and Alinor made some soothing response. The bed was soft and warm as heaven. Ian slept.

Morning brought disorientation and a moment of panic. From the exquisite bedcurtains, it was plain that he was in some great lady's bed—but whose? Full wakefulness resolved the panic into clear memory and a roar of laughter. Alinor pulled the bedcurtains aside.

"That is a pleasant sound to start the morning."

"And you are a pleasant sight to start the morning."

"How gallant. But you laughed before you saw me. Why?"

Ian hesitated, then grinned. "Because at first I could not remember whose bed I was in— And it is a gentleman's first duty to remember in the morning—"

Alinor giggled delightedly. It was the first sign she had that Ian was not a pious-mouthed prude. "Wretch! Well, you will not be troubled with that question again —not if you wish to keep intact the wherewithal to make a bed a place for other than sleep."

"Alinor!"

"Did you think I would not be a jealous wife?" she asked provocatively. "I have not a complaisant nature."

Somewhat dazed by that miracle of understatement, Ian had only strength enough to murmur, "I would never have guessed if you had not told me."

"I thought so." Alinor replied with enormous gravity as she put back the bedclothes to look at Ian's knee. "My disposition is so mild and yielding in general, that I was sure you would need this warning." A sidelong glance did not meet the indignation Alinor expected. She had underestimated her opponent.

With a totally bland expression, Ian agreed warmly. "Of course. Have I not had repeated demonstrations of your gentleness? I know you so meek and mild that a single angry word is too great punishment. I am sorry to hear of your jealousy, of course. However, since you are so biddable, so amiable, in all other ways, I needs must make the best of this small crotchet."

Beaten at her own game, Alinor could only laugh. She was relieved to see that the swelling was greatly reduced, although the blue, black and green discoloration seemed greater. Very gently, Alinor probed Ian's kneecap. He stiffened but did not wince away or protest. As well as she could feel, the bone seemed whole. This news was very welcome. Ian confessed he had felt it himself two days before but could make nothing of it. Then a lively discussion ensued. Alinor proposed that Ian remain abed; he swore in response that he would have his clothes off and bathe if it cost his life. Although Alinor knew this was the thin edge of the wedge, his need was very apparent. His skin was caked with dirt; she could see the lice in his hair; and he stank to high heaven—even to Alinor's hardened nose. Ian's proposal won.

The movement from bed to bath and out again seemed to do so little harm, even though Ian had to bend his leg a little in the tub, that it was far less unreasonable when he said he would go down to his guests.

"I must, you know," he insisted, forestalling Alinor's objections. "I dare not ask this one and that one to come up here to talk. Each will wonder what the other said, and also that would be an unhealthy tale to carry back to the king—and someone is sure to carry it. Worse yet would be for all the great lords to come together away from the tale bearers."

A compromise was reached. Alinor bound Ian's leg

to a splint that would prevent him from bending his knee, and he agreed to use a crutch. With this protection and the help of two sturdy menservants, he was got down the stairs in time to break his fast with the guests. As was natural, his arrival was greeted with loud and ribald jests about his reluctance to yield up his single state for married blessedness. Several warm offers to take his place were proposed, and various inducements were offered to Alinor to throw over so reluctant a groom and choose one more eager.

To the company's huge delight, this brought Adam to his stepfather's defense. He bounded up from where the young people were seated and proclaimed sturdily that Lord Ian *did* wish to marry his mother. Lord Ian had said so, and he was no liar. What was more, Adam insisted pugnaciously, Lord Ian had been occupied upon his mother's business, and that was what made him late. Ian's voice, gravely thanking his ardent supporter, over-rode various sounds of strangulation as the good-natured crowd smothered its amusement. Satisfied at routing the enemy, Adam returned to his proper place again, but that was the end of that sort of joke. Whatever animosities those in the group had for one another, few were directed at the bride and groom and, even if small spites that could be relieved by a jest existed, no one wished to distress Alinor's children.

Unfortunately, the next shafts of humor were less harmless. It started innocently enough with Robert of Leicester rolling his goblet of wine between his hands and complimenting Ian on the entertainment they were being offered. Ian raised a quizzical brow, unsure of whether this was a sincere compliment directed at Alinor or a prelude to some teasing remark. The lively, laughing Robert of Leicester seemed to be unlike his father, who had been a grave, ponderous man, slow of movement (except on the battlefield) and heavy of appearance. In actuality, both had the same keen, quick mind and the same steady, single-minded devotion to the quiet development of their own property and power. This apparently selfish motive produced really excellent results.

Neither of the Leicesters were violently acquisitive men, the younger Robert more because of the example of his father than from his own peaceable intentions. Thus, they were not prone to attack their neighbors for an imagined insult. This mildness had brought them huge increases in wealth and influence. During the violent upheavals of the civil war, when Henry sought to wrest the throne from Stephen, their lesser neighbors had voluntarily begged for their protection and had taken vassalage under them. Stephen, wishing to have at least one great baron who was not ready to leap to arms, confirmed these arrangements and even seissined more estates upon them. Because the restrained behavior was accompanied by a lively intelligence, a good strong arm when challenged, and a deep understanding of affairs, the property had remained intact and had even grown under Henry's and Richard's rules.

The Leicesters had always done the king good service and had been decently rewarded. What was often forgotten was that their loyalty, like Alinor's, was to their own lands and not to any king. Old Robert had been a favorite of Stephen's for many years, yet when he saw that Henry was the stronger and that, if a strong king did not soon curb the realm, complete chaos would result, old Robert changed sides and gave his strength to Henry. There had been no need to shift between Henry and Richard; that war was fought on the continent, and old Robert was a past master at evading his military feudal duties.

It was young Robert who faced the choice between Richard and John. He had not set a foot amiss. Sweet words were offered to both—and nothing else. Young Robert watched his herds increase, watched his serfs garner rich crops, listened to the contented talk of his vassals and thought to himself that his father's ways were good ways. Because he was a young man and strong of his hands, he fought gladly in the Crusade and in the wars Richard waged against Philip of France. England lay at peace, and it was cheaper to fight himself, leading his own vassals and men-at-arms, than to pay knights to take his place. When John continued the war so lamely that he lost Normandy, Robert was not among the army. And when the treaty had been signed with Philip, Robert went to France and made his own arrangements. Unlike nine tenths of the English barons who had lost their Norman lands, Leicester's still belonged to him.

Needless to say, Robert of Leicester did not approve of John's desire to invade Normandy in 1204. He had supported the barons' refusal, although he had not been among their spokesmen. Thus King John's wrath did not fall directly upon him, as it had upon William of Pembroke. Still, he could see the handwriting on the wall, and each year the taxes pinched him harder and took a larger number of cattle and sheep from his herds and a larger number of bushels from his grain.

"I make special remark of the richness of our entertainment," Robert said innocently in reply to Ian's half-cautious, half-questioning look, "because if you had delayed a few weeks in your wedding, I am afraid you would not have had the wherewithal to furnish us food and drink so lavishly."

Ian's eyes flew to Alinor and hers to him. Did Robert know of the grudge King John had against her? And if so, how did he know?

"You must think me a poor housewife to be so ill-prepared for the lean months of winter not to be able to feed my guests," Alinor responded with a laugh.

"Lady Alinor, I meant no such thing, and you know it," Leicester replied, more seriously than Alinor liked. "I have guested here often enough, and I know well your matchless skill at management. However, you cannot feed guests with that which has been taken away to enrich another's store."

"None can take—" Alinor began, bristling, but Ian laid his hand over hers.

"Are you trying to insult me, Robert?" he asked, grinning. "I never knew you to be so unkind or to add shame to a man already stricken down. Just because I fell victim to a child's trick and scraped my knee——"

"No," Leicester drawled, "I do not think a scraped knee, nor a broken one either, could hold you back from guarding your own—except against one single force. I have heard—from a good and reliable source—that the king will demand a thirteenth of our goods when he comes again to England."

Not only the high table fell silent but the tables at which the vassals and castellans sat also. As the words were whispered to the lower tables, farther and farther away down the hall, silence fell upon them also. This touched every man, down to the serfs, who were not present but would ultimately pay for all. The eyes of the silent faces were not turned toward Leicester, who sat three places down from Ian on the left of his own wife, who followed Lord Llewelyn and Joan in the seating, according to protocol. Everyone looked toward the Earl of Salisbury, who sat at Alinor's right hand.

He shrugged. "I cannot deny there was some talk of it. What was decided, I do not know. My wife sent me an urgent message that I must come home."

"I was very ill," Lady Salisbury's whining voice confirmed from her husband's side. "I had such beatings of the heart, such pains of the eyes and dizziness of the head that I could not lift myself from my pillow."

Alinor did not doubt that Salisbury had received such a letter. Probably he had received one exactly like that twice or thrice a week the entire period of his absence. Perhaps, Alinor thought, with a flash of amusement, she had overestimated Salisbury's good nature. It would be

a shame to rid oneself of such a good excuse to come
and go from the king's presence. While Salisbury wished
to be with his half brother, he had only to commit Lady
Ela's letters to the flames. When he wished to go, it was
only necessary to present the pathetic missive.

That was all less to the point than why Salisbury had
left John. It was possible he came early to England out
of love of Ian, to lend his presence to the wedding and
thus soften John's spite. Certainly, he had asked sincere
and anxious questions about Ian's lameness. There were,
however, more interesting reasons that could be suggested. Had Salisbury come to spread the news about
this new tax so that the shock when John announced it
would be less? Had he opposed his brother's will in this
matter and left either in pique or in disgrace?

"Of course it does not matter to me," Lord Llewelyn
remarked. "A thirteenth of nothing is still nothing. North
Wales is a poor land, and any man who wants a thirteenth—or any other portion—of its wild flocks can
come and hunt them through the hills. Still, I send my
people out to hunt *before* a war, not after. Money is
needed for fighting, not for peace. I understand, moreover, that the king had great success in this campaign.
Was there no booty?"

"Llewelyn," Joan murmured, "do not be so mischievous. This is not the time or place to make trouble."

"There could not be much booty," William of Pembroke's deep voice rumbled from the right of Lady Salisbury. "Since the lands were his to begin with, the king
could have no profit in stripping them."

Salisbury looked down the table. "That is generous,
Pembroke," he remarked.

"It is just," William replied stiffly.

"Still, there must have been rich ransoms," Leicester
commented. "I heard Montauban was stuffed with
Philip's nobility."

"You heard aright, but the ransoms did not go to the

king, beyond a moderate share," Ian pointed out pacifically. "I had my portion, as did all who took part in the assault."

"Well, that is true enough," Leicester agreed. He had made his point and did not wish to embarrass his host and hostess.

"It was kind of you to warn me, Robert," Alinor said swiftly, before anyone could introduce another sensitive topic. "Now that I know, I shall put you all to work for your dinners. My huntsman has reported a fine boar lies up only a mile or two into my forest. Who will come with me to bring him down for the table?"

A chorus of enthusiastic response covered Ian's startled oath. "You will not go to hunt wild boar!" he exclaimed.

"No, of course not," Alinor assured him softly. At another time she might have teased him by insisting she would hunt with the men just to see how angry he would get before he realized she was teasing; but that was for private play. "I must ride out, of course, but I promise I will not dismount."

"Do not stay too near," Ian cautioned. "If the boar should break away wounded, he will go for a horse as quick as for a man. *Peste!* I wish I had more wits than to fall off my feet like a puling infant."

"Do not fret, love," Alinor murmured. "I will keep my huntsmen by me. No harm will come to me."

There was no time for Ian either to respond to Alinor's endearment or to urge her again to be careful. The offer of a hunt brought breakfast to an abrupt end. Men swallowed what remained in their goblets at a gulp if they still thirsted, and crammed the remainder of their bread and cheese into their mouths if they still hungered. Most simply left what remained before them and rose to fetch cloaks or to change their fine garments to coarser wear.

Salisbury lingered a moment to bend over Ian and

murmur, "I have spoken to Geoffrey. Ian, I cannot tell you how deep I am in your debt. Ask, and what I have will be given, up to and including my life. He is not the same child."

"You do not do your own son justice," Ian replied. "He is exactly the same child. He is a brave and steadfast boy. I have done nothing for him except to make him happier and to improve his swordplay and riding a little. We are quits, William. I have given you a more contented son, and you have given me a squire I can trust to the uttermost. You owe me nothing."

Salisbury shook his head. "I will not argue with you. I have said what I feel and what I mean. There is something else I wish to speak to you about. I wish I could stay, but if I do, there will be too many odd looks over it. Just tell me, who is Lady Joanna?"

"Joanna! My daughter—I mean, Alinor's daughter. What——"

To Ian's surprise, Salisbury broke into a roar of laughter and clapped him so heartily on the back that he jostled his knee. By the time Ian had ungritted his teeth, unsure whether his still tender back or his sore leg hurt worse, Salisbury was gone. Alinor had already left with the other more adventurous ladies to change her dress. Ian cursed under his breath and signaled to a manservant whom he instructed to pull back the bench so he could hoist himself to his feet. A strong hand seized him under the armpit and hauled him up almost painlessly.

"My thanks," Ian grunted, turned his head to see who he was thanking, and controlled a gasp with some effort. "My lord Oxford, thank you again. And I have also to thank you for doing Alinor and myself the honor of coming to our wedding."

"There is no need for that," Aubery de Vere remarked with a self-conscious smile. "Rather should I thank you and your good lady for receiving an uninvited guest so graciously. The thing was that I was delayed in a necessary visit to Salisbury, and when I finally arrived, he was all but mounting up to come here. Naturally he returned within, but when he heard my business, he suggested I come here with him. I demurred, not being invited, but Salisbury said he thought he had enough credit with you to buy my pardon."

Ian laughed. "Neither you nor he need any pardon. Had I known you willing, you would have been asked. Truly we limited our asking for our guests' sakes. Simon, as you know, was no favorite of the king's. John had wished Alinor to be married to a henchman of his own. He was not best pleased when Simon took her. I do not know why the king should have any objection to our marriage, but if he should feel we have played some trick on him——"

"Why make trouble for your friends? Yes, I see."

While they spoke, Oxford had helped Ian to a chair by the hearth. A maidservant stopped gathering the scraps from the table into a basket, which would be given to the poor at the castle gates, and fetched a footstool. She was obviously afraid, however, to touch Ian's bad leg, and Oxford bent forward and lifted it gently.

"There is no need, my lord," Ian protested.

"Will you be tied by the leg for long?" Oxford asked, ignoring Ian's polite disclaimer. From his tone it was plain that the enquiry was purposeful, not a courtesy.

"I hope not," Ian replied sincerely. "It is already less swollen and painful. Alinor says I did not break the bone. A week or two should mend it."

"I am happy to hear it, although even a month or two more or less would not affect my interest."

"You have some work for me, my lord?" Ian asked cautiously.

"Let us say rather some enterprise in which you may wish to have a part."

If William of Salisbury knew of this, it could not be treason. Auberey de Vere, as much as Ian knew of him, was said to be an honest man. However, the need to discuss any enterprise so hastily and so privately that one would come uninvited to a wedding woke a strong feeling of reserve in Ian.

"If you propose it, I might, indeed," he said courteously, "but do you not wish to hunt? We will be here some two weeks more. I would not wish to spoil your sport when there will be time enough for talk."

"I may be discourteous enough to come to your wedding without invitation," Oxford said with a smile, "but I am not so rude as to propose an enterprise of war in my unsuspecting host's home without his knowledge and permission. This hunt I will miss while I lay the matter before you. I am not so young anymore that a hunt is of prime importance. If you are willing, I will propose what I plan to those others we decide would be interested and benefit thereby. If you are not willing, that will end the matter. I will be only your guest."

Alinor cast a bright glance around the outer bailey and then up at the sky. Everything seemed to be perfect. The dogs were yelping with pleasure, straining at their leashes; the huntsmen seemed no less happy and eager. The weather was ideal. It had not rained at all in the past few days, and it had been cold enough so that the ground was hard. William of Pembroke was overseeing the distribution of boar spears and bellowing Alinor's guests into some form of order. Fortunately, he seemed willing enough to take charge. It was that aspect of the hunt which had troubled Alinor the most. She knew well what should be done, but she did not think the noble huntsmen would take pleasure in being ordered about by a woman.

As the party rode out over the drawbridge and quickened pace a little in the open, the tension of the responsible hostess oozed out of Alinor and a new tension began to build. This was far pleasanter, an exhilarating sense of anticipation of excitement and danger. The dogs were still leashed but were straining madly, pulling their handlers along so quickly that some horses broke from a trot to a canter to keep pace. It would have been easier to loose them, but the men had been promised boar, and the air was so clear that all kinds of scents were running. The dogs might just as easily have rushed off after a fox or a hare or a stag. Game was exceptionally plentiful, because, owing to Simon's illness and Alinor's preoccupation, no one had hunted Alinor's forests for almost two years. Once in a while Alinor had ordered her huntsman to bring in a doe or a fawn or a wild piglet to tempt Simon's appetite, but aside from that, the beasts had developed unchecked.

They rode into the tongue of woods where Alinor's abductors had hidden and, almost at once, one of the dogs put down her head and began to bell. Alinor found her breath quickening. It had been so long, so long since she had ridden behind the hounds. The rache bitch was loosed, and then a few more. The huntsmen, having determined that the raches had picked up the correct scent, signaled that all the leashes be slipped. At once bedlam broke loose. Even the hounds began to bay, so strong was the scent. The horses sprang forward on the heels of the hounds, Alinor's spirited black mare along with the others.

"Have a care, Alinor," William shouted as he thundered by.

But Alinor was not in the mood for care, and she laid her whip to Velvet out of pure excitement, for the mare was eager enough without that stimulus. Now that the initial hysteria was over, the dogs were quieter; the raches belled their signal to the hunters, but the fighting hounds ran silent. It was dangerous riding. The horses shouldered and jostled one another into trees, and low branches whipped and tore at flesh and clothes. Alinor laughed with the thrill of danger as her headdress was torn from her head. Had the branch caught more firmly, she could have had her neck broken or been strangled by her wimple. Fortunately, the whole headdress was merely unseated. Impatiently, Alinor seized it, pulled it back up and then forward, off her head completely. Somehow the ribbons that bound her braids had become entangled in the cloth of the wimple. Ruthlessly, she tore those free also. Her long black hair streamed behind her as she rode, as wild as any maenad.

Suddenly there was a burst of barking from the alantes, mastiffs, and hounds. The boar had been sighted. The noble huntsmen called encouragement to the dogs and spurred their horses to greater speed. Alinor saw a man struck by a heavy branch fall from his mount. Caught in the passion of the chase, she did not even turn her head or wonder who it was. For some reason the boar had not remained in his earth. The beast had chosen to run. Behind she heard a crash. A horse had gone down. Caring nothing, shouting and hallooing, the hunting party careened on in pursuit of its prey.

Then the belling of the raches changed to excited yelps which told a new story. The boar had found a place to make a stand. As the riders came closer, they could distinguish the snarling of the larger hounds. The men called encouragement and leapt from their horses, automatically testing the soundness of the crossbars on their boar spears as they ran. If the crosspieces affixed about 18 inches up from the head of the spear were to give way, the boar would run right up the weapon to get at the man at the other end. Pain seemed no deterrent to the great fierce beasts; it seemed rather to stimulate them to wilder attempts to savage their attackers. Next, hands went to loosen hunting knives in their sheaths. With about 20 stone of struggling, slashing wild boar on the end of one's spear, a knife that would not come free spelled injury or even possible death.

With some difficulty Alinor checked the pace of her mare, but she did not stop completely. Her eyes gleaming, she allowed Velvet to fret herself forward. None of the other women had yet arrived, but she could hear their horses in the brush. The sound held no interest for her; she strained forward, watching the raches making little rushes forward and then retreating, yelping all the while. The larger dogs made more determined rushes, leaping and slashing. One, grown too bold, fastened his teeth in a bristly shoulder for one instant. The boar's head swung; three-inch tusks flashed; the dog screamed and fell away.

The beast had chosen well, either by knowledge or accident. No man was willing to denigrate the intelligence of the great, wild boars. Where a large old oak had fallen, there was a tiny clearing. In the angle between the huge trunk and the upraised roots, the monster stood at bay. Blood now stained the slaver from his jaws, and he uttered a coughing sound that was more roar than squeal. There was no terror in the little red pig eyes, only rage. Mouth open to tear, he shook his enormous head, flinging spume across the clearing and onto the bellowing hounds.

Among them there was also no fear. "Hold him, children, hold him," Alinor shrieked, wild with excitement. She did not think the dogs needed encouragement; she only needed to cry aloud.

The men had now ringed the clearing, dropping to one knee with the butt of the boar spears resting on the ground and the points angled up to about 20 inches. The earth would take most of the shock of the animal's charge. This time the men were fairly close together because the open area was small, but even if they had been more widely spaced, it would not have mattered. It was very rare for a boar to run between the hunters to try to escape. The instinct of this animal was to attack. Nor was it usually necessary for the huntsmen to prod the beast. The irritation created by the yelping, charging dogs and the shouting men was enough to enrage a boar into charging.

The signs were on the beast now. He shook his head and snorted, tore at the ground with his sharp hooves.

A short dash caught a large mastiff, a little slow because of his size. The big dog was tossed right over the boar's back, belly ripped open, to hang twitching, caught on an upended root. Blood streamed from the dying animal, staining the boar's black hide red and driving the other hounds into a frenzy. One leapt to the trunk of the fallen tree and down onto the boar's back, tore at it, leapt away. The boar shrieked with rage and charged, slashing right and left so that yelping, bleeding hounds flew in all directions.

There was not much space to charge, so that the boar could not work up any real speed. As it was, Alinor gasped between fear and exultation. Red eyes, red mouth wide, ivory tusks bared, the beast seemed to be rushing straight at her. She knew she should turn her horse and fly, but she could not. All she could do was curse herself for her empty hands.

"A spear," she cried, "give me a spear!"

One was thrust into her hands, but even as her fingers closed on the shaft, the final scene of the drama was playing out at a quite safe distance. To the boar, the kneeling men in their bright robes were a far more attractive target than the thin black legs of the mare. Nor did Alinor's voice draw the animal. All the men were shouting, some calling insults, some endearments, as their natures directed.

"Come, love, come!" Leicester bellowed, waving his right arm wildly.

"Son of a sow, here!" Pembroke shouted.

Lord Llewelyn, to Leicester's left, used no words. He uttered a sound almost identical to the boar's own shrieks and it was at him, head down, tail up, that the furious animal charged. It swerved out of the direct line so that it was headed just too far left of Leicester's spear to be caught and too far right for Llewelyn's to reach. A woman's terrified scream rang across the clearing. Joan, Alinor thought, as she herself uttered a gasp of horror and kicked her mare forward; the huntsmen

leapt forward with her. The boar was not seeking freedom; it had twisted again in a split second to slash at
Lord Llewelyn's unprotected right side.

There was no expectation that horse or huntsmen
could prevent what Alinor feared. They plunged ahead
in the hope of driving the boar from his victim before
great injury was done. But no injury befell the Welshman, who had run boar down afoot in his own hills with
no more than a few dogs to help him. As the animal
turned, Llewelyn had come to his feet; as it twisted to
slash at him, he jumped clear over its back, bringing
down his spear with an angled, overhand thrust that
forced the point in behind the shoulder and deep into
the chest. The knife was already out in his free hand,
but there was no need to seek for a death thrust in the
throat. Blood burst from the boar's nose and mouth,
and it sank forward on its knees.

A shout that shivered the bare branches of the trees
went up from the men's throats. Pembroke raised his
hunting horn to blow the mort. There was a concerted
rush of men and dogs toward the boar and Lord
Llewelyn. Simultaneously, at the other end of the dead
tree, there was a loud crashing among the branches. The
dogs went insane, snapping at the bloodied hulk one
instant and twisting to rush off toward the other side of
the clearing barking madly in the next.

"Ware! Ware!" the huntsmen shouted at once.

The noblemen whirled in their tracks. Out of concealment in the tangled branches of the fallen oak, burst
a huge sow and three half-grown piglets. Alinor heard
one man cry out in pain as a small devil tore open his
leg. William of Salisbury leapt to his aid, thrusting his
spear through the middle of the young pig's body in a
hasty attempt to prevent the animal from slashing the
fallen man a second time. Although it could not have
weighed above seven stone, its strength was enormous.
The stroke was not immediately fatal, and the pig twisted
madly, wrenching the spear from Salisbury's hand. Sir

John d'Alberin, rushing to help, was knocked off his feet by the haft of the spear. Two of Simon's castellans, just on Sir John's heels, finally pinned the already dying piglet to the ground.

Pembroke had caught the sow full in the chest with his spear, but the angle was wrong. The spear had touched no vital spot and the haft broke in his hands as he struggled to hold the enormous animal. A huntsman plunged forward, knife bared, only to be bowled over. Alinor wrenched her mare sideways, thrusting down as the sow threw Pembroke off a shoulder. The spear entered the thick neck midway between shoulder and head and passed down without obstruction. Alinor shrieked an oath, thinking she, too, had missed, but blood suddenly gushed like a fountain between the sow's legs. By chance, Alinor had nicked the jugular. The violence of the sow herself had burst the vein.

Leicester, who was farthest from the point at which the sow and her young had erupted, had had time to collect his wits. He was able to take decent aim and skewer the second young one without mishap. This, however, left him with nothing but his hunting knife in hand to withstand the charge of the third, who had followed hard on the heels of his littermate. Crouching slightly, Leicester swung the knife up in an underhand blow. He did not catch the throat as he had hoped, but he did deflect the charge of the piglet just enough so that Sir Giles of Iford could finish it off.

Slowly the chaos of squealing pigs, yelping dogs, shouting men and violent physical activity began to die down. Everyone stood, panting and gazing around at the little clearing which was now almost carpeted with bodies. Dead dogs and dead pigs lay everywhere. Injured men groaned and struggled upright. Pembroke passed a bloody hand across his face in a kind of stunned amazement, levered himself up on his feet, and looked up at Alinor. Slowly a beatific smile of pleasure spread across his now blood-streaked features.

"I think," he said, chuckling deeply, "I think now we can safely blow the mort? I should have known nothing you arranged would be so tame as a simple boar hunt. Can I blow? Are there any more surprises awaiting us in this quiet little wood of yours?"

CHAPTER TWELVE

Although Alinor stoutly and repeatedly denied she was in any way responsible for the advent of the sow, she was grateful for it. There was no need to think about safe subjects for conversation at dinner time. No one had any interest in any subject but the hunt. Every hoofbeat and spear and knife thrust was described and analyzed. When the head of the boar was brought in formal procession to Lord Llewelyn, his remarkable feat was sung by a bard, with Owain hastily translating between the staves for the guests who did not understand Welsh. The head of the sow was then presented to Alinor.

Until that moment Ian had been very silent, partly because he was very much interested in hearing the details of the chase he had missed, and partly because he did not trust himself to speak more than a word at a time to Alinor. She had returned, much disheveled, with her hair completely loose, full of sticks and leaves, and had, like the other ladies, retired at once to put herself to rights. The rights were almost more than Ian could bear with the circumspection necessary before a crowd of people. Just as she tossed aside the torn and dusty wimple and her bloodstained riding dress, Alinor had cast off the hoyden, even cast off the lovely and lively young woman Ian had always known. Garbed in a soft, deep-green tunic and rich gold cotte, her eyes a little heavy-lidded with fatigue, her lips reddened by cold and exercise, Alinor suddenly presented to Ian an image of sultry sexuality. He did not know where to rest his eyes and had some difficulty in keeping his hands to himself.

The presentation of the sow's head brought his seething desire, his sense of loss for the Alinor he had known, who seemed to have disappeared, and his terror at the remembrance of her wild heedlessness of her own safety all to a head. Completely forgetting himself, Ian flushed brick red and roared, "Alinor! Did you not swear to me you would not hunt?"

"Would you have me sit and watch my friends and guests trampled and slashed without raising a finger to help them?" Alinor flashed back in no more moderate tone than his own.

The men at the high table whistled, clapped, and stamped their feet, urging on their host and hostess as one would encourage a pair of fighting dogs. This, naturally enough, reduced the combatants to laughter, but the militant light did not fade completely from either pair of eyes. Good breeding required that the battle be carried on in private, and so it would be at the proper time and place.

However, the fight was not to be continued that night when Ian and Alinor went up. Ian abruptly dismissed the menservants who had helped him up the stairs as soon as they reached the antechamber, and closed the door leading to the main room.

"You could have allowed them to help you into bed," Alinor protested. "We could talk as well with you lying down. You look tired and you look as if your leg hurts."

"I will not sleep in your bed tonight, Alinor," Ian said stiffly. If he lay there this night on the sheets that smelled of the same spicy scent—rose and something else—that Alinor used on her body, Ian knew he would not sleep at all. "There is a truckle bed set up for me in there." He gestured with his head toward the small chamber where Alinor's maids usually slept. "Do not argue with me," he added sharply. "I will not need any attendance tonight. I have something important to say, however, before we sleep. Oxford, as you might have noticed if you were not too busy killing sows, did not join the hunt."

"First of all, I did not swear I would not hunt," Alinor began heatedly. "All I said was——"

"Never mind that now." Ian said quite unfairly. "Oxford, as we both knew, came for a purpose, and he laid it before me while you were out. What does on your Irish lands, Alinor?"

"What does not?" Alinor remarked disgustedly, at once abandoning argument in favor of business. "My chief vassal there is one Sir Brian de Marnay, and until three years ago we had no trouble. The lands were never of great profit. The people are rude and the country largely untilled. Simon went there—let me see, it was just before Joanna was born—to see why so much land yielded so little profit. He was well received and confirmed that Sir Brian seemed loyal enough and that no more could be wrested from the land without doing more harm than good. Then our *dear* king appointed this madman Meiler FitzHenry as justiciar, and all went awry. He has driven the lesser barons into so determined a revolt that de Marnay can do nothing with them. Now rather than little, I receive nothing. Sir Brian wrote to Simon begging for help, but that was after Simon fell ill, and I did not even show him the letter."

"That was right. You could do no other way. Alinor——"

"Perhaps. Perhaps not. My heart ruled my head there, for Simon could at least have advised Sir Brian on the best tactics, which might have been of help. However, I could not bear that he should know he was called upon for help and unable to go. He fretted so much over his helplessness. So I told Sir Brian what had happened and begged him to do his best. I think he does. Simon said he was an honest man, and Simon was not easily befooled. Nonetheless, things go from bad to worse. I do not wish to let the lands go, yet—I have a fear of Ireland, Ian. I suppose it comes from my mother and father drowning on their passage home from there." She shuddered.

In spite of the dress and the glowing look of maturity, the old Alinor was still there. Ian took her hand and smiled at her. "That is not like you, Alinor. Think how near you came to drowning yourself on your way to the Holy Land. Do you fear that? And I know you used to go sailing for pleasure."

"It is true, and it is also true that I do not fear the sea, nor fear drowning. It is Ireland itself I fear—and not, it seems to me, for myself. Ian, why are we speaking of Ireland?"

"Because that was Oxford's purpose. He has large property there and, like you, has had nothing from it except complaints since FitzHenry has governed there."

"Why should he be different? William has been half crazy over what is happening, Isobel tells me. He has begged and prayed King John to let him go and at least set Leinster to rights, but the king has forbade it."

"So Oxford says also. To say it in plain words, Oxford wishes to avoid the king's commands and for a group of us to go and make peace there—at least on our own lands. To me it seems——"

"No, Ian! Oh, do not go to Ireland. Not now! I fear——"

"Certainly not now," Ian soothed, kissing the hand he held. "I must be married first, you know, and then there are those castellans of Simon's to settle with. In any case, the decision does not rest with me. Your holdings are small. What Oxford desires is that William of Pembroke should go. That is why he was so hot to come here. He wished to talk to Pembroke without giving John cause for suspicion."

A brisk war between her fear for and love of Ian and her passionate possessiveness was fought in Alinor's breast. Calling a temporary truce, she asked suspiciously, "If he was not urging you to undertake this enterprise, why should he miss a hunt to talk of it with you?"

"Out of the perfectly reasonable feeling that he had no right to press William of Pembroke to this action under my—or rather our—roof without our knowledge. Oxford will not go himself. That is reasonable, too; he is too old to be of much use. His part, and Salisbury's, is to prevent John from commanding Pembroke to return home, or declaring him a traitor, or taking any other action that will interfere with Pembroke's success."

"Salisbury thinks well of this plan?" Alinor asked unhappily.

"So well that he brought Oxford here," Ian pointed out.

"I do not know. I do not know. It does sound right and reasonable. If FitzHenry continues unchecked on the path he has taken, we will lose the Irish lands completely. I wish you had not told me. This weighs like lead upon my heart, and yet my mind says it is good."

"I think what weighs like lead upon your heart is your tiredness, Alinor. If you will go pig-sticking and riding like a madwoman, with your hair all undone, you must expect a little heaviness of spirit at the end of the day."

"What!" Alinor exclaimed, the more readily diverted because she knew her forebodings were baseless and useless. "Do you think I am so aged and decrepit that a hunt can wear me into a lassitude? I will show you yet my strength and endurance. We will see, between the two of us, who first cries, 'Enough! Enough!' "

The deep eyes lit. Ian's grip tightened on Alinor's hand, and he pulled her close. "Mayhap I will sleep in your bed this night after all," he muttered.

"Oh no you will not!" Alinor exclaimed briskly, pushing him away and wrenching her hand free of his grip.

"Why not, Alinor?" Ian pleaded. "What is the difference between tonight and three nights from now? I have been long without a woman. I want you."

She let him see that she was stirred by his appeal, but she nonetheless shook her head. "There is a difference to me. You will have made enough talk by closing the door thus, but that will be mended when I open it, showing all plainly that we remain as we entered."

"If that is all that troubles you, I will be quick," he urged. "Who will know that we were a few minutes more or less in talk?"

Alinor laughed in his face. "That may suit your need, but what of mine? Quickness is no recommendation to me."

"I will content you! I swear it!"

"Not tonight, you will not," Alinor reiterated, but with considerable effort.

"What is it about me that is not to your taste?" Ian cried passionately. "No other woman has ever so denied me, and the others had good reason to do so. Why will you not have me? We are betrothed husband and wife."

"Do not be such a fool," Alinor hissed, stretching her hand toward the latch of the door. "You are greatly to my taste, and I will have you with great pleasure. I will not deny that I desire you as greatly as you desire me. But I will not yield to your lust—nor to mine either —three days before my wedding. What you desire will be all the sweeter in three days time when it can be had without shame or a closed door or huddling back into clothing hastily shed." She flung open the door. "Gertrude! Ethelburga!" The maids slipped into sight from where they had been waiting. "Put Lord Ian to bed," Alinor said shortly. "I will tend to myself."

The next morning Ian was down before Alinor rose. When she appeared in riding dress to break her fast after hearing Mass, he ground his teeth.

"More pig-sticking?"

"I hope not," Alinor replied, smiling sweetly. "My huntsman was told to mark some great stags."

He opened his mouth and then gripped it tight shut. Alinor noted his heavy eyes and giggled very faintly.

She had been too tired to lie awake, lustful and un-
satisfied, and she would be too tired again tonight after
the wild ride she expected. Ian's rangy, wire-hard body
desperately needed exercise even more than it needed a
woman. Alinor guessed that was more than half his
trouble, but he was tied by the leg. He would be wild
by Sunday. So much the better. She noted that there
had been no talk last night of his heart. All his attention
was centered elsewhere.

By Friday dinnertime, after still another day of
idling, Ian was not fit to speak with, as Alinor had
expected. The lesser men took to avoiding him; the
greater picked their words with care and confined themselves to political subjects that did not raise contro-
versy. At table, Ian had given his attention largely to
Lord Llewelyn's wife Joan, exercising such charm that
Alinor saw there was more reason than his beautiful
face why no woman ever denied him. She was not even
mildly pricked with jealousy. Joan was sufficiently
attractive, but she was no match for Alinor, who burned
like a flame that dinnertime and evening in shades of
crimson, silver embroidered and set with brilliants.
Moreover, the light in Ian's dark eyes matched Alinor's
dress on the occasions when he turned them on her.

Had Ian been Simon, Alinor herself would have suggested easing his tension by a premarital mating. There
was nothing in Ian, however, to suggest Simon's ability
to assess such a thing calmly. Something told Alinor
that for all his discomfort and bad temper, Ian prized
her resistance above any proof of tenderness that yielding would give. Perhaps it was because most women
were so easy to him; he was the one who suggested that
they were married already in faith, while Alinor es-
poused the Church-held view that the deed must exist.
Yet to Alinor it did not matter, and she was sure that
to Ian it did. He would equate yielding to him now with
the possibility that she would yield to some other man
for some equally specious reason in the future.

Nonetheless she was sorry for him. Her eyes dwelt fondly on him, and a half smile curved her lips as she watched him listening to some tale Sir Giles was telling. Briefly, Ian's eyes lifted, caught hers, moved back to Sir Giles. Alinor grew a little worried when Sir Giles turned away suddenly and then marched across the hall toward her.

"How have I offended your new lord, Lady Alinor?" he asked angrily.

"Offended him?" Alinor repeated.

"I asked if he would look upon my youngest son and then, if he thought him fit, recommend him for fostering to a good house. Sir Simon did so much for the older boys, and I thought it a reasonable request."

"Ian denied you?" Alinor asked in an amazed voice.

Ian was kind and generous to a fault, and never proud, but it flashed through Alinor's mind that she had seen him only with his equals or superiors in rank and with such lesser folk as the serfs and villeins or men-at-arms. Perhaps he was high in his manner to vassals and gentle-born inferiors. He might consider such a manner necessary to keep them in their place and obedient to his will. Alinor's vassals were not accustomed to such treatment, however. In a social situation, Simon, and Alinor herself, had always addressed her vassals and castellans as equals—as friends. They were good men and understood the difference between a conversation and an order.

"He did not *deny* me," Sir Giles replied flushing slightly. "He listened at first, then looked away and began to scowl, and then he asked if I equated my son with a horse, that he should need to inspect its paces before buying. He said that if I believed the boy was ready, he would believe it also. The words were fair enough, but—but—I will speak the truth of my heart to you, Lady Alinor. You have known me long and will not take what I say amiss. His voice and look were such that, had he not been your lord, I would have struck him in the face."

"Oh, do not do that," Alinor managed to get out, and then could control herself no longer and burst out laughing. Sir Giles stiffened still more, drew in his breath sharply, and began to turn away. Alinor clung to his arm, gasping. "Please, please, do not be angry," she begged. "I am not laughing at you. Indeed, I am not. Ian was easy enough until he looked away, was he not?"

"He looked a little as if his mind was elsewhere, but, yes, he was courteous enough."

"His mind *is* elsewhere," Alinor chortled.

"I am sorry if I intruded my small matter upon some great affair," Sir Giles said even more stiffly.

"His great affair is between his legs," Alinor remarked crudely. "His words were for you and meant as a compliment. His black look was for me. My lord is a little wroth because I insist that we wait for the priest's blessing."

A look of illumination spread slowly across Sir Giles face, and he broke into a broad grin. His eyes ran over Alinor. "Poor man," he said feelingly.

"I am sure he will do his best for your son," Alinor added when she stopped laughing at Sir Giles's sincere sympathy for a tormented man. "What do you desire for the boy?"

"You know I can give him nothing," Sir Giles responded soberly. "A horse and armor, a little money. If he does not have a place where he can get honorable service, he must go the tourney route or sell his sword in whatever war he can find."

"Let me think upon it," Alinor said. "William of Pembroke would have taken him, but that is no safe house for the boy to be in at this time. We will find something," she assured him.

Later in the evening she noticed that Ian had hobbled over and was speaking earnestly with Sir Giles. Alinor was glad he realized he had offended her vassal and was trying to mend matters. Still, she was very relieved when the good weather broke that night and Saturday was a day of pouring rain. They were all pent within the castle, which could and did lead to minor conflicts, especially among the younger men. Ian, however, had plenty of company and, from the bearing of the men who formed in groups around him, plenty to occupy his mind.

After dusk had fallen, a guest they had almost despaired of appeared, riding through the pouring rain. Alinor raised her eyes to heaven for help and prayed— it did not seem appropriate to curse. Peter des Roches, Bishop of Winchester, had at last come, as he had promised, to perform the marriage. With him, however, he brought two more unexpected guests, William, Bishop of London, and Eustace, Bishop of Ely, and Alinor had to find some suitable place to put them.

"We will be the firmest-wed pair in the entire realm," Alinor said to Ian as they parted for the night for the last time. "Three bishops should surely be enough to tie fast the knot. Which one of us," she teased, "did they think would seek to undo it?"

"Not I," Ian replied.

He was standing in the doorway to the small chamber in which he slept. This night he did not argue or plead. Although he ate Alinor with his eyes, he said no more. The silence, the hot eyes, came close to undoing her. Alinor found herself several paces closer to Ian before she realized that she had moved. Still silent, he had stretched out a hand. It trembled just a little. Alinor stared at it. Even his hands were beautiful, she thought. They were slender and long-fingered. Alinor thought of their touch on her body, uttered a small gasp, and fled.

That night, half laughing, half crying, Alinor blamed herself for her amusement at Ian's torments. She did not sleep well. The next day, however, was much easier for everyone. By custom, the ladies remained apart from the men. Bread and cheese and wine were carried up to them, and Father Francis came up to say Mass in an improvised chapel while the bishops officiated below. The morning was given to the examination of one another's dresses, to trying these jewels and those. Alinor's wedding gown, brocaded gold and orange velvet, was laid out and drew exclamations of envy and pleasure.

Midmorning, Ian's squires craved admittance and were bidden to enter. "Bride gift," passed from mouth to mouth, and the women clustered close. The small casket the boys bore was a work of art worth a king's ransom in itself, carved of ivory, bound in gold, and set with gems. It was deep for a jewel box. Alinor opened it carefully, looked inside, and drew breath. Pearls, glowing with a life of their own, marvelously matched for color, lay within. She drew them forth, and drew, and drew, while around her sighs changed to gasps. Someone took the box, and someone else piled the strand into Alinor's hands until both hands were full and the loops fell over. At last they found the clasp, a golden hook that fastened to a short chain that held another marvel—a glowing, sparkling, golden stone as large as a hen's egg, but flatter, carved into the likeness of a phoenix rising from a bed of flames.

That wonder kept them all occupied until it was time to dress in the finery that had earlier been displayed. Alinor could not help wondering, as Lady Llewelyn, Lady Salisbury, and Lady Pembroke wound the pearls around her neck, whether she would be able to support their weight, but they were not heavy. As light to bear, Alinor thought, as a strong man's body in the act of love. She was deeply grateful to Ian, not only for displaying the incredible value he set upon her, but for giving her a jewel that Simon had never favored. She wondered now whether this enormous celebration was only for political purposes. Ian was so very kind. He had known of her first wedding, bereft of all ceremony, bereft of guests and of any celebration at all, darkened by an angry King Richard and a miserable, weeping Queen Berengaria. Clever Ian. Had he planned that this should be as great a contrast as possible? that it should wake no unhappy memories?

If it was his plan, he had succeeded. It was impossible that Alinor should not remember Simon in this moment, but the memory was not sad or bitter. It was of something warm and good, strong and safe, but so very different from what was taking place, from what she felt and expected to feel, that it could wake no unhappiness in her. With brilliant eyes, half-smiling lips and light steps, Alinor went down to forge the first firm link in the chain of the new life she was making.

Everything was different from that first wedding. The happy chatter of the women as they followed her down the stairs, the affectionate kisses Isobel gave her as she placed Alinor's cloak over her shoulders; William's sober-sad yet honest approval as he lifted her to her horse; the road, bright in sunlight, frosty cold now that the rain had ended; the people lining the road, shouting joy for her, cheering anew as Ian and the men followed the train of women. The whole road, from the gates of the palisade around the keep to the town itself, was deep in common folk—first her own men-at-arms and the castle servants, many in tears; then the servants and retainers of her guests; then the serfs from the countryside, who threw wheat from their scanty store, the symbol of peace and plenty; then the townsfolk, the better and the lesser. Here and there a flower was thrown, a winter rose, a costmary, an iris, carefully nurtured at home for a little color and joy during the bitter winter months. In all the cold, Alinor was suffused with warmth; her people loved her and wished her well.

Nothing was a shadow of the past, not even her own voice or Ian's giving the responses. This time there were no doubts, no fears, no oppression. Alinor heard her responses, and Ian's, wing clear and firm to the outer circle of witnesses in the church porch, heard the happy *"Fiat! Fiat!"* of approval roar back in confirmation.

The women pressed around Alinor to kiss her and wish her well, and the men to kiss and embrace Ian. William of Pembroke said soberly, "God help you; she is a devil unconfined. But if you treat her ill, you must answer to me." At which Ian did not take offense. It would have been hard to find anything that would offend him that day. Besides, he understood. William had stood as father to the bride, Alinor being totally without male relations to protect her interests. He was not implying any distrust of Ian, as the first part of his statement indicated, merely affirming that he took his responsibility seriously. Sir Giles behind Pembroke laughed aloud. "Lady Alinor can take care of herself; you had done better to have warned Lord Ian to guard himself." Yet Ian had almost to fight for his right to lift Alinor to the saddle for the return to the keep. Part of the reason for the rush to assist him was, of course, concern for his lameness, but a good part was also affection for Alinor. No man wished her day to be spoiled, and all feared that Ian would falter and drop her.

He did not, and would not have done so to ease any pain. They rode back, side by side now, through the streets of the town where oxen, sheep and pigs were already near-finished roasting at bonfires on almost every crossing, and huge tuns of ale and coarse wine were being broached. Of all the businesses, only the bakeshops were open. Bread and cake and pies were to be had for the asking. On Alinor's wedding day, no man, woman or child would go hungry or thirsty or need to beg.

They were cheered for that, of course, but it was for more than that. There were those who ran along beside Alinor's mare to kiss her foot or her stirrup or the hem of her gown. Many she called by name. It was as well,

Ian thought, that he meant well by his wife. If he had ever doubted that she could have any man she did not like killed or maimed into a helpless hulk, he doubted it no longer. An enemy to the Lady of Roselynde would be safe nowhere, neither in the town nor in the country-side, nor in the keep, either.

It was plain from the surprise and delight with which Alinor received some of the wondrous dishes presented to her that, although she had planned the meal, she had not planned those. A representation of Roselynde Keep was presented to her, complete in every detail, its walls and towers of pastry, the moat filled with honey, blued with crystallized violets, the sea breaking in a froth of white meringue upon the rocks and beaches below. A representation of the wedding followed, showing the church front, the three bishops with their staffs (two having obviously been crammed in at the last moment), the bride and groom (Alinor smiled; her maids' tongues had been busy for her orange and gold gown and Ian's emerald green were faithfully depicted), and the crowd of onlookers. How many extra days and nights of labor, how much thought and ingenuity her people had willingly added to the already onerous task they faced only to give her pleasure!

The entertainment was as rich as the food. Minstrels had been summoned from everywhere Alinor's messengers could reach. They played, sang, juggled, danced, and performed miracles of tumbling. Trained bears jigged lumberingly to tunes and were fed honeyed tidbits in reward; dogs formed pyramids, danced together, leapt through flaming hoops. And another surprise awaited Alinor. To her chagrin, she had not been able to engage a true troupe of players. However, before the guests became stupid with food or befuddled with wine, Sir John d'Alberin rose from his place, bellowed for silence and a clear floor, and announced that some acts of mimicry would be performed. It was, he said, a token of affection from Alinor's vassals and castellans.

The pieces were hilarious. All, of course, dealt with marriage, and not too kindly, but the ultimate was one about a domineering woman who produced disaster after disaster with unfailing regularity, which her patient husband repaired with equally unfailing ingenuity.

"How do they dare?" Lady Llewelyn hissed across Alinor's convulsed husband to the new-made, maligned wife.

But Alinor was laughing as heartily as anyone else. She knew they dared out of love and trust. Those who wished to shake off her domination were not here. Every man who had come knew he would be expected to renew his vows of fealty publicly before three bishops, the king's half brother, and the greatest soldier England had, as well as before his brother vassals and castellans, who would thereby be sworn to join with his lady to punish him if he violated those vows. The ceremony was set for the following day, when all the guests would still be present. Some would linger for a few days or even a week more, but many had pressing business and would leave as soon as the swearing was over.

Through the whole day and the evening when, because Ian could not dance, he spent his time hobbling from group to group to soothe drunken quarrels, there was not a cloud on his brow. Moment by moment, he saw his fulfillment draw nearer. No doubt that Alinor grieved for Simon darkened Ian's mind, nor had he missed her genuine eagerness for the consummation of their marriage despite her resistance to a premature coupling. It was not until he saw the great ladies approaching Alinor to start the bedding ceremony that apprehension touched him.

It was not that Ian doubted his skill as a lover in a general way. He knew he was well able to satisfy any normally passionate woman, and he was quite sure

Alinor was perfectly normal. Nor was he reluctant to perform his marital duty; in fact, he thought wryly, watching his none-too-sober friends bear down on him, there was his trouble. He was a bit too eager. Again, in a general way, that would not have mattered—but this first time— Fool, he told himself, think of something else. You will be finished before they get your clothes off if you do not.

The immediate problem was solved by Ian's drunken escort. Ian had dispensed with his splint that morning, feeling that it would be an unwelcome adjunct to a wedding bed. His friends, however, were in no fit state to help him up the stairs properly, and the pangs in his knee served, temporarily, to cool his passion. The calming effect did not long outlast his arrival in the upper great chamber where, for lack of space in Alinor's bedchamber, the disrobing ceremony would take place.

Alinor, gowned and bejeweled and wimpled in a gold veil so fine that her white skin gleamed through, was an exquisite creature. Alinor quite naked, except for the black mane that hung to the middle of her thighs, was enough to bulge a man's eyes and stop his breath. Then the women drew back her hair and lifted it so that all her perfections and blemishes would be clearly visible. Ian's prompt reaction brought shouts of laughter, applause, snapping fingers, and stamping feet.

The jests flew thick and fast, the ladies as quick to laugh and top one sally with another as the gentlemen. There was no fault to be found with either party. Alinor's vigorous life had prevented her pregnancies from marking her. Except that her breasts were somewhat fuller, her belly a little rounder, and a few faint blue lines of stretching were apparent, she might have been an unwed maid. This fact drew some complimentary remarks, but it was Ian's condition, naturally enough, that called forth most of the comments. It was great fun, but in spite of the roaring fire, it was not comfortable in the month of December to stand naked for long. Isobel saw that Alinor was shivering, and pulled at her husband's sleeve to point out the bride and groom were cold. Wine had temporarily wiped Simon from Pembroke's mind.

"For God's sake," he bellowed, "let them go or they will both be as stiff and blue with cold as Ian's knee."

"Wait, wait," Salisbury shouted, as bedgowns were brought forward to wrap the chilled pair, "what if the knee remains stiff? Will you repudiate Ian for lameness, Lady Alinor?"

It was a serious consideration, but Alinor had had a few drinks, too. "No," she responded gravely, but with dancing eyes. "I take cognizance of all stiff parts, knees and otherwise, and I state before witnesses that I will not repudiate my husband if those parts remain stiff."

"Alinor!" Ian exclaimed.

"Quick," Llewelyn exclaimed, "into bed with them before they can begin to quarrel. I do not wish to spend any time making peace. I have an appetite that needs to be satisfied at once."

A few minutes more of chaos terminated with Alinor and Ian side by side in her big bed. One more flurry of laughter and some urgent calls for action, and they were alone. The silence, broken only by the hissing of the flames in the fireplace, was a shocking contrast. Alinor turned her head, still smiling at the last jests, but Ian was staring straight ahead into the dark outside the area illuminated by the night candle.

"Did I really offend you?" Alinor asked, striving to keep the chagrin from her voice.

"No, of course not." He turned now and smiled, but his mouth was stiff and his body tense. "I— I——"

"What is it, Ian?" Alinor asked, reaching toward him.

"Do not touch me!"

Alinor's eyes widened. That was a protest for a virgin maid, not for an eager man.

"Oh God!" Ian choked on laughter. "I do not mean that. I mean— Some nights past I swore I would content you. I am not so sure I can."

"What?" Alinor shook her head in disbelief and surprise. "How can you say such a thing? Two minutes ago you were showing the whole world how able and ready you are to content me."

"I am too ready," Ian cried, laughing helplessly. "I greatly fear that if I lay one hand upon you or you upon me, my overripe readiness will burst."

Alinor giggled, although her breath was coming short and quick. "Think of something nasty," she suggested, "disemboweled horses, slimy drinking water——"

But Alinor was not really worried. She knew it would not matter. She had been longer without mating than Ian, and the sight of him, the rough jests, were stimulation enough. She needed no preparing this night; she was as ready as he. He could hardly be too quick for her this time, unless he could not hold himself for even two strokes or three. She leaned closer, as if to whisper more horrors in his ear, and tickled it with her tongue instead.

That was enough. Ian pushed Alinor flat and flung himself upon her. The movement wrenched his knee cruelly, but he did not feel it then. Once, his shaft slid past her sheath. Alinor shifted eagerly and the second thrust brought him safely home. Together they groaned as if mortally wounded, but neither was dead yet. For one long moment Ian held his breath, straining chest and shoulders upward and away while his hips pressed down, perfectly still. Alinor held her breath, too. Then his head came forward, his eyes opened; his battle had been fought and won. Gently he let himself down upon her, sought her lips; slowly he began to move, seeking the position and rhythm that would bring her to joy.

"You are no oath breaker," Alinor said eventually. Her head was nestled comfortably into the hollow of

Ian's shoulder, her whole body pressed against the length of his. Both were exceedingly well pleased with themselves and with each other, but Alinor's satisfaction was somewhat the keener. For that, although she did not think of it, she had to thank Simon also. Among other bitternesses of loss Alinor suffered, not the least was the loss of the comfort of a warm, strong body beside her in her bed. That emptiness was now filled.

"It was a near thing," Ian sighed, grinning, "and I will give credit where it is due. You delayed me not at all in the performance of my promise." He sighed again, contentedly. Then the arm around her stiffened a trifle. "We left the bed curtains open," he said in a low voice

"What of it?" Alinor asked sleepily. "The children will not come in at this hour."

Ian's lips, parted for speaking, remained parted merely to smile. True enough. It did not matter. This was his bed, his wife, his right. There was no need to hide his desire or his satisfaction from anyone. His! Completely and entirely his! Not to be shared with a legal husband as so many "loves" of the past; all her beauty, all her passion—his. Ian drew a deep breath of happiness and gratitude, for what Alinor displayed was truly a clean passion, not lust. The enormity of her pleasure, the ecstatic cries and writhings were an additional joy to him and no sign of weakness in her. Knowing what pleasure she denied herself, yet she had been able to deny herself. The memory of Alinor's pleasure sent a flush of heat through Ian's loins. His arm tightened around her; his hand sought her breast. Quite unaware of the towering virtues with which she had been endowed—which would have given her great amusement had she known—Alinor made a sleepy, contented sound. Ian bent his head to kiss her, but found only her cheek. Satisfied and half asleep, Alinor had slipped back into the familiar role of long-time wife.

"Have you cried 'enough'?" Ian whispered.

The voice, rich and pleasant, but very different from

Simon's bass rumble, reminded Alinor she was a new-wedded wife. "I thought *you* had," she replied, stretching sinuously.

"I have only blown the froth off the beer," he said. "Now I am ready to drink in earnest." He started to turn toward her but desisted with a slight gasp.

Alinor could feel him gathering himself for another effort, and she put a hand on his shoulder to keep him flat. "You hurt your knee," she murmured. "I should have thought of that, but my mind was elsewhere."

"Mine also. That was how I came to hurt it. It does not matter," Ian insisted.

"No, of course not," Alinor agreed, "but there is no reason for you to be uncomfortable. Lie still and let me play the master. You will not regret it."

It was a novel idea to Ian. For one thing, his hasty couplings of guilt had left little time for experimentation. Even when husbands are known to be absent, there are always other prying eyes to avoid. For another, Ian had always automatically assumed the dominant role as a lover and, because he seldom remained long with a mistress, none had known him well enough or securely enough to suggest innovations for which there was neither need nor excuse. He did not answer, but Alinor could feel the tension of preparing to move go out of him.

She lifted herself on one elbow to lean over him, kissed his lips softly, moved her mouth to suck his throat and then his ear. Her free hand caressed his body, playing it as a skilled minstrel plays a harp. Simon was not a young man, and Alinor had been taught many tricks that wake and build passion. When Ian began to writhe and strain upward toward her, she left off what she was doing with her mouth to murmur, "Quiet. Be quiet. Your pleasure will be greater if you lie still."

He was wide-eyed and open-mouthed, gasping air, when she mounted him. Even then she played with him until he moaned aloud and whispered, "Please, please," but Alinor knew he had no desire to end the sweet torment. He could have ended it at any moment by gripping her and going into action himself. Instead, he cried for mercy, but he lay very still. Only it could not last forever. As Ian's passion mounted, so did Alinor's. There came a time at last when she could no longer think of him at all. The indescribable pleasure-pain of orgasm took her. She plunged upon him, unheeding, gripping his hair, crying aloud.

That time it was Ian who spoke first, when he had caught his breath a little. "Enough," he whispered, laughing feebly. "If you do that to me again, you will kill me. You have made good your threat. I cry, 'Enough.' "

CHAPTER THIRTEEN

"Have I ever told you that you are the most beautiful woman I have ever seen?"

In the act of pulling the bedcurtains shut, Alinor turned. "No, you have not," she replied tartly, "and it is just as well, because it would have given me grave doubts as to your truthfulness. Beautiful I may be, but I am no match for Queen Isabella and a goodly number of others."

Ian laughed and shook his head. "There are other things than perfection of feature that make beauty. Perhaps if you were both statues, Isabella would be lovelier, but I care little for statues. Come back to bed."

He laughed again at the conflict in her face—pleasure at the demand, a ready kindling of desire, concern for the lateness of the hour and the many tasks waiting. "I am sorry to disappoint you," he continued, "but I have no ardent intentions. Well, I do have, but I must needs master them. I have a good deal to tell you, and I do not know where else or when else we may be private."

"Ireland?" Alinor asked apprehensively, drawing on her bedrobe and returning to sit beside her husband.

"Yes, but not for me as yet. That can wait. The first thing is whether Adam knows his part in today's ceremony."

"Yes, of course. I have been over it with him often enough, and his armor and sword are ready. God forbid some devil will enter him and make him misbehave, but I do not think it. He is delighted with his own importance."

Ian's face softened with affection. "Even when he is a devil, you cannot help but love him. But I must warn you that Adam is like to put us into trouble. He has so enchanted Leicester, Oxford and Salisbury that I believe all *three* will offer to foster him."

"Mary have mercy!" Alinor exclaimed. "How can I say no to any one of them? Will they come to me today?"

"I do not know. I tried to put them off. I told them—what they knew—that the boy was too young, and then I said straight that I wished to be sure how the king received the news of our marriage before I burdened any one with a child of ours. I mean——"

Alinor touched Ian's hand. "Say what you will. If Simon can hear, it will give him only joy to know what you feel."

It was not Simon's reaction Ian was concerned with. Alinor had changed since the last time they had spoken of the children in this sense. Thank God for that, Ian thought. He knew he had been foolish. In the idle weeks of waiting for the reavers, or just waiting, desperate to think of anything except Alinor and incapable of drawing his mind far from her, he had planned this and that for "his" children. He had occasionally called them that even when Simon was alive, but now it was a habit. Had Alinor taken it ill, things would have been difficult. Do not be a fool, Ian reminded himself. Just because she does not fly into a rage over this and she coupled with you gladly, do not leap ahead too fast.

"Ian," Alinor continued after a moment of thoughtful silence, "he is too young, but mayhap it would be well to—to promise him to someone, someone the king will not be willing to offend. When the vassals and castellans have sworn to him, he must swear to John or you must swear for him. Once he is brought to the king's notice——"

"So you thought of that, too. I did not like to say it for fear of worrying you. Yet John is not all evil. He does not speak spite, or show it either, to Pembroke's boys, and he treats them full lovingly."

"That may be true, but they are older than Adam. Moreover, I do not want Adam in the king's train. I do not like what I hear about the men John has about him. I have had my differences with my grandfather and with Simon, too, on the subject of honor and duty, but when all is said and done I know that without them a man is no more than a two-legged beast. Adam——"

"You do the child an injustice," Ian interrupted hotly. "He has high pride, and his soul is clean of evil. A little mischief is nothing. He owns a fault bravely, even when he knows he will be whipped for it."

"Yes, because he has been taught honor, and he has had as examples only Simon and you—even Beorn has a rough honor. Perhaps you are right and he would hold fast to his early teaching, but why put such a burden on a youngling? Why tear his soul? Why make him ashamed of the master he must serve? There is another thing. Simon's lands are new bought and new seissined. There is no long loyalty to the Lemagne arms and name. Adam must know the art of war and know it well. He will need to overmaster his vassals before their loyalty is perfect."

"What the devil do you think of me?" Ian burst out furiously. "Will I let a man deny my son his right?"

"Ian, Ian." Alinor took his face between her hands and kissed him. "You cannot shield him forever. Some day he will need to face them, God willing he live to be a man. Once he has his spurs, he must fight his own battles. You cannot even go with him to advise him, or the men will credit you, and he will be nothing in their eyes."

He gnawed his lower lip, and Alinor remembered Simon doing that when his heart warred with his head. Likely Ian had picked up the habit from years of watching it. His face was rough with beard stubble, and it scraped her hands when he turned his head to kiss her palm.

"You speak so calmly of it." Ian's voice was husky and muffled by Alinor's hand across his lips.

"It is a woman's fate to watch her men go out, and pray in pain for their return."

Ian shuddered. "I do not envy you."

"It has its compensations. You do not know the joy of seeing the beloved ride home safe. Oh, such joy. Only in heaven, if what the priests tell us is true, can there be its equal."

"I do not know. It is said that women are frail, yet such pains and such joys would kill me. Well, that is not to the point. You are right, and in any case I will not live forever. I will do what I can, and you also must say what you can to discourage Oxford, if he should speak to you. He is too old. That leaves only Leicester and Salisbury."

"I suppose you think William—I mean Pembroke—a pox on so many Williams—is also too old? It would be easy to say that Simon had already promised—but then there is the trouble with the king."

"It is not that, nor that he is old. Oxford acts like an old man; he goes no more to war but sends his sons. I think that is why he desires a young one around the house. Pembroke is different. He will be active in the field until he dies, but he will not be in England—at least, I do not think so. That much is settled, that Pembroke will leave for Ireland as soon as he can gather a suitable force and the weather will permit. That will be no brief work. It will be a matter of some years. You spoke so ill of Ireland that I did not think you would wish Adam to go there."

"No," Alinor replied emphatically, "not to Ireland. Not Adam. Besides, Adam has no place there. The kind of battle that will be fought there will teach him little he will need to know. Simon's lands are all rich and well-castled and they are here in Sussex and in Leicester, near Robert's." She turned her head a little so that Ian could not see her eyes. "And you? Will you go?"

"I told you, not yet. I will provide a force—I have not yet decided whether to levy on the vassals or hire mercenaries. Later, when Pembroke knows what more is needed, I will go myself, bringing such additional aid as he will direct."

"And Oxford? And Salisbury?"

"Oxford will send men and, I think, his youngest son. Salisbury has offered to send men also, and that I cannot understand. He has no stake in Ireland, except— If you want my thoughts, he does this for John's sake."

"What!" Alinor exclaimed. "Ian, if it is John's desire to get Pembroke to go to Ireland, I must warn Isobel to stop him. And, as for you, you will not go even if I must——"

"Alinor!" Ian said sharply. "I will go where it is right for me to go, and where I have passed my word I will go, even if hell should bar the way. Fortunately, we will not need to quarrel over this. John has no desire for Pembroke to go to Ireland; he has thrice forbidden it. You did not understand what I meant. I believe it is Salisbury who desires Pembroke's absence so that John cannot demand of Pembroke something he cannot in honor give."

"You make my head go around," Alinor said irritably. "I thought the idea was Oxford's."

"Indeed it was, and I think Oxford brought the idea to Salisbury only to discover whether it would bring down John's wrath upon him. Salisbury then saw how great good for all could be gained. Look at it thus. John is already greatly hated and is not mending matters by this new tax. There is no man in England, or anywhere else, who does not honor Pembroke or who does not know how patiently he has borne the slights the king has placed upon him. If John should demand what is not lawful of Pembroke and drive him into rebellion, it is not impossible all England would rise with him. Even if it does not, the anger and bitterness of the barons will be a hundredfold increased. Each will see himself treated as Pembroke is."

"Ian," Alinor breathed softly, "is there no way to be rid of this king?"

"He is my king. I do not wish to be rid of him," Ian replied firmly. "I wish to control him so that he cannot do harm. I tell you there is good in him also. Salisbury is a clever man. He will send Pembroke to Ireland to tame the Irish. For a year or two, John will be sufficiently busy coming to terms with his new Archbishop of Canterbury to have no thoughts of one who is out of sight. Which reminds me, I have yet to tell you what brought *three* bishops to our wedding—but that can wait. Then John will go to Ireland with an army that need do nothing beyond marching about. Thus John will win a great victory, and in his pride he will forgive Pembroke—who will have done all the work— and all will be well again."

"I understand what you have said about John being an English king. Nonetheless, my gorge rises——"

"Swallow it, then! At least the king is coming to know he is no great soldier. If he can have the appearance of leading, he is content to leave such matters to Salisbury now. In many things he is hated for what is no fault of his own. John is greatly blamed for the rise in taxes, but if he had not received a kingdom deep in debt owing to Richard's crusade and Richard's ransom, the taxes would be much less."

"Perhaps, but you know, Ian, it is the man, not the money. Oh, I do not love to part with what is mine any more than another." That made her husband snort with laughter. Alinor was a good deal more reluctant than most to part with anything. She cast him a glance of amusement mingled with irritation, but it did not divert her from her subject. "It is what I said before. A man without honor is a two-legged beast, and not fit to be a king."

"I wonder if any man is fit to be a king," Ian replied slowly. "It is so large a thing. Those from the north want one thing; those from the south another; and a man raised to the customs of England thinks scorn on the customs of Wales, while those touched with the luxury of the East, those of Poitiers, condemn all of us here in England as barbarians. Yet the king must content all. And all the while he must watch those who would wrest his power and place from him—but he must not act unjustly. Is it any wonder that even a good man runs mad in the end. Hardly, even with good will, can he do what is right. If he yield gently to demands, he is called weak and scorned. If he forces order, he is called tyrant. Moreover, he is expected to spin justice out of his gut like a spider, regardless of his own humors or desires; yet he is condemned if the justice is tainted with bile or lust."

"What are you saying? That we should have no king?"

"God forbid! That way lies chaos and hell. No, but it seems to me that there should be some writing, almost like unto a marriage contract, whereby the two parties —on the one hand, the barons and the people, and on the other hand, the king—would know what is required of them. Alinor, think how little we have to quarrel about——"

That drew a spurt of laughter from Alinor, who knew that two people in love could always find plenty of grounds for quarreling. Ian laughed briefly, too, not being such an idiot as to believe that marriage to Alinor would be all sweetness and light. He foresaw already that there would be some raging contests over the question of his departure for Ireland. That, however, would be a quarrel that grew out of tenderness and love and fear for him. Whatever the outcome of the argument itself, however angry each was at the outcome, no bitterness from it would taint the long future. They both understood Ian's deeper meaning in spite of the laughter. Both thought at once of the ceremony of homage that would be enacted that day and thought it was an excellent example. If their marriage contract had not specified that Alinor would continue to take homage from her vassals, Ian might have expected to do so. Then a different kind of quarrel, one that might end in permanent separation or even in war, might have arisen.

"Doubtless," Alinor remarked, "between your temper and mine we will find the wherewithal for a few cross words. Nonetheless, I see what you mean. The difficulty——"

"I," Ian interrupted sententiously, "have a very sweet temper." They both laughed again, but Ian sobered quickly. "The difficulty, of course, is to convince the king to sign such a contract. He will see it certainly as a means to chain him down."

"Which it is. Is this your thought on how to cage the wolf, Ian?"

"Not mine alone, but I had some part in it. Contracts, as you may imagine, have been on my mind for some time."

"It is a good thought, but I cannot see, short of rebellion, how to force the king to sign."

Ian rubbed at the stubble of his beard nervously. "I will not have part in any rebellion. I am sworn to the king. Still, it might be managed. There are many things the barons say are their right that the king contests. The contract could be sweetened by chaining the barons, too."

"But then neither will be willing to sign!"

"I have some hope of it. It must be carefully written and not done in any haste. If each side thinks there is more of benefit in it for him—the Church might be of some help, and Langton, if he be chosen for archbishop— Alinor, this is no time to be talking of such matters. We will have time enough when our guests are gone. What must be settled is whether you wish to make some commitment either to Leicester or Salisbury about Adam and, if so, to which."

"It is no easy choice. Leicester would be kind to Adam and would not take his mischief amiss, having a merry nature of his own. His lands are not far divided from Simon's—Adam's, I mean—and he is wise in the management of his vassals. He is a good man of his hands also; Simon said he fought well in the Holy Land. I have nothing to say against him except that he leans to his father's teachings and will not fight in the king's wars if he can avoid it. This is good and wise, but no way for a boy to learn of battle."

"I do not think you need to worry overmuch for that," Ian remarked drily. "If what I fear comes, there will be fighting enough. In any case, there are bound to be disaffected vassals that Leicester must deal with or, in these times, attacks upon his vassals for which he must bring them aid."

"I suppose that is true, but I have come much to your way of thinking about Salisbury. Certainly he is a good man, and Adam could learn from him all there is to know about war, but against that, his lady could sour any young man upon marriage for life." Ian chuckled acknowledgment of that, but Alinor continued, "And also there is the problem that he is so much at court that Adam could almost as well go to the king."

"There is something else I had better tell you. It may be easier to put off Salisbury than Leicester. Salisbury can be told that you do not wish to make a double tie to one house—that will not give him offense; he will acknowledge it as reasonable. Salisbury desires to make contract for Joanna with his son Geoffrey."

"No!" Alinor exclaimed explosively.

Ian was shocked speechless for a moment. He had grown very fond of Geoffrey in the past few weeks and, although he had sense enough not to make any commitment to Salisbury, reminding both of them at the last moment that Joanna was Alinor's daughter and not his to dispose of, he had been delighted with the idea. The shock was of infinite benefit in that it gave Ian time to control his sense of outrage and permitted him to ask quietly, "Why no? Do you object to the boy's bastardy? Salisbury is mad for him and may well have him legitimatized. In any case, he is no pauper. Both the boy's grandfather and Salisbury have assigned property to be his, and I am sure Salisbury would find more to give him——"

"Do not be foolish. Why should I care that the boy is a bastard! His mother was not unknown or ignoble. We know his blood, and it is good on both sides. And you should know I do not care about what lands he brings, either. Joanna will be rich enough to marry as she pleases—and that is what she shall do."

"Marry as she pleases?"

Ian could have been no more amazed if Alinor had said Joanna would grow wings, fly off, and live in a tree. Girls simply did not choose their own husbands. Kind and thoughtful parents tried to match temperament and age so that their daughters would be happy. Ambitious parents used daughters as pawns to further their plans for increased power or land, without a thought for the girl's fate. Girls, after all, were born to marry to cement land boundaries or to breed children for a mingling of blood lines. Their feelings about the husband who shared those duties were totally irrelevant. Older women sometimes did make a free choice, as Alinor had—well, almost free—but not young girls.

Intemperate words rose to Alinor's lips, but before they poured out she realized that they might also be cruel words. Certainly on this day, it would be a bitter thing to remind Ian that her first marriage had been to her own pleasure; indeed, that she had followed Simon halfway around the world, scaling mountains and crossing deserts only to be near him. To say that at this time would imply that she had married Ian only from necessity—and it was not true. That thought and the memory of her recent pleasure washed away her quick anger.

"You would not wish Joanna to be unhappy, would you?" Alinor asked softly.

"Wish her unhappy! You know how much I love her. That was why I was so pleased when Salisbury suggested Geoffrey. Think how suitable they are in age and in disposition also. You do not know the boy as well as I, but he is kind and gentle, with a most loving heart— and he is drawn to her. That was what gave Salisbury the idea. He could look considerably higher for a wife, even for his bastard, as well you know. The thing is, Salisbury is most anxious for Geoffrey's happiness. He feels he has done the boy a wrong, and he will go far to amend it."

Alinor could only be grateful that she had held her tongue. It was plain from what Ian said that he was considering Joanna's happiness. Nonetheless, she had no intention of contracting her daughter until she was sure of Joanna's preference.

"Unfortunately," Alinor sighed, "a woman's heart is not always a reasonable thing. I am sure what you say about Geoffrey is true, but if he does not wake her heart and body, he might be a saint and as beautiful as the morning and still make Joanna bitterly unhappy."

Ian's expression froze. "I see," he said quietly.

"My God," Alinor cried, having fallen all unaware into the pit she thought she had avoided, "you do not think I mean me as well!" She smiled at him. "Did I seem cold to you last night?"

He had to laugh, even though doubt still clawed at him. One thing he knew, Alinor had not been unhappy in her first marriage. What could she know about the subject then, unless— Well, he guessed she had not welcomed this marriage. Perhaps she had been unhappy and then had come to terms with her fate. But if so, all the more should she realize that Joanna would also adjust. Women did adjust. Yes, but Ian knew very well that sometimes they did not adjust, and then they cast their eyes around and betrayed their husbands—and that did not make them happy, either. It was not impossible that Alinor was right.

"What am I to say to Salisbury? Do you wish to speak to him or shall I deny him outright?"

"Do not deny him."

Alinor had been thinking over the subject, and she began to come around a little to Ian's point of view. The boy was a dear. His connections were wide and mighty. If Joanna could be inclined in Geoffrey's direction, there could be few more excellent matches.

"You say Salisbury is desirous that Geoffrey should be happy," Alinor went on, "and that he asks for Joanna because he sees his son is inclined toward her. Well, tell him that I feel just so about my—our—daughter." She took Ian's hand. "Now that I have had a moment to think of it, I am aware that it was your thought for Joanna that made you wish to bind her to Geoffrey. And Joanna, although she has spirit enough, is not such a hellion as I. If she casts her eyes upon him, I will be very happy in the match. No, certainly do not deny Salisbury. Say to him only that there is no unhappiness equal to that of a husband who loves his wife when the wife does not return his affection."

Ian's jaw clenched just as if Alinor had incautiously probed a painful wound, but she did not notice. She was looking past him, thinking of Joanna and Geoffrey and their behavior toward each other that day they had been together in the keep. Alinor had not had the time to observe them since Ian had brought Geoffrey back with him, but from what she had seen herself she was sure that Salisbury was right when he said there was a liking between them. Alinor was one of the few who did not feel that was enough. She flicked a glance at Ian that took in the tumbled hair, the long lashes on downcast eyes, the sensuous mouth, clear and fine in the black-stubbled face. A physical pang of that combination of lust and affection that is called love twisted her middle just below her heart.

There was underneath Joanna's apparently placid exterior a passion as hot as the child's red head, Alinor suspected. How could it fail to be so when she had it from both the mother's and the father's side. Alinor would not deny her daughter either the joy or the pain that came with love. But Joanna was malleable. If the love could be directed toward someone who would return it and be good to her, so much the better.

"Tell him also," Alinor continued, "that I will do what I can to fix Joanna's heart on Geoffrey so that both may be happy. But I will not countenance a contract for two reasons. The first is plain. If Joanna cannot love him, she must not marry him. The second is a little more subtle. I believe Joanna and Geoffrey do like each other. So, if the children know they are contracted, they may well plod along together in mild contentment. That is not enough. It is dangerous. If both do not burn for each other, there may come a time in the future when one, or both, will burn for someone else." Her eyes sought Ian's and did not find them. "Ian," she demanded, "look at me."

He raised his eyelids. The dark eyes were wary, guarded against hurt.

"You know, none knows better from what I have heard, what comes of such feelings. Do you want to see Joanna in the place of the women you have bedded?"

"Alinor! Joanna is no slut!"

"She is not now. Were those women sluts at nine? Before boredom or bitterness had eaten away their souls?"

"Do you blame me for their state?" Ian asked heatedly. "I assure you I picked no unripe fruit. What I had fell of itself into my hand."

"No," Alinor laughed, "no man is guilty for the face with which he was born."

She was glad of the turn the conversation had taken. Having said all she wanted to protect her daughter, Alinor wished to cozen Ian into happiness again. Something had hurt him. He looked tired suddenly, and he leaned back against the pillows on the bed with drooping shoulders. It was true he had spent such a night as might make a man weary in the morning, but there had been no sign of it until their discussion of wedded love began. It had been a mistake, although an unavoidable one, to bring his mind back to the woman he could not have. Alinor touched his nose with the tip of her finger.

"A face like yours might seduce a saint, but if it seduces anyone new—when I am by—it will look quite different after I find out."

"Where did you think I would find the strength for such a thing—when you were by?"

"I noted no feebleness in you, even after you had falsely cried 'enough.' Shame on you for disturbing my well-earned rest."

"Shame on me!" Ian exclaimed. "What did you expect?"

Alinor did not answer that except with a laugh of acknowledgment. Unaccustomed to the usages of the marriage bed, Ian had been wakened when Alinor pressed herself against him or threw a thigh and an arm across his body. He had responded as a lover instead of as a husband, rousing himself to caress Alinor into another coupling instead of merely accepting her embrace as a sleepy sign of contentment and affection. Alinor had not corrected him, partly because by the time she was sufficiently awake to explain, she had also been sufficiently roused to welcome his advances and partly because she judged, quite rightly, that he would have been hurt by her refusal. There would be plenty of opportunity to clear up the misunderstanding when they were both more secure in their relationship, if Ian did not come to understand without any explanation.

However, Alinor had accomplished her purpose. She did not know whether she had really driven his lost love out of his mind or merely turned his thoughts into pleasanter channels, but his expression had lightened. He pulled her close and kissed her, which gave Alinor the excuse she sought to change talk to action. She gave a brief, enthusiastic response and then pulled away.

"Hedgehog," she remarked. "Of course, I have never kissed a hedgehog, but I imagine it must feel like kissing you right now. Let the barber come in and shave you, Ian. And, oh heavens, look at the light. Surely we have missed both Masses."

Had this been Alinor's first marriage, the noble ladies and gentlemen would have come early to waken bride and groom and to display the bloodstained sheets that were evidence of the bride's virginity. Since this proof could hardly be expected from a woman who had been thirteen years married and had borne four children, the second part of the bedding ceremony had been dispensed with.

"Do you want me to bind that leg now, or will you be shaved first?" Alinor asked after having clapped her hands sharply to summon her maids.

"I can do without the binding," Ian assured her, releasing her a little reluctantly.

Alinor twitched aside the covers and burst out laughing. "I will put a lock and key on it," she teased. "How dare you cry lack of strength." But her eyes had already shifted to his knee, and she realized Ian had been speaking the truth. Even though the splint had been off all the previous day, there was almost no swelling and the discoloration seemed a little fainter. The knee was mending. Still laughing, she pulled the cover over him again and sent one of her maids off to summon his squires. "It would be too shocking for Gertrude and Ethelburga," she teased. "You are not decent. More-

over, I would not wish them to think that you were so
ill content with me that you have remained in that sad
condition all night."

With that she fled from the room, leaving her husband half exasperated and half enchanted. One thing
was certain. He was not likely to be bored even if he
was pent in the keep alone with Alinor all winter.
Doubtless she would find some deviltry to amuse him,
but this was no morning for guessing games. It was all
very well, he thought, easing himself out of the bed, to
say she would send his squires to him. No doubt they
would be useful in getting his clothes and armor on—
provided he or they knew where his clothing and armor
was. Ian certainly did not know. Alinor and her maids
had been seeing to his needs for the past five days. All
he knew was that perfectly exquisite raiment, most of
which he had never seen before, appeared each time he
needed to dress. The truth was that half the time he had
been too cross to ask where the things had come from,
and the other half he had had something more important to talk about.

As soon as Owain and Geoffrey arrived, Ian realized
he should have known Alinor better than to suspect
anything, including a wedding night, could divert her
from practicality. Before he said a word, Owain found
and presented the chamber pot. Ian laughed so hard he
almost missed it. Lock and key indeed! Alinor had
known well enough what his need was. In the next moment, seeing Geoffrey heading for the other chamber,
he shouted for him to stop.

"Where are you going?"

"For your clothing, lord. Gertrude said to come to
her for it."

"Oh, well, do not enter the chamber. Lady Alinor is
dressing in there."

The boy blushed and hurried out. Ian raised an eye-
brow. If Geoffrey was still as innocent as he seemed, he
might need a little urging in the right direction. Owain

helped his master into his bedrobe and then to a chair by the newly replenished fire. The barber entered on cue. Owain went to help Geoffrey with Ian's armor, which was heavy for the younger boy. By the time the barber's task was finished, Geoffrey was back. He slipped his master's feet into maroon chausses. Ian smiled at the feel of the cloth, a fine soft wool more fitting for an outer garment. Alinor obviously intended to impress the vassals and castellans. Even though he knew it, he whistled at the silk shirt that came next, and the undertunic. It matched the chausses, obviously cut from the same piece of cloth. He fingered the gem-set, embroidered neckband.

"This is ridiculous," he protested. "I will strangle myself if I try to lace up my hood."

"But there will be no fighting today. The hood will lie open, lord, and think how beautiful it will be." Geoffrey's voice was quivering with excitement.

Ian smiled at him and did not argue further. It was true enough. He was to be an image of grandeur today, not a working warlord. The hauberk, which was offered next, made Ian laugh again and jestingly hold up a hand to shield his eyes. It had been polished until it glittered like silver in the firelight. Every steel ring had been scoured and scrubbed and polished free of the rust and blood and dirt and grime that had accumulated in the weeks they had spent in the field.

"This is a piece of work," he praised. "I cannot think how many hours were spent over it. To whom do I offer thanks?"

"Lady Alinor, I suppose," Owain said, laughing. "She came and saw to it that it *was* well cleaned. Three times we had it back. If you mean whose fingers and nails scraped and scratched at every speck, we took it in turns, Geoff and I mostly, but Jamie helped, and even Beorn."

That brought Ian such a feeling of warmth that he

was silenced. He had achieved what was to him a near heaven. Alinor's passionate attention to every detail of this magnificent costume was not only the mark of a good wife but showed that she did not intend to out-shine him, which she could have done most subtly. It was, of course, his squires' duty to clean his armor, but whether or not Owain was joking about the thrice-returned mail, that duty had been carefully and lovingly performed. What was more, the love and pride the boys had for him shone in their faces this morning. To top all, that Jamie and Beorn should help with a task well beneath their stations, a thing Alinor would not have asked of them, displayed a heartfelt devotion. Because of what had befallen Ian before he came into Simon's hands, he needed love. Here it was being poured out on him, and for a little while his joy was such that he could not speak.

His attention was recalled by hearing Owain murmur to Geoffrey, "You do it. Your hands are lighter."

That might be true, Ian thought, realizing the boys had reached the point in dressing him of tying his cross garters, but Owain did not like to be scolded. It was a pleasure to see Geoffrey reach unhesitatingly for the scarlet laces, to see his eyes flick up briefly but trustfully as he warned, "Say if I hurt you, lord." Just right, Ian decided. He loves me, I him, and both of us love Joanna. Somehow Alinor must be brought round to see how valuable such a strong blood bond would be.

"Let me help you up, lord," Owain urged.

"Good God," Ian exclaimed as Geoffrey brought his surcoat, "all I need is a halo and I can be one of those painted images they use in the churches of the Holy Land."

The garment was magnificent, scarlet velvet, gold em-broidered and set with—Ian lifted the border close so that he could see—pearls that, he would swear, had been added later. A notion dawned on him that made him purse his lips into a whistle again, but the sound never came, because at that moment Alinor swept into the room.

"Two halves make one whole," Ian said appreciatively, staring at her.

Alinor smiled at his quick comprehension. It had certainly been her intention to give the impression that they were mirror images of each other. Alinor's gown matched Ian's tunic and chausses; her tunic matched his gown. The embroidery on both sets of garments was the same pattern, and the row upon row of pearls that had been Ian's bride gift were bold sisters to those that glowed in the neckband and borders of Ian's garments.

"Quick," she said as she opened a chest, "take that gold chain set with topaz and put it on. It will finish you nicely. Wait. See also if you can find some rings in there that will go on your hands."

"Whose are these?" Ian asked.

What little he had left in the way of gems and gold were in his northern stronghold. All the remainder had been sacrificed to pay for Alinor's pearls.

"Who knows," Alinor replied. "Mine, I suppose, if you mean who owns them. I guess they were my father's. My grandfather never wore such things at all, and Simon either. He was quite right of course; they would have befitted him like a silk panache befits an ass. I always thought it a great waste, though, that they should lie unused. It is a pleasure to see them on you, Ian. You do them honor."

"But Alinor," Ian protested, "to dress me in borrowed plumes——"

"Borrowed from whom? As long as you and I live, they are yours. When we die, they will be divided among our children."

Ian opened his mouth to protest further, but was interrupted by Joanna's voice craving admittance from the outer chamber. "Yes, come," he said, and then, "Holy Mary, Joanna, how beautiful you are!"

Even all unformed as she was, one could see the woman that would ripen. She was dressed in the same dark red as her mother, and it was a surprise to Ian how well the color suited them both. Of course, Alinor's dark hair was hidden under her gold wimple, and mother and daughter both had the same very white skin, but the dark red seemed to make Alinor's eyes glow gold and deepen the gray of Joanna's to a blazing blue. Impulsively, the child ran to Ian, and he embraced her and kissed her, suffering as he held her a total reversal of his eagerness to make contract for her marriage. It did not seem to Ian that any man would ever be good enough to deserve Joanna.

He was saved from voicing any such idiocy by Adam's indignant demand for attention. Ian released Joanna, who went to her mother to have her dress twitched and patted into more perfect folds. Adam, except for the jewels that bedecked Ian, was a small version of his stepfather. In fact, with his dark hair and changeable eyes, he could more easily have been taken for Ian's son than for Simon's. With Adam, Ian wasted no time on praise. The boy was as fine as a cockatoo and knew it.

"Stand," Ian ordered. "Now turn. Yes. Hitch that sword more forward so the hilt is readier to your hand. Let me see you take it. Quicker. Grab the scabbard with the left. Higher. So. Draw. So. Now let me see——"

"Ian," Alinor warned, "do not you dare kneel."

He laughed. "You see how much better it is. I had forgot for the moment. Owain, you are the taller. Kneel to him for me. Yes. Let me see you touch him with the point, Adam. Gently! Very well. Sheath. Thank you, Owain. You and Geoffrey had better go and dress and be quick about it. I want to see you before you start to serve. Adam, come here."

"Do not bother to go down," Alinor said to the squires. "There are new garments for you both in the chamber opposite and Gertrude and Ethelburga will help you dress. Tell Gertrude where your arms are, and she will send a manservant for them."

Ian turned away from showing Adam how to adjust the hang of his cloak so that it would not impede his sword hilt. "My squires, too?" he said uneasily.

"They must stand behind you. I would have all meet and fitting. You did not leave the boys' baggage with me, and even if the clothes were once fine enough, I can imagine the condition of dirt and raggedness they are in now. It was easier to make all new than to think of cleaning and mending what they had in the midst of the guests."

"Very well, but their fathers are well able to afford new finery for them. I will charge them with the expense."

"Oh, Ian, let me gift them. They are so kind to Adam —are they not, Adam?"

"Yes," Adam the irrepressible replied, "but if you want to gift them, Mama, I know what they want more than clothes."

"Do you, love? How clever. Tell me."

"Owain wants a jeweled eating knife, like the one Ian used the night he wore the green gown. And Geoffrey is crazy to have a lute. He has been borrowing the minstrels' when they would lend them. He plays very well." Adam lowered his voice. "The queen took his away. She said it was not fitting. Ian, is it not fitting to play the lute? Mama has told me that King Richard played and sang, too."

"That silly boy!" Ian exclaimed. "Why did he not tell me?" Then to Adam. "Of course it is fitting. If I had the smallest ability, I would play and sing myself. Perhaps Geoffrey did not understand just what Queen Isabella meant. Perhaps he played at the wrong time or place."

But Ian's eyes were furious when they met Alinor's over Adam's head, and she knew he had excused the queen only so that Adam would not hear something he was too young to estimate wisely.

"Can you keep a secret, Adam?" Alinor whispered. The boy nodded excitedly. "Very well. Perhaps Owain will have his knife and Geoffrey his lute for Twelfth Day presents. Now, do not tell or you will spoil their pleasure, and that is a bad way to repay their kindness to you. Ah, here are our attendant gentlemen. Well, Ian? How do they look?"

Ian grunted approval, more interested in correcting the carriage of weapons than in appearance. Alinor straightened the folds of the tunic at Owain's back and pulled at Geoffrey's to even the hemline. Ian promptly undid Alinor's work by resettling both sword belts, but eventually he was satisfied and stood back. Owain was tastefully attired in two shades of soft blue; Geoffrey in shades of green. Both looked well and would neither conflict with nor outshine the principal actors.

"Thank you, lord," Geoffrey said, going to his knee to kiss Ian's hand.

Owain echoed the gesture and the words.

"No thanks to me," Ian remarked, tousling both heads gently. "To my shame, I did not even think of having your clothes sent back to the keep to be cleaned. Thank Lady Alinor for both thought and labor."

Both went to kneel, but Alinor forestalled them by drawing them into her arms. "I am very happy to welcome you into my family and into my heart. I know you are too old to need a mother, yet there are some things a man wishes to tell or to ask a woman, and a mother is a safe person to listen to tales and troubles. If I can help you, remember I am most willing."

Ian gathered the group with his eyes. "You go first, Adam. Then Joanna and Alinor. Owain, lend me your shoulder. I can stand but I am not sure of the stairs. Geoffrey, do you follow, and be ready to grab my belt if my knee should fail. I do not desire to enter the hall on my face."

CHAPTER FOURTEEN

It was a marvelous ceremony, marred only for Alinor, who had to struggle frantically to control her tears when Adam took the vows of his men. He was so very small, his tiny hands engulfed in the large ones of the men who knelt to him. A pain stabbed from Alinor's throat down into her breast until she felt literally that her heart would break. Simon, her painful heart wailed, Simon. But there was no answer, not even the vision of him that, in the past, used to rise in her mind's eye to calm her when she was frightened or sad. There was only Ian's voice, following Adam's treble affirmation of the vows of fealty, Ian's voice, sure and strong, repeating again and again, "I, Ian, Lord de Vipont, do warrant and stand surety for my son by marriage."

Fortunately, Alinor had taken the fealty of her dependents so often that the words and gestures flowed from her without need for thought, and however forgetful Ian had been in the matter of his squires' dress, he had obviously not failed to instruct them in their duties. As each vassal or castellan swore, Owain or Geoffrey, by turns, came forward to receive and carry to safety the token of homage. Sir John of Mersea's offering of five fish, three eels, and two oysters; Sir Giles of Iford's two couple of hunting dogs; Sir Henry of Kingsclere's tall lance; and Sir Walter of the Forstal's sparrow hawk had been accepted before Alinor really was conscious of anything beside her own misery. She had not even heard the roars of *"Fiat! Fiat!"* that shook the rafters after each swearing.

She came to herself swiftly enough, however, when

270

she detected an odd note in the voice of her castellan from Clyro Hill. In the moment, she was aware of Ian, who stood just at her left shoulder. Although his right hand did not move, his left slid down to grasp the scabbard of his sword as if to ready it for drawing. Even Joanna, who Alinor saw had remembered her part and came to stand at her mother's right hand, noticed something amiss and stiffened. Alinor said her say, leaned forward and gave the man the kiss of peace, but it made her no easier that he would not meet her eyes. He waved his squire forward with his token, a clutch of pheasants' eggs and five leeks, and Alinor accepted them with the formal words. The witnesses shouted *"Fiat!"* Sir Peter stepped down from the dais, but Alinor's eyes followed him speculatively until she had to give her attention to Sir Alfred of Ealand.

Then she was free to step back. It was Ian's turn. This taking of homage was, of course, totally unnecessary in the sense that nothing had changed Ian's social position or his relationship with his vassals. However, it was a good idea to renew oaths of fealty as often as possible on general principles; the repetition seemed to increase loyalty. Moreover, renewing the oath at this time would obviate the complaint that Ian would be busy with his wife's lands and might neglect his own without warning his vassals of his new responsibilities. Alinor paid little attention. Although technically she was Ian's heir, because he had no other family, she was not yet concerned with the idea of holding his lands if anything happened to him.

Midway in the swearing, there was a disturbance at the back of the hall. Alinor's head lifted sharply, but apparently the men-at-arms crowded into that section had either explained what was going forward or had otherwise silenced the intruder. Completely freed from her earlier oppression, Alinor's heart leapt with expectation. If this was the king's messenger, God had favored her in a most singular way. There could not be a better time for his arrival.

Alinor had, of course, hoped it would happen this way, but there had been no way to arrange it surely. She knew her huntsmen would not leave the man in the forest until it was light, for fear the beasts that roamed there would harm him, but after that all was conjecture. How long would he take to free himself? How long would it take him to find Roselynde? How long would be needed to convince the castle guards to let him enter, all ragged and dirty as he must now appear? Alinor's eyes rested on Ian a little ahead of her and to her left. If this was the king's messenger, God had truly given his blessing to this marriage. Ian would be shielded by the evidence of strong witnesses from having had any desire to flout the king's wishes. After all, how could he know that the king had other plans for the lady he had married if the messenger carrying the information had not arrived until after the wedding.

A quick survey of other possibilities for the disturbance left Alinor with little doubt as to how she must act. As soon as the last *"Fiat!"* died away, she stepped forward.

"Who broke the peace of this swearing?" she called sharply. "Let him be brought forward."

Ian, who had been looking at his vassal, had not noticed the brief swirl of activity at the end of the hall. From the surprised looks and random head turnings, Ian judged that few others had noticed either. He put a hand on Alinor's arm.

"Be gentle," he warned her. "This is not a day for severity."

"I am not angry," she declared, not loud, but in a clear voice that would definitely carry to the important witnesses who stood just in front of the dais—the three bishops, the earls, and Lord Llewelyn. "I am concerned. Yesterday, during the entertainment after dinner, one of my foresters brought me the king's seal and a demand for ransom for a king's messenger. He said a man he did not know had caught him from behind and, at knife point, had bid him carry the seal to me and ask two marks for the man and the message that went with the seal."

"What?"

The startled word was no indication that Ian had not heard her, only that he did not believe his ears. Alinor could only hurry on, hoping that Ian would have sense enough not to contest anything she said in public.

"I gave him the money, and a guard to see that he did lay it where he said he was told to leave it. I did not tell you. I—I did not wish to look a fool, if I had been choused out of my money."

Ian's eyes opened as wide as they could go, and he swallowed convulsively. The idea of Alinor doing or thinking anything so simple-minded and passive was inconceivable. It was plain as a clear day to Ian that she was up to some deviltry, but he dared not say or do anything to mark his suspicion. In any case, the man had already been brought forward. Ian listened, silent and totally incredulous, to the tale that poured out of him.

He had been seized by outlaws. What outlaws? Ian knew he had cleaned out the only nest of men in the area and had cleaned it out before the messenger had been taken. Of course, it was possible that there was a small group living in the forest off game and the few pence they could wrest from low-born travelers who were afraid to complain of their experiences at the castle. It was possible, but not likely. The idea that Alinor's huntsmen or foresters would miss such a group was very farfetched. The idea that they would deliberately betray their mistress, as King John's foresters in Bere had done, was laughable. King John was far away and very unapproachable; he might come to Bere once in a year, if so often. His men were in little danger that the king would discover their dishonest doings. Alinor was close at hand, a good mistress who listened to her people's complaints readily; she had many faithful servants who would run to her with news of another servant's cheating.

He had been stripped of his clothes, his money, his horse and arms, the messenger cried passionately. Even the message had been defaced, the seal torn from it. Alinor interrupted to confirm this last and to say for all to hear this time that the seal had been brought to her as a token and she had paid the ransom required, not daring to refuse when the king's messenger and the king's orders were at stake. She received tearful thanks. They would have killed him to conceal their crime if she had not paid, the messenger said. The large ransom, they had told him, was to enable them to flee the country. They had laughed at him when he told them they would be hunted high and low for interfering with a king's messenger. Not in France, they said contemptuously; King John's power did not stretch to France.

Eventually, having unburdened his soul of its fears and frustrations, the man handed over his defaced scroll. Alinor begged that her guests would forgive her while she opened and read it at once. It had been overlong in coming, and she desired no more delay before the king's wishes were attended to. Ian bit his lip until he was able to control his mouth. Then he gave low-voiced instructions to Owain to see that the messenger was cared for, allowed to wash, fed and rested, and provided with decent garments instead of the foul rags he was wearing. Ian was happy to have something to hold his attention. He was not sure whether it would have been possible for him to control his expression when Alinor displayed the consternation and regret almost certainly called for by the message. Ian was not even sure what his expression would display because he was so torn between horror, anxiety, relief, and amusement.

He did miss Alinor's first fulsome regrets that it was

impossible for her to obey the king's order, but he could not escape it all. She turned to him to grasp his hand with a pretty display of feminine appeal.

"He cannot break our marriage, can he, Ian? He could not part us now?"

Ian could have murdered her in that moment, not for what she said but for the way she was lying with her voice and her body, playing on the sympathies of the witnesses to make them believe she was a weak and frightened woman. There were a few faces, he knew, that had set like stone. Those men knew Alinor for what she was—William of Pembroke, Sir Giles of Iford, perhaps even Robert of Leicester—but none of those men would betray her. What was worse, she had maneuvered him so that he was forced to draw others into a tangle he had made himself with open eyes and felt was his to struggle with alone. Nonetheless, she had been too clever for him. If he did not fall willingly into the trap Alinor had set, he could destroy them both.

"I am no churchman," he replied stiffly, "but I am sure marriage is an affair of the Church and not of the king."

"Is this true, my lords?" Alinor cried to the three bishops.

Before Ian could guess what she would do, she had released his hand and run down from the dais. Ian could feel the color rise into his face. He thought he had been clever enough, answering without requiring confirmation from anyone. Now he saw he had played exactly as she expected, into her hands. All three bishops were assuring her aloud that what God had joined no man, save God's vicar on earth, the Pope, could part asunder.

"And there must be a real reason, must there not? Such as consanguinity or some other holy cause of wrong for the Pope to annul a marriage? It cannot be just for a political purpose?"

Peter des Roches of Winchester looked into the eyes

of the woman he had just been—as he thought—comforting. It was fortunate for Alinor that he was a clever man with a marked sense of humor and a keen eye for a beautiful woman. He, too, saw the corner into which he had been backed. Before this crowd of witnesses, it was impossible for him to say aloud—what everyone knew—that political considerations annulled many more marriages than holy causes ever did. He shook his head infinitesimally, knowing Alinor would understand the signal. This once she had caught him, and he would do as she wished, but she was not to play such a game with him again.

"There is no reason of consanguinity or other holy cause to annul *this* marriage," he said, yielding graciously since he had yielded. "And no fate of nations—which, although political in a sense is also a holy cause in itself—can possibly rest upon it. Therefore I can say, and I believe London and Ely will confirm my words, that the king has no cause to ask that this marriage be set aside."

"I am most humbly grateful to your lordships for giving me this reassurance," Alinor said clearly so all could hear. "I hope I am a faithful and loyal subject; thus, it gives my heart ease to know I will have no occasion to contest the king's will. I am not sure he has the right to name a husband to me, but even so, I would have preferred to obey him and—to speak the truth—I could not have done so. However good and devoted servants Fulk de Cantelu and Henry of Cornhill are to the king, I could not have accepted either as a husband."

There was a gasp that echoed around the whole audience of men and women. Ian ground his teeth. That was what she had been aiming for from the beginning. Obviously she could not read the king's message aloud to the group. She had to find a way to communicate to them a piece of information that would enrage every well-born man and any woman who had any feeling softer than hatred for her. Sir Fulk and Sir Henry were the king's lickspittles and dogsbodies. They were low and brutal, lechers and sadists who were employed on those tasks any man of honor would flatly refuse even from the king.

In the minds of Alinor's guests, it was an offense that stank to heaven, that such men should have been proposed as suitable to marry Alinor. True, most of the male guests were indifferent to the brutality of the proposed grooms. What was offensive to them was that the men were outsiders, crude and common, whom, nonetheless, the king preferred to themselves. It was upon Fulk and Henry that favors were heaped. It was to them the king turned in his idle hours. And, if they realized that it was so because Fulk and Henry obeyed John without question, without remonstrating about honor and legality, so much the more offensive was the king's act. After all, the king's nobles were his natural advisors. It was his duty to take counsel with them and to act according to their advice.

The women, except for Isobel, were simply horrified by the thought of the life Alinor would have led. Isobel, who knew Alinor very well indeed, thanked God that such a marriage had not brought the sin of murder upon her friend. She might have wept and prayed and endured. Alinor would, Isobel knew, either kill the man herself or arrange to have him removed out of her way. Yet Isobel was in no way offended by Alinor's pretense of fear and frailty. Weakness was a woman's rightful weapon. Isobel had rather see Alinor using that than a knife.

The initial shock over, the guests crowded forward to offer oblique sympathy and, a few, open support. Alinor's vassals were at one on that subject. Many of them were fond of their overlady, but that was not their reason. The thought of having Fulk de Cantelu or Henry of Cornhill as their liege lord increased their loyalty to Alinor and Ian to fever pitch. Neither their wives and daughters nor their lands would be safe with such a lord.

Ian's vassals were less happy. They did not desire the enmity either of the king's favorites or of the king. Nonetheless, they came forward to pledge their support to Ian. It occurred to them that, Alinor now irrevocably being Ian's heir, if harm came to him they would be inherited along with her by any man to whom the king chose to give her. They had no more sympathy with the king's apparent choice than Alinor's own vassals; de Vipont was a good lord, honest in his dealing and quick to come to the defense of a man in trouble. Had they known the king's pleasure, they would have protested against this marriage, which would be contrary to it. However, none had known because of those accursed outlaws—and those, mostly, existed by the king's fault —so now it behooved them to stand firm behind their lord.

William of Salisbury was furious, but his anger was not directed against any person. How could it be? Plainly, Ian was as surprised and appalled as he himself was at what Alinor had done. Yet he could not blame poor Alinor, who was equally plainly frightened out of her wits by the choice of husbands offered her. Probably Ian should have warned her, Salisbury thought, not knowing that Alinor had read his letter, but he understood why Ian had not done so. Salisbury could not even blame John, poor John, who could never judge a man or a situation aright and who invariably and consistently did exactly the wrong thing. He would have to go to John as soon as he arrived in England, Salisbury thought, and explain what had happened. If he could convince John to accept this marriage graciously, little harm would be done. The king's kindness in forgiving a subject would overshadow his lack of good taste in desiring to enrich his faithful servants.

Shortly after dinner, before he departed, Salisbury said as much to Ian and asked about the disposition of

Adam and Joanna. To Ian's relief, he did not seem at all put out by the inconclusive answers he received. He said he understood that Alinor would scarcely be able to give her mind to such matters in the midst of her own wedding. Ian had to be a little less discreet, but Salisbury still did not take offense. He said he was sorry not to have Adam, and then remarked with a laugh and in plain words on what Ian had phrased most delicately.

"Alinor is wrong about my wife. She will have to come to know Ela better, but I can see that attendance at court might not be what is best for a young boy of such high spirit, more particularly for Adam if my brother takes this marriage ill—which I hope he will not. And it is reasonable not to make double ties in one direction when there are only two children. I may hope, then, that Lady Alinor will agree eventually to the marriage of Geoffrey and Joanna? She has no objection to Geoffrey?"

"As to that, none at all," Ian replied, and then, since Salisbury had been very frank, he added, "She said plainly that she would be glad of him even landless and without legitimization, if he could take Joanna's fancy. Moreover, she added she would do whatever was in her power to turn Joanna's eyes in Geoffrey's direction."

"Then I am content."

Salisbury mounted the horse held ready for him and waved farewell as he clattered over the drawbridge, following his wife's party. Ian stood looking after him for some time before he turned and hobbled back toward the keep. It was a relief to know that Salisbury was not offended and that he would do his best to smooth matters over with John. That had been implied, of course, in his letter. Nonetheless, it was good to have his renewed promise in the face of the animosity toward John that Alinor had deliberately raised.

Ian was never deluded into believing in the band of outlaws, but he credited Alinor with even greater skill in management and duplicity than she had. All day, busy speeding parting guests and entertaining those who remained, Ian vacillated between fury at the way Alinor had used her guests and relief that the cause of the king's anger—if John decided to show his spite—would be well and widely known. That night, as soon as Alinor's maids had gathered up his discarded clothing and left the chamber, he turned on his wife.

"What outlaws? How did you dare?"

Alinor made no reply, quietly braiding her hair into two plaits as thick as Ian's wrists. Ordinarily she did not braid her hair at night, but it had got in her way when she mounted her husband the previous night. As Ian had been on his feet a good deal this day and his knee seemed, from the way he was standing, to be painful, she thought it just as well to be prepared to play the more active role in lovemaking again.

"Did you hear me?" Ian snarled.

"I am not deaf," Alinor rejoined calmly.

"How dared you trap the bishops, Oxford, Llewelyn, your vassals and mine, even John's own brother and daughter into an open disapproval of the king's act?"

"Because it was an act worthy of disapproval."

"That is not what I meant," Ian bellowed. "You cannot befool me! There were no outlaws in the forest. I scoured it clean, and I know it was clean. It was your men who took the messenger. How dared you do such a thing?"

"I thought it better than adding open defiance of the king's will to the spite he already has against me. The messenger came to no harm. No blame can fall upon him for what clearly was not his fault. No blame can fall on us for what was not our fault. Where have I done wrong?"

"You have lied with your eyes, with your mouth and your voice, with your body. You——"

"I will confess and do penance," Alinor said indifferently.

Ian choked. "Father Francis must have the penance

for that engraved deep in his heart," he remarked bitterly.

Having finished with her hair, Alinor twisted in her chair to look at her husband. "Not really. I am not a liar by nature," she teased.

Ian's fists clenched, but he made an enormous effort of will. "Alinor," he said softly, "how long do you think two marks will keep the man silent? Will he not soon ask for more, and then for more?"

"What man?"

Her husband took a step forward, obviously near to losing his control. "You may lie to whom else you like, but not to me. Not to me!"

"On Simon's soul," Alinor replied, "I have spoken nor acted no lie to you in this room here and now—nor any other time. What takes place in this chamber is between your heart and mine, and I do not and will not lie."

That cooled Ian like a cold douche. What Alinor swore on Simon's soul was true; she might risk her own damnation, but not Simon's. His hands opened. "Let me understand you," he said reasonably. "Your men took and held the messenger prisoner?" Alinor nodded confirmation. "By whose arrangement, if you did not bribe him, did he come into the hall just after the swearing so that his business would be known to all so conveniently?"

"By God's or the devil's," Alinor replied soberly. "I swear it was not by mine. I told my men to release him this day, so much was my doing, but I made no other arrangement. How could I? I will confess that, could I have arranged such a thing, I would have gladly done it, but it seemed impossible. How could I know where the woodcutters would be working? How could I know whether a sheep might have strayed here or there to bring a shepherd after it? Without such knowledge, I dared not tell the huntsmen exactly where to release their prisoner. Then, he had to be left bound lest he try to follow those who had held him. How could I know how long it would take him to loose himself? Or how long it would take him to find his way here? I bade them leave him near the edge of the wood, but they could not leave him too near. He could have turned about and gone completely astray."

"Who knows of this business?"

Alinor thought that over, then shook her head stubbornly. "They are mine, to me," she said. "They will not betray me. They have never betrayed me, no matter what I bid them do."

"And you think I will betray them?" Ian's voice rose again.

"Of course not," Alinor assured him seriously. Then she smiled. "You will confuse them. In your desire to save me from myself, you will either forbid them to do such things another time, or you will bid them come to you for confirmation of such orders from me, or you will try to explain to them the danger to me in their obedience in performing such acts. In another place or with a different woman, it might do well enough. But I am the Lady of Roselynde, and these people have obeyed my lightest breath for nigh on twenty years— no matter who was my husband."

"Now you listen to me, Alinor!"

She rose and went to him, grasping his upper arms gently. "No, Ian, you listen to me. I do not do this to dim your pride or to make my power blind your eyes. I trust you. I know you would never do me any hurt for any reason. But think. It is not a natural thing for men, even such men as these, to obey a woman. I dare not break their habit of obedience. Some day Joanna will be the Lady of Roselynde. If she marries Geoffrey and he lives, all will be well and you may say my care was wasted. But if she marry another, or Geoffrey should die and some king should press upon her some brute— There may not be a kind Ian to protect Joanna as you have protected me. Even if her vassals are loyal, what could they do? The day that a small band of vassals could raise rebellion is over. It is the small people of Roselynde who will be her bulwark—the huntsmen with their long bows; the thieves from the stews of the town, with their long knives; the fishermen with their boats that overturn and their nets that tangle. They must know only that the lady's word is the law."

That appeal silenced him. He was not so sure that the day a band of vassals could raise rebellion was over, but he was not going to put that idea into Alinor's head. In any case, it was horrible enough to think of Alinor in the power of a Fulk or a Henry, but Ian knew Alinor for a strong and resolute woman. The idea of Joanna, whom he had cradled in his arms and who still appeared to him as fragile and helpless as a new spring flower, faced with such a threat was inconceivably worse. His arms came up and drew Alinor close against him. She laid her head against his breast. After a moment, however, she lifted it. It was most unwise to allow Ian to think over their conversation at any length, or he would begin to find new doubts. A healthy distraction was in order.

"Ian, did you have speech with Sir Peter of Clyro Hill? He was avoiding me these past few days, I think, although I cannot be sure because—" she bit Ian gently, "—because I was taken up with other things. And today, after the swearing, I wished most earnestly to speak with him, but Lady Ela nearly drove me out of my mind. How Salisbury has not murdered her, I will never understand. First she would not go because she was too weary, and after dinner was too late to begin a journey. Then she would go because the packing was all done, and it was too much to draw forth the garments she would need for the extra time. Then she would not because all the worry had made her breath short. Then——"

"Enough," Ian laughed. "She may have been a trial to you, but Salisbury sets a great value on her and is fond of her beside. He speaks well of her always, although he knows her failings."

"Now I can understand how he loves the king. He has a disordered brain. But what of Sir Peter?"

"He could not avoid me," Ian said slowly as he steered Alinor toward the bed, "but I learned no more than we both guessed at the swearing. Something has made Sir Peter very, very uneasy. Perhaps it is only that something is brewing in Wales, and if Pembroke goes to Ireland, a strong hand will be lifted from the cover of that bubbling pot. It may not be *all* spite that made the king deny Pembroke's desire to go to Ireland. Even though he is stripped of all authority, his presence makes men think twice about creating a disturbance."

"Sir Peter heard of that plan?"

"Not from me or Salisbury or Pembroke, but Oxford's tongue can run away with him once it is oiled by a little wine. Moreover, Llewelyn might well have told him for his own purposes."

"But Lord Llewelyn is very fond of you. And you cannot tell me *he* has a loose tongue."

"Not without purpose, no. Get into bed, Alinor. It is cold."

Alinor cocked her head at him. "Ian, I want to hear the end of this tale of Sir Peter and Lord Llewelyn and Wales, and if we get into bed, we will stop talking."

He laughed, pushed her into the bed, and got in beside her. "I am not trying to divert you. The tale— if it is a true thing, and not of my imagining—is quickly told. Llewelyn would think it no hurt to me if one of your castellans should try to shake loose your hold when Pembroke is no longer there. Whether Sir Peter is so much a fool as to think I would not come and settle with him—with or without Pembroke's assistance—I do not know, but doubtless what Llewelyn hopes is that Sir Peter will appeal to Lord Gwenwynwyn for support, offering to do him homage and be his man instead of yours. That would give Llewelyn an excuse to rush to my aid and incidentally to challenge Gwenwynwyn, which is what he really seeks."

"Lord Llewelyn does not think I would mind my castellan defying me?" Alinor asked in a rising voice.

"Now, now, do not fly into a rage. The whole idea is that you would get your land back and be rid of a castellan of very doubtful loyalty, Llewelyn would have done me a favor by aiding me in ousting that castellan, and——"

"And he and you and Gwenwynwyn will fight a war all over my property so that my people will be killed, their crops and flocks destroyed, and more of my rents will be in arrears just when the king plans to raise taxes and will probably lay a fine upon me for marrying you. I hope you thanked Llewelyn for his generous thought."

Ian looked somewhat taken aback by Alinor's mercenary analysis. "I said this was all my guessing. I do not know whether Llewelyn has anything at all to do with Sir Peter's odd behavior. In any case, the war would not be fought on Clyro Hill or, at least, no more of it than necessary to drive out Sir Peter which, if he is not loyal, would be needful anyway. Llewelyn has his eyes on Powys, not on your lands."

"Quite right," Alinor replied tartly, "and my eyes are on my property, not on Lord Llewelyn's ambitions. I would prefer he found his excuse for quarreling with Lord Gwenwynwyn elsewhere than on my land. It would be better, if Sir Peter is disloyal, to find a way that he should not return to Clyro Hill at all rather than to fight a war to oust him from it."

"Now wait, Alinor," Ian protested, "the man swore his oath and presented his token fairly enough. You cannot make any move against him, after accepting those and giving him the kiss of peace, without offending all your other men. And I say again, this may be all my imagining. We are building a mighty castle out of the wet sand of one odd expression and a seeming avoidance of our company. There may be perfectly innocent reasons for that, or I might have misread him."

"I do not think you did, for I read his face the same way. And I know full well I cannot move openly against him now." Suddenly, in the midst of her thought, she laughed and laid her lips on Ian's shoulder. "If I had not been thinking of other matters, I might have seen his disaffection—if it is disaffection and not some other trouble—sooner. Then I could have refused his oath—but my mind was elsewhere."

"Am I to blame for that?"

"Assuredly. If you were hateful to me, or nothing to me, would I not have applied myself to business to drive you from my thoughts? As it was, Sir Peter tried to speak to me—twice, I think—but I put him off and I cannot remember a word he said."

Whereupon, quite reasonably, instead of blaming his wife for her carelessness, Ian kissed her soundly, and Alinor's prediction came true. They stopped talking. Ian thought no more of the subject of Sir Peter that night. His application to his new business of being a husband was too intense to leave room for worrying about another man's affairs. However, the ominous note in Alinor's flat statement that she "could not move openly now" remained buried under Ian's pleasure and came to the surface again the next morning.

Alinor had left the bed quietly soon after a predawn bout of lovemaking. Ian, expecting that she had gone to relieve herself and would soon return, slid off into sleep again. He slept heavily for a little while, but as the effect of his immediate exertions passed, he drifted upward toward consciousness. It did not take much rest to restore him. He was a strong man, accustomed to hard physical labor, and if anything, he had been too much rested in the past few weeks. Alinor's voice, low but not unclear, brought Ian to full wakefulness. His first reaction was an intense anxiety that almost brought him up and out of bed at once. A second woman's voice dispelled that impulse. Ian lay quiet, because he was still a little sleep-dazed and was trying to decide what made him feel so worried. The thought came to him that Alinor would not order her maidservant to kill anyone.

That idea, naturally enough, restored his anxiety in full measure but with a definite object. Ian had no idea how long he had slept. That hellion he had married could have ordered ten or a hundred murders by now.

"Alinor."

In a moment she was at the bed, putting back the curtains. She wore only a soft green bedrobe that made her eyes look the color of the sea over pale sand and exposed her white throat. Her expression was as sweet and compliant as any man could desire; her voice, as she asked in what way she could serve her lord, was as soft and musical as if it could never snap as viciously as any whip. All Ian wanted to do was pull her down beside him and caress her. He steeled himself against the tempting weakness.

"Send your maid out," Ian said.

Alinor raised a brow but made no protest. She sent Gertrude away, then returned. Her expression was still sweet, a half smile still curved her lips, but her eyes were wary.

"What I desire now is that you remember what you swore to me here, last night, that in this chamber there would be no lies. Then tell me what you have done about Sir Peter."

"Done? About Sir Peter himself? Nothing."

"Alinor——"

"If you do not believe what I answer, why do you bother to question me?"

The green of Alinor's eyes was hard as emerald now; the voice, still flexible and expressive, nonetheless held a note of steel.

"I will believe that you have not personally attacked Sir Peter with knife or sword. I want to know what orders you have given about him."

"About him? None."

Relieved of his most pressing fear, Ian grinned. It was rather fun to match wits with Alinor. He could see that she did not wish to anger him by refusing to answer, and he believed that she would keep her word and not tell a flat lie. In this chamber she would speak the literal truth. The trick was to recognize when the literal truth was as good as a lie, to ask such questions as would not force her into a stubborn silence and yet would produce answers that could be pieced together to mean something.

"Will Sir Peter be allowed to leave here in peace and to arrive at Clyro Hill in possession of his health, his wits, and all his limbs?"

Alinor stared at him blankly and then began to laugh. "It would serve you right if I made you waste half the morning drawing from me piece by piece what you want to know. Why do you not ask outright? I have told you the exact truth."

"I am sure you have. So exact that if what befalls Sir Peter is one hairsbreadth to one side or the other of what you have said, I will not be able to call you a liar. As to asking straight—" Suddenly Ian's face became bleak, his eyes distant. "What can I do if you refuse to answer me? Do not mistake me, Alinor. It is not you I fear but myself. I have seen what follows when a man uses his strength against a woman."

Stricken by sympathy, Alinor nearly assured her husband that she would keep nothing from him. Good sense restrained her at the last moment so that she only said, "I have nothing to hide on the subject of Sir Peter. He has served me well and faithfully in the past. His looks were strange, but that could mean many things. Also, when I bethought me of what you said, I came to see the truth of it. What is more, the man has a wife and children—" Her eyes hardened again. "Whom, you will note, he did not bring with him."

"That has no meaning. It is a long way and he might

fear to leave the keep unguarded or fear the weather or the dangers of the road. These days the safest place for a woman, unless a man has a large retinue, is in her own keep."

"Yes, that is true. So, thinking of those matters, Sir Peter will go in peace and come home hale and hearty— or, if he does not, it will not be by my doing or even my wishing."

Amusement had returned to Ian's eyes. "Alinor, I find it hard to believe you have done nothing at all."

"I do not ask you to believe it. I have sent messengers —who will surely outride Sir Peter—to the garrison of the keep, civilly informing the men of my marriage and the fact that my husband, Lord Ian de Vipont, is my deputy and, thus, to be obeyed above the order of any other man. I reminded them that my marriage changes nothing, that their first loyalty is to me, and that if Lord Ian seeks entrance to my keep and it is not opened to him, with or without Sir Peter's permission, my vengeance will fall upon them, and not lightly." Alinor paused and examined Ian's face. "Now what is wrong?"

"To suborn Sir Peter's men——"

"They are not his!" Alinor exclaimed explosively, her eyes wide, her lips drawn back from her teeth. "They are mine! Mine to me!"

"Alinor!"

She drew breath. "They are mine," she said more quietly. "Every year, except when I was in the Holy Land and the one year when Simon was ill, I have gone myself to pay them and to give them, as agreed, a suit of clothes and shoes. I have seen, I myself, not Sir Peter, that their mail was sound, that their food was good. I have listened in private to their complaints. I have taken their oaths—oaths to me!"

"I am not contesting your right," Ian said slowly, "but to go behind Sir Peter's back——"

"To do what?" Alinor snapped. "Have I bid my men disobey Sir Peter in any reasonable order? If he be loyal to me, they will be loyal to him."

"It is right," Ian sighed, "yet I wish it were not needful. I wish men would stand better by the oaths they swear."

"I, too," Alinor replied tartly. "It would save me a great deal of time, effort, and money." Then her expression softened. Ian was not so worn by the world as Simon had been. He still looked for men to be what they should be instead of what they were. It would be best for him if he thought no more of Sir Peter and his doings, but what would divert him? She could not send him out to hunt.

"Ian," Alinor said, "we overlooked a matter of some importance yesterday. We must send word of our marriage to the king. Or do you think we should just wait until he hears of it?"

"No, we must send word at once. And I did *not* overlook it. Until I had time to speak to you about your game with the messenger, I was not certain of just what I would need to do."

"Will you write to him? Or should I write, since the message came to me?"

"Both of us, I think."

Alinor giggled. "Oh, good. I have already begun a letter. I am glad my labor need not be wasted."

Ian hid his face in his hands and groaned. Alinor laughed aloud, saying she would fetch her letter while he went to piss. She returned to find Ian sitting in a chair with a long-suffering expression on his face.

"Listen," she urged. "If there is anything you do not like, I will change it. I thought to break the matter to him gently, so I began with 'From Alinor, Lady of Roselynde.' I can still say that, it does not matter that I am now Alinor de Vipont instead of Alinor Lemagne. Right?"

That was certainly a good notion. Ian nodded.

"Then I said, 'Dear my dread lord and king, I am sorry for the long delay in replying to your kind letter, but it is owing to no negligence upon my part nor upon the part of your messenger. As you foresaw and wrote to me about, trouble has come upon me because of the long sickness of my late lord and husband. My lands have become infested with bands of outlaws who prey upon my people and upon the merchants from the town. These fiends, lost to all sense of order and reverence, did take your messenger prisoner and hold him to ransom. As soon as this word came to me, I paid to gain his freedom, but by that time it was too late for me to comply with your most considerate and thoughtful offer.' "

"Really, Alinor," Ian protested, almost horrified, although he was laughing. "Do you think he will swallow that?"

"If you think not, it will be altered to your taste, but why not? Is any flattery too gross for this king's taste? As to the words 'considerate and thoughtful'—the man he offered me the first time was a decent man. I have not been to court since John has been king. Why should I know that those he mentions this time are not fit to be eaten by worms?"

"Hmmm." Ian was no longer laughing or horrified. There was considerable sense in what Alinor said. "Would I not have told you that they were monsters?"

"Why should you? Why should anyone, now that I am safe from them? What purpose would it accomplish other than to make me hate the king? Unless you were about to turn rebel, and Salisbury's presence here must convince even John that you do not have any such intention, your desire must be to make me think kindly of him. This letter, I hope, will show how well you have succeeded."

"Could I have succeeded, considering what passed between you and the king?"

"On my part, why not? He did me no harm and, for

all his threats, he did Simon no harm. Why should I not believe he has forgiven my transgression? And, you know, Ian," Alinor laughed, "it is a rare woman who hates a man for calling her beautiful and making advances. Resistance does not betoken hatred."

"Yet you hate the king."

"Certainly not for attempting to lie with me. Besides, I am not sure hate is the right word. I fear King John— not so much for myself, but—but he would eat the world if he could, and yet he hates it and everyone in it, I think."

"He is not so bad as that. He loves one, at least. Go on with your letter."

Since it was impossible for Alinor to define her feelings about the king, she began to read again. " 'Not knowing, my lord, that in the midst of your victories and the heavy business that must fall upon you, you would still find time to think of my insignificant troubles, I had accepted an offer of marriage from one of your most loyal servants. Ian, Lord de Vipont, and I were betrothed on the ides of October and married on the first day of December by Peter des Roches, Bishop of Winchester, with William, Bishop of London, and Eustace, Bishop of Ely, assisting. I hope you will pardon this unknowing disobedience and I hope you will believe that I intended no disrespect. Indeed, knowing Lord Ian to be high in your favor, my lord, I thought this union would be pleasing to you. Allow me, my lord, to sue humbly for your approval of my good intentions and to subscribe myself your faithful, loyal servant and vassal, Alinor.' And so on and so on. There, what think you?"

"I do not think I like that 'sue humbly,' " Ian bristled. "We did no wrong. I even paid for leave to marry who I would."

"You shall change it to what you like," Alinor soothed, "but for a woman such words come easier than to a man. I am willing to 'sue humbly' if it will buy me a little peace."

Ian scowled as he got out of the chair, and Alinor began to help him dress. She was right, and yet he found it offensive that she should humble herself before such a man as John. He stalked off finally to see what guests were up early while Alinor was dressed. She watched him. He still limped, but he was walking more easily, and there was no doubt that no permanent damage had been done to his knee. Alinor picked up the parchment from the small table upon which she had laid it while she dressed her husband. If only she could be even a little as hopeful that no permanent damage would be done to his life by this marriage, she would be much lighter of heart.

CHAPTER FIFTEEN

The habit of Alinor's servants was to carry out their mistress's orders as quickly as was humanly possible. Although she was not so unreasonable as to punish a man for bad weather, neither was it wise for a messenger of hers to sit down beside a river and wait for a flood to subside. Thus the trusty man that carried her letters and Ian's found King John at La Rochelle, where he was making preparations to return to England. It was a great relief to the messenger not to have to pursue the king, for John, when he was not sunk into lethargy, moved from place to place almost as swiftly as his mother had done. Moreover, the messenger's task was essentially over. Fortunately for him, in the city of La Rochelle full court protocol obtained, and this protocol forbade the direct approach of so insignificant a servant to the king, except in a dire emergency. Alinor's man had only to see the court official Ian had designated and deliver the letters to him.

Ian had taken a good deal of pleasure in deciding to whom to deliver the letters. There were so many of the king's favorites he disliked, and John was notoriously unrestrained in his behavior toward the bearer of ill tidings. The first idea had been to let Fulk or Henry carry his own rejection, but Ian reluctantly had to abandon that notion. Neither of those gentlemen was above lifting the seals with a hot knife, murdering the messenger and destroying the letters, so that Alinor's seeming refusal to reply to the king's orders would make the marriage seem an act of defiance. Not that most of the other gentlemen of the court were *above* lifting a seal,

294

Ian told Alinor wryly. It was just that no other would think the danger of discovery worthwhile when the letter did not concern him.

Having given the matter some careful thought, Ian grinned wickedly and bid Alinor's man to deliver his burden to Hugh of Neville.

"From whom?" that gentleman asked disdainfully, not reaching a hand for the proffered packet but signing a servant to take it.

"From Alinor, Lady of Roselynde," the man-at-arms repeated, bowing low and humbly, "and from Ian, Lord de Vipont."

His accent was uncouth; his clothes were mud-splashed, salt rimed, and sweat stained; he smelled to high heaven. He knew he was offending the great lord, but his instructions had been clear, and he was obeying them.

Neville frowned as he turned the packet over in his hands and looked at the seal. He was not the man to do even a friend a favor if it would not benefit him, and he certainly had no intention of accepting for delivery to the king anything that would upset John's temper. It was not that John was ill-humored at this time. In fact, he was particularly cheerful, as if he anticipated some pleasant event, and, of course, the queen was breeding, at long last. Neville, however, knew the king well enough not to depend on that. Once John roused into his active stage, his mood could not be trusted from one moment to the next.

Ian de Vipont was known to Neville. He did not like the man, but the king did not seem to dislike him. The seal, however, was even less meaningful than the lady's name. At least he remembered there had been some talk of a Lady Alinor being recently widowed. Neville's face cleared. Doubtless the lady wished to marry again. That would mean a fat fine if the choice was her own or a prize to be given away to a loyal henchman. Fulk? Hugh Neville looked down at the packet with an instant of doubt. Poor woman. Perhaps— No. It was no affair of his. All that mattered to him was that the king would be pleased. His eyes flicked over the messenger. Even if there was a reply, there was no need to use a dirty worm like that. The king's instructions must be carried by a more worthy instrument.

"There will be no reply," Neville said curtly. "Begone."

Not given to watching the reactions of his inferiors, Neville missed the expression of relief on the messenger's face. His lady had told him not to wait for a reply, but to return to Roselynde for further orders after delivering the packet. He had been troubled by that order. Usually he was told to do what the recipient of the message told him. He had wondered what would become of him if the lord who took the letters bid him stay? Caught between the fire of the lord's wrath if he disobeyed him and the lady's wrath if he disobeyed her, he would have been consumed either way. Now he was free. He bowed again, and backed gratefully out of the chamber. His horse was waiting, and there was a ship in the harbor due to sail for England on the evening tide. He would be on it.

Neville waved a hand as if the motion could dispel the scent of the messenger. Stupid woman, he thought, she deserves Fulk. Why did she not tell the man to clean himself before presenting himself to his betters? The air was redolent of the creature's stench. He rose unhurriedly. Actually, this was as good a time as any to deliver the messages to the king. The odor would be gone by the time he returned.

Entrance to the king's chambers was gained readily, and Neville was well-satisfied at the way John's eyes lit when he named Lady Alinor. John had been somewhat surprised when he received no reply to his letter. He had half expected a long screed pleading for a reversal of his decision or for delay on the grounds of the recentness of her widowhood. He really did not care what she did, however. Silence or an open defiance would have been equally satisfactory. Either would be a perfect excuse to use the force he was bringing back from France to break open Roselynde. He could have her declared a rebel and have her entire estate, instead of needing to divide it with others. John shrugged as he broke the seal. The delay probably meant that she had been seeking information about the two he had proposed as husband to her.

John's first real doubt came when he became aware of the weight of the packet. This was no simple letter. Was the bitch cleverer than he thought? Was this some kind of legal argument based on custom and precedent that she hoped would make her immune from his right to choose a husband for her? The first lines of the top scroll, which bore the lady's name, caught his eye and gave him a momentary taste of victory. Stupid slut, did she think that if she pretended to reverence him and spoke of her troubles, he would forget what had passed between them? The fleeting satisfaction made the shock and fury engendered by Alinor's announcement of her marriage so much the more violent.

"Bitch!" John shrieked, throwing the packet onto the table so that its contents spilled out. "Whore! Foul, stinking, cod-swallowing whore! Shit-eating sow!"

The blazing eyes roamed around the room, but living prey was gone. The servants had been sent to wait outside when Neville asked for audience. Neville himself had gasped and slid out of the doorway at the first darkening of the king's countenance. If the doubt he read on the king's brow cleared, he would be just outside, waiting to re-enter. The shriek of rage, however, told him his best safety lay in retreat. As he hurried back to his quarters, a doubt flickered through his own mind. If the messenger had been kempt and well-dressed, he might have been bidden to stay or to carry the packet to the king himself. Had the stinking, ill-garbed creature been a trap? Where was he now?

Neville sent servants scurrying through the castle to inquire regarding the whereabouts of Lady Alinor's messenger. Whether they found him or not was not important. It was the excuse he needed for having left the king's presence.

Temporarily bereft of something that would scream when violence was done to it, John looked for something that would crush, break. The table before him was clear of all such objects. All that lay on it at the moment were the scattered parchments. He snatched up Alinor's letter again, but he did not cast it into the fire. His rage and frustration were such that he froze with the document in his hand, leaning forward against the table. The pressure across his loins vividly recalled all the pain and shame inflicted upon him by the author of the letter he held in his hand.

The memory did not spark another bout of rage. It was so vivid that John reacted as if the paroxysm he had suffered 14 years past had just taken place. His chest heaved and his legs felt oddly shaky. He sank back into the chair he had risen from, staring blindly and fixedly at the parchment he held.

"Mealymouthed bitch," he muttered as he reread the letter carefully. Nonetheless, the submissive tone calmed him further, and he began to think. "Three bishops," he said next. "Much good that may do you. As soon as John Gray is consecrated Archbishop of Canterbury, they can be brought to heel."

But that was not important. John had no intention of annuling Alinor's marriage in so peaceful a fashion. He dropped Alinor's letter and took up Ian's. His expression darkened again. Here was no submission. John had a quick vision of the man who towered over him in height, of the proudly held dark head, the contempt that sometimes flashed across the handsome face, curling the beautiful lips into an unaccustomed sneer. No, the annulment of de Vipont's marriage would not take place tamely through the church. As John began to contemplate the various methods he could use to destroy Ian, calm returned to him. He picked up the marriage contract and felt even better. He could ask a tenth of Alinor's property as a fine and not be considered greedy. With the thirteenth he was asking as a tax on top of that, she would be pinched enough to pinch her dependents in turn. That would be the first. As soon as de Vipont was dead, she could have her choice of husbands again, and he could take another tenth as a fine. John passed his tongue across his lips slowly. Almost three tenths. That was very nice.

The frown returned to his brow, but it was thought, not rage. Why should he be content with three tenths? Just to satisfy Fulk or Henry? Piss on them! He could now have the whole if only he could think of a way to arrange de Vipont's demise so that it looked like treason. Suddenly John's eyes lit, and he smiled. What could be better? What could be more natural? Of course. He would cross from La Rochelle to Portsmouth and then go to Roselynde, hard by. He would do Lady Alinor and Lord Ian the great honor of being their guest as a gesture of forgiveness—and they would treacherously attack him, so that it would be needful to take Roselynde. De Vipont, of course, would die in the struggle, perhaps in the very act of attempted regicide. Alinor would be taken prisoner and held at his pleasure. John licked his lips again, but his mouth was so wet that little bubbles of spittle hung at the corners of his lips.

There was a daughter, too. Very convenient. The son would have to die, but the daughter could be put to better use. John looked down at the parchments on the table and smiled at them almost fondly. All in all, that stinking sow had done him a favor by this marriage. It would give him a good excuse to rid himself of de Vipont, who had been taking entirely too much of his brother Salisbury's attention, and would drop two handsome estates into his hands. De Vipont's property was mostly in the north, too, which would give John a foothold among some very loudmouthed and rebellious barons.

The good humor that these plans generated in the king was markedly increased by the discomfiture of his "dear friends," Fulk and Henry. He not only enjoyed their rage when they saw the rich prizes they had counted their own disappear, but had the additional pleasure of laying the groundwork by which they themselves would permanently remove those promised prizes from their own grasp.

Both Fulk and Henry hated Ian for what he was. They hated him worse because, unlike many others who had treated them with contempt and disdain from the first, Ian had been reasonably friendly. He had been quite willing to overlook their unknown and possibly ignoble ancestry. After all, Simon had risen from nothing and was a fine man, whereas his own wellborn father had been nothing to boast about. Why should not these men also be worthy of friendship, whatever their birth? There was a gradual development of disgust toward them that Ian took no pains to hide, and this was more exacerbating to Fulk and Henry than the mingled fear and loathing with which John's other noble vassals had always regarded them.

It was not difficult for John to play on those feelings. Although vanity, spite, and greed often blinded the king and distorted his judgment so that he did foolish things, he was by no means a stupid man. When he had done with his henchmen, they were ripe for anything—but John strictly forbade assassination. Whatever befell Ian, he warned his men, it must have the appearance of a legal death or an honorable challenge based on reasonable cause. If it did not, he threatened, it would be necessary for him, no matter how great his regret, to sacrifice those who were guilty of harming de Vipont in order to keep peace with his barons. Ian was known as a faithful vassal, and he had played a prominent part in the victories achieved in France. The king would not be able to ignore his murder or allow his murderer to escape.

Unfortunately the king's sunny temper did not long outlast his arrival at Portsmouth on the 12th of December. The first blow fell when the messenger he sent to announce his visit to Roselynde returned to say he would not be welcomed there.

"What?" John shrieked, utterly delighted. "Do Lord Ian and his lady defy me? Do they cast my favor, my wish to do them honor, back in my teeth? By Christ's toenails——"

"No, my lord, no!" the messenger cried, blanching and backing away slightly. "They are not there. No one save a few men-at-arms and the serfs are there. The keep is bare of provision, the garderobes are full and stinking. No insult was intended."

That was the last thing that John wanted to hear; however, his rage was held in check for an instant by the notion that he might take Roselynde Keep without loss or trouble. The happy thought did not hold him long. The noblemen with him would never countenance such an act perpetrated against a loyal vassal; it would cause more trouble than murdering de Vipont outright. Fortunately for the messenger, his next remark suggested an equally satisfactory notion.

"They are gone to Iford, my lord, on progress."

"Iford?" John purred, suddenly alert.

It had been Sir Giles of Iford who pretended to concur with his wishes and then had betrayed him, who had helped Simon trick the garrison of Kingsclere into admitting them. Once in the keep they had wrested Alinor, who was John's prisoner in her own stronghold, from his hands. John had not forgotten Sir Giles. Well, the move to Iford did no violence to his plans. If anything, it was helpful. Sir Giles could die at the same time as de Vipont. In addition, it would be safer to do the work at Iford. The king realized he could rid himself of most of the noblemen who were inconveniently hanging to his tail. Many would crave leave to go home of their own desire; the remainder he could send on to Winchester with Isabella. The less traveling Isabella did in her breeding condition the better. That would leave him free, with none but the mercenaries accompanying him or those witnesses whom he knew to be safe, to pay his "visit" to Iford.

The renewed sense of satisfaction lasted four days. John was impatient to taste his joys, but he restrained himself. He could not hurry Isabella's pace in traveling for fear she would miscarry, which, after her long barrenness, would be a tragedy. Nor could he appear to fret lest he hint at some purpose and wake suspicions in his courtiers. With so happy a goal to dwell upon, John found the day they spent resting at Portsmouth and the second day they spent resting at Netly Abbey more bearable than he expected. Had he known what had occurred minutes after his messenger left Roselynde, he would have been far less content.

Cedric had made his way up to the great hall and into the smallest and least-convenient wall chamber. He knew that the young man who lodged there was in some sense a prisoner and not to be mentioned to anyone who came to the keep. Sir Guy, of course, had no authority, but the lady had sent him on a mission, which he had performed to her satisfaction, and the new lord had spoken to him kindly. Cedric had an idea that he must do something about the arrival of the king's messenger; he knew it was important, but no instructions had been left for him about what to do. It was his instinct to seek orders from the gentlefolk. Since no one else was there, he would ask Sir Guy. The response he received was so much what he had thought was right himself but had been afraid to do without authority that he had no further doubts. A messenger was dispatched posthaste to Iford to inform Lord Ian and Lady Alinor that the king was close by Roselynde and had sought lodging there.

As it was, John's sky was unclouded until, on the road from Netly Abbey toward Winchester, he saw an entourage bearing his brother's colors. Salisbury! The man of all men whose company he did not desire at this moment. It was not that John feared William would ever betray him or play him false, but William had developed a most irritating affection for Ian de Vipont, and William, from long years of experience, was a most astute smoother of troubled waters. It would be virtually impossible either to goad de Vipont into a genuine insult or attack or even to manufacture a pretended situation in William's presence.

"I thought," John said caustically, as soon as Salisbury had kissed his hand in greeting, "that Ela was at death's door. What do you here?"

Salisbury laughed and looked a little surprised. "You know she recovered in her usual way as soon as I came home. She has been very well since then. She even came with me to de Vipont's wedding."

"You attended the wedding?" John asked as the cortege got under way again.

"Certainly. It was a very grand affair. Pembroke was there, and Oxford and Leicester and Lord Llewelyn rode all the way in from Wales. Your daughter seems very happy in her marriage, John. That was a well-made match. He is a born maker of mischief, but she curbs him very well with a word and a sweet smile."

John was not to be diverted, however. "How dared you attend that wedding! You should rather have stopped it. You knew I intended her for Fulk or Henry."

Now Salisbury stared at his brother purposefully. "I heard you make some jest about them, but I never dreamed you were in earnest. We were all drunk, and the last thing you said was that it would be best if the lady made her own choice and paid a fine. I did not believe you could have meant it. She is a gentle, well-born dame. Fulk and Henry are— I know you need such men, brother, because of the state of the realm, but Fulk or Henry and the Lady Alinor— It is unthinkable! Even her daughter would not be safe from them."

"What is that your affair! You did not think me serious, even after you heard what was in my letter?" John snarled. "Or did the gentle, wellborn bitch conceal the fact that she was defying my order?"

"I know you did not like Sir Simon," Salisbury soothed, "but do not let that spill over onto his wife. She did not defy your order. Your letter did not come until the day after they were wedded and bedded, too. The messenger, all draggled and torn, arrived during the swearing of the vassals. He *was* kept prisoner, John. I went and questioned him myself. He was near a week hidden in some outlaw's den."

"My dislike for Lemagne has nothing to do with it," John raged. "You are not such a fool as to forget where Roselynde lies. I need a faithful man in that keep."

"Ian de Vipont is a faithful vassal. He has answered every summons you have sent promptly and with the full number of men in his tail. He has fought bravely in each action. You need fear no treachery from him. I am so sure of that, I will stand warrant for him if you desire. If you must be angry at someone, be angry at me. I knew de Vipont had an eye for Lemagne's widow—well, not so much for the widow, in fact, as for the children whom he speaks of constantly as his own." Salisbury did not really believe that any more. He had seen Ian's reaction to Alinor. It seemed a safer idea to present to John, however. "When you said the lady must marry soon and might choose for herself, I wrote to tell Ian to push his suit."

For a moment John looked as if he would burst. Then he laughed. "Much good your warranty would do me. Do you think I could harm you even if he turned traitor? Do not talk like a fool. But I am angry, William. I acquit you of malice. Nonetheless, you have done me an ill turn. Go home and cosset your wife until my temper cools."

"Do you mean I am not to come to Winchester for Christmas?" William asked, his voice low and hurt.

"No, of course not. If you wish, you may accompany Isabella there. I am angry, but I am not unjust. In fact, I had talked myself around to accepting this stupid business. If you had not come here with your talk of a grand wedding—and a fine bunch of rebels you have been consorting with——"

"Rebels? I? Oxford? And Leicester is no rebel, no matter how much he sits on his own lands instead of coming himself to support you as he should. He will help no other man, either."

"And Pembroke? And Llewelyn?"

"Of Llewelyn, who can say? Even de Vipont, who is some kind of clan blood brother, does not know from day to day what the Welshman will do. For now, you may trust to Joan. But as to Pembroke—you know we do not agree. Pembroke is no rebel. He even spoke for you in the matter of the costs of this war."

"William," John said, his lovely voice high with exasperation, "shut your mouth! If you cease to talk, perhaps I can bring myself to do what I had intended, which was to put a good face on this matter and pay Lord Ian and his wife a visit of honor. If I have to listen to you argue, I will go straight to Winchester and——"

"But brother, where are you going if not to Winchester?"

"I *was* going to Iford, where I have heard Lord Ian and his lady are now staying," John snapped.

Salisbury smiled warmly. "That is truly kind and generous. How glad I am that I rode down to meet you."

The words sparked a question in the king's mind that he had been too angry to voice or even to think of before. "Ah, yes, how did you know I was come? I sent you no word of it."

"I knew from de Vipont," Salisbury answered easily. "That is why I said I was glad I had come. I have saved you a useless journey. Ian wrote to tell me that you had arrived in Portsmouth on the twelfth and that he had decided to go to Winchester to meet you. I suppose Lady Alinor will come also, although he did not say so, and she has the children to consider. Naturally, they are both distressed at having disobeyed your wishes and desire to make their peace with you. They must be there already. Ian said they would lodge with the bishop there."

John stared woodenly ahead. Rage boiled in him, but there was no heat in it, only a cold deadliness that needed no vocal or physical outlet. "Who put that idea into his head?" he asked softly. "And how did de Vipont hear of my coming?"

"Word went out from Roselynde. You must have meant to visit them there and sent a messenger. That was good of you, brother. Truly, I was somewhat afraid that you would cherish a spite against them. I came to welcome you, of course, but also to beg you to be generous in your dealing with de Vipont and his lady."

"Just a few minutes ago you were warranting his loyalty. Are you warning me now that he will turn on me?" John purred.

"Not de Vipont—barring any—er—insult to his lady." Salisbury's eyes shifted. He had hated to say that, but Alinor was very beautiful, and he knew his brother. "He is still young," Salisbury added apologetically, "at least in that way, and very proud and passionate. No, the danger does not come from de Vipont. I am sorry for it, but I must say there was some ill feeling when word of whom you offered as husband to Lady Alinor spread."

"And how did that come about?" John snapped. "Did my loyal vassal Ian de Vipont cry it aloud to excuse his disobedience."

"Now, John, you know there was no disobedience. I

have explained that already. And, no, he did not say who you had offered to her," Salisbury soothed. "Well, what could he say? He was married already. He could not say he was sorry for that—not with the lady standing beside him. What happened was that your letter frightened Lady Alinor. She sought reassurance from the bishops that you would not put her marriage aside. When they said it was a Church matter in which you— er—" Salisbury hesitated. He was too wise to repeat the bishops' assurances that John *could* not interfere with the Church. "In which you would not wish to meddle," he went on, "she was greatly relieved and said she was grateful for it because she did not wish to disobey you but she could not have brought herself to accept Fulk or Henry."

"Lady Alinor was frightened, was she?" John said neutrally.

Salisbury glanced at him, but the king's face betrayed nothing. "She did not say it for any purpose," he assured John. "It was only a woman's thoughtlessness. In her fear she was heedless of what import her words might have."

"And what import did they have?"

After a longer look at his brother, Salisbury shrugged. "What did you expect? I will say the truth. I was disgusted myself. There are enough decent men who are bound to you by tie upon tie and would be faithful in the face of any temptation to reward with such a woman and such estates. Why in the name of God did you choose those two? Every man and woman there was outraged, and the vassals of both de Vipont and Lady Alinor clustered around them to swear again what they had just sworn—support to the uttermost. Whatever use Fulk and Henry are to you, John, this is no way to reward them. You will turn every nobleman away from you."

"What is it their affair?" John snarled.

"They have wives and daughters, too," Salisbury

pointed out. "My own belly churned. Do you think I wish to fear that Ela will end in such hands?"

"Nonsense," John said, almost laughing at the idea. His surface irritation was considerably abated by the thought of his sister-in-law in the hands of his henchmen, but the cold hate for Ian and Alinor lay coiled inside him like a snake.

"For me, perhaps," Salisbury replied, having no idea what had changed John's mood except that he believed his brother was warmed by realizing he could be a strong protector to Lady Ela. "For others who are not so sure of your love and favor, it is a more real fear."

"Oh, very well. There will be no more talk of it. I have told you already that I plan to make the best of the marriage. I will take no more than a tithe from Lady Alinor as a fine, and I will show de Vipont my favor."

"And I may come with you to Winchester?" Salisbury asked with a slight hesitancy. He feared the implication that he did not trust John, but that was indeed the case. John had lied to him often on such matters, concealing his rancor and then inflicting his revenge when Salisbury was elsewhere.

"Of course," John laughed aloud. "If you think you can get so far before Ela's heart begins to beat too hard or her head pains start again."

Salisbury laughed also. Perhaps his suspicion that John's spite was directed against Alinor was incorrect. If so, the worst was over. "I do not fear it," he said gaily. "She started before me to meet us there. She looks forward to cossetting Isabella in her present condition. I declare, that news made her recovery more swift and sure than my homecoming."

Lady Ela was indeed in Winchester, settled into a house her husband had purchased soon after John became king. Salisbury owned similar houses in London and Oxford, other favorite royal places of residence. Of course, his rank and relationship to the king, and John's affection for him, could have commanded a lodging in the castles themselves, but his wife complained so bitterly of the noise and crowding and their effect on her fragile health that private residences seemed necessary. They were also convenient, Salisbury admitted to himself not long after he had been whined and pleaded into the purchases. Ela was always indirect and she never admitted she did anything for his good, but he found himself far better off with a retreat from the court.

Within a day of her arrival, Alinor received a note requesting that she pay a visit to the Countess of Salisbury at her earliest convenience. She was a little surprised. She had not taken to Lady Ela and saw no reason why Salisbury's wife should seek her company— except, perhaps, as Salisbury's wife, carrying some message for him. With Ian's reputation what it was, it would be unwise for Lady Ela to invite him to her house when her husband was away. Alinor knew she would have to go, but Ian was out and she did not know where to reach him. Alinor sent a page for the bishop's secretary, told him where she was going, and asked him to inform Ian when she had left and her destination as soon as he returned. She then threw a cloak over herself, summoned Beorn and ten men-at-arms, and declared herself ready to follow the messenger to the Countess of Salisbury's house.

The first thing that struck Alinor when she entered Lady Ela's home was the immaculate precision with which she was welcomed, divested of her outer garments, her men-at-arms were arranged for, and she herself was shepherded upstairs to the countess' solar. The house did not look like the dwelling of a lazy sloven, and the servants did not act like those of a careless mistress. Lady Ela, however, was reclined on a well-cushioned article of furniture, the likes of which Alinor had never seen before and which gave her a strong desire to giggle. It was a cross between a chair and a bed, narrow, with a high back and arms but with a long footstool attached so that the lady could lie down or sit up as best pleased her. Ela held out a hand, not to be kissed, as Alinor had at first suspected with a quiver of resentment, but to clasp Alinor's.

"It is so kind of you to come and visit me," she sighed. "I should have come to you—a stranger and new-married as you are—but you know my sad health makes even such pleasures a painful effort. And the bishop's house is so large and draughty, and there are so many people coming and going that I cannot bear the noise. Oh, please, do sit down, Lady Alinor."

Alinor complied with the invitation promptly. Now that she was no longer distracted by worry about Ian and the myriad problems of being a hostess to a large and complex group of guests, the expression in Lady Ela's eyes, so much at variance with her whining voice and silly conversation, came into sharp focus.

"You do me honor to invite me, madam," she replied cautiously.

"Oh no, not at all. I will always do for you and Lord Ian anything in my power. William told me, you see, that if it had not been for your husband's help, he would not have returned to me at all."

The voice was so different that Alinor's eyes widened.

"Did Lord Ian not tell you?" Lady Ela continued. "That is a generous man, generous to foolishness."

"He did tell me," Alinor replied after an instant of swift thought, "but what he did is meaningless. He would have done as much for a common man-at-arms, and Lord Salisbury would have done the same for him. There is no debt. I never thought of it again."

"That is generous of you, and kindly said, but I think of it. Of course," Lady Ela's voice changed suddenly again, taking on its normal high-pitched whine, as if she had given Alinor a signal and now wished to see whether she were clever enough to pick it up, "I do not know why I should care. You see how William misuses me, sending me off all alone to face the dangers of the road and to open the house and order the servants and all things, rushing off to greet his brother as if that is the most important thing of all. So cruel, when I am so weak and so troubled by a dizziness behind my eyes and a strange ringing in my ears."

The lips were petulant, the hands fluttered idly and helplessly, but Alinor was not looking at those attention-demanding distractions. Her eyes were fixed upon Lady Ela's, taking in with amazement the bright and mischievous twinkle that dwelt in their pale depths.

"Do you not think William is grossly unkind?" Lady Ela insisted.

Alinor opened her mouth to utter an appropriate platitude, but a giggle came out instead. She gasped and choked. Not a muscle quivered in Lady Ela's face.

"I am sure he does not mean to be unkind," Alinor got out. "Men seldom consider the burdens we women must bear. Look at Ian, inconsiderately spending his time ridding my lands of outlaws instead of staying at home to help me make the wedding arrangements and take care of the guests." Alinor's voice quivered and she uttered another gasp as she strove to steady it. "And never a word to tell me whether he was alive or dead."

"Men are dreadful creatures, are they not?" Lady Ela sighed, as if she were expiring. "They never seem to care about talking at the top of their lungs of the most private things right in the midst of a crowd. It makes my head ache. I can never do so. And men act as if strange servants had no ears and the noise does not trouble them at all. How they do not misunderstand each other more often is a marvel to me. I cannot think, much less talk sense, in such a situation."

"Yes, indeed," Alinor murmured, all desire to laugh gone.

This was the second time Lady Ela had stressed noise and crowds. The meaning finally penetrated to her. How incredibly stupid she had been, but it was a long time since she had been at court and, at that time, no one

had been interested in the doings of one young girl—
at least not interested in the sense of setting spies on her
to hear what she said. In addition, the court had been
different in those days—except for the few months when
old Queen Alinor had sparred with the Chancellor
Longchamp. Richard never felt he needed to set spies
on his subjects. He was willing, even eager, to meet any
rebellion or treachery they planned head on in battle.
There was no need for his subjects to spy upon him.
Whatever faults Richard had, concealing his feelings
was not one of them. John was different entirely. He
was deceitful by nature and totally paranoid. Spies were
as natural to his court as ants to a honeypot, and probably as frequent.

"How stupid of me," Alinor exclaimed involuntarily,
and then, her own eyes twinkling, "here I have been
feeling quite out of sorts, which you know is most unusual to me, and I did not know what was troubling me
until you brought it to my mind. I am quite unused to
the rush and hurry of a court. I think, perhaps, if it is
decided that we will stay, I will have to seek out a house
where I may have a little quiet."

"So wise," Lady Ela agreed. "And then if one has
any little ailment that needs physicking, it may be
attended to easily in decent privacy and comfort."

The question of how often Salisbury, who was as
strong as an ox, might need "physicking" flashed across
Alinor's mind, but it would be both dangerous and ungrateful to ask. Instead she said, "Now that you have so
kindly solved this problem for me, Lady Ela, perhaps
you would be so good as to help me with another. It is
many years since I have been to court. I am sure the
modes and manners are much changed from the time of
King Richard. If it would not weary you too much,
would you tell me how I must bear myself in Queen
Isabella's presence?"

"I am seldom wearied by talking to one person at a
time in a quiet place. Indeed, I find that a restorative to

my health and just the kind of quiet liveliness that is best for me. And I am never, never wearied by giving advice."

That time Lady Ela's lips twitched with amusement, and Alinor was betrayed into another giggle. However, both returned immediately to practicalities. On the subject of when to bow, what form of address to use, and similar matters, Lady Ela's advice was clear and direct. She spoke directly, too, of the queen's exquisite beauty and how great a pleasure it was to tell Isabella how lovely she looked and how well her clothes and jewels became her. It was never necessary to lie or force a compliment, for the queen's taste was excellent, and the king was very generous in supplying his wife with any adornment she desired.

Constant flattery was necessary, Alinor noted mentally, interpreting Lady Ela's complimentary remarks quite correctly.

"The only thing I find distasteful, and that is my fault, is that the queen's ladies are so much interested in the affairs of the realm. The queen is in no way to blame for it. To her credit, she does not listen to such talk and grows quite cross with the ladies when they wander from the more important subjects of clothes and jewels. I cannot but help agree with Isabella. It makes my heart beat much too hard to talk of those matters that are more fitted to menfolk." The whine in Lady Ela's voice was particularly pronounced. "Those foolish women think it a mark of a husband's or lover's affection that he have a loose tongue and tell them all his business. If that is true, I must be sure that William loves me dearly despite his lack of consideration of my feeble health. He is always wanting to speak of such matters to me, but I cannot bear it. It makes my breath catch and my head ache, and the dizziness behind my eyes becomes so great that I must send him away and lie down."

"How fortunate you are," Alinor murmured dulcetly, "both in your husband's affection and in the afflictions that save you from any chance of speaking unwisely. Now I myself am most curious about such matters; I was accustomed to be a scribe to old Queen Alinor and so I grew a taste for state affairs, but Ian will never mention a word of them." Alinor stared wide-eyed into the keen eyes that looked so steadily back into her own. She had neither the intention nor the expectation of being believed, but she was satisfied by the approval in Ela's glance. "I suppose it is because we are so lately married, and he has as yet no trust in me. Perhaps I can learn something to his benefit from the ladies, especially those in the queen's confidence. Then he will trust me better."

"Some of the ladies," Lady Ela twittered, "are more in the king's confidence than the queen's."

"Do tell me," Alinor whispered, hitching her chair a little closer to Lady Ela. "I must pay especially close attention to them."

CHAPTER SIXTEEN

As word of King John's arrival and destination spread, noblemen and their ladies poured into Winchester. Alinor was very grateful to Lady Ela. Owing to her advice, she had been in time to rent a small house not far from the castle. Ian had been hesitant at first, not wishing to offend either the Bishop of Winchester, who had offered them accommodation, or the king, if John should offer lodging. However, far from being offended, Peter of Winchester thought the notion excellent. Though he laughed heartily at Alinor's excuse, no lady to his mind being less likely to be disordered by excitement or exertion, he said he thought it would serve well enough for those who did not know her.

Ian waited on the king as soon as word came that John was ready to receive his noblemen, and came home very puzzled and worried. He had been greeted with what was, to his mind, suspicious blandness. Even though Salisbury had caught him as he entered the great hall to say he had smoothed matters over, it seemed unnatural to Ian that the king made no reference to his marriage except to ask whether Alinor had accompanied him. He had been almost tempted to say she had not, but too many people knew the truth. After a few minutes of pleasant talk, John had dismissed him with an invitation that amounted to a command, for himself and his lady to attend the great feast on Christmas Eve.

More puzzling than the king's apparent indifference was the casual manner of the court at large. The king, as Ian knew all too well, was practiced in the methods of deceit. However, Ian's friends seemed glad to see him and neither hinted obliquely at trouble nor warned him openly of it. His enemies, an even better indicator, seemed healthily enraged by his profitable marriage. There were scowls and snide remarks where there should be and, although he was as watchful as he could be, Ian neither saw nor sensed hidden smirks among the king's intimates that would suggest a secret knowledge of retribution to come.

Alinor could make no clearer sense of what to expect than her husband, even after she had an interview with the king two days later. She had been summoned to a judicial session in the normal manner to make restitution to the king for marrying without her overlord's permission. Ian went with her, full armed, which was not the usual attire for answering a summons from the king. John, however, gave him hardly more than an indulgent glance, as if to say he understood the protective spirit of the gesture but that it was not necessary. And so it proved.

Alinor pleaded the danger to her estates and her son's inheritance from reavers and disloyal and disaffected vassals and castellans in extenuation of her hasty marriage. She added that, the king being at war in France, she did not know where or how to reach him or how long it would be before he returned. If John remembered that Alinor's messenger had found him without the slightest difficulty to announce Simon's death, he did not mention the fact. He allowed the plea of necessary haste and disallowed the plea of inability to request permission on the reasonable grounds that Ian had known quite well where he was and that the fighting was over by that time. Then he set the fine at a tithe—one tenth the value of the income from her estates. It was a heavy fine, but by no means unreasonable.

"You would have done better to take the man I chose for you," John said with a smile when Alinor had bowed her acceptance and given surety for payment of the fine. "William of Wenneval is still alive and hearty."

"It was not a matter of choice for me," Alinor replied softly. "I was married before your offer was put to me by King Richard's order in the Holy Land."

That was, of course, the only answer Alinor could make, but she and Ian discussed the king's remark at length. It was so natural, so reasonable a comment that, had any other person made it, they would have taken it as a signal that all was forgiven and forgotten. Neither could quite believe it of John. He was famous, or perhaps infamous, for never forgetting an injury or an insult. The court at large might take what had been said at face value because they did not know how deeply and personally Alinor had injured and insulted John. To Alinor the mention of the incident was a deliberate reminder that John had not forgotten. It seemed to her that the emphasis on Wenneval's living was a threat that Ian would not live long.

Ian shrugged that off indifferently. He agreed that John had probably meant Alinor to think that way, that the king no doubt wished to frighten her. He pointed out that there was little the king could do to implement the threat.

"There are long knives in dark corners," Alinor snapped.

"Nonsense," Ian rejoined. "The whole court now knows the story of our marriage. Do you think any would doubt where the order came from if aught befell me? In the heat of anger, when he first heard, the king might have thought to be rid of me that way, but he is cool now. He would never give so good an excuse for complaint to the noblemen, who are still whispering about what happened to Arthur. Especially now before he declares a most unwelcome and heavy tax. I think we are safe for now, at least until the Twelfth Day festivities are over. It is then he will declare the tax of one thirteenth, I am sure, and he will desire no cause for outcry until that is safe in his purse."

"Perhaps you are right," Alinor said, "but there are at least two others who are not clever enough to associate your death with the king's tax and who probably believe that the king would not be sorry to hear that you had died of trying to breathe through holes in your carcass."

After which, she drew forth a marvelous thing that had once been Simon's, a shirt of mail with links so thin and fine that it bulked scarce larger than a woolen tunic. It would not turn a sword blow, but under a man's tunic, it would give fair protection from the thrust of a knife. From then on Ian wore it when he went abroad without armor, and Alinor breathed a little easier. However, the precaution was not necessary. Fulk de Cantelu and Henry of Cornhill looked daggers at Ian but drew none with their hands.

On Christmas Eve, Alinor and Ian again appeared dressed as two halves of a whole. It was a day for magnificence, and they were as grand and bejeweled as the greatest lords of the land. It was just as well they had made the effort, because soon after they entered the great hall, a page came running up with a message that places had been set for them at the first table before the dais.

"By whose order?" Ian asked sharply.

"The king's, my lord," the page replied.

"He does me great honor," Ian responded automatically, feeling Alinor's grip tighten so hard that her nails bit into his wrist.

It was far too great an honor. Ian de Vipont was a baron, but there were many with higher titles who should sit closer to the king in the hall by the order of precedence. In spite of their knowledge of John's character, Alinor and Ian had had some hopes that Salisbury's persuasions had induced the king to take the fine and content himself with that, at least for the present. This mark of favor ended that hope. John might swallow his spite enough to ignore them; he would never honor them. The king's character could not change that much. What the king intended, however, remained a mystery until the crowd was finally seated for dinner. Then, before the first course was served, King John pounded the table and shouted for silence. When he had their attention, he announced that a great tourney would be held on Twelfth Day to celebrate the season, their victories in France, and the hope that the queen now carried for the future well-being of the realm.

The room exploded in honest roars of joy and approval. A tourney was always a welcome diversion, and everyone was truly overjoyed to hear of the queen's condition. John was over 40 now. However little he was loved, if he should die without a legitimate heir, civil war was certain. That was even less inviting a prospect than a continuation of John's reign. The noise quieted rapidly again as the king held up his hands.

"Now this is a most joyous occasion," John said, smiling on his subjects, "and I would not wish it to be marred by any personal spites. Thus I have chosen as my champion a man beloved by all and, in addition, newly married. Rise up Ian, Lord de Vipont, and accept my glove as token of your charge and of my love and pardon of any fault that may have come between us."

Ian rose as requested and stepped over the eating bench. When he reached the dais to accept the glove, he was smiling broadly. It was a great relief to Ian that John should take out his spite in this harmless way. He did not doubt that the king hoped he would be well-trounced or even killed, but he was reasonably sure that John would engage in no large-scale plots against him. He might well indicate to his cronies that he would be well-pleased if Ian came to grief. Even if the king tried to do more, Ian was not worried. He had friends enough to back him.

Because all eyes were on her husband, Alinor had a chance to gather her strength and pride. She knew the

king had seen the first stricken whiteness of her face.
His eyes had been on her, not on Ian, whose reaction
he could well predict. Alinor hoped that her expression
of fear would give him pleasure and convince him she
was a silly, helpless thing. Without surprise she heard
the king name William, Earl of Salisbury, and William,
Earl of Pembroke, as judges of the tourney, thereby
removing Ian's most powerful friends from any chance
of fighting in his party. She had not had any expectation
that John would overlook so obvious a move, particularly when the choices would seem to prove the king's
favorable intentions toward Ian. After all, choosing a
man's friends to judge him could hardly be thought of
as showing animosity toward him.

Twelve days, Alinor thought, I have twelve days. In
that time Sir Henry could come from Kingsclere and Sir
Walter from the Forstal. Probably the time was not
long enough to allow Sir John to come from Mersea, but
she would send out a man to summon him anyway. If
Ian should come to harm—Alinor drew a deep breath
and held it to prevent herself from panting with fear—
she would need some loyal vassals. Sir Giles was close
also, but Adam and Joanna had been left with him at
Iford when word of the king's arrival had come. Alinor
did not wish to weaken Iford's defenses in any way, and
Sir Giles' lady was not one who was capable of defending her keep. Ian's nothern vassals and his Welsh ones
also were too far away to be of any help.

That depressing thought gave birth to a far more
hopeful idea. There were a number of northern barons
present. They were not especially friends to Ian, largely because they thought him too close and too loyal to
the king, while they were well on their way to being
outright rebels, but one thing was sure. They would not
kill Ian from behind on the king's orders. The problem
was how, in 12 days, to convince them to fight on the
king's side behind his champion. Normally they would
be in the opposition party. Alinor knew she might do

a little herself during the dancing and entertainments that would celebrate the Twelve Days, and she might do a little with the wives of those men who had wives, if they had brought them to Winchester. However, a woman's word counted for little in such matters.

Alinor needed a man, a man loyal to her, who would not be overly scrupulous in what he hinted about the king. Sir Giles would have been perfect, but Alinor had already decided he must stay where he was. Besides, Sir Giles had been involved in the original trouble with John. His sudden appearance at court would arouse sharp suspicions in the king. It might even spark so much animosity in him that he would forget appearances and move openly to attack Ian.

More cheering drew Alinor's attention. The king had appointed William, Earl of Arundel, to lead the "loyal opposition." It was another nice touch. Arundel was a competent man in battle, who was certainly no enemy of Ian's or Alinor's. He had known Simon well, and they had worked together in the administration of Sussex where Arundel held large estates when Simon was sheriff. Alinor curved her lips into a smile, acknowledging to those who bothered to look at her that she approved the king's choice as a suitable and yet not dangerous opponent for her husband. Suitable he certainly was—for the king's purposes. Alinor knew Arundel fairly well herself. The only subject upon which he was competent was fighting. For the rest, his head might as well have been a block of wood. Still, Arundel in himself was not dangerous, even if John should manage without his knowledge to seed his party with men who hated Ian. They were opponents. Ian would be prepared to guard himself against them. What Alinor feared was those who would join Ian's party, either to run him through from behind when no one would see or to desert him at a crucial moment.

Arundel, Arundel. The words seemed to echo in Alinor's mind, and pleasantly at that. Was there something she had not remembered about Arundel himself that might help Ian? It was, after all, seven years since she had spoken to the man. Then she smiled again, a real smile, not a mechanical curving of the lips, and her eyes brightened. It was an appropriate moment. Ian had just returned to his seat beside her. He was delighted at her self-possession and her seeming pleasure, although he was sure she was not deceived by the king's words and manner. However, Alinor's expression had little to do with Ian and, had he known the reason for it, he would have been appalled. Alinor had remembered what it was about Arundel that pleased her. Sir Guy had sold the king's messenger's horse in the town of Arundel, and Sir Guy was obviously just the man she needed for what must be done.

The next ten days were furiously busy for both Alinor and Ian, but the pressure was inordinately greater on Alinor, who dared not give the appearance of doing anything more than waiting on the queen, buying at the enormous fair that had opened to cater to the court, and visiting friends. The fair in particular was a godsend. It was there that she was able to meet a young knight-errant who sported a close-clipped beard and mustache in King John's style. Alinor complained sharply that he had ridden across her path so suddenly that her horse shied. The young knight apologized most sincerely, saying his mind had been elsewhere. The lady would not be so easily appeased. Low-voiced, she continued to scold. The knight-errant apologized again, at length, even dismounting to stand beside the lady's stirrup. Still she scolded, and, murmuring assurances, the knight remounted and rode along with her to her destination. If anyone had noticed the young knight when he arrived at Winchester, they might also have noticed that he was much richer after that chance encounter—but no one did notice. Word of the king's tourney was spreading, and every knight-errant within riding distance was making his way toward the town to take part in it. There would be rich prizes in horse and armor ransom with so many of the courtiers competing.

The one important piece of good luck Alinor had was that Ian was too busy to pay much attention to her. He and Arundel had met with Pembroke and Salisbury the day after Christmas to arrange for how many would compete, which field they would use, and such details. They had to meet again to rearrange everything. For one thing, the king had suddenly requested a day's jousting to precede the melee; for another, the tournament was arousing more interest than anyone had expected. Owing to the short notice, both Ian and Arundel had assumed only the knights at court would take part. Obviously someone had taken care to spread the word widely abroad. Every younger son who wished to add ransom money to his thin purse was besieging either Ian or Arundel for a place among his men. Before they could refuse and set hard limits, a message came from the king that no one should be refused; all were to be welcomed to this celebration of joy.

At first, Ian tried to keep this information from Alinor, but the queen's ladies were not so considerate. It was not that all of them intended to be unkind, merely that many would not have cared one way or another about the fate of their husbands in similar circumstances. Moreover, Alinor had gone to considerable trouble to impress upon them and upon the queen that her feelings were exactly similar. Ian was a convenience. He had saved her from the king's henchmen—Alinor did not hide her abhorrence of Fulk and Henry, but she couched it in terms that would surely please Isabella; she pandered to the queen's pride by decrying their low birth. More, even, she affected a bright-eyed, excited interest, saying, quite truly, that she had never witnessed a tourney before. This opened the gates of speculation among the ladies, and Alinor gathered a great deal of information that her husband would have preferred she did not have.

When, at last, Ian found a chance to draw breath and look at his wife, it inevitably became apparent that Alinor knew what was going on. Ian was shocked by her apparent calm. Rumors of his wife's indifference to him had already reached him via a number of thoughtful ladies who felt such a man to be wasted on so cold a wife. Considering the source, Ian had paid no attention to the hints and invitations. Nor did he now believe Alinor to be indifferent. She might not love him as she had loved Simon, but she certainly did not wish to be a widow again—not here, when she would be almost completely in John's power. Then, Ian deduced, if Alinor was calm, it was because she had some little plan working.

However, he did not see what it could be and he did not dare question Alinor, on the very slim chance that she did not understand that, as the size of the tourney increased, so did the danger. When Sir Henry rode in from Kingsclere and Sir Walter from the Forstal, he was rather relieved. No man disdains two loyal and worthy fighting men at his back. If Alinor's plan was to call in her knighted vassals and castellans to support him, Ian had no quarrel with it. When Leicester came in with four of his vassals the day before the start of the jousting closed the lists, Ian was a little annoyed. Calling up one's vassals was one thing; begging help from friends was another. He could say nothing to Leicester, of course. Had Leicester simply wished to fight, he would have signed in much earlier. For Ian to comment that Leicester had offered himself only in response to Alinor's pleas would impugn the earl's courage. Ian accepted his offer with suitable expressions of pleasure and vowed to himself to have the matter out with Alinor as soon as he saw her.

Later in the day, however, Leicester's action was put out of his mind by an even more curious event. As he was returning home for dinner, Ian was accosted by Eustace de Vesci, one of the leaders of the rebellious

barons of the north. Ian knew him and his two companions, Robert de Ros and Peter de Brais, fairly well.
They were brave men, and Ian had nothing against
them personally. However, their training and attitude
toward government were diametrically opposed to his.
Ian had long accepted Simon's concept that the good
of the realm must be considered equally with or, sometimes, even above one's own interest. These men, like
many others, did not disdain the good of the realm;
they merely assumed that if their own interests were
served, the realm would naturally also be served. Vesci,
to Ian's amazement, offered himself and eight other
northern knights as participants in Ian's party.

"You are very welcome, gentlemen, very welcome
indeed," Ian responded with a quizzical lift to his brow.

"We would crave the honor, Lord Ian, of positions
directly behind your banner," Vesci continued.

Ian stared into the broad, heavy face. A stubble of
red beard showed on cheeks and chin, betraying the
strong admixture of Norse blood. Briefly Ian wondered
whether these men were taking this chance to remove
someone known to be loyal to King John, who would
make a weak link in the chain of northern strongholds
that were to be committed to rebellion in the not-too-
distant future. But Vesci's eyes met his purposefully,
and Ian put that unwholesome thought aside.

"If you desire it, I will do my best to arrange the
matter," Ian agreed slowly.

"We northerners must stand together," Vesci said
pointedly. "If we do not, we may be picked off one by
one. We thought it best to serve in the king's party this
time. We wish to display our appreciation for the love
the king has shown to one of our countrymen."

That remark was not so palatable, but Vesci and his
friends gave Ian no chance to reply. They wheeled their
horses and rode off, shouting "Till Tuesday," leaving
Ian to digest the various implications. The most obvious
was that they wished to draw Ian into their group by

associated guilt even if he was not a member of it in fact. That would be the more believable if the king began to show any resentment over the marriage. Ian rode home, sourly contemplating that idea, and presented it to Alinor. First she looked startled, but finally she shrugged her shoulders.

"Likely that is in their minds. They think that the king, who already has a cause for spite, will become more suspicious of you, treat you worse, and drive you into their arms. I wish it were so—not that you should be a rebel, but that the king *could* hate you worse than he already does. I greatly fear that nothing they or anyone else can do will alter John's feeling toward you now." She looked away across the room. "I have done you an ill turn by yielding to you, Ian."

Cursing himself for a fool, Ian took Alinor's hand. "You have made me very happy. The rest does not matter. John's nature being what it is, sooner or later I must have fallen foul of him. Look at Pembroke, who fought for John's right to the throne, who has been loyal in every way. He is hated merely for giving honest advice. At least I have a prize worth the whole world and more to me as compensation for the king's hatred." And then, seeking for something to distract Alinor, Ian added, "But I wonder what Vesci meant by that bit about their appreciation for the king's love. You know, Alinor, the matter can be read in another way. Vesci could mean to hint to the king that if favor is shown to the northerners, they will 'fight in the king's party'; that is, they will be loyal."

Alinor nodded. "I am sure they would take no exception to that reading. It can do them no harm, and will place no restraint upon them, either."

There was, however, still another interpretation, one that did not occur to Ian until suggested by a not-too-welcome visitor. After dark, Robert FitzWalter craved admittance. Ian and Alinor exchanged startled glances, and Ian rose from his chair beside the fire with a black scowl on his face.

"I will go down and tell him you are not well and I cannot receive him," Ian growled. "I could not prevent him from signing on to my party, but I do not have to receive him into my house."

FitzWalter was also no friend of Ian's, but there was a difference in Ian's feelings toward him and toward Vesci and his group. This was based largely upon an act of cowardice or treachery that had been instrumental in the loss of Normandy in 1203. FitzWalter and Saer de Quincy, his boon companion, had surrendered without a blow a key spot of defense of the province, the great fortress of Vaudreuil, to Philip of France. Thus they had opened the whole area to easy and uncontested conquest. FitzWalter had excused his act by saying he had appealed to the king and had received neither any help nor even any answer.

This was perfectly true. John had acknowledged the plea by paying FitzWalter's and de Quincy's ransoms and had not punished them in any way for yielding the castle. However, it did not mitigate the act in any way in Ian's eyes. Everyone knew that John was in one of his periods of lethargy. Had FitzWalter closed up the fortress and fought, it was entirely possible that John would have been aroused and come to his support. Even if the king had not wakened to action and the fortress had to yield in the end, the battle would have depleted the French forces or even delayed Philip so long that the change in season would have put an end to the fighting and saved the province. To Ian's mind, FitzWalter was guilty of either cowardice or treachery —and that was a far cry from Vesci's bold and open agitation against the king. Ian disagreed with Vesci, but he did not dislike him.

The firelight and the ruddy glow of the candles concealed the fact that the color had drained from Alinor's cheeks. "Wait," she said. "FitzWalter does not come here after dark on a winter night to make idle conversation. It cannot be wise to turn him away, no matter what you feel. Let him come up."

A moment's consideration convinced Ian that Alinor was right, and Owain, who had come up with the message, was sent down again to show FitzWalter in. The immediate shock of hearing that FitzWalter was to fight in Ian's party having passed, Alinor's complexion had returned to normal, but she kept her eyes lowered to hide the blaze of animosity in them. FitzWalter was a very likely candidate for an attempt to run Ian through. He must be paying in a variety of ways to retain John's favor now that every attempt to retake Normandy had failed.

"In what way can I serve you," Ian asked coldly, when Owain had brought a chair and FitzWalter was seated.

"Not at all," FitzWalter replied smoothly. "On the contrary, I have come to serve you, Lord Ian. I have heard some rather disturbing rumors about this tourney."

"Nonsense," Ian snapped, glaring angrily at Fitz-Walter. The man was a coward and a treacher, but no fool. Doubtless his purpose was to make Alinor as unhappy as possible. "I have the greatest confidence in the honesty of Salisbury and Pembroke, and Arundel is too much a man of honor to lend himself to any irregularity."

Ian started to rise, as if to show his guest out, but Alinor said, "Things can be done without the knowledge of the leader of the party. Of course, the rumors may be false. One need not believe them. Still, deliberate deafness can also be a mistake."

"As your lady says," continued FitzWalter, "I do not necessarily believe what I have heard, yet— There is a knight-errant of the 'loyal opposition' who is suspiciously rich for so young a man and one who has no great name. As with others to whom wealth is unusual, he has spent more than he ought on wine. He hints that there is a party within that party who has been paid—and promised more—in lieu of what ransoms they might have taken, so that they will devote themselves to making sure that the king's champion will not come alive from the field."

Ian ground his teeth, bitterly regretting that Fitz-Walter was seated in his own home so that he could not smash his mouth shut. Worse, the man was not even of the opposing party, so that he could take out his rage upon him on the tourney field. He was so furious that he could say nothing, but Alinor's voice came smooth and unshaken.

"We thank you for the warning, my lord. It was kind of you to come with it. May I hope that you will also carry word of this rumor to the Earl of Arundel?" She took a vicious pleasure in the look of discomfiture on FitzWalter's face, then rose gracefully with her hand extended. "I know you are in great haste to do this, so do not allow us to detain you."

Like a sleepwalker, Ian also rose. FitzWalter had no choice but to follow suit and was shepherded out of the solar by his mute and fuming host. Fortunately, Ian's squires were well-trained. Owain was occupied, but Geoffrey was waiting in the small antechamber into which the stairs rose, and Ian was able to hand FitzWalter over before his temper erupted. With scant courtesy, he turned away to hurry back to his wife. Alinor was leaning back in her chair with closed eyes.

"It is nonsense," Ian said furiously. "And even if it were not, I am not a child. I have fought in enough wars where my blood rather than a ransom was sought. I am well able to take care of myself."

Alinor opened her eyes slowly. "I do not fear your ability to guard yourself against Arundel's party," she sighed, "but FitzWalter came here for a purpose, and that purpose was not to warn you against treachery."

"Of course not. He is John's creature and came to frighten you—oh, and me also, I suppose."

"No," Alinor said. "At least, that was not his main purpose, although it might be a welcome side benefit."

"Now, Alinor——"

"Listen to me," she cried, getting to her feet. "His purpose was to fix your attention on Arundel's party——"

"That is ridiculous. Where else would my attention be?"

"It should be on your own back," Alinor exclaimed. "If you look for treachery in Arundel's party, you will be blind to it in your own. You said FitzWalter is the king's creature. Is he above running you through from behind? It has been dry for weeks. The grass is dead and brittle. How long will it be before the dust is so thick that the watchers will see nothing——"

"They are likely to see a hole in the back of my mail," Ian put in caustically. "Do not be so silly, Alinor. That is the last thing the king would desire."

"Oh, FitzWalter will not be alone in it. Perhaps he and the other favorites of the king, for whom it would be natural to fight in the king's party, will have some arrangement whereby the hole is in the front. You will be surrounded by men seeking your blood. You must— Ian!"

Alinor's furious and despairing cry was wrung from her because her husband, who had been looking more and more blank, had suddenly burst out laughing, slapping his thighs and stamping around in a circle.

"The king's love," he gasped, when he was able to speak, "that was what Vesci meant by appreciating the king's love. I did not think Vesci was the kind for tortuous planning. And Leicester!" He began to laugh again. "I was furious with you, Alinor. Leicester came to me today and offered himself and four of his knights, and I thought you had gone to him and asked for his help. Now I see. Leicester and Vesci must both have heard what FitzWalter came to tell us." Then he wiped the tears of mirth from his eyes and sighed. "You need not worry about my back. There will be Vesci and his party, Leicester and his, and Sir Henry and Sir Walter."

"Do not trust overmuch to Sir Henry," Alinor whispered, fighting tears.

"You are not going to tell me that Sir Henry will try to harm me," Ian said sarcastically.

"No," Alinor found a wavering smile. "Do not be so silly, but he becomes blind with fighting and cannot keep more than the battle he is engaged in in his mind. He will be no guard for you." Behind the words, she was thinking that she would need to get word to Sir Guy to watch especially for FitzWalter and any close companions. Then she knew she could hide her fear no longer. She went to Ian and put her hands on his forearms. "Let us go to bed, Ian," she whispered. "I am so cold—so cold."

Her hands struck like ice through his velvet sleeves, and he did not protest that it was very early or that a long night of love play was no way to recruit a man's strength for battle. He gathered Alinor to him and carried her to the bed.

CHAPTER SEVENTEEN

The day of the jousting dawned clear and fine, as so many days before had. The weather had been remarkably dry and mild through the entire autumn and winter. In the long hours of the night, while Alinor lay carefully still beside her sleeping husband, she had occasionally prayed for rain—heavy, pouring rain—but there was no conviction in her prayers. It could not rain forever, and the moment the weather eased, if only to a drizzle, the tourney would be held. Just as uncertainly, Alinor at one moment prayed that Ian's knee would not be able to withstand the shocks of jousting, and at the next that it would be totally unaffected. If she could have believed that injury to his knee could keep him out of the melee, she would have been more wholehearted about her prayers. It was far more likely that he would fight anyway, crippled or not.

The jousting did not arouse the same terror in Alinor as the melee. There was much less chance for treachery in jousting. Although she did not doubt that some of the men who challenged Ian would try to kill him on the king's instructions, Ian was no novice in the art. If he was not as deadly a jouster as Simon or Pembroke had been in their youths, because his slender body did not carry the same weight, he was nonetheless very skilled. She had seen him joust against Simon before Simon's illness. It was a common sport for them in those days. Simon said he needed the exercise; Ian said he needed the experience; both simply joyed in the activity, and Alinor's initial nervousness that one or the other would be hurt by accident had soon dissipated into pleasure at watching two experts in a magnificent performance.

It was thus not difficult to greet Ian's easy waking with a smile, to watch him dress and arm, to ride with him and talk easily of whether they should send for their clothing and change at the castle or whether there would be time to return to their house. Ian insisted on the house, saying with a laugh that he would need to bathe to rid himself of the dust he would be rolled in, and it would not matter if he was a little late for dinner, as, king's champion or no, he did not expect to win the prize for jousting.

They parted at the edge of the field. Ian rode toward the tent where the jousters could replace their armor if it was damaged, get a drink, or be treated for an injury. Owain and Geoffrey, leading two spare destriers, followed him. Alinor, trailed by Beorn and Jamie and four other men-at-arms, rode toward the loges where seats had been set for the king, those noblemen who were not taking part, and the women. A three-sided, tentlike structure had been erected over the benches to keep off the wind and charcoal-burning braziers warmed the area within. Hot stones were available for the feet of those who felt the cold.

Having dismounted and looked around, Alinor realized with a quiver of distaste that the space left vacant at the king's right was for her. She should have known that it would be so. Ian's appointment as king's champion made it mandatory that his lady be seated in a place of honor. Her heart sank a little as she saw Isobel seated to the left of the queen. She had hoped that she could sit beside her friend, who would offer a word of courage or sympathy to support her, but she lifted her head and came forward to sink into a deep curtsy before the king and another before the queen. Isabella smiled at her quite graciously. She knew her husband did not like Alinor and, in general, she was not overfond of handsome women herself, but Alinor was very pleasant and amusing. John smiled also. Alinor watched the flash of his teeth beneath the dark mustache and wondered why they were not pointed more sharply. Surely a ravening wolf should have sharper teeth.

"Oh, do sit down, Lady Alinor."

The high-pitched whine drew Alinor's eyes before she needed, in courtesy, to lift them to the king's. It was Lady Ela, well-wrapped in furred garments, with a maid standing behind her so that she could lean back on that support if sitting upright became too exhausting. Another maid hurried up to remove a packet of cooling stones and thrust some newly heated ones beneath her mistress' feet.

"Do sit down," Lady Ela repeated, a trifle impatiently. "The wind has been blowing right through the space left for you, and my left side is aching with cold."

Instinctively, Alinor looked up at the cloth of the tent, which was perfectly unmoving, and then, as she turned to sit, at the pennons, which hung limp in the still air.

"I think I must have been mad to come here," Ela whined. "It is all William's fault. He insisted I would take pleasure in seeing the jousting. Why should I take pleasure in it? It will serve him right if I fall ill and die of this cold. And I know I will have a painful ague in my side for weeks and weeks, and he will say—oh, he is a monster about such matters!—that no one could have taken cold on so mild a day."

"I do not feel very cold myself," Alinor admitted, "but I am used to riding out in all weathers."

"Oh, you should not do so," Isabella put in, leaning forward across her husband to discuss this entrancing subject. "It is dreadful for the complexion to expose it in that way."

"Ladies, ladies," John urged in his sweet, mellow voice, "please allow Lady Alinor to watch the proceedings. After all, she must have a sharp interest in them, even if you have not. Her husband is playing a noble role here."

"But nothing is going forward now," Lady Ela whimpered after the barest moment of hesitation. "And I do not believe Lady Alinor is large enough to keep the wind off me. I feel a dreadful stiffness in my arm already. Ah! A twinge! I feel a twinge in my side!"

A hysterical giggle rose in Alinor's throat, and she quenched it sternly. "Perhaps if I sit a little closer to you, Lady Ela, I will be able to warm you somewhat," she suggested.

Ian dismounted when he reached the head of the lists and looked toward the loges, the rein loose in his hand. Before his eyes found what they sought, the rein jerked and there was a shriek of consternation behind him. The evil-tempered gray destrier had launched a vicious kick at someone who had passed unwisely close to his heels. Uttering a resounding oath, Ian grabbed the bridle and hung on to it, forstalling an attempt to rear, while he brought the loose end of the rein up to slap the nose of the stallion as it snapped at his arm.

"A very spirited beast," Salisbury remarked, strolling over.

"Lord Rannulf's strain," Ian grunted, holding the rein under the animal's lower jaw in a determined grip. "I swear the devil sired each and every one, but they know their business and are strong in work."

"He will need to be," Salisbury said drily. "You are remarkably popular for a man who is not famous as a jouster."

"What?" Ian asked distractedly, wrestling with his recalcitrant mount.

"I said your horse will need to be strong in work. There is a list as long as my arm that wish to joust against you."

Snorting and stamping, the gray destrier at last gave

over showing his displeasure at wearing an empty saddle by trying to kill everyone in reach. Although Ian did not relax his grip, he was able to turn toward Salisbury.

"I have come prepared," he said neutrally. "My squires hold two other destriers. My horses will not fail. For myself," he shrugged, "I will do my best."

"I am sorry," Salisbury remarked obliquely. "If I could have turned some of them away, I would have done so, but for the jousting that is not allowed."

Ian understood well enough, but he had known John would encourage and possibly even pay any man willing to enter the jousts. It mattered very little to him. John might take pleasure in seeing him tumbled from his horse. It was a cheap and meaningless pleasure. Ian did not have the kind of pride that rested on invincibility. He had been tumbled by Simon too often for his self-respect to be damaged by a fall in jousting. His attention wandered toward the loges. Alinor, he saw, was in earnest conversation with Lady Ela. Salisbury followed his eyes and smiled.

"Ela told me your lady has not been to a tourney before. Do not worry about her. Ela will take care of her."

"But Alinor is—" Ian began and then closed his mouth on the information that she was inured to a lot bloodier sights than a tournament. If Alinor wished to be thought of as sheltered and weak, she had a reason for it.

"She is not so incapable as you think," Salisbury encouraged. "Keep your mind on your own business."

At that moment the trumpets sounded, fortunately drowning Ian's brief hoot of laughter. Salisbury hurried away to his duties, and Ian shifted his grip on the rein preparatory to remounting. After another brief tussle, he made it into the saddle. The heralds were calling his name at one end of the field and Arundel's at the other. Ian settled his tilting helm over his mail hood and touched his now-docile mount with his heel to ride forward and take the lance Owain was offering. He fewtered it and watched Arundel do the same through the eye slits. The trumpets blew again. The heralds cleared the field. Ian eased his rein and touched his horse with the spur. Eagerly it leapt forward.

The impact of Arundel's spear on his shield was minimal. It, as his own, was deliberately ill-aimed and slid off easily over his shoulder. The horses pounded past each other, slowed, turned, and trotted back to their positions. The second and third passes were identical. Conversation in the loges was hardly interrupted. This was the formal opening of the tourney, and everyone knew that neither man had the smallest intention of unseating the other. The only thing that could have altered the result was if one of the horses had been clumsy and slipped on the dry grass.

Formally, the heralds announced no result, offered another three passes if a conclusion was desired. Formally, Ian and Arundel declined, saluted each other, and rode back out of the lists. Two young and inexperienced knights took their places. Ian lifted off his helmet, rested it against his saddle, and watched with mild interest. He would need three new castellans for Adam's property, as soon as he ousted the three who had not come to do homage. He had one man in mind, but if he saw a young knight of unusual promise, he might use him in the fight to regain the keeps and then, if the man was as good in battle as in the tourney, give him one of the smaller castles to hold.

The first two were useless. One did throw the other, but Ian shook his head in disgust. He would never have permitted so ill-trained a squire to be knighted. He was sure the stroke was luck on one side and sheer inability on the other. Owain, he thought, could do as well. Another pair came forward. One was a little better. He held his spear well and threw himself forward almost at the right moment. His opponent went down on the first pass, but that was more because his defense was poor than because the blow was of any moment. Not good enough.

"Challenge to the king," the herald called. "Sir William of Barnsley will challenge the king for three acres of arable."

Ian hissed with irritation as he replaced his helmet. He had forgotten that there might be genuine challenges, or that the king might offer restitution of contested property to those who would prove their case on his champion. Ian did not know Sir William. He watched the man carefully as he rode toward his end of the field. Not so bad. He rose a hair higher to the left when he moved to his horse's gait. His left leg was stronger than his right. Once again, as the trumpets blew and Ian clapped spurs to his mount—a good deal more firmly this time—he wished he weighed two stone more. Since that was not possible, his trust must be in Lord Rannulf's horse.

Nor was the trust misplaced. The speed that the gray stallion could achieve in a short distance was totally incompatible with its thick legs and heavy-set body. Ian was two thirds of the way down the field, and his opponent's horse had not even hit its best stride when his lance took Sir William well left on his shield. The point slipped, caught a boss; the shaft bent as Sir William hung precariously. Then, as the man's legs braced against the pressure, the stronger left leg, involuntarily reinforcing the push of Ian's spear, tipped him over the cantle. Ian slatted Sir William's lance off well to the side and rode on past.

The loges applauded a neat piece of work. The crowd shouted happily. The heralds called the result aloud. By prowess of his champion, the king was confirmed in his possession of the contested three acres of

arable. Ian cursed John under his breath. He had no
way of knowing which challenges were bribes. Had he
known, he would have taken as good care as he could
not to unseat an honest challenger. An inconclusive result on the field would leave the case open for settle-
ment in the courts, where such cases belonged.

Alinor watched the pass with smiling approval.

"A well-placed stroke," the king said to her.

"Yes, my lord," Alinor replied gravely, her eyes
demurely lowered so that John would not see the
amusement in them. "It could not be otherwise, for he
was trained and practiced by my late husband, Sir
Simon who, as you know, was one of the great jousters
of his day. Until Simon fell ill, he and Ian spent hours
each day jousting. You remember, I believe, that Simon
was as great a master of the tourney field as Lord
Pembroke. Of course, Ian is too thin to be as fine a
jouster as Simon, but——"

"I do not like it," Lady Ela whined. "I do not like
the way the dust is starting to rise. Just look. If the
wind shifts, it will blow upon us. It is very bad for me
to breathe dust. It causes a catch in my throat."

Alinor turned to her other neighbor. "It seems to
be settling very fast," she soothed. "If it should drift
this way, you can cover your nose and mouth with a
veil, and I will fan the air away."

The ridiculous interruption was very apt. Alinor was
reminded that King John was not the right person upon
whom to exercise her teasing wit. She had said enough
to prepare the king for Ian's continued success so that
he would not be betrayed by temper into displaying his
peculiar displeasure at his champion's triumphs. At the
immediate moment, it had also given John time to reconsider his next remark. In view of all the attentive
ears so close around him, the king said something
quite unexceptional about how fortunate they were in
the mild weather. By then, Sir William had been helped

from the field, his horse caught, and the heralds were calling the next joust. Conversation lapsed.

The next challenge was again for the king's champion, but this was only "to prove valor." Ian knew this opponent and grinned in the safe concealment of his helmet. Young ass, he thought, as he braced his lance. He deserves to be set on his ear on the first pass. However, one makes allowances for the son of an old friend, and for a young man, some ten years younger than oneself. Ian hardly touched the gray destrier with his spurs on the first pass. He was a little surprised at the power of the blow he received. It rocked him back against his saddle-tree before he tilted the lance off his shield. The young grow up, he thought. Little Robert de Remy was 21, not 11—and he was a second son, a good boy, well-raised. Perhaps Robert would like a castle of his own to hold.

"Come," Ian muttered to the gray horse, "let us have a little more, but not too much."

The ears twitched back, and the beast snorted. Plainly, it was accustomed to being spoken to. The easy tone, Ian realized, did not communicate what he wanted. "Ha! Ha!" he urged, and the stallion increased his stride. Ian's lance took Sir Robert's shield exactly right, a little off center, so that the impact forced it toward the body. He threw himself forward just as the gray destrier came down on his forelegs. Sir Robert slid sideways out of his saddle and grabbed at the pommel, releasing his own lance. Because Ian had made no attempt to slat off Sir Robert's spear, it caught the young knight a violent blow as it responded to the pressure of Ian's shield and completed the work of knocking Sir Robert out of the saddle.

Ian wheeled his horse to see whether Sir Robert had landed awkwardly; the stallion, more a warhorse than a tourney mount, promptly reared, forelegs flashing dangerously to strike the unhorsed man. Roaring blasphemies, Ian wrenched his mount's head around and called an apology. He was relieved to see Sir Robert climbing to his feet as he rode back out of the lists. Owain ran forward with a fresh lance.

"Send Geoffrey with my compliments to Sir Robert, the man I just unhorsed," Ian instructed quickly. "Tell Geoffrey to say that I was greatly pleased with the improvement in Sir Robert's jousting and that if he is interested in serving under me, I will have some work in hand early in the spring. Whenever he is ready, we can talk of it."

He was about to add a little more—that Geoffrey should tell the young man where they lived and when was the best time to catch Ian at home, but the heralds were calling for the king's champion again, and he had to ride out to meet the challenge. It was another young knight, and Ian unseated him on the first pass. Then there was still another, not so young this time, a jouster who had seen many tournies. Neither unseated the other, but the blows his opponent delivered hurt and numbed Ian's shield arm, which was a little tired by the repeated shocks it had taken in close sequence.

Breathing under the tight-closed tourney helm was also becoming less easy. Ian was gulping air through his mouth, and he was growing dry for a drink as the activity warmed him, so that he sweated freely. He heard the king challenged again, "for the steading of Westfield in Norfolk," and recognized the name of the challenger. Sir Thomas was no young lightweight either. Ian turned the gray horse toward the lists again, felt the lag in the animal's stride. He wondered whether he had been wise to send Geoffrey to Sir Robert. It began to seem as if he might not be in any condition to receive him—or anyone else. The tip of his lance quivered, and Ian eased his grip on the shaft. He was tiring and clutching it too tightly.

Careful, Ian warned himself, careful. This man probably has a good right to what he challenges for. It was a cursed mischance that brought him up against an opponent he was not willing to unseat when he was too tired to judge his blows nicely. The first and second passes were successful. His lance slid off Sir Thomas' shield, and the blows he fended off did not shake him severely. The third pass was a disaster because his lance was flawed. It shattered as soon as it made contact with the opposing shield. Thus, the impact he endured was not diluted by any counterpressure.

Ian gasped with pain as his left arm was slammed back into his chest, but long training held. He forced the arm up, tilting his shield, allowed himself to lean backward into the cantle of his saddle, and pressed his knee urgently against his destrier's side. The horse turned sharply away from his opponent. With a scraping screech the lance point slipped upward. Painfully, Ian wrenched his head further aside, lifted the shield still higher, and finally thrust it outward as the lance fell away. At the same time he threw down the end of the shattered shaft he held and gripped the pommel of his saddle.

The wonderfully even stride of his mount, and instinct, held Ian in the saddle. Unguided, the horse slowed and turned as it had each previous time. Sobbing breaths brought air back into Ian's laboring lungs. Sufficient strength returned to his right hand so that he could lift his rein and bring his horse back into position, but he was in serious trouble and he knew it. If the challenger for the steading of Westfield demanded another three passes, he would never withstand them. The heralds were calling something. Ian shook his head, trying to clear the buzzing in his ears.

Something was wrong with his timing, Ian thought dazedly. He should have had a few minutes' respite while the challenger arranged for the next three passes. Then he thought resentfully that more was wrong than just his sense of time. He should have been accorded the courtesy of accepting or refusing the renewed challenge. Technically, he had the right to refuse and to

demand a different form of combat to settle the
question. He was too numb, however, to argue. Peering
glassily through the eyeslits of his helmet, Ian tried to
find Owain with a new lance. The squire was nowhere
near. Ian wondered if he was so dazed that he had mistaken his position. He swung his head right, then left.
No Owain, but his vision and hearing were clearing
well now. He saw Sir Thomas at the far end of the
field, arguing vociferously with Pembroke while two
other knights were in position at the ends of the lists.

Knowing his face was hidden by his helmet, Ian
closed his eyes and uttered a short prayer of thanksgiving for his faithful friends. Pembroke must have
known he was badly shaken. Doubtless he had raised
some technical point of honor that prevented an immediate challenge and then said that the tourney
should continue while it was settled.

"Lord?"

It was Geoffrey's voice, just a trifle too loud and
assertive. Ian hoped he did not look as pallid as he felt,
but he had to breathe air unfouled by his own gasping.
He lifted off his helmet and looked down. Geoffrey was
holding up a bowl of wine, his hand shaking just a
little.

"Are you well, lord?"

"I am glad of a chance to catch my breath," Ian
replied. "My thanks for the thought," he added, taking
the wine from Geoffrey. He drank, shuddered. "Child,
it is not watered," he exclaimed, then laughed shakily.
"I am not so faint as to need that. Go bring me another,
but more water than wine. I am athirst, but I do
not want to add my drunkenness to my opponents'
abilities."

When Geoffrey returned, Ian drank more slowly.
"Where is Owain?" he asked when the bowl was empty.

Anger made Geoffrey's eyes lighten to a flashing
gold. "He is going over every lance inch by inch with
Jamie to help him. He was like to die of rage when

that one broke at the first touch. It was my father who sent me for Jamie. The lances came from the king's armory. They should have been———"

"Enough," Ian said sharply. "A flawed shaft can escape any armorer's eye now and again."

The three passes were over, but two other contestants had taken the places in the lists. Salisbury had now joined the conference between Pembroke and Ian's challenger. Ian watched them for a moment longer, then reached out to tousle Geoffrey's hair.

"Tell Owain to leave Jamie to check the lances and come back to his place. I am ready to joust again now, and I will have to settle with the gentleman, who seems to be determined to win Westfield over my body."

It was not completely true that Ian was ready to joust again. His shield arm still ached, and it trembled slightly when he lifted it. He was tired, too, but he could not allow Pembroke and Salisbury to delay the challenge much longer. The king, Ian could see, was staring in their direction. He rode slowly around the edge of the field. His horse, he noted, seemed to have recovered faster than he and was quite light and easy in movement. The devil took care of his own.

"But my dear Sir Thomas," Salisbury was saying, "this is not a trial by combat. This is a tourney to celebrate several happy events. The king has graciously consented to show his love and respect for Lord Ian by permitting himself to be challenged, but no provision has been made for bringing such matters to a final conclusion. And there are so many others eager to try———"

"Lord Arundel was offered a second passage," Sir Thomas grated furiously, obviously repeating something he had said before.

"But Lord Arundel———"

"Please, Lord Salisbury," Ian interrupted. "Sir Thomas has what he believes to be a just quarrel, and no fault can be found in him because my lance failed. If he desires another passage of three, I have no objection to it."

"There is no time, Lord Ian," Pembroke protested. "We will be here long after dark."

Ian smiled. "I think what is best will be to take the matter to the king. I am sure Sir Thomas and I will both be satisfied with his decision."

What Sir Thomas might have replied to this mischievous suggestion would never be known. Before he could open his mouth, another voice spoke with asperity. "May I ask what goes forward here?"

The four men, who had been concentrating on one another, were all startled. All heads turned sharply. Salisbury and Pembroke bowed. Ian and Sir Thomas, who were mounted, bent their heads. Salisbury began to explain the situation as succinctly as possible.

"If Lord Ian and Sir Thomas both desire to conclude the matter," the king said without allowing Salisbury to finish, "I do not see why they should not."

"Very well, my lord," Pembroke agreed stiffly, "but that will make it necessary to allow any gentleman to do the same. In which case, those men who came late to challenge will need to forgo their chance. The days are short. It will be dark long before we come to the end of our list."

Something flashed briefly in John's eyes. It might have been his dislike for Pembroke, but Ian did not think so, because the cold black stare passed over him briefly.

"I see," John continued. "That would be most unfair. Some of those who came late to challenge have ridden a far distance to join the sport. I am sorry to deny you, Sir Thomas. You rode well. It would have given me pleasure to see you ride again. But your cause is not lost. Perhaps something can be done to return Westfield to you."

This last sentence was dismissive. Sir Thomas could do nothing else but thank the king and ride away.

"Your wife seems to be enjoying herself," John then remarked to Ian.

No doubt he meant to convey that Alinor did not care what happened to her husband. Ian's lips curved a little. John had closed that gate to jealousy himself with his offerings for her next husband. Even if she had hated Ian, he knew Ian was better than Fulk de Cantelu or Henry of Cornhill.

"I hope she continues to enjoy the jousting," Ian replied, but there was suddenly a note of strain in his voice.

It had just occurred to him why the king was anxious for the last challengers to have their chance. He bowed again and touched his horse gently. Perhaps it was the sweat drying on his body, but suddenly he was chilled. Fulk and Henry were both fine jousters. They, if anyone, would have the skill and would take real joy in laying Ian in the dust. They were here, at court, although Ian had not seen them, probably because they were avoiding him. Why had not their names appeared at the head of the list? Because they were waiting until the end to catch him at his weakest, a weary man on a weary horse. Dimly, Ian heard the start of another run. To kill him, he wondered. So that Alinor could be offered as the tourney prize the next day?

A cry of pain and the roar of the crowd drew Ian's eyes. He saw only the end of it, the torn belly, whitish pink guts spilling out and the bright red gushing blood, but he knew how it had happened. An ill-held shield had tipped the lance-point into the soft abdomen instead of past the ribs. The ache in his shield arm made him set his teeth. An ill-held shield— Oddly, it was not the fear of death that stung Ian at that moment. It was that ridiculous remark about Alinor enjoying herself. She was enjoying herself because her husband was, thus

far, a victor. Alinor had great pride. She would not
enjoy seeing her husband die, but she would not enjoy
seeing him tumbled into the dirt, either.

Since Ian's thoughts were conducive neither to ease
of mind nor to lightness of spirit, it was just as well
that the King's champion was called for soon after the
dying knight had been carried from the field. Owain
was ready with a lance, muttering grimly that if this
one did not hold he would skewer himself on the blunt
end. Ian managed to smile and say it was not Owain's
fault, but his mind was not on his squire. He found
himself ridiculously nervous, just as he had been the
first time he had jousted at a tourney. He was not
frightened in the sense that he was afraid of being hurt
or dying; he was nervous of making a fool of himself,
of doing something that would arouse contemptuous
laughter.

So fixed was Ian's mind on the various stupidities
that had moved him to laugh at inexperienced knights,
that he very nearly committed the most gauche of all
on his first run. He aimed his lance so poorly that it
caught in his opponent's and was nearly wrenched from
his grip. He did hold on to the weapon and, presumably, the watchers thought he had tried some tricky
refinement that had not worked, because there was no
laughter. Ian felt his face grow hot beneath his helmet,
but his shame was a private matter. Whether embarrassment would have led to further awkwardness, Ian
never discovered. On the second run he realized why
his lance had not been wrenched away. For sheer incompetence, no other rider he had seen that day
matched his present opponent. His guard was awry;
his seat in the saddle was terrible; in fact, he should
never have been allowed on the field. What idiot had
knighted this idiot?

Diverted completely from any fear of incompetence,
Ian inserted his lance cleverly between the man's body

and his shield arm—so open was his guard—and lifted him from his saddle bodily. Then he dropped him, contemptuously—unhurt and relatively gently—onto the field. To his dumb amazement, this neat, comic by-play was received with only the commoners' roars of laughter. Instead of riding back to his place, he went over to Salisbury. The earl grinned at him and shrugged, motioned to him to bend down, and repeated the name Ian had not caught. That explained it. One of John's passel of bastards. Before Ian could make any remark, the king's champion was being summoned by the heralds again. Salisbury looked at him blankly.

"We will rest you as we can," he promised. "There were fortunately few *gentlemen* who wished to challenge you, unless they had a cause to do so, but there were others——

It was all he or Pembroke could do. Ian lifted a hand in salute and went to take a fresh lance. The encounter with John's foolish, vain son had restored him. His shield arm ached, and he was still tired, but fatigue was not unknown to him. To his surprise, the fatigue did not seem to increase much in the beginning. For that he was sure he had Pembroke to thank. Simon's old friend was a tourney master equaled by no other, and he could judge a jouster most finely. There would be two or three easy passes and then a hard one. Invariably, after that Ian would have a period of recruitment while other knights ran against each other. Robert de Remy was one of the most active, and Ian noticed with pleasure that he was really very good, better than his run against Ian would indicate. Probably he had been nervous; it was not an easy thing to challenge a man one is accustomed to thinking much superior to oneself.

Alinor had been mildly alarmed when Ian's lance broke, but mercifully she did not realize how badly he had been shaken. For some time she was able to watch the jousting continue without any real anxiety. Even when Ian changed his horse, although she knew he was being punished as severely as his mount, she could see no change in his graceful seat and outwardly easy handling of his lance. Worry began to prick her at the second change of mount. It was not only that she began to realize how bruised and achingly tired Ian must be. In addition, she recognized the horse. The gray stallions might all look the same to others, but Alinor had known each of them since the day it was foaled. Small differences in color, in characteristic behavior, identified them to Alinor. Ian had not changed to the third fresh destrier; he had remounted the first animal. That could only mean that he was saving the third stallion for some severe trial he knew to be coming.

A young knight screamed, blood showing as he went down under Ian's lance. Alinor shuddered and drew her furred cloak closer around her. It was horribly clear to her that Ian was too tired to manage his lance properly now. He would never deliberately harm a virtually unknown youngster. She saw him throw down the weapon and call something to the attendants, ride over, curbing his horse to speak to the fallen man.

"I am so cold," she whispered.

Immediately there was a furor of activity. A brazier was moved closer; new hot stones were fetched to warm Alinor's feet. A spate of words poured from Lady Ela's lips, mingling "I told you so's" with personal complaint. Alinor's hands were seized by a maid and rubbed briskly. Before quiet was restored, Alinor had her terror under control. If her smiles of thanks to those who attended her were stiff, they were still smiles, while the brisk patting applied to warm her cheeks had also brought color back into them. Moreover, often repeated in the spate of words was the pointed remark that the sun was well down in the western sky, it was overtime for dinner, and Lady Ela was hungry.

She said it so often, and her high whine was so car-

rying in spite of the noises of the watching crowd and
the other people in the loges, that the disaffection began to spread. Some of the courtiers began restlessly to
look at the sun. The queen leaned over and whispered
to the king. He made some soothing answer, but
Isabella, once alerted to a desire of her own, was difficult to quiet or divert. She replied pathetically, her
hand going to her abdomen. John cast a glance of
venomous dislike at his sister-in-law. If Isabella left,
the ladies would go with her, even Alinor, and half his
planned pleasure would be stolen. He had waited long
and patiently to watch her as her husband fell. Isabella
spoke again, her voice rising on a sob so that Alinor
caught her final words.

". . . silly sport, that you care nothing for the harm
my hunger may do your heir. We will not speak of me!
I do not matter! And do not tell me that you will have
food brought. I ache from sitting so long on this hard
bench. I know I do not matter, but——"

John took her hand and patted it. His voice was an
indistinguishable soothing purr as he spoke directly into his wife's ear, but the tone was unmistakable. Isabella subsided. Alinor stared unseeingly at the field, her
small hope that Isabella would force her husband to
declare the jousting at an end seemingly killed. However, it was immediately apparent that the queen had
accomplished part of her purpose. John rose and signaled to a herald, who hurried over. Soon the trumpets
blew, and word was called across the field that, owing
to the lateness of the hour, all challenges "for valor"
would be dismissed. Such matters might be as well
settled in the melee the next day. Only those who had
a real quarrel or a challenge for the king would be allowed to joust.

Through the announcement, Alinor sat quietly, apparently unmoved. She had heard what John ordered
while his attention was on the herald, and her doubts
and fears were now under control. Her mind squirreled

around behind her impassive face. Was it better for Ian?
Worse? If many real challenges for the king's champion
were unanswered, it would be far worse. Ian would
have no rest at all. Alinor swallowed nervously. In the
shelter of her heavy cloak, her hands twisted together.
Ela's whine in her left ear was a meaningless cacoph-
ony, but she was glad to turn her head toward it, glad
that her blank, blind eyes would give no satisfaction
to the monster who sat on her other side.

To Ian, the announcement meant nothing beyond a
few more moments to sit still. He had reached the stage
of exhaustion where his mind was not functioning beyond the recognition of his own call to action and the
performance of acts so drilled into him over the years
that they were mechanical. He saw Salisbury and
Pembroke hurry toward each other, the herald who had
charge of calling the combatants join them. He did
not wonder what they were about. He simply did not
think at all. When the sun's glare pierced through the
eyeslit of his helmet, he merely turned his head a little to block out the ray. He did not realize that only
when the sun was very low in the west, would it strike
at that angle.

The trumpets blew again. The herald began to call a
challenge aloud. Suddenly, the primitive instinct of
self-preservation pierced the fog in Ian's brain. He had
recognized the names of the challengers. The challenge
itself was incredible! Fulk de Cantelu and Henry of
Cornhill were joint challengers, demanding that the
king make good his promise to them, of which King
John claimed to be absolved by the Lady Alinor's marriage. If Lady Alinor was not free, they claimed an
equivalent heiress must be offered in her place. Even
Ian heard the roar from the loges. He was awake now,
unmercifully aware of the grinding pain in his left knee
and left arm, the miserable ache of his whole abused
body. He was aware of a dry mouth, of laboring

breath. Whatever the king's purpose, those two men intended to kill him if they could. Then no equivalent heiress would be needed. Alinor herself would be the sacrificial lamb.

Ian touched his tired horse with a spur, then had to rowel the beast harder to make it move. Just as he started, he caught sight of Owain running across the field toward the herald. He almost called out to him to stop, bothered by some vague notion that his squire would say he was too tired; then he remembered the arrangements he had made when he was still capable of thought. The herald called a pause while the king's champion changed horses. Ian caught just a glimpse of a horseman riding up to Pembroke as he went around the back of the tent where the fresh destrier was tethered. He felt a single flash of amusement. That must have been either Fulk or Henry protesting. Whoever it was would receive short shrift from Pembroke. The sluggish gait and hanging head of the mount he was riding were mute evidence that Ian was not seeking any unnecessary delay.

His amusement evaporated when he needed to dismount so that his saddle could be shifted. Owain and Geoffrey had to help him, and if Owain had not held him upright, he would have fallen when Geoffrey ran to get him a drink. He did not protest that the wine was not watered this time. In fact, from the way it burned going down his gullet, he suspected it had been liberally laced with usquebaugh. Mounting was even more hellish, but once in the saddle, the rearing and bucking of the fresh stallion made him feel better. It was as if some of the horse's fierce energy was transmitted to him. Still, it would be a very near thing if he managed three passes against Fulk and Henry. These were not country squires trying to regain a parcel of land nor fresh young men seeking to establish themselves as jousters.

As soon as Ian came around the tent, the trumpets sounded. That was a piece of luck. It permitted him to start his horse some dozen yards from the head of the list. Another time and place or against another man, Ian might not have seized the advantage. Now, he jabbed his horse hard and fewtered his lance as he moved. There was no need to look for weaknesses; he doubted his opponent had any.

The shock was appalling. Ian heard his saddletree creak as he slammed back against it, but his arm held, his own lance held. His teeth clenched as he felt his body lift, and he forced himself forward against the pressure. Crack! The sound was as sweet as an angel's voice, and the pressure against him released suddenly. Another crack. That was not so sweet. His own lance splintered also. He heard the roar of appreciation from the crowd as the forward leap of his destrier saved him from falling forward. One pass.

Ian brought his horse up short, turned and galloped back to seize a new lance. The wine burned in his blood. He was ready before Henry and deliberately fretted the impatient stallion, so that the moment the other started and he could loosen his rein, it leapt forward almost at a full gallop. The second shock, to his surprise, was not so bad. He was not even moved in his seat and, although he did not unseat his opponent either, he did slat off the lance and have the pleasure of seeing Henry twisted under the impact of his own spear.

The third time it was Henry who started first. Ian was a little surprised, because Owain had been right at the head of the lists with his fresh lance. Even the gray devil Ian was riding could not compensate for the speed Henry's horse had developed. Desperately, Ian swung his legs back a little to brace against the impact better. His knee screamed as he gripped the saddle, but his eyes remained fixed on the point of the bobbing shield that he must hit. Bad! He could feel himself tip. It would be a bad fall! And then the blessed crack of overstrained wood again. One more desperate effort——

It was the roaring of the crowd that told Ian he had unhorsed Cornhill. The effort he had expended had brought brilliant flashes and black spots to obscure his vision. He tightened his rein, felt the speed of the horse slacken. Oddly, in spite of the peculiarity of his vision, he did not feel faint. There was no need for him to clutch at the pommel of his saddle to keep from falling. Three passes.

Only three more. For the first time, a little spark of hope that he might succeed flickered in Ian. It seemed to set the drink he had taken afire in his blood again. Think of it! Instead of seeing him humiliated, John would have to give him the prize. Ian was not sure how many men he had unhorsed today, but he knew it was many more than any other jouster. If only his vision would clear completely. Intermittently now he could see, but his eyes were still not trustworthy. No, he would not be granted time enough. Owain was thrusting another lance into his hands just as the trumpets blew. Ian's jab at his horse was vicious.

He was not surprised when he felt his lance slip along Fulk's shield. He knew he had not been able to keep a steady aim. Instinctively, as the metal screeched among the bosses of Fulk's shield, his legs tightened to hold him steady against the blow he would receive, but the pain in his knee was nearly unbearable. His right knee thrust all the harder, and the horse, war trained, veered sharply toward Fulk's mount, snapping and trying to rear midstride to strike with its hooves. The shock of contact twisted Ian in the saddle, but the abrupt change of angle produced by his mount's action and the response of Fulk's destrier allowed the lance to slip away. Four passes.

Because he knew there was no point in being first at the head of the list, Ian checked his stallion's pace and walked it back. He did not care what anyone thought now. Every man who had ever fought at all understood what his condition must be. To walk the horse might gain him a minute or two of rest, and that might gain him a victory. He was so close now. When he reached down to take the lance Owain held, he shook his head slightly. The squire could not have looked more worshipfully at God. And he has served with me long enough to know better, Ian thought. Nonetheless, even though he knew better himself, it was a spur to his pride. No matter how foolish, it was a more cogent reason to succeed than all the real good that might be accomplished by a successful run.

Ian fewtered his spear and, quite deliberately, allowed his shield to tip inward, as if his arm was too weary to hold it straight. This was near to the truth, but not quite true. He knew his left leg was beyond use to brace him. Thus, he could not endure the full impact of a tilting lance. He could only use the desperate device Simon had once shown him. He could hear the rich bass voice.

"Only if your arm be broken or your collarbone, and you cannot hold any blow off with the shield. Then, when the lance strikes, you must twist so, and lift your right elbow out so, and then, if the shield swing free enough and your timing is very nice, very nice, indeed, then the lance will slip off between your body and your right arm. Of course, if your timing is not so nice, you will have your belly ripped open or your right arm torn off. It is not a device I would recommend. In war, if death be the only other way, a man might use it—I have. In a tourney, better, far better, take your fall and pay your ransom; you can afford it."

Only the ransom to be paid this time was too high— King John's gloating satisfaction, the light in his squire's eyes, a whole day of battering and torment gone for nothing, Alinor's safety, or if not hers, that of some other innocent woman. No, Ian would not pay that ransom. He roweled his destrier and took as steady an aim on Fulk's shield as he could. He had to hit fair this time. One more time, he told his tired body. One more time pays for all.

CHAPTER EIGHTEEN

Alinor did not know whether she wanted to kill or kiss Lady Ela. She never saw the last pass of tilting that overthrew Fulk and won Ian the rich prize the king had offered. Quite suddenly, when that pass had started, Lady Ela had cried out, "I am shivering! I am shivering!" Alinor's eyes had been drawn to the sharp sound involuntarily, and when she looked back toward the men, there was a maid standing right in front of her, blocking her view of the field while she rubbed Lady Ela's hands. By the time Alinor had shoved the maid aside, it was all over.

At least Alinor had no doubt, even momentarily, about what the outcome was. The roars of approval from the loges would never have been uttered for Fulk, nor, even if the man had been well-loved instead of well-hated, would they have been uttered for a fresh challenger who overthrew a much tried and overworn jouster. Besides, among the roars, she heard one angry mutter that the "stinking, slimy snake had what he deserved for so scurvy a trick." Alinor realized that Fulk had tried some device of which the noblemen disapproved. If Ela had known of that through some rumor, she had done what she could to save Alinor from seeing her husband struck down. She had also saved Alinor from displaying any overviolent pleasure in the outcome and thereby exacerbating the royal temper even more.

The latter problem was eliminated when Geoffrey came tearing across the field to summon Lady Alinor to her husband's assistance.

"My lady, he came down from his horse smiling and and then he fell, and we could not wake him," the boy whispered, trembling all over.

Alinor rose at once and curtsied to the king, who did not even bother to hide his satisfaction. Angry words rose to her tongue, but it was more necessary to get to Ian at once than to tell the king what she thought of him. And it did pass her mind also, that it would do Ian more harm than good to show John openly her hatred and contempt. She made some brief formal apology, which was accepted with a self-satisfied nod.

The king had hoped that Ian could be finished in the jousting, but he was not really surprised or disappointed when that did not happen. An experienced jouster, even a tired one, is seldom killed, although if Fulk's trick had worked, it might have been fatal. Had Ian been unhorsed, the chances for a sad outcome would have been much greater; for example, a man could be trampled when his opponent returns to help him. Ian's own horse had nearly killed a young jouster early in the day. However, John had far more elaborate plans laid than an "accident" while jousting. His one concern had been that Ian might be severely enough injured, instead of being killed, to prevent him from fighting in the melee the next day. He knew that had not happened. Everything was working out for the best. De Vipont would be sore and stiff and clumsy, but he would have no wound to which he could point as an excuse. Tomorrow, he would fight, and die, and no one would be able to point a finger of blame at anyone.

Lady Ela watched as Alinor and Geoffrey moved toward the jouster's tent, but her eyes were on the boy. Alinor's hand rested comfortingly on his shoulder, and her head was bent as she spoke to him. He looked different than the glimpses Ela had caught of him when he was in Isabella's service. She had not helped him then, when he needed help so badly. Now she blamed herself bitterly for refusing to take him into her home, but at the time she had still been childless, and she had had some crazy fear that William would try to make Geoffrey heir to her father's lands and would come no more to her bed. Now she had a son of her own, and she could also judge her husband more rationally. She had been a fool to hate that poor woman, dead before Ela herself had married William, and to transfer her spite—as she had done—to the innocent child was unforgiveable.

William had accepted her refusal to take his bastard into her care without argument, but he had not really forgiven her—not until he saw the boy at Alinor's wedding. That was another debt Lady Ela owed Lord Ian and his wife. Her eyes slid sideways toward her brother-in-law. How she hated him! Sometimes when she and William sat beside John at state dinners, she became really ill with the passion of hate that burned in her. Somehow, someday, she would show William what that creature really was. Somehow, someday, she would destroy that doting love that still saw only an unhappy baby brother instead of the poisonous viper into which the child had grown. William still sought to save John from himself, but it was far too late for that. There was nothing left to save.

Meanwhile, Alinor was saying comfortingly to Geoffrey, "I watched most carefully. Lord Ian has taken no fatal hurt, I promise you."

The promise was easy enough to redeem. When she and Geoffrey arrived, Ian was already sitting on a campstool, cheerfully arguing with Salisbury and Pembroke about attending the king's feast that evening.

"What?" he was protesting, "will you deprive me of receiving in person the one and only tourney prize I am ever likely to achieve?"

His lips were smiling, but when his eyes moved to Alinor, their expression curbed the hot speech she was about to utter. Later that night, she called herself a fool a hundred times over for yielding to him. Had she known why he insisted on attending, she would have set her men on him to hold him down by force. When they first reached home, however, the idea did not seem so unreasonable. Although Ian's knee was swollen, and he groaned dismally on getting into a hot bath, he seemed lively enough. Alinor did wonder whether his eyes were too bright, but he was taking so much pleasure in recounting the maneuvers that had saved him one time or overthrown an opponent another time that she had not the heart to bid him be still.

Later, she blamed herself for not recognizing the feverish activity of exhaustion. She had seen it often enough in Adam, but she did not expect it in a grown man. It carried Ian through the ride back to the castle, which he made on a quiet palfrey with his left leg hanging out of the stirrup, and through the groups that rose from their places at the tables to greet and congratulate him and to ask anxious questions about why he was using a crutch. They were rather late; the meal was on the table and half eaten, but portions were eagerly provided for them. Alinor began to have doubts when Ian would not eat, but he was still talking and laughing feverishly. When the prize was brought to him, nervous energy lifted him to his feet to make a speech of acceptance.

"I thank you, my lord, for the honor you have done me, and I accept this prize as a token of the far greater prize I have won. Remember, my lord, that by overthrowing those who claimed her, I have won on the field of battle God's sanction to my marriage with Lady Alinor and, more than that, His sanction, to which I am sure you will add yours, that Lady Alinor will be forever free of any forced choice of husband. If I should die tomorrow, or the day after, or even ten years, or twenty, or fifty hence, Lady Alinor, by God's will, must be free to act as she chooses—to marry or not to marry, and if she marry, the man to

be of her free choosing, not from any proffered list
of suitors."

The hall was as silent as if it were empty. Men and
women with food in their mouths forebore to chew;
men and women with cups at their lips forebore to
swallow. All waited on the silent, staring king.

"Come," Ian urged in ringing tones, "I have saved
you a mort of money and contested lands this day.
Will you confirm my prize to me before this honorable
concourse of gentlefolk?"

What answer the king would have made had he
been left to his own choice was questionable. However,
into the silence came a low whisper from the back of
the room: "What was won today will be lost tomorrow." Had even a draught stirred the hangings that
voice would have been lost, but in the aching silence
that followed Ian's challenge to the king, the words
hissed through the hall like the whisper of the Father
of Evil.

Eustace de Vesci got to his feet. "Confirm his prize,
my lord," he shouted.

And first half, then three quarters, of the men in
the room were on their feet. "Confirm!" they roared.
"Confirm!"

Old King Henry would never have gotten himself
into such a situation. King Richard would have shouted
the whole hall down. In the face of force, John yielded.
With his yielding, the impetus that had driven Ian
disappeared. He slid back into his seat, the fire fading
from his eyes, the color from his skin. As surreptitiously as possible, Alinor put an arm behind him, fearing he would fall off the bench. After a little while,
as the lesser prizes were being distributed, she coaxed
him into drinking some wine, and that revived him
enough to sit upright until the ceremonies were over.
After that, stubborn courage lifted Ian to his feet. The
courage might not have been quite enough to carry
him out of the hall, however, had Robert of Leicester

not come over, ostensibly to say a word about the
melee the next day. A companionable arm around Ian's
shoulders also managed to provide considerable support.

Outside, Alinor abandoned pretense, ordered Beorn
and Jamie to lift their master into the saddle, and told
Jamie to ride pillion behind him to keep him there.
Ian began to protest, and she turned on him with blazing eyes.

"Shut your mouth, you fool!" she raged. "Well for
you I am too well-bred to say what I think in public.
What did you think you were doing in there? What did
you expect to gain? Do you think the king more likely
to keep this promise than any other?"

"No, you bad-tempered bitch, I do not," Ian responded, temporarily invigorated by fury. "But I do
think he will be so angry at me that his spite against
you will be pale by comparison."

This logical piece of insanity so enraged Alinor that
she became quite speechless. She did not say another
word nor, in fact, make any sound until, in their bedchamber, she had stripped off Ian's clothes. Then she
uttered a cry of consternation. In the hours that had
passed since Ian had been bathed, the redness Alinor
had noted on his flesh—and put down to the warmth
of the bath and the irritation of the heat in his armor—
had darkened into hideous bruising. His left arm and
breast, his right wrist, elbow, and rib cage were all
blue and purple, shading to black. Ian's eyes followed
Alinor's.

"Oh, hush," he sighed wearily. "What did you expect when I was battered nearly insensible. It is nothing, only bruises. Let me sleep."

Nothing, Alinor thought, as she pulled the bedcurtains closed, he says it is nothing. But he must fight
again tomorrow. How will he lift a shield on that arm?
How will he sit a saddle firmly when his knee will not
hold him? Wildly she wondered whether she could

give him some drug that would keep him out of the battle, but such an idea was only a mark of the temporary hysteria of fear that had gripped her. To do such a thing would be the end of their marriage. Ian would leave her. Love, if he loved her, would not outlive the dishonor she would bring upon him.

It was an interesting choice, Alinor thought, crouching shivering before the fire. Would I prefer to lose Ian by death or by hatred? But even as she posed the question, Alinor knew her preferences were irrelevant. It was Ian's life. Although she might manage that in small matters, she had no right to interfere in this. There was no doubt in Alinor's mind that Ian would far rather be dead than dishonored. Nor was he deceiving himself about the possibility he would die the next day, Alinor knew. That piece of divine lunacy about directing the king's hatred to himself was no more than a sugared comfit for her. Alinor was no fool, once her sudden rages abated. What Ian had done in the hall was to announce publicly that he knew there would be an attempt made to kill him and to pledge every man there to safeguard his wife's freedom.

Alinor whimpered aloud in her pain. Ian, too? Ian, too? She could not bear it. She had hardly finished weeping for Simon, and now she must begin to weep for Ian. And this weeping would be bitterer by far. Alinor had nothing to reproach herself for in Simon's death. He had died peacefully and willingly. But she had murdered Ian, as surely as if she wielded the sword or mace that would strike him down. In her lust and her fear and her loneliness, she had leapt at his offer of marriage—and now he would die for her weakness. And there was nothing she could do—nothing.

A groan from the bed brought Alinor's self-recrimination to an abrupt end. Idiot that she was to sit lamenting what had not yet happened! She rose from the hearth and hurried to the antechamber where she gave orders that sand was to be obtained at once, and jars of cold water. The sand was to be heated, then poured into soft sacks, and cloths must be found for soaking in the water. While these preparations were being made, Alinor went softly to the bed and opened the curtains. So deeply was Ian sleeping that his eyelids did not even flicker when the light touched his face. Alinor fetched her chest of medicinals and softly, carefully, she began to apply unguents to Ian's bruises. Even then he did not stir, although from time to time he groaned.

It was a night that would return to Alinor in nightmares for many years, but toward morning her total despair began to lift. Not only did Ian seem to be sleeping more lightly and naturally, but the hours of application of hot and cold to his bruised body appeared to be having an effect. He was shifting himself more easily, and his groans had faded into silence or an occasional grunt of discomfort when he turned onto a tender spot. Two or three hours before dawn he even roused and looked blearily at Alinor.

"What are you doing?" he muttered querulously.

"Treating your bruises, so that you will not be stiff as a plank of wood tomorrow," Alinor snapped.

He passed his tongue across his lips, and Alinor held out an imperious hand. A maid hurried to put a cup of watered wine into it. Alinor lifted Ian's head and put the cup to his lips. He drank thirstily, then reopened his eyes, squinting against the light.

"Come to bed," he complained. "It is very late. Leave the maids to tend to me. I cannot sleep when you are not beside me."

Alinor repressed a hysterical giggle. What had he been doing until now? On consideration, however, it seemed like a good idea. She had slept very little the night before and not at all this night. She knew she would have to sit beside the king again during the melee. Whatever happened, she did not wish to give him the satisfaction of seeing her distress. Also, if the worst happened, she would need a clear mind to plan what to do. A few hours of sleep would be a great help.

In the end, Alinor had more sleep than she expected or intended. At last, however, a half-recognized sound disturbed her, and she woke with a start to an empty bed. Terror seized her. "Ian!" she shrieked, leaping out into the room.

"Alinor!" Ian exclaimed.

And William of Salisbury, who had just closed the door behind him—that being the sound that had wakened Alinor—politely turned his back.

"I beg your pardon," Alinor gasped, retreating hastily to the shelter of the bedcurtains, where she drew on her bedrobe.

"You need not," Salisbury replied with a grin. "So lovely a sight can never offend."

"Lovely," Alinor laughed, quickly gathering up her hair and plaiting it. "All unkempt as I am, I must look like a witch."

"Madam, if witches looked like that, I could be easily reconciled to the unholy brood."

"Stop trying to seduce my wife right in front of my face," Ian said with amusement. "Draw up a chair and join me. I am sorry to tell you to serve yourself, but my knee will not serve me."

Despite the complaint, Alinor's spirits lifted as she looked at her husband. The gray pallor of exhaustion was gone, his eyes were bright, but normally so, and, best of all, he had already consumed what appeared to be a massive meal and seemed to have every intention of eating still more. True, his movements were stiff and, Alinor guessed, painful, although his expression gave no evidence of it. Nonetheless, Alinor was reasonably sure that once his muscles were warmed by activity, they would serve him faithfully. Salisbury's appearance, however, was far less satisfactory. Now that his startled pleasure at Alinor's nude appearance had passed, he looked decidedly uneasy.

"You are early astir," he said to Ian.

"Early?" Ian was surprised. He glanced toward the window, which was bright with daylight. "It must be well after the prime. I must be on the field to place my men before terce."

"You are sore overworn. Surely you will yield your place to another man. There are several who have offered to stand in your shoes this day."

Ian looked even more surprised and a little offended. "I had some heavy work yesterday, but what is that? A night's sleep has restored me—you can see that."

"But you said your knee was injured. That——"

"My knee will not serve well for walking, but that is no reason why I cannot sit a horse. For jousting, perhaps, such a thing is a disadvantage, but there will be no play with lances this day," Ian said sharply.

Salisbury glanced at Alinor, who had just filled a goblet with wine and handed it to him. Her face was set like stone. "Do you wish me to retire, my lord?" she asked stiffly. "I will, if it will make you more easy, but I assure you that you can tell me no more about my husband's danger than I already know."

Uncomfortably, Salisbury stared down into the contents of his cup, turning and turning it in his hands. Ian glanced sidelong at Alinor, but said nothing to contradict her. He went stolidly on with his meal, leaving the next move to Salisbury.

"Why did you do it?" the earl asked at last, the words wrenching themselves unwillingly out of his throat. "He did not deserve it. Oh, perhaps he did encourage jousters to go against you. He was angry that you had stolen so great a marriage prize and would have taken pleasure in seeing you overthrown, but——"

"Let us pretend that you did not ask that question,"

Ian said softly. "Let us say that you did me the courtesy to come and see if I was well enough to fight, so that you could ask the king to appoint another leader if needful. You have seen that I am quite well. Tell me something more important. Does Oxford hold to his intention about Ireland?"

"Ian," Salisbury said painfully, "please answer me."

"What do you want me to say?" Ian asked furiously.

"It must be plain, my Lord Salisbury, that my husband felt an urgent need to enlist support for me," Alinor put in smoothly. She liked Salisbury, and she was sorry for him, torn as he was between his love for his brother and his fear for Ian. He had tried to save Ian; he had offered him an easy way out. It had given Alinor no flicker of hope; she had known Ian's answer before the suggestion was made. "The king has a long-standing grudge against me, and perhaps I deserve it. Many years ago, he offered me a compliment that I took amiss. I am sorry to admit that I have a very hot temper. I lost control of it, and I struck him with an embroidery frame. The Angevin memory is very long. Ian fears for me."

Salisbury did not lift his head. He raised the wine to his lips and set it down again untasted, as if he could not swallow. "You are very kind to take the blame, Lady Alinor," he muttered. "I understand that Ian wished to protect you. What I do not understand is why he felt the need to be so urgent. It does happen, of course, but it is not common for men to die on the tourney field."

Ian slammed his eating knife down on the table. "The king is your brother and my liege lord," he snarled. "It is scarce fitting for me to answer you. Go ask of his enemies."

"I know what his enemies will say," Salisbury whispered. "I want to know the truth."

"I do not *know* the truth, William," Ian said more gently, "and I do not wish to know it unless it be to the king's credit. I wish only to protect myself and my wife. I could not do other and, look you, if I live through the day—which I expect, for I have taken this and that precaution—no more harm will be done than that men will think I have a suspicious mind."

"No more harm?" Salisbury repeated blankly. "Do you think John will love you after this?"

To that, Ian made no reply. He picked up his knife again, looked at the roast haunch, and then laid the knife aside as if his appetite was gone.

"I see," Salisbury said. "If you believe what you do, how can you be faithful?"

"The same way you love. There is the small matter of *my* honor also. I have given my oath, and I will stand by it as Pembroke stands by his," Ian said coldly.

"I beg your pardon!" Salisbury exclaimed, rising so suddenly that the chair crashed backward and the goblet he had been holding tipped, pouring wine over the table.

"My lord," Alinor cried, hurrying over to him and laying a hand on his arm. "Ian did not mean that."

"Mean what?" Ian said, looking amazedly from the dripping wine to Salisbury's white face. "William, i r God's sake, what did I say?"

"It—it sounded as if you implied that Lord Salisbury was a part of—" Alinor's voice faltered away.

"I did not mean that nor, indeed, any offense to you, William. I meant that love and honor do not always have a perfect recompense or, for that matter, a worthy object. Many men love unworthy women and cling to that love even when they know they have been betrayed. Many men make idiotic, harmful vows and fulfill them to their own and other's harm—look at King Richard and that stupid Crusade. Sit down, William."

Salisbury righted the chair. Alinor picked up the goblet and refilled it, more to have something to do than because she expected Salisbury to drink. When she thought over the words that had produced so violent a reaction, she realized that only Salisbury's feeling of guilt could have misinterpreted them. Added to what Salisbury had said when he first came in—his suggestion of excuses for Ian to withdraw from fighting in the melee—his behavior was near proof of guilty knowledge. It was natural that he should be very sore on the point of honor. To know what he knew and not to act or speak out was not honorable. Yet Alinor could feel no contempt. It was bad enough for men like Ian and Pembroke to serve faithfully such a master. What hell it must be for Salisbury, who not only served but loved him.

"Of course," Ian continued, with a faint smile, "I do not think I am so bad as Richard. I have a good practical reason for what I do, in addition to my sworn oath. I said to Alinor some time since that it was necessary to put aside personal liking and sometimes even personal good for the good of the realm at large. Whatever the king feels toward me, he loves this land. It is his native place, the seat of his affections. I have said also, more than once, that much ill for which the king is blamed is no fault of his, and he has done much good—for example, reforming the courts of law from the corruption of Richard's reign."

Some color had returned to Salisbury's face. He lifted the cup of wine, and drank. His expression was eager, although a shadow still dwelt in his eyes. "Yes, that is true," he agreed urgently, almost pleadingly.

"You need not feel that I will fail in my faith," Ian said firmly. "Not for liking nor disliking nor insult. I may well withdraw from the court—it may be necessary for me to do so, as you point out what I have done could not be pleasing to the king—but in any time of need I will stand firm."

A sigh that trickled out of Salisbury told the other half of the tale. He had come to warn Ian, but he had also come to bind Ian tighter and tighter to the man who plotted his death. Standing quiet behind her husband's chair, Alinor warred against showing her flash of resentment, but it soon faded. Salisbury's effort was superfluous. Ian had given her his reasons long ago. He would be faithful to King John despite any cause to rebel, because there was no one else.

Salisbury finished his wine and stood up. "God bless you," he said softly and then, with bitter fervor, "God keep you."

When she had seen their guest out, Alinor returned. Ian had not moved. He was staring at the dark stain the wine had made on the table. Alinor began to dress without summoning her maids. Ian turned his head to look greedily at the firm, white body. He did not want to die. There was a great lust in him to live, to sup more fully of the pleasure and the treasure he had waited for for so long. Shift and tunic obscured what he never seemed to have enough of, even the moment after he had spilled his seed into her. He lifted his eyes to his wife's face.

"Would you consider remaining here, or even setting out for Iford?" Ian asked slowly.

Fear clutched at Alinor's throat so that the one word she forced out came in a gasp "No." Ian was looking again at the wine stain. "Do not ask it of me," she begged when she had regained mastery of her voice. "Do not condemn me to wait and pray in this silent house."

"No, I will not." Ian looked up again, smiling a little. "I should have known you would rather see the blood spill."

"Not yours."

He smiled more broadly. "Doubtless a little will be let, but not, I believe, so much as the king hopes." Then he frowned. "What I do not understand is how Salisbury came to hear of this. Men do not tell him such tales of the king—and he knew. He all but begged me to refuse to fight."

Memory stirred in Alinor, memory of repeated insistence on Salisbury's unnecessary attendance on the king. "I think the tale came from a woman," she said, and then, after a pause, "I would lay long odds that it came from his wife. It comes to my mind that Lady Ela does not approve of her husband's close association with his brother. I misjudged that woman, Ian. She is very clever."

But Ian was not listening. He was staring at the window, and his eyes had the faraway look of a man who sees a vision. "A woman," he said softly, and then more softly, so that Alinor would not have heard if she had not been aware of the faintest whisper of his voice, "I had almost forgotten."

On the words he pushed back his chair hurriedly. He limped across the room, unlocked the coffer where the jewels lay, and searched roughly among them. Alinor was so surprised that she could not say a word, nor did she notice then what he extracted from the chest.

"The men will see you to the field," he threw over his shoulder at her. "I have an errand—a call I must pay. Fare you well."

Frozen, mute with disbelief, Alinor watched him go. She heard his halting step down the stairs, heard him calling orders to his men and his squires, heard him mount and ride away alone—and still she could not stir nor utter a sound. A woman he had almost forgotten. He has left me, Alinor thought, perhaps to go to his death, without a kiss, or a tender word—without a look. This, I shall have to remember: a "Fare you well," cast at me like a clod of earth because his whole being was bent upon another woman.

CHAPTER NINETEEN

If Alinor had seen Ian's face when he emerged from a house somewhat larger and more elegant than her own, she would have been saved much grief. He did not look like a man who had parted tenderly and sorrowfully from the love of his life. Amusement and satisfaction mingled with puzzlement on his face. The lady he had visited, with whom he had, indeed, once had a long and satisfactory, if quite intermittent, relationship had talked freely enough once her throat was lubricated by the very pretty and very expensive necklet Ian had brought her. Ian did not doubt her facts. Saer de Quincy, FitzWalter's bosom friend, was one of her steady clients, and she had an uncanny ability to extract information from men. Ian blushed to think of the things he had told her from time to time. What she said, however, left him thoroughly confused.

Apparently, there must be two quite separate plots to eliminate him. One, the one Lady Mary had so obligingly disclosed, was easy enough to accredit to the king, for it bore the mark of the way his mind worked, although it could never be brought home to him. In any case, proof against John was the last thing Ian wanted. That plot—a neat and deadly combination of attack by acknowledged enemies among the opposition and treachery by two or three knights enlisted under his own banner—might well have worked had it not been for the other. Ian cast wildly around in his mind for someone he could have hurt or offended enough to desire his death, who was also of such monumental stupidity as to hatch so inept a plot.

It did not matter, of course. The device had no chance of working once it was known, and it had no chance of remaining unknown by its very nature. When gold is scattered freely among poor knights-errant before they have accomplished their mission and are therefore bound to remain in the place, tongues are bound to wag over wine pots and in bawdy houses. It was this talk that had brought Vesci and Leicester to fight under Ian's banner and which FitzWalter had betrayed. A good move, that, Ian acknowledged. For FitzWalter, it would have been better if no scent of treachery had fouled the tourney atmosphere, but, once the smell of it was abroad, he could hope to cut his losses by fixing Ian's attention on the expectation of a mass attack from the opposition.

By the time Ian reached the tourney field, his amusement had abated. Plot and overplot that revealed each other might be funny. It was also true that the likelihood that either plot alone would be successful was greatly decreased by the fact that it was known. However, the men involved in the king's plan were quite intelligent enough to put two and two together. If they held off their attack until the mass attack was launched, the combination might well overwhelm Ian, Vesci, Leicester and their followers. While he donned his armor in the pavilion assigned to his forces, Ian worried the question of revealing what he knew to the others. Either alternative was equally unpleasant. If he spoke, he would blacken the king's name in a dangerous way; if he did not, he might endanger the men who were trying to help him.

Owain proffered a tilting helmet, which Ian stared at blankly for a minute. Then he thrust it away impatiently. "Not that one," he snapped. "This is fighting. I have to breathe." And then, furiously, "My God, do you mean to tell me you have not brought my battle helm?"

No one intended to tell him anything when he was

in that mood. Owain rushed to make a pretence of searching while Geoffrey was already out of the tent and on a horse, racing back to the house to rectify the mistake. It was fortunate for Ian's squires that Sir Henry and Sir Walter chose that moment to arrive. Had Ian not been so furious at Owain and Geoffrey and still so undecided about what to do, he might have noticed the slightly overhearty manner in which they greeted him. He returned the greeting courteously enough, but his face was as black as thunder. The men glanced at each other. They had gone to Ian's house in good time to ride with him to the field and found him gone. This had provided them with the dubious pleasure of escorting Alinor, who was in such a temper that they had been heartily glad to be rid of her.

"Er—it is a fair and pleasant day," Sir Henry assayed.

"The weather holds most mild," Sir Walter agreed uneasily.

Ian looked from one to the other and made a quick compromise. "The weather may be the only thing that smiles upon us," he remarked. "As you may know from yesterday's events, there are a few who believe I have done them a wrong. In fact, it has come to my ears that a large party will be marshaled especially against me."

To Ian's surprise, expressions of intense relief, which were quickly masked, appeared on the faces of Alinor's vassals. Both assured him they would watch for any sign of such a move and hold their places beside him as well as they could. Ian could only assume that they, too, had heard the rumors and, for some reason, were reluctant to speak of the matter. Then he realized there was no need to warn Vesci and Leicester. Obviously, they already knew the part of the plot that might endanger them. Of the treachery from his own side, Ian dared not speak. Perhaps it would have been safe to tell Leicester, but Vesci and his followers would actively seek proof that John was involved in it—and they would seek the proof for treasonable purposes.

As if on cue of his thoughts, Vesci stuck his head into the tent. "Oh, you are here. Arundel's men are forming up."

"And so would mine be if I had other than idiots for squires," Ian replied, but his voice was lighter.

He was a great fool to worry about Vesci and Leicester. They were competent fighters and, moreover, no one wanted to harm them. The worst that would befall them was the need to pay horse and armor ransom. Ian stepped out of the tent and cocked an ear to the imprecations of a coarse voice. They were saddling one of the gray destriers, and the grooms were obviously having trouble. It was a pity there was no way to place the saddle on the horse with a rider in it. It was also a pity that one could not explain to a horse the difference between a saddle empty because the rider had not yet mounted, or had dismounted voluntarily, and empty because the rider had been hurt or killed.

The others had heard the grooms also, and they all moved by one consent to watch. The audience did nothing to calm the horse, and even when the saddle was firm and Ian in it, the creature kicked and bucked for several minutes. By then, fortunately for all concerned, Geoffrey was able, breathlessly, to hold up Ian's battle helmet. There were comments on the advantages and disadvantages of the open style of helmet, and on the use of so finely trained horses, while the men rode off all together in the best of tempers.

The field, where most of the participants had arrived already, lifted spirits even higher. The sun glanced back from helmets and from mail-clad arms, winked on the bosses of shields and the metal of the horses' harness. Brilliantly dyed surcoats and brightly painted shields glowed in the clear morning light. The only dull thing was the earth itself, but the slippery, dry grass had mostly been torn away and broken to dust by the previous day's jousting. There was less danger of slipping. That was good, but there was also nothing at all to hold the dry earth down. That was not so good, because the dust, disturbed by the horses' hooves, would soon obscure from the judges and the audience much of what was happening.

Ian guffawed briefly when the thought crossed his mind. Much good the judges could do him, even with the best will in the world to help and even if they did see what was happening. Their power was limited to calling a foul and depriving the guilty party of horse and armor ransom. Since dead men do not pay ransom, the point was moot. Of course, theoretically, the judges could also stop the fighting if they saw any-large-scale dishonorable action. The notion made Ian laugh again. Stopping the fighting in a tourney was not like picking apart two small boys who were in a squabble. It took time to stop a tourney, and in that time the work on him might be finished three times over.

"You are in good spirits, my lord."

Ian turned his head to look at FitzWalter. "I am indeed," he remarked blandly. "The nice thing about being battle leader in a tournament is that the responsibility ends once the sides are chosen and marshaled on the field. In a war, a leader must continue to worry about the safety and the movements of his men, you know—or do you know?"

FitzWalter's face turned purple. His ransom had been paid by the king, but many of the men from Vaudreuil still languished in French prisons. Ian's remark was an open insult, and he had spoken quite deliberately to see how far the man would go. He went the full route.

A grimace that was meant for a smile pulled at FitzWalter's lips. Choking on the words, he replied, "You are very merry, my lord, very merry, and a little excited, too, I think. Too excited to weigh words care-

fully at this moment. Let it pass. In view of what I
had to tell you two days ago, I have come to ask to
fight near at hand to you."

"How kind of you," Ian said icily. "You know, I
begin to think the threat you heard was some jest. So
many ears have heard it—here are Leicester and Vesci
and others, too, all asking to ride behind me. Surely if
harm was intended me, a little more care would be
taken to keep the secret. However, if you can find a
place in the crowd of well-wishers, you are welcome."

With some satisfaction, Ian watched the expression
that remark had brought to FitzWalter's face. It might
well be that he had taken the heart from the king's plot
with those few words. Besides, he noted with amusement, FitzWalter was not exactly finding a welcome.
When the man turned to look for an opening, Sir
Henry and Sir Walter nudged their horses a little closer
to Ian's. Leicester's men also drew together, and the
earl advanced a few steps, as if to say something to
Ian, but he did not speak. FitzWalter moved off to Ian's
left and found a place beyond Vesci's men.

Mild winter or not mild, Ian thought, glancing at the
sun, it was getting cold sitting still without a cloak. He
could feel his sore muscles tightening, and he watched
with displeasure as Pembroke and Salisbury engaged
in still another conference. Ian looked at the colors of
the knight who had apparently raised a question. Devil
take him, it was that young scapegrace Robert de Remy.
Now what was he about? The decision was apparently
negative, with some allowance. The young man said a
word of thanks for the grace given and then turned his
horse and galloped across to pull up before Ian.

"My lord," he said, "I have been to the heralds, but
I am not allowed to change sides. I tried to see you
last night, but your lady sent a message that you were
engaged——"

"A polite tale. I was abed groaning over my bruises,

some of which you gave me. Now quick, I am freezing, what is it you want of me?"

"Just to say I am sorry to fight against you, my lord, and I hope you will not hold me to blame and—and I am most anxious to take service with you——"

"Robert," Ian said exasperatedly, "do not talk as if you were one instead of twenty-one. How can you be to blame for which side you take in a tourney. This is no grudge fight."

The young man's face was partly concealed by his helmet, but it seemed to Ian that his expression changed, possibly was marked with concern at those words. He could do nothing but ignore it. "Just see that you fight as hard as you can against me. I will love you all the better for it. And for God's sake, and mine, do *not* come to my house tonight. Wait until tomorrow at least. My offer of service will not fly away. Now let us start this battle before I become frozen into my seat. And Robert," he added, his expression softening, "have a care to yourself. I want you whole and undamaged."

"You also, my lord. Have a care—" He stopped, then leaned closer across the horses. "Have a care especially to your back," he whispered.

That was odd, Ian thought, very odd. How could the boy know anything about that second plot. But at that moment the trumpets sounded, and Ian abandoned any thoughts beyond those of immediate action. All along the line, shields were swung forward, swords or other weapons drawn from their resting places. For those men to whom nervous speech was natural, voices were raised in meaningless jests and remarks. The herald came to the center of the field and began to read the formal phrases.

". . . the honorable Lord William, Earl of Arundel, and, for the king, the honorable Lord Ian, Baron de Vipont, have chosen . . ."

Ian's eyes wandered to the loges, and a qualm of

worry seized him. He had not thought once of Alinor since he left the house. He wished she did not have to sit beside the king. It was all very well for Salisbury to say Lady Ela would take care of Alinor. Ian doubted whether Lady Mary, the Queen of Heaven, would be able to stop Alinor's tongue if she saw him struck down.

Alinor's thoughts were running in the same pattern as her husband's. It had been some years now since Alinor had worried about her tongue betraying her. During the time Richard had been king, Alinor had been much at court and had added to the training she had had from the old queen. With people she trusted, she was still prone to let hot words fly before she thought, but not with others. She feared herself now, because her rage at Ian was like to spill over onto everyone around her.

The frozen shock that had held her silent when Ian left her so abruptly had melted into a bitter storm of tears. Since their wedding night, Alinor had not given a single thought to the rival she once believed held Ian's heart. There had not been the smallest hint that his love for her was shadowed by another image. Most often he did not even close his eyes in loveplay. Some woman who loathed her husband had once told Alinor that was how she endured his embraces—she closed her eyes and imagined another man. The remark had not made much impression at the time; Alinor closed her own eyes, not to imagine another man but to concentrate better on the one she had. After she mastered her weeping, however, she thought back over the month of her marriage, seeking signs and portents in every remembered word and act.

Nothing had betrayed another interest. And I am a fool to have wasted time thinking of it, Alinor said to herself. Ian's own words had confirmed his satisfaction with his wife. "I had almost forgotten," he had whispered. What kind of love is it that could "almost forget"? Alinor did not "forget" Simon. She did not think of him all the time; for that matter, she did not think of Ian all the time. But Simon was always there, just as Ian was always there. Never by any stretch of the truth could she say she had "almost forgotten" either of them. It was insane to be jealous of a woman, of a love, that could be "almost forgotten." Yet, no matter what she thought or what arguments she offered herself, the hurt remained. That he could go that way, without a single tender kiss or look, to bid another woman farewell was unbearable.

Alinor's spleen spilled out over her maids, who were well-slapped for nothing, and over her castellans, who raised their eyes to heaven and thanked God that they were not tied to her closer and that the ride to the tourney field was short. It would have spilled out over Lady Ela also, but she was too clever to give her fulminating neighbor a chance, and a strong, basic sense of self-preservation—even stronger than rage— made Alinor clamp her teeth into her lips and shake her head at any comment the king addressed to her. Let him think her afraid, if that would give him satisfaction. If Ian came alive from this venture, she would have the last laugh over this running sore of a king— and over Ian, too.

The trumpets drew her eyes from her own knotted fingers to the field. If Ian came alive from this—if—if. Cold fear fought with the roiling rage. Alinor sat still as a graven image, staring with blind eyes at the herald, who recited the old, formal phrases:

". . . in God's name, do your battle!"

The trumpets blew; the ranks of men moved toward each other, the brilliant shields and surcoats giving something of the appearance of two beds of flowers that had suddenly become mobile. Down the lines occasional good-humored challenges were called between members of the opposing parties. Even in the

central party around Ian, the first minutes before contact were slow-paced and easy. Ian and Arundel again
engaged each other in a rather formal duel. The thrusts
and slashes were powerful enough, but they were aimed
where it was certain they could be easily caught on
shield or opposing sword.

For Ian, the formal opening was a mercy. The
bruised muscles that Alinor and her maids had tended
faithfully through the night had stiffened. The blows he
launched did not have the power he usually commanded, and his responses to Arundel's attack were
painful and dangerously slow. As if he recognized the
problem, Arundel held Ian longer than normal, pressing
him harder and then a little harder still, increasing the
tempo and force of his blows, making Ian stretch and
bend to guard himself and riposte. At first, Ian was
scarcely aware of the favor, his attention being wholly
absorbed by his own physical pain and his efforts to
prevent it from interfering with his action.

As he warmed, Ian recognized his opponent's consideration and knew it for what it was. Tourneys were
not like chess games or wars. The capture of the "king"
of the opposition would not end the play or bring victory to the opposing party. Of course, quite honest
efforts would be made to capture him, Ian knew, because the horse and armor ransom of the leaders was
higher than that of any other knight on the field. It was
assumed that the man chosen as leader would be the
best and most skillful fighter, and thus the reward for
defeating him must logically be the highest. Ian uttered
a bark of laughter as that thought crossed his mind. It
would be very funny if he should be unhorsed and
taken prisoner by some innocent bystander with a
mighty arm who would, all unknowingly, frustrate his
king's intentions and win royal animosity.

That he should permit or encourage such a solution
to his problem simply never occurred to Ian. Subcon-

sciously, he was incapable of failing to defend himself to the uttermost in a battle situation. He could hold himself back from fighting at the peak of his skill and power—as he did toward the end of the duel with Arundel, as he did in any training session with his squires in mock combat—but he did not know how to fake a defense. Moreover, such an act would smack to him of cowardice. However reasonable and logical it might seem, however unlikely that anyone but himself would ever know what he had done, he could not do it nor even think of it other than as a jest. He would know. He would be smirched in his own eyes. He would begin to sink down into what his "unremembered" father had been.

Besides, Ian was enjoying himself. As activity loosened his cramped muscles, his normal pleasure in combat swamped any thought outside the duel itself. The field was opening up as pairs of fighting knights advanced and retreated beyond the original close-packed lines. Pembroke's nephew, Sir John Marshal, moved in from the right to engage Arundel, and Ian found himself challenged by the Earl of Wenneval. He had never crossed swords with the gentleman before, although he knew him as one of John's and Salisbury's intimates. A decent man, although not too clever, was Ian's judgment. Nonetheless, he fenced cautiously. Stupidity did not necessarily imply inability in arms. Look at that blockhead Arundel. He was as fine a fighter as you would look for anywhere.

The paradox did not exist in Wenneval, however, Ian soon found. The man was mediocre in skill as well as in person and mind. Ian feinted viciously with his shield and, as Wenneval brought his own shield wide to counter the blow, raised his sword to strike Wenneval's weapon from his hand from the inside. At the last moment, however, Ian remembered that Wenneval had wanted Alinor once. Having gained that greatest of all prizes for himself, Ian was ready to forgo the lesser one of Wenneval's ransom. Let one of the poorer knights to whom the money would mean something take him. He tapped Wenneval's fingers and wrist—not too gently, but not hard enough to hurt him or to knock the weapon from his hand—turned his sword and thrust at the exposed ribs on the right.

Without touching Wenneval, Ian pulled his sword back, lifted it slightly in salute, and kneed his destrier into a sharp turn to the left. Had Wenneval wished to continue engagement, he could have followed; that he did not probably indicated that he had known himself outclassed. Ian's eyes ranged over the shields immediately available, seeking the device of a man with whom he would enjoy matching skill. Sir Walter, who had been on his left, was now behind him, and Sir Henry had charged right past Wenneval and was fighting well ahead, bellowing like an enraged bull. Alinor obviously knew her men. Where Leicester was, Ian had no idea, but Leicester had a cool head. Still further left, Robert de Ros was fighting two knights of the Earl of Warenne's retinue. Ian spurred the gray destrier in that direction, calling a challenge.

The young knight was no match for him. Ian had him unseated in six strokes, but he did not pause to take his yielding. If the man could catch his horse and mount again, let him go on fighting. Ian did not care a pin who won the day—he had done all he was going to do in the king's name—and he certainly did not want to take horse and armor ransom from someone who might have to borrow to pay it. He never knew whether his gesture had any effect beyond transferring the ransom he had spurned to someone else's purse, because he was set upon by two knights he did not recognize. Plainly, they were fighting as a team and, equally plainly, they planned to take him if they could.

Their skill, however, was not equal to their intentions. Ian brought both knees forward and prodded his mount hard in the shoulders. Up went the destrier, shod hooves slashing at the head of the closest horse. Well braced against the move, Ian did not even look in that direction. Instead he repeated the move he had made against Wenneval on the second knight. This time, however, he did not hold his hand. His concession to the spirit of the tourney was to turn his blade so that the edge would not sever fingers and wrist. A most satisfactory yowl greeted the landing of his blow.

"Yield," he shouted, as he presented the point of his sword at his disarmed opponent's chest. Simultaneously, he swung his shield back and up to guard a blow from the other side.

"Yielded!" came the reply. A name followed, but Ian did not heed. If the man was honest, he would seek Ian out after the tourney was over and make arrangements to pay his ransom. If not, he would ride back home, less a sword and with a shadow on his conscience. To Ian, it did not make any difference. His attention was all for the other knight of the pair, who was a somewhat better swordsman. That duel took longer, but eventually ended the same way. Again Ian did not wait for assurance of whom he had bested. Ahead he could see the colors of Philip of Albini, a gentleman whose fighting skills he respected as deeply as he deplored his politics. Albini's head turned toward Ian's shouted challenge, and he spurred forward eagerly. Ian drew breath. This would be a duel worth while.

Neither fear nor rage can remain at fever pitch for very long, particularly in a warm and open person. Very soon after Ian crossed swords with Arundel, Alinor found herself more interested in the action than in her own emotions. Idiot though he was, she could not forbear a swelling pride in her husband. If Ian did not have the enormous strength of Simon, he was quicker and more graceful. It was thrilling to see him hold so famous a warrior as Arundel at bay more and more easily. Nor was the generosity of Ian's rescue of Robert de Ros and his failure to demand yielding of his opponent lost upon Alinor.

Still, she had not forgotten Ian's danger. She uttered an oath under her breath when she saw Sir Henry charging ahead to engage, all careless of his lord's safety. Sir Walter, however, was not far from Ian, and Robert of Leicester, although well to the right, seemed to be forcing his opponent in Ian's direction. Vesci's men, undisciplined and caught up in the battle, were scattering. Anxiously, Alinor's eyes turned to the opposing forces, seeking there the insurance she hoped she had purchased. At first, she did not find what she sought, and fear made her bite her lips again. Hurriedly, she looked back at the place Ian had held. A gasp was drawn from her as she saw the team of knights bear down upon him.

"Too soon," she told herself, "it is too soon. Nothing will be done so early. The stinking cowards will wait until he is tired and until the dust rises enough so that their filthy treachery will be better concealed from all eyes." Nonetheless, she watched with quickened breath until it was certain that Ian was in no trouble. Then her eyes searched the field again. Surely, surely, her trust had not been misplaced. But she could not find the drab surcoat, the battered and besmirched shield with half-obliterated emblem that had been decided upon as the best concealment for Sir Guy's real identity.

He had to be there. He had to be—unless the young fool had been carried away by the fighting like Sir Henry. I will kill him, Alinor thought. If Ian dies because of his carelessness, I will kill him by inches over years and years of torture. Perhaps it was not his fault. Perhaps he had been attacked and taken prisoner. Would that young fool's honor keep him off the field? Would he let Ian die for some stupid point of proper behavior? What of the other men Sir Guy had been supposed to enlist to help him? Where were they? And

who were they? She had not had time to discuss the
details with Sir Guy. There was a limit to how often
one could go to market and, worse, each meeting increased the chance that someone who had heard Sir
Guy's tale would see their meetings and guess the
source of the rumors he was spreading.

One more fruitless sweep and Alinor could look no
longer. Ian drew her gaze like a magnet. A tense moment when she could not find him at his old position
melted into relief when she saw him safely engaged
with Albini. A hysterical giggle rose in her throat as
her own words echoed in her mind. Imagine calling a
duel with Albini being safely engaged! Albini was a
clever and powerful warrior. He had had Simon's
respect, and that was not easily come by. In the heat of
a spirited combat, Ian might well be severely injured.
But not killed, Alinor thought. Albini would be no part
of that kind of treachery, even though he was of five
or six different minds about whom he would support in
any political crisis.

There was a particularly ferocious passage of arms,
which brought both Albini's destrier and Ian's to their
haunches so that the horses were nearly as much engaged in battle as the men. Alinor sobbed aloud once as
a cloud of dust arose and obscured the combatants.
Perhaps it was not safe for Ian to be engaged with
Albini. All his attention would be concentrated on so
worthy an opponent. The fierceness of the action would
conceal him from his friends. His back would be naked
to anyone despicable enough and sufficiently lost to
honor to attack him.

Alinor knew that was a silly idea even as she thought
it. No matter how concentrated Ian and Albini were,
they were too much men of war not to see someone
attacking from behind. In any case, the very violence
of the duel drew the attention of the fighters nearby,
so that some, by mutual consent, suspended their own

battles to watch, and even those who were too near the conclusion of their own fights to give over, drew away. A space opened around Ian and Albini, and the shouts and general clangor of metal against metal diminished until only the battle noises of the principals were loud in that area. No one could now approach without being entirely obvious to spectators and judges alike. The cloud of dust diminished also, since there were no other horses, no other furiously moving bodies to keep it suspended.

Both men were now clearly visible, and both had been slightly wounded. A trickle of blood blackened Ian's sapphire blue surcoat from the ribs of his right side. A similar trickle stained Albini's high on the shoulder. Neither seemed aware of, or in the least impeded by, the cuts. At the moment, the horses were almost still as both men stood in the stirrups and hammered at each other with great, slashing strokes. Then, almost as if by some mutual signal that no one else could see, the destriers plunged into violent action again.

As the horses reared, Ian launched an overhand blow. Albini lifted his shield to catch it, simultaneously leaning out to the right to gain a freer swing at Ian's unprotected side. Possibly the edge of his shield struck the horse, or possibly the rider's position unbalanced the animal, but Albini's destrier gave a terrified neigh and crashed to the ground. Ian uttered a cry of consternation, loosed the handgrip of his shield and grabbed for the rein that was fastened to his pommel. In his efforts to prevent his horse from savaging the fallen rider and mount, he almost brought the beast down. By a contortion that very nearly unseated Ian, the gray kept his feet, plunging and snorting with fury.

In the moments that it took Ian to get his horse under control, Albini had extracted himself and was urging his destrier to its feet again. Ian rode back. The unmounted man raised his shield, but Ian's sword hung straight down, clearly signaling that he would not strike.

"Are you all right?" he asked anxiously.

Albini lowered his shield. "I will thank you for the courtesy if you will give me leave to mount."

"My lord, that horse is not fit," Ian replied, watching the destrier's struggle to rise. Then he laughed. "If you will have it no other way, I will yield to you."

That drew an answering laugh from Albini and assuaged his angry frustration. "If it could get me one of those gray devils you ride, I could almost bring myself to accept. But you teach me courtesy, de Vipont. I yield me."

"No you will not," Ian responded promptly, "for a mare's son has failed, not your mother's. You as near overmatched me as I do not like to admit. We will meet some other time."

The horse was now on its feet, but something had been severely strained, for it was limping. So, Ian realized, was Albini. He must have hurt his leg when the horse fell. Without more words, Ian accompanied him to the edge of the field to be sure no one would try to take advantage of his condition, and then took his leave with a few polite platitudes. He was in the best of spirits. The battle with Albini had been most stimulating, but also rather exhausting. It was very convenient that Albini's horse should fall. It had provided him with a needed restful interlude. He held his horse a moment, scanning the field. The dust was much worse. He had not the faintest idea where his friends were. On the other hand, most probably his enemies did not know where he was, either.

In the next few moments it was proved that the latter expectation was too sanguine. As soon as Ian realized he would not be able to pick a likely candidate for his attentions from the sidelines, he rode toward the nearest opening in the mass of battling men and moving horses. He was a little surprised when no one rode out to meet him. He had assumed that, since he could be seen, someone would hurry to make capital of the fatigue from his recent exertions. However, it was not until he was swallowed up into the dimmer air near the center of the field that anyone showed an interest in crossing swords with him. He was again challenged by two knights, and this time he had little hope of an easy or quick victory over them. Fulk de Cantelu and Henry of Cornhill were not novices, and they were seeking to revenge themselves for their unexpected loss in the jousting lists. If they were successful in their enterprise, Ian knew he would not come alive off the field.

Nonetheless, Ian had none of the sense of despair that had gripped him the previous day. His experience in war was wide and varied. He was still relatively fresh. The nick in his side was giving him no trouble. Cheerfully he shouted aloud the names of his attackers, swung his horse wide and spurred it sharply, so that it leapt forward toward Henry's right side, leaving Fulk, who was on Henry's left, blocked by his own partner. The surprise generated by this move and the unexpected angle of Ian's attack permitted him to land two mighty blows. One caught Henry on the helm, and the other smashed into his ribs. Both helm and mail held—the armor was of the best quality—but Ian heard the man cry out and knew he was hurt.

Wisely, Ian made no attempt to follow up that success with any further effort to belabor his opponent. Henry was hurt but by no means unable to fight back or defend himself. Prodding with his left knee and spurring with his right heel, Ian turned his mount still further in the direction he was headed so that he was now behind Cornhill. Meanwhile, Fulk had recovered from his surprise and ridden forward around Henry to come up on Ian's left side. The move was grossly unimaginative; in fact, it was exactly what Ian hoped and expected.

Because Ian had sense enough not to linger in his

duel with Henry, even though it seemed to hold the promise of the quick elimination of one opponent, Fulk found himself behind his intended victim. His joy at seeing Ian's unprotected back did not last long. Ian had leaned forward, swung both legs back and prodded his stallion's haunches. Promptly the beast lashed out with both hind legs. It did not catch Fulk's mount in the head, as Ian hoped, but one shod hoof did make contact with the other stallion's shoulder. In response, the animal reared and Fulk's hopeful stroke went awry.

Shouting curses, Fulk wrestled his horse down, prepared to strike again at a man he thought unable to turn in time to defend himself. But the moment Ian's destrier had his back hooves on the ground, Ian made him rear upright and turn on his hind legs. Fulk's sword met a ready shield, and the horse, coming down, struck Cornhill's mount on the left hindquarter. Startled, Henry's destrier plunged away to the right, again leaving Ian momentarily with only one opponent.

Not for long, Ian thought bitterly, as his eye caught half a dozen knights riding through the press of fighting men. They looked neither right nor left for opponents. They rode straight as an arrow's flight toward Ian and his two challengers. John's hired killers, Ian thought. Viciously he spurred forward. This was no time for the niceties of tourney fighting; this was war, where the only good enemy was a dead one. Invigorated by rage, he launched a fusillade of blows at Fulk while he roweled his horse unmercifully. Too busy guarding himself to spur his destrier forward and out of the way, Fulk came suddenly to the end Ian had planned for him. The gray horse struck Cantelu's mount just in the barrel of the belly. Instinctively, the stallion curved its neck to bite and tried to rear. Ian thrust hard. Fulk twisted to present his shield, leaned back—and the horse went over.

Never pausing a moment in his roweling, Ian charged toward the oncoming knights. Suddenly, from behind

him, he heard his name called aloud twice. A rush of
relief was immediately swamped by shock. The voice
was not that of Leicester or Vesci. It was FitzWalter,
who was shouting for reinforcements. Ian knew his one
real fear had been realized. The two plots against him
had been combined, either deliberately or by accident.
The bitter realization nearly undid him at once. Turning his head to see if it was really FitzWalter not only
provided him with proof that it was, but added the unwelcome information that Saer de Quincy was already
at FitzWalter's side. Ian had no delusions about how
this must end. Six before and two behind were more
than any one man could handle. And turning his head
permitted Cornhill, who had mastered his horse and
his own hurts, to strike a blow against which Ian was
unguarded.

A shout of triumph from the oncoming knights was
an unexpected blessing. Ian's sword came up in time to
deflect Cornhill's blow, which would certainly have cut
his throat if it had not completely severed his head
from his body. It took him in the shoulder, but glancingly. The gasp Ian uttered had nothing to do with the
pain of the blow. It was a sound of sheer surprise as
the six-man ram that had been thundering toward him
neatly split in two, detoured around Henry and himself and, three on a side, took on FitzWalter and de
Quincy.

It took Ian ten minutes to finish off Cornhill instead
of five, because he was so consumed by laughter that
half his blows were ineffective. In spite of his amusement, he was horribly aware that his danger was not
materially decreased. The fact that one set of plotters
had eliminated the second set in the mistaken belief
that they were coming to Ian's rescue, did not change
the fact that there were six men behind him who intended to kill him. Finally, Ian struck the sword from
Henry's hand and had the satisfaction of hearing him
yell again and seeing that he made no move to reach

for the mace fastened to his saddle. Ian let his horse run past, then wheeled it round.

Cornhill was already gone, hopefully to nurse his broken fingers. Saer de Quincy was just going down. Ian saw one of the attackers drag the shield from his arm, another seize his sword. He braced himself for a new onslaught, but there was no need. Without a glance in his direction, the three rode off, losing themselves in the mass of fighting men and clouds of dust. Thoroughly bemused, Ian looked toward FitzWalter, who was still heavily engaged. He was faced with a ridiculous point of honor. Technically it was his duty to attempt to rescue the man.

Like a gift from heaven came a single knight who called a challenge. Blessing the man, whoever he was, Ian caught the stroke he launched and attended to his own business—but not too energetically. Fortunately, his opponent was not his equal, because Ian was still shaken, now and again, with most untimely mirth. But, between fits of laughter, he watched FitzWalter's battle. It did not last long. Shield and sword were wrenched from him. Ian parried the blows his blessing aimed at him with inattentive precision. The behavior of the first trio of knights was suggestive but no guarantee of the behavior of this second group. And, for a moment it looked as if they were, indeed, of a different mind, for they turned from FitzWalter and rode toward Ian. However, they did not pause. Swerving off to the right, they left Ian to his mismatched fight.

With a few powerful strokes, Ian disarmed the country squire who had sought to try his strength. He did not listen to the man's name. All desire to laugh had left him. He had recognized one of the shields. Sir Robert de Remy was one of the second group of three.

"Now that," a pleasant voice behind Ian said, "was very odd, very odd indeed."

Ian ground his teeth. "I swear it was none of my doing. I—"

Leicester laughed aloud. "You need not tell me! Do I not know Lady Alinor's fine and elegant fingers stirring a pot of soup when I see them? But so far, so well done. Let us finish it now," Leicester said, not realizing he had stricken Ian mute with his insight. He raised his voice, calling at the top of a pair of healthy lungs, "À Vipont! À Vipont!"

CHAPTER TWENTY

The remainder of the tourney was an anticlimax to both Ian and Alinor. Although she had been spared the sight of Ian being prepared for the slaughter by Cantelu and Cornhill, she knew when the worst danger to her husband was past because she saw his enemies ride and limp from the field. When FitzWalter and de Quincy followed soon after, stripped of both swords and shields, it was apparent to her that her plan had worked. Relief from fear should have brought her joy; the king's barely controlled chagrin should have given her pleasure; instead the only emotion that seemed to remain within her was rage.

That emotion had its benefits. She sat in a rigid silence, giving no indication that she knew her husband was now safe—or as safe as one could be in the midst of a tourney. No matter when he glanced at her, John could not find any sign of relaxation or satisfaction. As much as he hated it, the king was forced to believe that Alinor had no knowledge of any special reason for her husband's good fortune. Pure accident or his own skill had saved Ian de Vipont. Had there been tampering with the tourney, John might have found a way to turn it against Ian. He could not bring himself to believe that so besotted a loon as de Vipont could keep any plan he made from his wife. In fact, it was obvious from the strain Alinor was laboring under that she knew the rumored plot against him.

That thought made John utter a faint, high-pitched whine of rage. When he found out who had fouled his plans with so asinine an arrangement, he would inflict such tortures on them as had not yet been devised even in hell. The phrase, a mere outlet for his current frustration, led to an idea that might be profitable and certainly was pleasant. He could and would make open search for those inept plotters. He would catch them and punish them so that damnation and an eternal sojourn in hell would be a pleasant reprieve from his attentions—and thereby he would clean his own name from any stain of treachery against de Vipont. Good! That was very good. Moreover, Salisbury could do the hunting. Salisbury's affection for de Vipont was well known. No one would doubt he was honest in his search, or that the king was in earnest about catching and punishing the guilty. And William's heart would be made easy, too.

All in all, John decided, the black look easing from his face, perhaps this was for the best. After that scene at dinner last night, if de Vipont had not come safe away, nothing could have stopped men from believing the worst. I should not have allowed my rage to push me into desiring so quick a revenge, John thought. Sooner or later, and it could not be much later, de Vipont would be embroiled in some war or other. Had not William said something about rebellious castellans? Could not the king send help to a loyal vassal? If the help was rejected, perhaps with violence, would not that be treason? Details would need to be arranged—a call for help, perhaps—to lend verisimilitude, but that did not discourage John at all. It was exactly the kind of planning he enjoyed most.

Despite his total lack of interest in it, Ian was a strong runner-up for the melee prize as well as the prize for jousting. His battle with Albini had been in the heroic style of the romances all loved to hear, and after he had absorbed Leicester's remark, he was so furious that he hewed down everyone who crossed his path. In the end, the prize went to Arundel, largely because of the unspoken agreement between Pembroke and Salisbury that

it would be unwise to cast two days of success for Ian
into John's teeth. It was just as well they made that
decision, because Ian did not even wait to hear the
results. As soon as the trumpets sounded the end of
battle, he rode off the field and directly to his house
without even stopping to tell his squires.

Behind him he left consternation. Owain and Geoffrey
had come with Alinor. They saw their master ride off
at a spanking pace and had no idea whether to follow
him or wait upon his lady. If they left her to come home
alone, he would slay them; if her vassals were to accompany her, however, it was their duty to follow Lord Ian.
Worse still, if he wanted service and no one was at hand,
there would be trouble. Before they could even discuss
the matter, a number of bruised and bedraggled combatants were converging on Ian's colors to render up
their pledges for horse and armor ransom. The situation
was one neither squire had ever faced before. Was it
their duty to take the pledges? How should they explain
their lord's absence?

Salvation came to them. As welcome as the Mother
of Heaven, Lady Alinor rode up just ahead of the
slower, more reluctant, defeated knights. A swift question and a frightened answer made the situation all too
clear to Alinor. He had gone off to tell his lady he was
alive—so delicate a lady, too refined to gird her spirit
to see her love die, if that was what was needful. Alinor's face was set like marble, her eyes and smile as
blank and empty as any statue when she greeted Ian's
defeated opponents. To each man she apologized for
Ian's absence, pleading some urgent and unexpected
business and begging that they do them the favor of
calling at their house on the next day.

No one believed her; that was not important. No one
took offense, either. Several men expressed sorrow that
Ian had come to grief and offered any help they were
able to give. These offers Alinor rejected graciously and
ambiguously, never denying that Ian was hurt and never

admitting it, either. Sometime during the procession, Sir Henry and Sir Walter arrived. Had they been less brave men, they would have turned tail and fled when they caught their first glimpse of Alinor's face. If Ian were sore wounded, they could in some measure be blamed for it, since Alinor had summoned them specifically to support her husband. They waited in an agony of apprehension until the last defeated knight had departed.

"My lady, my lady, where is he?" Sir Walter begged. "How came he to be so sore hurt? I saw him not an hour since fighting strongly."

If Alinor recognized who was speaking to her, she gave no sign of it. "Who said Lord Ian was hurt? Not I. I thank you for your service, it was well and loyally done. You are welcome to stay and pleasure in the court now, if that is your will, or to leave, if you so desire."

Sir Henry stared at a mistress he did not recognize. Cold thanks were not Alinor's way. She could be icy in disapproval or blazingly angry, but thanks were always given with smiles and embraces, with laughing eyes and a flooding of warmth. Something was desperately wrong, but he could not even guess at what. "I will stay a day or two," he said roughly. "If you have need of me, my lady, do you send to my lodging, and I will come."

"I also," Sir Walter echoed.

"Very well," Alinor agreed tonelessly. "I thank you."

Then, without a farewell or a look at the squires who waited uneasily in the background, she turned her horse and rode away. There was a mad scramble to follow her, men mounting and gathering up equipment that could not be left behind. Her castellans watched her retreating back with open mouths. Such heedlessness of men and property was totally unprecedented in Alinor.

The act, however, was not a result of heedlessness, shock, or even rage. Alinor simply wished to arrive home without any witnesses. If Ian were not yet there, she would not need to make excuses or explanations. She could retire to her solar and leave Ian to explain his own actions. In fact, her precaution had been totally unnecessary. As Alinor mounted the stairs, she heard the crash of a metal cup striking either floor or furniture, and as she entered the antechamber Ethelburga also burst into it as if she had been catapulted out of the solar. Her exit was followed immediately by a louder crash. Doubtless the wine pitcher had just followed the cup. Light flickered in Alinor's blank eyes, and a quiver moved the corner of her set lips. It seemed that Ian had not been received exactly the way he had expected.

"Madam, madam," Ethelburga whispered, clinging to Alinor's arm as she started forward toward the doorway. "He is gone mad. Let him cool. Do not go in."

Alinor unloosened the maid's fingers from her arm. Her eyes flashed green fire. "I can give as good as I get. Do not fear for me. Meantime, get you below and order water to be heated and the bath to be brought up." She had not bothered to lower her voice, and the response was immediate.

"Alinor!" Ian bellowed, appearing in the doorway. "Get in here!"

The maid, who had been about to plead with her mistress again, uttered a gasp of terror and fled. Alinor raised blazing eyes to Ian's face, but decided it would not be wise to infuriate him more by refusing to obey him. It was not fear that made her docile—Alinor had been beaten before and, although she did not like it, she did not fear it—it was the pain under the rage in her husband's eyes, and the blood, some of it still bright and red, that stained surcoat and armor. Nonetheless, she hissed with irritation when she entered the solar. The rug and the floor were stained with wine, a chair and table were overturned, a valuable pitcher and cup were dented and damaged.

"Where have you been?" Ian snarled at her.

"I have been fulfilling your duties," Alinor replied quietly. "I have been telling the knights you defeated to come here and speak with you tomorrow."

"What! You interfering bitch! Did it never enter your greedy mind that I did not wish to take their pledges? How dared you?"

"Greedy?" Alinor shrieked, her sympathy swamped by renewed hurt and rage. "I am greedy? You took my jewels to give another woman, and you call me greedy! How have I interfered? You disgusting, inconsiderate animal! You defeated those men on the field—and they are honest men, for they came to redeem their honor—and you left them as if you thought them of no more worth than beaten, mangy curs. Are you the only man in the world with skill or pride?"

The real truth in Alinor's argument doused the more uncontrollable flames of Ian's wrath. He had not thought of how his action might appear from the point of view of the beaten men. He stood, clinging to a chair, panting with frustration and fatigue. "How could I take their pledges," he gasped. "How could I look any man in the face after what you have done?"

"What I had done?" Alinor repeated, totally at a loss. She could not imagine what Ian was talking about. "What have I done?"

"You have shamed me and dishonored me." His voice was trembling, and tears glittered in his eyes, magnifying their dark luster. "You have compounded with my opposition and bought my safety as if I were some feeble half-wit unable to defend myself."

"Half-wit!" Alinor exclaimed. "If you can say such a thing, you give yourself overmuch credit. You have not so much as half a wit."

"Do you mean to tell me you had no part in the action of those six knights who fell upon FitzWalter and de Quincy? Do you mean to deny that you were the 'enemy' who was buying knights to fight 'against' me?"

"No, I do not claim to be innocent of any such thing at all. There is nothing wrong with my wits, however addled yours may be."

"I thought that plot stank to heaven. It was so foolish, so crude, that it had to be a jest——"

"A jest? That was an expensive jest! Of course those men were acting for me. In whose pay did you think they were? The king's?"

"Why?" Ian pleaded. "Why did you put such a shame on me?"

"Oh highty-tighty, high and mighty," Alinor spat, "because—fool that I am—I would rather stand here and listen to you babble like an idiot than mourn over your dead body. Is that a fair answer?"

"Do you not think me able to fight my own battles?" Ian roared, stung to rage again.

"Who interfered with your battles?" Alinor shrieked in reply. "Who lifted a sword, even once, to aid you? Did someone distract Arundel? Did someone aim a blow at Albini during your duel? Did anyone draw away one of the knights when you alone fought two? I ordered one thing and one thing alone—that you were not to be stabbed in the back by men of your *own* party. Chew that cud, you ox, before you grunt of shame and dishonor."

"I will not be made a party——"

"To what were you made a party?" Alinor cut him off furiously. "Name a dishonorable act that one of those men performed, and I will see that he is called before you and punished as you see fit. Did one launch a single blow at any man in his own party? Say Fitz-Walter and de Quincy were honest men, riding to your aid because they saw you overmatched. Would the action of those six knights have been wrong? Oh, you braying ass, I have dealt with men like you all my life. I know the meat of honor."

"You cut the meat very fine, but your slices stink nonetheless."

Alinor shrugged indifferently. "So honor is a bloated corpse here. I am not the one who killed it, and you know that. Will you tell me there was no plot to have you slain on that field?"

"If there was, it was none of your affair. It was my business."

"Oh yes?" Alinor sneered. "And what arrangements did you make to settle that business?" She turned away, then back again, her eyes blazing. "Since you speak of honor, let me remind you of one oath you gave that you seem willing to set aside most lightly. You came to me and offered me marriage that you might shield me and my children from harm. Perhaps the king wished me ill then, but it is nothing to what he feels for me now. You forget full easily that your life is *not* your own to spend as you please. With you *I* fall, and Adam, and Joanna. That makes your business my business most nearly."

At first Ian did not answer. He came around the chair that he had been holding onto and sat down heavily. His eyes slipped, almost as if he were too tired to hold his gaze steady, from Alinor's face to the floor.

"I was not unaware or uncaring," he said softly at last. "I did what I could. I spoke out, as near to accusing the king as I could, and took his promise——"

"Pish tush," Alinor snapped. "I know what you did. I was there. Belike he would not press me to a new marriage. Instead, before a week was out, some fault would be found in me to lay me in prison. And there I would starve to death, and Adam would die also, and Joanna would be used as a bawd before he threw her to some dog he had chosen. Only——"

"Stop!"

The cry of pain and horror brought Alinor to her senses. She bit her lip. She had not meant to say that. Ian was the kind to carry horrors around in his mind and embroider upon them. He seemed to have bad dreams enough without adding to his store. Alinor came across the room and laid a hand gently on his shoulder.

"Very well. There is no need to speak of what is past and no longer possible. I did but wish you to know why I meddled in your affairs. Forget it now. In a week we will be gone from here and safe on our own lands. If affairs of state grow hot enough, the king will forget us."

Ian's chest was heaving as if he were still in battle. "I cannot bear it," he muttered.

Subduing the temptation to remark nastily that he would not have to bear it, since he would be dead, Alinor unlaced Ian's mail hood and pushed it back. "If you mean to go to the feast this day, you had better let me sew up what needs sewing."

It had occurred to her that Ian's bad temper had not been generated by any unkindness on the part of his "lady love." Perhaps he wished to bask in the approval of her smiles. Alinor knew it was impossible to determine which woman it was by watching the court ladies. At least a third of them constantly cast languishing glances in Ian's direction. Now that she was aware, however, she might watch to see where Ian's eyes went. She had already given the matter some thought, but could not recall a single particular look. Possibly he had taken especial care, but it was more possible that she had not noticed because she was preoccupied with other matters and, previously, unsuspicious.

But Ian shook his head. "I cannot go," he said, and swallowed sickly. "Alinor, let us go away from here. If we ride out now, we can be in Kingsclere before midnight."

Alinor was aware of thinking along two different paths at the same time, as one can stand at the fork of a road and see two separate tracks leading out of it. One path thought contemptuously that either Ian had "forgotten" his "lady" again or that one glimpse in a year was sufficient to sustain that holy passion. With the other part of her mind, she castigated herself for her unwise speech. It was absolutely impossible to do as Ian wanted. It would be an open insult to the king to depart without craving leave after they had been received with so much apparent favor. It would be treasonous as well, implying that they had fled because they believed the rumors of plots against them. Worst of all, it would give John the right to recall them and declare them in defiance.

There were other, lesser reasons also: the men who would come to render their pledges the next day; Sir Robert de Remy, who was to be taken into service. Ian had made an appointment to discuss the Irish matter at the end of the week. As clearly as she saw all the reasons, Alinor also saw that Ian was temporarily beyond reason. She sighed softly. He was so much more difficult to deal with than Simon. He was softer. Everything hurt him more, and he reacted too often with his gut.

"You can ride nowhere tonight," she said, avoiding all issues, save that upon which a woman was customarily considered fit to speak. "You are hurt and tired beyond your own knowing."

"I cannot go to the feast. I cannot. I cannot go to court tomorrow. I cannot. I cannot face the king—I will spit upon him! I cannot, I tell you."

"Nor you will not," Alinor agreed. "You will take to your bed."

"But I am not hurt—a few cuts and bruises——"

Alinor could not help laughing. "That is what you think now, because the wounds are fresh, and in some measure the heat of fighting is still on you. Wait until tomorrow. You will be glad enough of your bed. You will wish you were dead."

The laugh soothed Ian in some indefinable manner so that Alinor's words made an island of sense in the turmoil in his mind. It was true enough. He would be as sick as a horse the next day, and he was tired. If he could sleep and forget— He began to fumble with the buckle of his swordbelt, but dropped his hands when Alinor's firmer grip unloosened it. He watched her as she began the familiar process of disarming him. He

would say no more, ever, about what had happened at
the tourney, although he still felt so shamed that he did
not know how he would speak to the men who came to
render up their pledges the next day. His mind flinched
away from her reasons and clung to the assurance that
there had, in fact, been no real violation of the code of
honor. Only its heart was broken, and that was nothing
new in King John's reign.

Ian's investigation into the nonexistent plot might be
over, but another was under way. Salisbury, horribly
aware of the rumors of Ian's planned death, had not
taken his eyes off Ian for a moment. He hoped that by
interposing himself personally, he would be able to
bring about a miscarriage of the plot. Thus, he had seen
Cantelu and Cornhill challenge Ian, had seen FitzWalter
and de Quincy ride up, and had seen their discomfiture
by the six knights-errant. He had assumed that Leicester's arrival had been what prevented the six from attacking Ian when they were finished with FitzWalter
and de Quincy. And he, too, had recognized Robert de
Remy's shield. As soon as Salisbury could free himself
from the closing formalities, he had enquired where de
Remy lodged, and when he had the information, had
gone there and accused de Remy to his face of conspiring treacherously to harm the king's champion. To his
surprise, Sir Robert burst out laughing.

"I? Harm Lord Ian? By God's ten toenails, no! Lord
Ian has just offered to take me into his service. I would
be mad to take any action against him, even if I could,
which I dare swear I could not." Then he sobered and
said seriously, "Why should you say such a thing to me?
You know I came and begged leave to change sides
before the melee so that I could fight in his party."

"The better to strike him from behind, perhaps,"
Salisbury snapped.

Color rushed to Sir Robert's face. "That is not my
way, Lord Salisbury. If I did not know you were very
much Lord Ian's friend and those words were spoken

for his sake—Oh, this is ridiculous! Lord Ian has been my father's friend for years. I have known him since I was a child. You need not take my word upon it. Ask Lord Ian; he will vouch for me, I assure you."

Salisbury was desperately puzzled. The clumsy, inept plot that Ela had described to him did not sound like John's doing, yet he could not think of any other of Ian's enemies who was desperate enough and stupid enough to concoct such a mess—unless it was Cantelu and Cornhill. But he could not believe that Sir Robert would have anything to do with them, and he was certainly telling the truth when he said he had no intention of harming Ian. Yet he had to probe further.

"Then what were you doing when you held off Fitz-Walter, who was going to Lord Ian's assistance."

This time there was no laughter. Sir Robert stared at the king's half brother. Hot words rushed into his mind, but he closed his mouth upon them. It had been made very clear to him that, if information about what had happened came to the king's ears, the matter would be twisted to Ian's detriment. Sir Robert knew also that, although Salisbury seemed a friend to Ian, his first love and loyalty was to his brother. No matter that the plot was the king's. There could be no proof of that now. To gain proof, they would have needed to allow FitzWalter and de Quincy to strike and, even then, who would take their words—a few poor knights-errant—against the words of close companions of the king? It had all been explained very carefully to Sir Robert, and he knew what he had to say.

"That had nothing to do with Lord Ian," he replied sullenly. "I had a private grudge against FitzWalter."

There was a false note in that, Salisbury thought. What sort of grudge could this young man have? How could he even know FitzWalter? "Oh, really? Yet he was on the field all day, and you chose just that moment to attack him. If your love for Lord Ian is what you say, it is strange that you should fall upon one coming to his assistance when he was locked in combat with two opponents."

"You may believe what you choose, but the truth is that I did not find FitzWalter earlier. As for Lord Ian, I account him well able to take care of himself, especially against such louts as those."

"What is your quarrel with FitzWalter? Does he know of it?"

"He? The whole world knows of it. He gave away Normandy, and with Normandy *my* patrimony. I am a second son, Lord Salisbury. My heritage, such as it was, lay not far from the walls of Vaudreuil. I decided to take back a small piece of what FitzWalter or Saer de Quincy owed me in horse and armor ransom." He shrugged. "Perhaps it was not absolutely fitting that three of us went at each of them, but they owed us all and it seemed the best way. We shared in their defeat, and we will share in their ransom."

Salisbury hesitated. It was a sounder and more logical answer than he had expected and might well be true. He asked for and received the names and lodgings of the other knights involved. Four more he found without difficulty. They were all of a type—wholesome and seemingly honest young men, none of whom, except Sir Robert, even knew Lord Ian. They had come casually to the tourney to pick up what money they could in the way of knights-errant and had been drawn together by their common grievance of loss of lands in Normandy. That was the story he had from all—but the sixth knight he never found. That one had not returned to his lodgings after the tourney, and no one knew any more than his name—Sir Guy.

If there was any mystery, Salisbury learned, it was connected with the missing Sir Guy. It was he who had drawn the other five young men together, yet he never said for certain that *he* had lost lands. Over the next few days, Salisbury made diligent search for the source of the rumor that someone had bought men to kill Lord

Ian. Few were willing to speak to the king's half brother of any plot, but when their minds had been set to rest with assurances and after all tales were traced back to the source, it was to this same Sir Guy. He seemed to have spread the tales of knights-errant hired to kill. And when the tales of poor knights with money to spend were also followed to their source, it was clear that the money was Sir Guy's. A return to Sir Guy's five companions produced nothing. They did not know the man, except for having joined him for the stated purpose. They certainly had no money, above the bare minimum they needed to live, and they had received none, nor any offer of money, from Sir Guy. It was true Sir Guy had spoken of the rumored plot with them, but as a rumor, not as if he knew any more than they did. To them he had shown no riches. His lodgings were as poor as theirs; his horse and armor no better. Salisbury was at a standstill. There might be thousands of Sir Guys in the country, and very likely Guy was not the man's name at all.

Of the men of note Salisbury questioned, none except the principals had seen anything. All had been busy with their own duels. The only item that raised any suspicion in Salisbury was the eagerness with which Cantelu and Cornhill, FitzWalter and de Quincy all accepted the version of the story offered by Sir Robert and his companions. Since the suspicion raised was not one Salisbury was willing to entertain, he did not pursue the matter. Leicester was as little help. When pressed for an opinion, he laughed consumedly but said, between the gusts, that, if he were Salisbury, he would accept Sir Robert's story and be done with it. If one turned enough rocks, he remarked enigmatically but suggestively, with a raised brow and a cynical twist to his lips, one was sure to find slimy worms.

On the third day, Salisbury came to put what evidence he had uncovered before Ian. He found him still abed, with blue marks under his eyes that spoke clearly of little sleep. The amenities past, he said, "On this matter of a plot—" but got no further.

"There was no plot," Ian interrupted tonelessly.

"No," Salisbury agreed, "it seems not."

He was about to explain further, but Alinor looked such daggers at him across the bed that he held his tongue. If it was ever necessary, he could always give Ian the details at some other time. There was only one thing he had to know.

"I spoke to Robert de Remy, who was one of the men involved. He said you knew him from a youth and were about to take him into your service and would vouch for him. Is this true?"

"Yes."

"Then that ends the matter," Salisbury said briskly, but he was uneasy. The lifeless quality of the answer disturbed him. "Ian, are you ill?"

That drew a faint smile and lit a spark in the dark eyes. "No, only sore and very tired still. I have not had so sound a drubbing since Simon took me from my father. I hope the king was not offended at our absence from court."

"No," Salisbury replied, then grinned and shook his head. "You know John. He was pleased. He felt avenged for that you made him angry. He wished to beat you, as one lessons a child, and that was accomplished. You will have no more trouble with him, I think. He was really outraged at the rumors that flew about. He set me to ferret out the truth—Good God, Ian, what ails you?"

"Nothing, an incautious move. You would not believe how I ache. It seems to grow worse instead of better. William, I am not sure I will be able to come to the meeting with Oxford and Pembroke tomorrow. Except for reserving myself from setting out in my own person, I think you can take for granted my agreement to almost any plan Pembroke puts forward. I believe he knows the extent of Alinor's lands there and therefore what it would be sensible for us to commit to him in men and money."

"Remember, Ian, that you have the matter of the three castellans to settle—and there is also Sir Peter of Clyro. We will need men here, too," Alinor interposed.

Salisbury looked at Alinor in amazement. She had been so still, except for that one admonishing look she had cast at him, that he had forgotten her existence, as he frequently forgot Ela's. That Alinor should interpose a military suggestion was odd enough—even Ela, whose wit Salisbury respected deeply, had never done that. Even odder was that Ian took it as a matter of course, merely assuring her he had not overlooked the matter.

"I had intended to call out Simon's—I mean, Adam's —other men as a levy, Alinor. I cannot see that the king will engage in any new war this year, so I will not need them for that purpose. And it will be salutary for them to fight under my orders and to punish those others who were once their equals, until they broke faith."

She thought about it, her lips moving a little, then nodded. "It should be enough—about five hundred men, I make it. The keeps are small. I doubt they hold more than one hundred and fifty or two hundred, even stuffed and garnished."

"I make it only four hundred, or a little over," Ian agreed, "but you may be nearer right than I. As for Sir Peter—I am still not certain he is unfaithful. Assuredly, he must be tested, but not with an army, Alinor. What will that tell us except that he knows when an overwhelming force is facing him? So he might well yield in order to be able to work his own will another time. I will need to go with my own troop only, as if, perhaps, to visit Llewelyn. Then, if I smell trouble, I can use my Welshmen and call men in from the north."

"Can you levy upon your men to fight my castellan?"

Ian smiled faintly again. "I am not sure what it says in law, but those devils will not argue point of law with me for that cause. They will merely cease from fighting one another for a while so that they can enjoy the pleasure of fighting someone new."

Salisbury's eyes had been flicking from husband to wife as if he were watching a game of pitch the ball. "By God's bright eyeballs," he said with a slight flavor of resentment, "I wonder why you trouble yourself about 'her' men, Ian. It seems to me Lady Alinor knows almost as much as you about the art of war. I am surprised she does not don armor and dispense with a husband entirely."

"For Mary's sake, William, shut your mouth," Ian groaned and laughed at the same time. "Did you not know that was why I married her? She was all prepared to do just what you said. I thought I had driven the matter out of her head, and here you are reminding her of it."

"He jests," Alinor explained. "I had no intention of donning armor. All I said was that——"

"Alinor," Ian interrupted, shaking his head, "you are making matters worse. All she said, William, amounted to the fact that two experienced men of war and a young, but not childish, vassal needed her guidance in the matter of taking three small keeps."

"Well," Alinor responded tartly, "now you have met Sir Giles, Sir Henry, and Sir John—was I wrong?"

Ian uttered a bark of laughter that checked on a gasp of pain. "No, you were not—at least, not in the matter of their need for guidance. I beg leave to think that mine will be better than yours, however." But the last sentence was spoken sharply, no longer in a light tone of teasing.

"Yes, of course," Alinor replied flatly.

Another flicker of pain crossed Ian's face, but Salisbury did not think it was caused by any twinge in his body. Ian rubbed his hand across his mouth, then dropped it, and the lips were set hard.

"I am sorry to intrude our affairs upon you," he said

formally. "Please assume that my choice will be the same as Pembroke's in the Irish matter."

"But why should you pledge yourself blindly? Would it not be better for us to meet here, if you are not well enough to come to Oxford's house?

Salisbury could not conceive what had happened between Ian and his wife. He had thought there was some constraint in Alinor's manner when he came in, but he had dismissed it as anxiety, either about the plot against her husband or about his health. At first they had seemed easy enough in talking to each other about settling the trouble on Alinor's son's lands, but then this touch of bitterness had crept in. Salisbury wondered whether Ian had some reason to suspect Alinor's loyalty to him. The offer to move the meeting was an easy test for that.

"If you think the others would be willing, I will be most grateful," Ian responded promptly.

Then it was no desire to keep Alinor ignorant of his participation in the Irish expedition, Salisbury thought, as he arranged to send a messenger to let Ian know what time they would meet.

Ian made an effort to smile again. "Any time will suit me. I will be there." Then he frowned slightly. "But I hope not abed for much longer. Do you think I can have leave from the king to go, William? I need to visit the strongholds that have been neglected since Simon fell ill, and I would like to do it before summoning the men to war in the spring. I will need to spend some time in each, so the sooner I start the better I can manage."

"I am sure John will grant leave. In fact, I think he intends to depart in a day or two himself. Let me ask him, and I will tell you when we meet tomorrow what he says."

With the words, Salisbury rose. The atmosphere had grown so glacial that he feared he would freeze to death, despite the roaring fire and the generally mild weather, if he stayed any longer. Not that the icy disapproval was directed at him. Salisbury was sorry for Ian, because he did not look in proper condition for the blast of cold wrath that seemed about to strike him. However, kind of heart as Salisbury was, he had no intention of trying to interfere. He had learned better during his 40-odd years of life than to interpose himself between a husband and a wife. Ian had married the woman, let him deal with her.

To Ian's horror, however, Alinor did not say a word when she returned from seeing Salisbury out. She went directly to the window and sat down before her embroidery frame. If Ian had been less proud, he would have wept. He had said the most provocative thing he could think of. He had spoken as if Alinor's property were his, as if he intended to go to her castles alone and establish his authority over them. He had said it, moreover, in front of a stranger, deliberately, to enrage her further. He did not doubt that he had succeeded in making Alinor bitterly angry, but it seemed as if he had failed in his real purpose. She would not quarrel with him, any more than she would quarrel with a total stranger.

For three days this nightmare had continued, ever since he had awakened the morning after the melee. Ian stared sightlessly into the fire across the foot of the bed. Alinor was attentive, polite, kind, gentle in cleaning and dressing his maltreated body—and as distant as the moon. If he spoke to her, she replied—politely. If he cried out, she was there at once with a cool cloth or a soporific drink. If he chose to jest, she curved her lips. She was no shrew, for she did not quarrel; she was no nag, for she did not scold; she was not Alinor, for her soul had withdrawn from him.

Yet no matter what he suffered, Ian knew he could not yield to her in this battle of wills. He could understand her reasons; he could not approve her act. He

could not say he was sorry he had berated her. He was
not sorry. What she had done, however wise, was against
his principles, and to yield would make him less than
himself—less than a man. Some instinct told him that
if he could prod Alinor into a rage, into any strong
emotion, he could break through the wall that held her
prisoner. Ian took no special note of the name his
thought had given to Alinor's condition, because he was
too absorbed by his own turmoil of emotions, but the
name was the most significant point in his whole thought.

In fact, every other part of Ian's conjectures about
his wife was wrong. Alinor never minded being berated
and cared not a pin for either his approval or his principles. She never expected him to say he was sorry he
had disapproved of her; had he beaten her, she would
not have expected him to apologize. Her plans had been
successful. She was pleased, and she dismissed all
extraneous matters from her mind beyond taking wry
note of Ian's delicate sensibilities, so that she could use
better care not to affront them the next time. Actually,
Alinor was more horrified by her own behavior than
her husband was. At least half her abstraction was
owing to her self-castigation and her effort to break
through the ridiculous resentment that held her natural
emotions in bonds.

Alinor was not jealous in any ordinary sense of the
word. She knew Ian was faithful to her with his body,
and even with his heart, in an everyday, practical way.
She had little doubt that he would always be faithful,
excepting, of course, for the whores or serf girls he
might use when they were separated. To deny him that
comfort, by Alinor's way of thinking, would be the
same as telling him not to urinate or move his bowels
when he was away from home. Nor was she angry. There
was nothing to be angry about, beyond the crude way
he had left the house the morning of the melee. That
was a little thing, resulting from surprise and absence

of mind, no intended slight. Alinor knew she had only to mention it and Ian would beg pardon—so it was not worth being angry about or mentioning.

Yet, no matter how Alinor strove with herself—telling herself how good her husband was, how loving, how honest; telling herself what a fool she was, how unreasonable, how unfair—she could not control that inner withdrawal. She had not said a cross word, she had smiled and served him with all compliance, yet he sensed the change in her. It broke her heart to see the hurt in his eyes, to hear him start a conversation or tell a joke and then drop it, and look away. She tried and tried to respond naturally, but the effort seemed to make her more wooden. As she sat by her embroidery, working with the frantic energy of frustration, Alinor was so angry with herself that she could not find a corner of her heart or mind to be angry at what Ian said.

The worst of it was that Alinor could not understand what was wrong with her. Never in her life had she been petty or spiteful. She had never blamed her grandfather or Simon for being what they were. She put up with their male idiocies, working around their quirks to accomplish her purpose—if possible with due care not to offend their upright souls. Why was this one small quirk of Ian's different? Obviously, he did not wish to spend his time sighing at his lady's feet; obviously, he wished with all his heart to live normally with his wife, enjoying her and pleasuring in her enjoyment of him. It was so unimportant—a dream that once in a while mistily haunted a man's mind.

But Alinor was spoiled in a deeper and more basic way than mere yielding to a woman's whims could spoil her. From the time she had had a woman's emotions, she had been the very center of her men's existence. They could revile her, beat her, fling themselves upon horses and ride away, vowing they would part from her, but they knew and Alinor knew that they could not live without her. She was the core of life, the beating heart in the body, the lodestar of the mind. That she was everything else in the world to Ian, his comfort and his happiness, made no difference. She had tasted the joy of being the light of a man's soul; if she could not have that, she did not want the man. Reason could tell her she was a fool; will could drive her to behave cheerfully and kindly; nothing could cure her inner shrinking.

CHAPTER TWENTY-ONE

It was not yet dawn, but Ian was wide awake. He lay with his hands behind his head, watching the eastern border of the sky pearl just a trifle before the first faint streaks of pink appeared. The tent flap was drawn, and it moved a little in the mild breeze. It would be dry and hot, Ian thought, but probably that would not matter. If all went well, they should have the keep before the worst heat of the day. The weather, at least, had returned to normal. After a December and January of quite unusual mildness and dryness, February had concentrated all of winter into one blow.

They had been very fortunate to escape with so little loss. In the beginning of the month, all the rain heaven had stored through the autumn and early winter seemed to fall, and on the 27th the wind had come. That had been a wind to end all winds. Serfs' huts had been lifted bodily and flung to earth miles away. There would be no lack of dry firewood for years. Trees, whole forests of them, had been uprooted. The greater fell where they stood, but the lesser had flown through the air like gigantic, bewitched besoms. Ian had seen one forced, roots first, through the wall of a house. And then, to add to the misery of the homeless and bereft, it had snowed and snowed and snowed.

Warm as he was, Ian shivered a little with memory. He had ridden home to Roselynde through it, his horse belly deep at times, so that he had to dismount and struggle along on foot. It was as well he had. Although his fears that even the great keep of Roselynde could not withstand that fury of wind and water had been groundless, he had found two frantic, terrified children who clung to him, begging assurance that their mother was safe. He had assured them, but he had passed two days of purgatory until a messenger had struggled through with the news that Alinor was indeed safe with Lady Ela at Salisbury.

It was just like Alinor, Ian thought, to have chosen that particular week to go to Salisbury to meet the woman Lady Ela suggested as a companion for Joanna. But that is not fair, he told himself. Alinor could not have known that God would send such a storm. She did not do it to spite him. There was little conviction in Ian's reproving thought. It seemed to him that anything Alinor did since that tourney was done to spite him. With an effort, Ian thought about the woman she had brought back to Roselynde with her and, after a moment, he smiled. Lady Margaret was a pleasant thought, one to induce smiles. Plump and cheerful, practical and placid, she was the ideal person to have charge of the children.

There was no tragedy about her story, although she was a widow with grown children. Her son had not cast her out, as sometimes happened. Her daughter-in-law adored her. Both had pleaded with her to stay, but Lady Margaret was no fool. As long as she remained, she managed the keep, and her daughter-in-law remained a child and a toy. Besides, Lady Margaret craved young ones to teach and to guide. When her grandchildren were of an age to need her and her daughter-in-law had more confidence, she would return. At present, she was happy to come to Roselynde.

Her coming had left Alinor free to go on progress. Ian was annoyed with himself for allowing Alinor's name to come back into his mind. That woman was like a sore, sharp-edged tooth. You could no more keep from cutting your mind on thoughts of her than you could keep from cutting your tongue on the bad tooth. Again he wrenched his mind away from his wife, concentrating instead on the dull, regular thuds of the trenchbuts as they flung boulders against the walls of the keep. There was a new sound to one place, a creaking screech that told of crumbling mortar and slipping stones. Ian listened and smiled again when a second blow produced a similar sound sooner than any trenchbut could be reloaded. Someone had ordered that two or more be played on some weakening spot.

Yesterday had been a good day all around. The channel to drain the moat had been finished. During the night, the fragile dam that held back the waters had been breached. Nothing but a stinking ditch would be left now. The ramps to span the ditch were ready, as were the scaling ladders—six days from the time he had arrived and demanded that the castellan yield the keep. Not bad. Each leader of the troops he had summoned seemed sincere in his efforts. Ian suspected there was a feeling of righteous spite spurring them on. Doubtless, all had considered rebellion, at least passingly, when news of Simon's death had come to them. They had decided against it, some out of respect for their own oaths and honor, but some out of a fear of losing what they had. Possibly, as the months passed and the rebellious ones were not brought to heel, they had regretted their "cowardice." Now they would not only prove themselves brave but, more important, right.

Then there had been that letter from Alinor. Ian shifted on his camp bed and it creaked. He was aware from the corner of his eyes that Geoffrey had sat up, but he lay still in his new position and the squire lay down again. Owain still slept. Owain had been at more than one keep-taking; when he woke he would be eager and alert, but not as excited as Geoffrey. Alinor had asked after the squires and sent them kind messages and some small comforts—a new shirt for each and a pair of hose, and sugared plums. Ian laughed softly as he remembered how the boys had fallen upon the treat, making a fool of him who had wondered that Alinor should send his squires, who were nearly men, a child's sweetmeat. Clearly, she knew what would give them pleasure.

Ian shifted again. She knew what would give him pleasure also. Few and brief, but very kind words ended that letter. "Have a care to yourself, my lord, and write to me often. Joanna and Adam beg news of you ten times a day, and, as for me, I wish I had it as many times as that and more." Perhaps when this keep had fallen, he would ride back to Roselynde for a day or two. Sir Robert could be left to reorganize the defenses and see to the repair of whatever damage had been done. Perhaps their long separation, while she had been on progress and he had been gathering these men and examining the keeps for the best way to breach their defenses, had softened whatever core of anger she still nursed against him.

It would not do to think too much of that. Once before he had hoped and been cruelly disappointed. Ian listened to the sounds of the camp. Men were astir, but he had no desire to give any sign of nervousness or distrust by being too early abroad. He had given his orders and designed the attack the previous night. To meddle now would be a mistake. All should be ready, or near ready, before he came to oversee the results. The sky was lighter now, and pink. Ian turned his head on his arm.

"Go and get me some breakfast, Geoffrey, and kick that lazy slugabed awake."

"Lazy slugabed" woke other memories. The king had fallen into a lethargy again a few weeks after that dreadful storm in February. No one had really been surprised, for John had showed himself at his very best immediately after the storm struck. He had ridden madly all over the kingdom, directing rescue work, controlling the lawlessness that any disaster brought in its wake, and bringing aid and comfort to the deprived and bereft. It was only normal to rest after such exertions. Although the king continued to move from place to place after the crisis had passed, and had done the most necessary business that was pressed upon him by Salisbury and others, he had seemed content to sleep till the day was far advanced, talk idly to the queen, pat her swelling belly during the afternoon, and futter a remarkable number of women through the night.

Had Ian been given to thinking in those terms, he would have said that God was showing His favor to the righteous. The lazy fit could not have fallen at a better time. Pembroke had been able to gather men and leave for Ireland without the slightest hindrance. When Oxford announced his departure, John had said no more than, "Better he than I." Now, however, Alinor wrote, the monster seemed to be stirring. Ela had written to Alinor that John had been asking sharp questions about Pembroke's doings abroad. So far, according to Salisbury, he seemed merely interested, not angry, but Ela did not trust her husband's interpretations of his brother's moods.

Ian had been able to write reassuringly to Alinor. He did not trust Salisbury's perspicacity about John's intentions any more than Lady Ela did, but he had information on another event that would doubtless divert John from any consideration of Pembroke's doings. The Pope had kept his compact with the bishops and had definitely and positively annulled the election of both Reginald, subprior of Canterbury, and John, Bishop of Norwich, as prospective Archbishop of Canterbury. After considerable pressure had been applied to the monks of Canterbury, who had come to plead the case of the subprior by the Pontiff, he had secured the election of Stephen Langton and, to obviate any slip twixt the cup and the lip, had himself consecrated Langton as archbishop on June 17.

The news had come to Ian from Peter des Roches, Bishop of Winchester. Peter was the king's man and a very loyal servant to John, too loyal to allow the king to bring disaster upon himself by the appointment of a man like John Gray. He understood his master, understood that he must be curbed if he was not to drive the country into rebellion and chaos. John Gray would be nothing, a tool to bend the Church to the king's will. Without the hope that the Church would mediate fairly, the barons would be driven into despair. They would feel that there was no place they could turn to have justice and that the only solution to their troubles was to rid themselves of the king entirely.

Peter des Roches was no holy man of God; he was too intent upon the affairs of every day. Nonetheless, he was sufficiently a priest to regard his obligations seriously. He had known Ian a long time, had been his confessor years before at John's court when John was only Richard's heir. When Ian had written to him, shortly after Simon died, and described his desires and his fears regarding a marriage with Alinor, Peter had considered the matter seriously, including the king's probable disapproval. Still, he had decided it was best that Ian marry the woman. Thus, he had a sense of obligation regarding the marriage he had forwarded. He had informed Ian late in January of mild feelers, which he had done his best to discourage, about an annulment. Now that an Archbishop of Canterbury, who could grant an annulment, was appointed, he felt Ian should be kept abreast of affairs.

Truthfully, Ian was not much concerned that John would try to annul his marriage. He suspected things had got beyond that stage in John's mind. Nonetheless, he was glad of Winchester's news. John might accept the *fait accompli*—Ian knew the Pope had baited the lure well with a rich gift of four magnificent rings and other precious jewels set in gold. In that case, there would be a period when all the king's attention was given to testing and coming to terms with his new archbishop. Or John might defy the Pope, and his rage would be directed to winning a far more serious contest than one with a single vassal. Ian sincerely hoped John would accept Langton—at least superficially. He had an enormous respect for the man, but, beyond that, it would be better if John's mind was occupied with a battle of wits near at hand. Letters to and from Italy took too long. In the waiting periods, John was all too likely to take out his spleen on some local issue. Probably the king would not bite off as large a piece of trouble as interfering with the Earl of Pembroke, but, Ian suspected, he and Alinor would make just the right-size mouthful.

It was a little surprising, in fact, that he did not yet have news of the king's reaction to the election of Langton. Ian shrugged and sat up as Owain brought his clothes and armor. At the moment there were more pressing matters to attend to. Dressed, Ian stepped out of the tent and sniffed the air. Geoffrey, bless the boy, was obviously providing something more substantial than bread and cheese and wine for breakfast. Then Ian joined the crowd of men drifting toward the back of the camp. A small bell rang; they all quickened their pace. Ian picked his way through the ranks of kneeling men to join Sir Robert de Remy and Simon's loyal castellans. With one eye on the sky and one on Ian, the priest began Mass just as Ian bent his knee.

On the last "amen" Ian was on his feet. He stepped toward the priest and nodded at him. The priest rang his bell again, more emphatically. The men farther back stood, the ones nearer by hunkered back on their heels. The silence, Ian noted cynically, was more profound than during Mass. Of course, that was not completely fair. No one expected to understand the words of the Mass; it was sufficient to be there as an act of faith. Being there brought God's blessing upon you; it was magic, and not meant to be understood by men. On the other hand, everyone expected to understand what Ian said, and it might be that their lives would depend upon his words.

"The battle places of each party and the duties of each I will leave to be explained by your own captains. I have only a few words to say. This is not an action of war. There is to be no looting. The keep is the property of my son by marriage, and I will not have anything of his despoiled. Swift and painful punishment will fall upon the man who steals or damages more than necessary anything in the keep. For the same reason, quarter is to be offered to any man-at-arms who desires it and to the castle servants if they offer no resistance. In fact, any person who does not resist, among the common folk, is not to be harmed in any way.

"On the other hand, I am not unaware that eager service must be rewarded. It is my understanding that the castellan here has amassed a considerable personal fortune. This, of course, does not belong to Adam and may justly be distributed among you. No man will be permitted to seize it all, and I will see to its fair distribution, including my share, which will be reserved to increase the prizes of the twenty most daring and valorous men."

A cry of pleasure went up. Two men, or even more, depending upon fatalities, from each group would come away from this battle with gold and silver, perhaps enough to buy a wife or a farm, if that was their desire. Ian knew well what he was doing. Under his arrangement, no man needed to be first and best. No penalty would attach to helping a friend, nor would there be any profit in slyly harming a battle comrade who seemed to be stronger or more successful. More, in fact, could be gained from attaching oneself to such a comrade and trying to increase his success so that you might shine by reflected light.

"As to the castellan and his family, I leave that to your own judgment. If you desire to take him prisoner in hopes that ransom may be paid by someone, by all means do so. I have no particular lust to see him or his family dead. However, I will not pay nor lend him a mil to preserve him. He has violated his oath to his dead overlord and sought to win advantage from a helpless widow and child. He is filth in my eyes, less than the beasts who have not God's law and precepts of honor to guide them."

Ian knew he had almost certainly condemned the man to death and his womenfolk to rape and murder. He hoped there were no young girls in the man's family, but it was not going to give him second thoughts or sleepless nights. Not only was he truly offended at the castellan's dishonorable act, but he also had two more keeps to take and a lesson to administer to the loyal castellans. When news of this castellan's fate reached the ears of the two other rebellious men—and Ian would make sure that it did reach them—the chances were greatly increased that they would yield without further resistance. To do so would ensure them of their lives and their family's lives. What they would do to live afterward was questionable, but possibly they had families that would take them in or they could try the tourney trail. Life was sweet.

In addition to the possibility of saving his own men future death and injury, Ian was planning on nipping future rebellions in the bud. He had gone to great trouble to be generous, mild, and affable to the castellans who had loyally answered his summons to fight for him. It had not always been easy, as his mind seesawed up and down according to Alinor's whim, but he had succeeded. The men were comfortable with him and trusted him. Now he wished them to see the other side of the coin. It was not sufficient to say "I am terrible when angered." It was far better to say nothing, to smile and show how ill those who broke faith fared.

"And now," Ian smiled as he looked out over the men, "I am sure you are as eager to break your fasts as I am to break mine. Eat hearty. If you do your work well, we will have dinner in the castle. If you are slow, you will miss your dinners altogether. Good fortune. God bless you all."

He turned to say a few courteous words to the priest while the men dispersed. Ian's chaplain was a sensible young man, not nearly as good or learned as Father Francis but also far less likely to preach a sermon on the evils of violence just before men went into action. In fact, he never preached sermons before battles, only offered the men the mystical comfort of the Mass. And when he did preach, few of his sermons failed to include the themes of upholding honor and righteous wrath, nor was he above wearing armor and wielding a mace to defend his Bible and chalice and holy relics. Father Jocelyn, Ian believed, would rise high in the church—and he would do the best he could to help him. Ian finished what he was saying, and the priest began to fold up his traveling altar.

"My lord——"

"Yes, Robert?"

"I need to talk to you."

The young man's eyes were bright, his color high. He was almost as excited as Geoffrey. It occurred to Ian for the first time that Sir Robert might never have been involved in taking a keep before—he had never thought to ask. It did not matter, because he was part of Ian's own personal fighting force and Ian had no doubts at all about his courage, but he wondered under whom he had trained.

"Very well. Come and share my breakfast. We do not have much time. Nothing is wrong with the preparations?"

"Oh no, Lord Ian. The ramps are in place, covered with brush, and the scaling ladders are in the ditch covered with mud. They need only to be lifted to the ramps."

An expression of acute distaste crossed Ian's face. "Whose brilliant thought was that?"

"Mine, my lord," Robert replied apprehensively. "I

thought it would save time. They cannot be lost in the mud, I swear. They are all marked, and the men who are to lift them know well where they must seek. Have I done amiss? I fear——"

"No, no," Ian laughed. "The thought was wise. If it works as planned, it will save time. But, Robert, in God's name, think how we shall all stink!"

"Stink?" Robert repeated blankly.

Of course they would stink, covered with the mud from the drained moat, which was rich in half-decayed feces and garbage. But what had a stink to do with anything? Everyone stank anyway, after working in the heat all week, with no chance to wash and no change of clothing.

"Never mind," Ian soothed, "it is a personal oddity in me. Sit."

He gestured toward a second campstool, and Geoffrey hurried over with a large wedge of cold meat pasty and half a fowl.

"I am sorry, lord," Geoffrey said. "That is all I saved from dinner. I did not think——"

"Bring bread and cheese and another cup, and we shall do well enough. Leave it. I will serve. Go arm yourself."

Ian broke the fowl into pieces and cut the pasty in half with a slight smile on his lips. He had sent Geoffrey away for a purpose. He did not misunderstand the boy's trembling, but Sir Robert from the superior level of his 21 years of life might do so. Six parts excitement, three parts eagerness, one part fear was what Ian judged Geoffrey's affliction to be. He would do well enough once he had duties to perform.

"What did you want to talk to me about, Robert?"

"The women." The young man choked a little around the mouthful he was eating. "You said no word about the women. The men will think they are free to do with them as they please."

It was, of course, exactly what Ian wanted them to

think, but how did one say that to an inexperienced young man who had been raised in a decent household? Sir Robert's precepts about women were clear. A serf girl might be raped in a field; a gently born woman might be seduced, but must not be forced. When you married, you could beat your wife for a fault, but she must be protected against harm by anyone else. Moreover, even in a war, the gentleladies were not to be assaulted or insulted—they usually brought good ransoms. Ian rubbed the back of his neck under his hood. His situation was particularly difficult because only a few days earlier he had had a long discussion with Sir Robert on the finer points and deeper meaning of honor, stemming from what happened at the tourney.

"I know. That was because I did not know what to say," Ian temporized. "By his act, the castellan has put himself beyond the law, has made himself less than a man, and that which is his is lessened also, its quality destroyed. He gave oath before God that he would faithfully administer his trust and return it on demand. He has stolen this property, and to make it worse, stolen it from a child of seven, as well as violating his oath before God. He is not an honest enemy as might be if he were, say, Philip's vassal and I John's, and we came to blows. Then he and his would deserve to be treated with honor, no matter how bitter the conflict between us. If I ordered the women to be spared, where would be the difference between honorable war and thievery?"

"I see."

"Robert," Ian said, amused by the fact that the young man's appetite was in no way diminished—his concern had apparently been more that he should not transgress his lord's sensibilities again than for the women involved —"if you can and you wish to shield the women, it will do you no particular disservice in my eyes. That will be your business and nothing to do with me—ever. Remember, if you cannot find a relative to take them, you will be burdened with them. Every man must know, you also, that although I will strive with all my power to help and protect a faithful vassal, I will not mitigate the punishment of an unfaithful one by so much as a hair."

Sir Robert merely nodded acceptance, his mouth being too full of meat pasty to make a reply practical. Ian gnawed the ends off the thigh bone of the fowl and sucked experimentally at the marrow. He heard the battle leaders urging their men to form up. Sir Robert heard also. He swallowed hastily, gulped down the remains of his wine, sketched a salute to Ian, and went off to attend to his assigned duties. Owain and Geoffrey appeared by the side of the tent with Ian's shield and helmet. He got to his feet and smiled at them.

"Owain, you will hold your place by my left shoulder. Do not be carried away. If a blow takes me on that side, God help you."

"He will need to, my lord, for I will be sore hurt or dead. I will not fail you."

"No, I do not suppose you will. Now, Geoffrey, you may draw your sword if you wish, but you may use it only to defend yourself at need. I do not wish you to become embroiled in the fighting. You must be free to carry messages for me. In such a battle, where the parties are hidden from each other, this is a most singularly necessary task. It is dangerous—I am sorry for that—but you are fittest for it. You are a small target and light on your feet. I tell you again, your first duty is to deliver the message and bring back a reply. Do not stop to help the wounded or try to save a man overmatched by others. This may be a hard thing, for you will doubtless see pitiful sights that you might amend or avert, but that is not your purpose. Do you understand?"

"Yes, my lord."

There was disappointment in the young face. Doubtless Geoffrey had envisioned himself a full-blooded warrior. He was not far off at that, Ian thought. Geoffrey's improvement in fighting technique was nothing short of spectacular. He made up in speed and ferocity, in pure determination to excel, for any deficiency in size. He was very nearly as good as Owain, who was two years older, although he was less powerful, of course. But the boy was beginning to grow now. He would be taller than his father, a good size, not so awkwardly tall as Ian was himself—if he lived long enough.

"Geoffrey," Ian warned sharply, "if you fail, we may lose the day. If I give order that a troop attack, or yield ground, and you do not give the message in the time I allow, my plans will be fouled. Do not forget yourself."

"No, my lord."

It was not really so serious a matter. Sir Robert had been instructed to keep an eye on Geoffrey when the assault was first made and the fighting was heaviest. Nonetheless, Ian hoped the boy would obey orders. Courage was a good thing, but a sense of responsibility was equally necessary for a man who would rule extensive estates and, very likely, be high in the councils of the king—if not John, then the next king. There was no sense in wondering. The matter would be put to the proof soon enough. Ian put on and fastened his helmet, slid his arm through the shield strap, and grasped the handhold. It would have been more convenient to use a round footman's shield for this work. Obviously, horses did not climb ladders to scale walls, and knights and men-at-arms would all be afoot. But Ian was so accustomed to the weight and feel of his own shield that he chose to put up with its unwieldy size rather than trust to an unfamiliar protection.

A glance at the sky, where the sun was now well up, assured Ian that they were in good time. The attack could not be a complete surprise. The men in the keep must realize that once the moat was drained, an assault would soon follow. Ian hoped, however, that the leisurely pace of the morning activities in his camp would convince the defenders that the attack would not take place that day. It was the reason why the ramps and ladders had been so secretly prepared and so carefully hidden. Doubtless, there would be sentries who would cry a warning as soon as the ramps were thrown over the drained moat, but, if most of the men on day duty were at breakfast, it would take them a few minutes, at least, to come to their positions.

The slow pace and leisurely start had also given time and confidence, Ian hoped, for those who had stood guard all night to go to bed. Full half the men had been on night duty. Ian had left instructions that all the serving men, dressed in the men-at-arms's armor, should be up and stirring, forming groups in a purposeful way from time to time, as if a night assault was being planned. It would take those men even longer to reach the walls. Whether or not they slept in their armor, some time must be lost shaking sleep from one's eyes, grabbing up weapons, and coming from the sleeping places. Ian looked around the camp and toward the castle walls. So far so good. His men were milling about in seemingly occupied groups, a few parties wandering toward the moat. No alarm had yet been sounded.

Ian walked slowly toward the nearest party of men while he watched the groups approaching the moat. Some, of course, he could not see because they were around the curve of the wall, but those he could see were only a few paces farther from or nearer their goal than the others. He had reached his own party by then, and he could feel himself tensing, could hear Owain and Geoffrey just behind him breathing harder and faster. Almost simultaneously, two men in each of the parties bent down.

"Ready," Ian warned softly.

As he spoke, he could see the men-at-arms in each group all turn toward the castle. The men who had bent suddenly flung the brush off the ramps and lifted. Then everything happened at once. Alarms rang out all along

the keep walls. The fighting parties began to run toward
the ramps they were supposed to cross. The ramps continued to rise as the men walked forward, lifting. Other
men aided them from underneath, pushing and walking,
pushing and walking, until the long plank bridges were
perpendicular. The guards on the wall were winding and
firing crossbows now, but there were few and poor targets, most of the men being shielded from the missiles
by the bulk of the ramps. Finally, the ramps were over-
balanced and fell over, the violence of their drop dig-
ging them well into the soft muddy clay of the banks. It
did not matter even if the ramps broke. Their only
purpose was to save the men from slipping and being
bogged in the mud, which was a foot or two deep.

A loud cheer went up from the fighting parties of
men-at-arms, who ran faster, a selected few lifting their
shields over their heads to form a "turtle." Under this
protection, the men who had buried the ladders came
forward. More and more arrows were flying down and
out now. Thus far, the turtles were not damaged, but it
was not long before one who stepped out from under
their shield cried out and fell. Another took his place at
once. The long ladders began to come loose from the
mud that covered them and caused them to adhere to
the drained moat. One end was laid across the ramp.
Willing hands pulled, pulled. Braced against the crosspieces of the ramp, the ladders lifted sluggishly, wavered, wavered, fell against the wall.

Around the curve of the wall, Ian heard shrieks of
disappointment. One of the ladders, at least, had over-
balanced and fallen to the side instead of against the
wall. "Now!" Ian called to those who followed him, and
ran onto the ramp. The turtle parted before him, and he
set his foot first on the ladder. He had not drawn his
sword. One does not climb a slippery, muddy ladder in
full armor without at least one hand to grip the rungs.
He did not raise his head to see how close he was to the
top, either. That would be an open invitation for an

arrow full in the face. Ian's back itched with apprehension as he climbed, although probably his mail would be firm enough to protect him at the angle he presented to the wall.

Right at his heels Owain climbed. He had his sword unscabbarded, hung from a leather thong at his wrist. Ian could hear it clink dully against the ladder from time to time. He hoped Owain would have sense enough to stay back sufficiently far that he did not get kicked in the head. He hoped the loose sword would not catch on a rung and either tear free or trip Owain. He hoped the free-swinging blade would not strike Geoffrey, who was directly behind Owain. Then the ladder swayed alarmingly. Ian could hear the overstrained wood groan as men on the wall hooked the top struts and tried to push it outward.

Panting slightly with effort, Ian struggled to increase his rate of climb. He did not think the ladder could be pushed outward and overturned. The angle at which it lay against the wall had been carefully thought out—Ian was no novice at wall-scaling. But if it could be lifted from its rest position, it might be tipped sideways, or the weight might be shifted completely onto one strut. If so, the pegging and lashing might not hold, or the foot of the strut might break. The only protection against that was to have sufficient weight at the top to prevent the ladder from being shifted. Ian drew a deep breath and moved his eyes from the rungs of the ladder to the side. He was no coward, but, when fully armed, he feared heights. To die in battle was one thing. To be crushed and broken and, perhaps, live to mend all awry and to be crippled—that was something else again.

The distance of the ground below at once brought relief and cold sweat. In the next moment, the easing of the pressure on the ladder was a warning. With a desperate effort, Ian lifted his shield over his head. A blow struck it and then another, but Ian laughed. The edge of the shield had not caught the wall. He was up!

Viciously he swung the shield out, mounted one more rung, swung sideways so that he could place a buttock on the wall. A single blow caught him on the upper right shoulder. He gasped with pain, although he had half expected it, lashed out with his mailed fist, and dropped down onto the safe stone surface of the wall. Three men leapt at him, but his shield was up, and under its cover he drew his sword.

The noise was now so loud and so general that Ian did not know whether any of the other parties had been successful in scaling the wall. He disabled one of the men who opposed him and moved right. Owain dropped beside him, his sword already swinging; he moved left. Geoffrey dropped safely between them and scuttled behind Ian, drawing his lighter weapon. For the moment, there could not be any messages to run. A solid wall of men opposed them to the right, where lay the entry to the left-hand tower that guarded the drawbridge and portcullis.

The number of defenders was not important, except in the long run. Because the walls were only eight feet wide at this level, only two or three could advance against the invaders at any one time. If the other parties scaling the walls were unsuccessful, however, the supply of fresh defenders could overwhelm Ian's party by exhaustion. Right now that problem was far from Ian's mind. He was concentrating on keeping his side clear and pushing the defenders back. What inhibited them worked even harder against Ian. If he and the few men who had come up the ladder did not push the defenders back, no more of his party could come over the wall to help. There simply would not be standing room for them.

Jamie and two other northerners were up now. They had taken over Sir Robert's and Owain's positions and freed those two to come to Ian's aid. It was on his side that the pressure and danger were greatest. There was neither time nor space for niceties of technique. Ian merely protected himself with his shield on the left, while his right arm rose and fell as regularly as if he were working a pump handle and with about as little aim. A man screamed; another fell.

"Cry quarter," Ian shouted. "You will be spared. Cry quarter!"

"Yielded," a man whimpered.

"Throw your weapons over the wall," Geoffrey ordered, "and get out of the way."

The offering of quarter, shouting the offer as a battle cry, had been planned to take the heart out of the rebellious castellan's men. In general the idea was a good one, but it had its drawbacks. Each man who yielded increased the crowd and blocked the space that Ian's fighting men could occupy. Nonetheless, the offer had to be made before rage and bitterness aroused stubborn resistance in the defenders. A body gave softly under Ian's foot and nearly overset him.

"Get the dead out of the way," Ian shouted at Geoffrey.

The boy was intelligent enough to know that his master did not expect him to lift the weight of a man and armor over his head alone. This was a "message." He slid back, past the crouching, yielded man to pass Ian's order to the men-at-arms who were now coming over the wall. They began to pull the fallen men out from under the feet of the fighters and toss them over the wall. One man screamed as he went over. The men-at-arms were not investigating the difference between dead and wounded too closely; if the body lay still and had weapons, it went over. Geoffrey shuddered, but he did not interfere. His business was to get back to his lord so that he could carry further commands.

The harsh order had another effect. Men who were slightly wounded and who might have fought on, showed an increasing tendency to throw their weapons away. Soon there was no comparison in the will to fight between defenders and invaders. For the invaders there was little choice. Once upon the wall, it was more certain death to try to go down the ladder than to fight. For the defenders, quarter was protection. Once yielded, if they saw the invaders taking the worse, they could escape down the ladders without much fear that their unyielded comrades would waste blows or arrows on them.

The pressure behind Ian was growing greater than the pressure ahead of him. Owain, thrusting around his master from behind, could still use his sword, but Ian was doing more damage with his shield than with the blade, because he had so little room to strike. Inexorably, as much by weight as by skill, he was pressing closer and closer to the door into the tower. Sir Robert smashed his sword hilt into the jaw of the man opposing him, stepped forward the width of the body, and was pressed sideways so that he faced the inner edge of the wall.

"There is fighting in the bailey," he shouted. "We have breached the wall."

The defender who had thrust Sir Robert sideways hesitated, with his sword raised for a blow, and also looked over the wall. What he saw gave him no comfort. He threw down the sword and cried aloud, "Yielded."

After that, what resistance was made was a mere token. Before the men of the first wave up the ladder felt the need to stop and breathe, they had won to the door and down the steps of the tower. In the guard room at the base, the fighting would be more determined, Ian thought. There were a number of men standing to the defense of the drawbridge mechanism. Ian measured his opponents warily. They were fresh and, he decided, ready to make a last stand. These were probably relatives of the castellan or squires grown up in service, not to be bribed into yielding by offers of quarter.

"Geoffrey!"

"Here, lord."

"Tell Sir Alfred, or whoever else you can reach, to make all haste into the other tower and open the portcullis."

It was surprisingly quiet in the tower, the thick walls blocking the shouts and clang of arms from the bailey and from the walls above. Geoffrey's boots on the sanded stone floor could be heard clearly as he took to his heels. Ian also heard the heavier steps of men-at-arms coming down the stairs into the tower base.

"Coward," one of the defenders cried passionately, "you will overwhelm us with numbers."

Ian laughed. "I do not extend the courtesies of honor to thieving dogs who steal from children and widows."

A cry of rage answered Ian's contempt, and the knight leapt at him. Ian laughed again. It was what he had wanted. Others surged forward after the leader, and the solid ring of defenders was broken. Ian's men charged forward also, some to engage and fight, but others worked over the handspikes holding the draw-bridge up. The sound of the blows used to loosen the spikes pierced the rage of Ian's attacker. With a shriek of anguish, he realized he had been taunted into his own defeat. Unwisely, he glanced toward the winch he was supposed to defend. Ian laughed one last time and caught his opponent's neck where the turn of the head opened a space. The armor was good; the head was not sheared away, but the man was dead in the next instant anyway, and Ian had to wrench fiercely at his sword to free it from the collarbone.

There was, in fact, no particular need for haste in freeing his weapon. The man who lay dead at his feet was the castellan's son, and the others were going down rapidly. Soon the noise of the drawbridge descending was reinforced by the screeches of the portcullis going up. Geoffrey came pelting back with word that the castellan himself was also dead. He had been at the breach in the walls and had been killed in the bailey.

No one had bothered to close the forebuilding, and so far as Geoffrey could see in his hurried trip back, there were no defenders there, so that the keep itself, if not already taken, was open to anyone who wished to walk in. Ian shook his head and stepped out into the bailey. Behind him, he heard Jamie mutter "Stupid bastard," in the coarse northern dialect.

Sir Robert came up wiping his sword on a strip of tunic he had torn from some prisoner. Puzzlement was written large on his face. "My lord," he protested, "there were far too few men, and the keep was ill prepared for war. What did the fool think he was doing, to defy you in such a case?"

"I do not know," Ian replied. "Make all secure, Robert, calm the servants and set them to work again. Let us not look a gift horse in the mouth."

It was all he could say under the circumstances, as, above all, he did not wish to look this particular gift horse in the mouth. Stupid the castellan might have been, although it was not Simon's way to appoint stupid or untrustworthy men—unless he had done it as a gesture to pacify "someone" in authority. Still, not even an idiot would have raised rebellion with his keep so undefended against retribution. The man had had time enough to prepare, heaven knew. And yet he did not prepare. Why? To that, there was only one answer. Because he did not expect that any attempt would be made to take his keep, not even when an army camped around it. Because he had expected help that had not come.

CHAPTER TWENTY-TWO

"Alinor," Isobel said suddenly, "you must stop mourning for Simon. He has been dead near a year. You are making Ian very unhappy."

"But I do not mourn for Simon," Alinor replied, lifting startled eyes from her work. "I never did mourn for him—he was very glad to die—I mourned only for myself, bereft and alone."

"You will not succeed, so do not waste your time in trying." Isobel spoke rather sharply, for her. "I am not a man, whom you can send off on a false scent with a twist of your tongue. It has taken me a long time to find the courage to say this, and I will not be turned aside. That is a good man you married, and you are making his life a bitter hell."

"It has nothing to do with Simon," Alinor sighed, tears rising to her eyes. "And you cannot say worse to me than I have said to myself. But it is not always so bad as it was yesterday. You saw us at our worst time. The first few days of our being together are very hard. In the letters we write, we cannot see each other's eyes, you know. My words are kind, his are cheerful. Perhaps I should not write at all, yet there is news I *must* send him and advice I *must* have from him. And I know he is unhappy, and I worry dreadfully that he will not guard himself properly, so I beg him to have a care and I say I miss him—I do miss him. Then he rides home, or I must send for him for some purpose—it is even worse when I send for him—and we meet—and——"

Alinor burst into tears, and Isobel stared in blank amazement at her friend's heaving shoulders. Then she rose heavily, for she was far gone with child again, and came around the embroidery frames. For a moment or two she caressed Alinor wordlessly. Then she drew her toward the bed where they could sit side by side, touching.

"Every word you say speaks of love. You miss him. You worry about him. What then ails you, Alinor?"

"A stupid, unimportant thing that I cannot drive out of me—a nothing, a shadow, and it is ruining my life and Ian's."

"A shadow— Alinor, surely you cannot believe that Simon would disapprove or would deny you the———"

"I told you Simon has naught to do with this." Alinor uttered a choke of laughter in the midst of her tears. "Would I, for any reason, call Simon a nothing? If Simon knew what I was doing to Ian and why, he would rise from his grave to beat me for such a stupidity. But I cannot help it. I try and I try— Oh, let it lie, Isobel. I swear that scolding me will not help. Here I come to comfort you and———"

"Comfort me? I thought you had come to help me bring another joy into the world. All goes well with me, Alinor, as you know. I do not have your fear of Ireland and, indeed, my news from William is excellent. As soon as I am lightened of the burden I carry, I will go to him there." She cocked an eye at Alinor. "What, no outcry? You are not using all your powers, my love. You are allowing me to come back to the matter you wish to divert me from."

Alinor could not help laughing again. "It is not that I do not wish to talk of it, only that I can see no sense in hearing from you what I have already told myself so many thousand times."

"Now that shows you are not thinking clearly. You would never hear from me the things you would say. Never would I demean myself to use such language as you do, Alinor. No, now, seriously, my love, you are plainly treading the same path around and around like a blindfold ox milling corn. Tell me the tale. If I see only the same things you do, then you have wasted an hour's time. No more harm can come than that and, after all, we have naught better to do. We must wait until my little one decides he wishes to look upon the world."

It did not take long for Alinor to give Isobel a more complete version of Ian's proposal than she had written, to describe his reluctance to return to the keep before they were married, and the events at the tourney. Isobel shook her head over Alinor's interpretation of the events, but she did not contest it. She wanted the meat of the present matter.

"So he might have some foolish, half-formed dream left over from childhood. Well, what of it? Simon loved the queen just so, and it did not trouble you."

"How did you know that?" Alinor asked in amazement.

"It was written in his eyes for all to see."

"Perhaps." Alinor shrugged. "But when he needed to choose, he chose me and not the dream."

"Well, if you are not the greatest ninny! Who do you think Ian would choose, if it came to the point?" Isobel was well-satisfied with the faint flush she saw rise in Alinor's cheeks. Obviously, the very unoriginal idea she had stated had not occurred to her friend or had been deliberately overlooked. "What I want to know is not what Ian dreams but what has passed between you since you conceived this notion."

Alinor shuddered. "I tried to hide what I felt. I swear I did. But he sensed it. He knew that I knew. He tried every way—except renouncing the dream—to ease me and please me. Then he grew angry, which I did not blame him for in the least, and we parted. I went on progress to the keeps I had not visited since Simon's illness, and he went to look over Adam's lands and to examine carefully those three strongholds which he meant to wrest from the rebellious castellans."

"I do not desire an itinerary of your travels, Alinor. What do you mean, you tried to hide what you felt— what *did* you feel?"

"Nothing." Alinor's eyes were desolate. "I am not angry or jealous—that much a fool I am not. I do not know how to say it, but it is like hearing a joke you do not understand. You laugh with your mouth, but inside you are not laughing. When Ian speaks to me, I answer, but only with my mouth; there is nothing inside. I serve him willingly, but with the same courtesy I would use to a stranger. I——"

"Have you denied him your bed?" Isobel asked sharply.

Despairingly, but easily, as if from frequent practice, Alinor began to cry. She was shivering uncontrollably, and Isobel put her arms around her and held her close. After a while she quieted and shook her head.

"Of course I have not. What cause have I for such a thing? It is horrible, horrible. Sometimes I cannot answer to him no matter what he does. That is not so bad, because I can pretend. I do not know if he is deceived, but it is not so awful as when he does arouse me. Then I am taken with such fits of weeping as I did not suffer even when Simon died."

"Some women are taken that way," Isobel suggested.

"Not I, and Ian knows it. It was very sweet between us, Isobel, until that accursed tourney."

That was the first really important thing Alinor had said. Isobel had wondered, despite Alinor's denials, if she was making up excuses not to love Ian because of some stupid idea about being faithful to Simon. It seemed that was not the case. The problem really lay between Ian and Alinor. But what the problem was, Isobel still did not know. She was willing to credit that the trouble had started with a convulsion of hurt pride, but Alinor was not the type to hug her hurt to herself and inflict pain to soothe her spite.

"Well then, you were hurt by Ian's inconsiderate

departure, but if it was so sweet between you, how could you allow a little thing like that to overset you?" Isobel wondered.

"I do not know," Alinor moaned. "I knew I had no cause to be jealous or angry. He never said there was no other woman. He never went to her but that one time. I have tried and tried to conquer my coldness."

"How?"

"I have not let a cross word pass my lips. Even when Ian is furious and says cruel and dreadful things, I do not quarrel with him. I answer softly or give him his way. Isobel, never in my life have I been so obedient, so compliant to any man. I fulfill his lightest wish, no matter how foolish, without hesitation or any complaint."

Alinor was staring at her hands in her lap and did not see the growing expression of horror and astonishment in Isobel's face. Her first view of it was when Isobel interrupted her catalogue of penances with a cry of "Oh, poor man!"

"How poor man?" Alinor snapped, bristling at the unappreciative remark. "Since when do *you* think sweet compliance a wrong?"

"Since you, against your nature, have adopted it. Compliance is for such hearts as mine, not for such as yours. Alinor, how could you! How long does Ian know you?"

"I am not sure. Some seventeen years. How can that matter?"

"And in all that time, how have you responded when you thought he was foolish or unreasonable?" Alinor was silent. Isobel nodded and put it into words. "You have told him, no doubt in language better fitted to one of your men-at-arms, what you thought of him, of his plans, of his brains, his ancestry, and everything else. And you did the same to Simon, right in front of Ian— since you did not regard him as a stranger or one to whom polite behavior was necessary. Am I right?"

"Likely you are right, but I do not see what that has to do with my present trouble."

It was the very core of her trouble, Isobel believed. Alinor was of a totally open nature in her dealings with those she loved. When she was hurt or angered, she spat out her pain and thus relieved her heart. It was her crazy conviction that she had no right to lose her temper or be her own passionate, unreasonable self because, however she denied it, she *was* jealous without cause. Naturally, every time she checked the hot words that rose to her lips, she reminded herself of the cause of her restraint and became jealous all over again. In addition, the projection of so much sweetness and good nature was doubtless curdling Alinor's sharp and pungent soul. But Isobel was not about to say anything concerning that. It would only give Alinor a new guilt to brood upon.

"I do not know what to say about your trouble," Isobel replied obliquely, "but I see clearly a way to make Ian less unhappy. You say he senses your coldness. Perhaps—if so, you are mistaken and there is no other woman, not even a dream of one. A man does not sense such things unless his very soul is bound to their cause. If his inmost heart is fixed elsewhere, he sees only what is on the surface. But what is on your surface tells a clear enough tale to anyone who knows you well."

"But I tell you, I smile. I do not scold or complain."

Isobel burst out laughing. "Scold and complain you never did, but smile and be meek? Alinor, if you had suddenly become meek and obedient to Simon—before he fell ill and knew the reason, I mean—what would he have done?"

A stricken expression came into Alinor's eyes, and after a pause a giggle shook her. "He would have called the best physicians to attend me, believing that I was dying. Oh, Isobel, he did so once. You know, when I am breeding, toward the end I become very soft and satisfied. The first time, Simon grew near frantic. He hung over me and asked me every other moment whether I ailed and what troubled me. I thought he was run mad, until he finally spoke out and told me I was so complaisant he thought I was growing too weak to argue."

"It is plain enough that you are not in the last stages of breeding nor in any way enfeebled. What then must your poor husband feel when he knows you so well and you behave in such a way? He rages at you, and you return sweet replies. He knows you are only polite to people you hate or do not know. Do you wonder all your kindness is making him miserably unhappy?"

"But I do not feel like quarreling with Ian," Alinor wailed.

"Who cares what you feel? You have hurt him enough to do what will content him, without regard to your own desires. Moreover, if you continue as you are going, you will drive him to make real this dream—if there is such a thing, which I am more and more sure you have made up out of signs that could mean anything. More likely, you will drive him to seek a woman who *will* quarrel with him when he desires it. Remember what you yourself told me made Berengaria useless to Richard—she would not be a safe butt for his rage. Do you know where Ian was going when he left here?"

"Yes, of course."

"Well, recall him. And when he comes, tell him you do not like the way his nose sits on his face. Tell him his feet are too big. Tell him anything so long as it will make him angry."

Although Alinor's eyes lit at Isobel's suggestion, she shook her head. "No, I cannot do that. He has gone to settle some dispute on his northern lands. I cannot call him away from a serious business. But I do not think the matter will keep him long. He will doubtless return to see how you do and to see me back to Roselynde."

* * *

Had Ian's business taken as long as he expected, he would have done just what Alinor predicted. However, by the time he arrived at the seat of the dispute, he found matters settled very happily by a marriage instead of a war. There was no more for him to do than dance at the wedding and gift the families with the marriage fine as a hint to his vassals in general that he preferred weddings to wars. In fact, everyone seemed to be abnormally content and peaceful. Ian was reduced to cursing his vassals for their good behavior as vigorously as he usually cursed them for their constant bickering.

Not that Ian took any pleasure in seeing the land ravaged by war, but he could not bring himself to face Alinor again so soon. After a few weeks of separation or of being together, the pain dulled. When together, they sank into a polite, formal relationship in which they could discuss business matters pleasantly and even with enjoyment. The only difficulty was that they still slept together. Ian both hoped and feared that Alinor would tell him to move to another chamber. Many times he vowed he would initiate the move himself and take another woman to his bed, but there was no woman he wanted when Alinor was there. So he lay with her, and cursed himself when she pretended so ignorantly or responded and then wept hysterically, creeping out of the bed when she thought he was asleep, so that he would not offend her further by offering comfort.

It was with the bitterness of such a meeting in his mouth that Ian had ridden hastily north, accompanied by only a small troop. His troops lay in seige under Sir Robert de Remy's control around the last of the castles held by a rebellious castellan. The first had fallen quickly; the second had yielded without a fight. This keep, which, like Roselynde, fronted on the sea, was the best supplied, the hardest to take, and was ruled by the most stubborn castellan. Ian suspected that the man was receiving supplies, men and encouragement from "somewhere," but he was careful not to investigate the suspicion, and to order Sir Robert to ignore all hints on the subject.

They had still been probing and testing for weaknesses in the defenses when Ian had received the appeal for "justice" from his vassals in the north. With the message, which had been sent on from Roselynde, was a letter from Alinor asking that, if he decided to ride north, he would stop by Roselynde and give her his company as far as Monmouth, where Isobel expected to be confined within a week or two. Without more ado, Ian had abandoned the direction of the siege to Sir Robert and the eldest and steadiest of the loyal castellans, and had ridden home. It was unfortunate that he was so torn between hope and fear that he did not recognize the cold hand and averted eyes Alinor offered were a duplication of his own unhappy emotions. In that instant he had flown from disappointed hope to rage, and when he woke no more response in his wife than silence or a faltered apology for her inability to please him, despair had swallowed reason.

Perhaps it should have been as clear to Ian—who had known Alinor as long as Isobel had—that no clash of wills could produce such results. Alinor simply avoided contests of will by doing what she liked and facing the consequences when they came, or she argued loud and long. Ian knew it, but, in the throes of the pain, he never questioned *why* he was suffering. He endured what he could and ran away when he could endure no more. Now, with his affairs settled so unseasonably soon, he was faced with a renewal of his agony before his wounds had scabbed over. Moreover, he had not received word from Alinor, who would, he was sure, write to tell him of Isobel's condition and delivery. That meant the child had not yet been born. Ian had no intention of cooling his heels in Monmouth while he awaited this event.

Desperation lent spurs to memory, and Ian recalled

Sir Peter at Clyro Hill. The man had received Alinor
willingly enough when she went on progress and had
made no other hostile move. Wales lay quiet also, so
Ian had put the matter out of his mind. Now it seemed
reasonable enough to stop at Clyro, which was only a
few miles out of the direct route back to Monmouth,
and test the welcome he would receive. He stopped a
night at Caergwrle and spent the next night at Powys,
making no secret of where he was going. He had no
objection to Sir Peter receiving word that he was on
his way. It would be interesting and significant, in fact,
if news was sent from Powys to Clyro Hill.

Word of his coming had certainly gone before him,
Ian decided, but he was welcomed with such obvious
pleasure that, at first, his suspicions were allayed. Sir
Peter was delighted to see him. He had been on the
verge of bidding the castle chaplain to write to ask him
to come. There was a matter, Sir Peter said, that needed
to be carefully discussed. Ian professed himself very
ready to listen, merely remarking that Sir Peter should
remember final decision on any subject lay with Lady
Alinor.

"But she will assuredly do as you bid her," Sir Peter
said.

Ian smiled, about to say he would take no wager on
that, but he repressed the words. He did not wonder at
the moment why Sir Peter should assume something so
foreign to the character of a mistress he knew very well,
because a fascinating idea had come to him. It was the
only thing he had not yet tried. Thus far he had only
threatened to deal with Alinor's people on his own.
Actually, he had not even accompanied her on her
visitations to her own domains, and he had consulted
with her on what he planned to do on Adam's property.
Perhaps if he actually moved without doing her the
courtesy of consulting her——

"Very well. Let me hear what troubles you."

"Oh, my lord, not tonight. You have had a long ride

and doubtless are tired. The matter is not so pressing as that."

To Ian that sounded the first false note. When a man has a problem great enough to merit summoning or asking help from his overlord, it is a problem he is all too ready to speak about day or night, timely or untimely. Yet Ian could not doubt Sir Peter's real pleasure and relief at seeing him. Perhaps the problem was personal or embarrassing in some way, or perhaps Sir Peter knew it was a matter that would be displeasing, like an inability to pay what was due from the estate. In such cases, he might well wish to be sure his overlord was rested, fed, comfortable, and in the best humor. Poor man, Ian thought, if he wishes to wait until my mood grows merry he will have a long wait.

"I am not so frail a flower," Ian remarked, "but if you wish to leave it for tomorrow, I do not mind."

"You will stay a little while, I hope, my lord?" Sir Peter ventured. "When does Lady Alinor join you? You will stay a few days, at least?"

"A few days if you like, yes, but Lady Alinor will not come unless there is some special reason." Ian's voice almost checked, but he forced it on smoothly enough. "She is assisting at the lying in of the Countess of Pembroke."

Something was rotten, very rotten. Whatever it was had to do with Alinor. Sir Peter could not, even as much as the dictates of politeness ordered, conceal his intense chagrin when he heard that Alinor would not come. Ian's initial reaction was pique. Did Sir Peter account him for so little? Did he think Ian would not understand what Alinor would? As the first angry sensation subsided, Ian realized it was no generalized contempt for his powers and veneration of Alinor's. Sir Peter's assumption that Alinor would obey her husband was genuine. Perhaps there was the seat of the trouble— Sir Peter felt that Alinor was too much under Ian's influence. But in what way was that Sir Peter's affair?

And how could it matter to him? And what would be changed if Alinor did join them? Ian knew his reputation was good, and if he had wished to influence Alinor to change her castellans, he would have done that before she renewed the oaths of fealty.

Ian answered polite enquiries about Isobel in which neither man was very interested. He had a substantial fund of small talk, as any courtier did, but made no effort to introduce it. Let Sir Peter choose the subject. Ian stretched his long legs toward the fire. Although it was mid-August now and even the nights were warm, summer never really passed the massive stone walls that wept moisture constantly from their rubble filling. Fires burned all year round, smaller in summer, but welcome nonetheless. Rolling his wine goblet between his hands and sniffing occasionally at the rising aroma, Ian looked as relaxed and contented as a big cat. And, like a cat, he was quite ready to spring from quiescence into activity on the instant.

The inner alertness seemed out of order when, having exhausted the subject of the Countess of Pembroke's family and childbearing, Sir Peter asked, "Do you think this quarrel between the king and the Pope is like to grow into a dangerous matter?"

"Yes," Ian replied soberly. "Both men have gone too far to retreat gracefully. I am sorry for it. I know Langton—the new archbishop—and he is such a man as should have that power. Also, I will say plain that I did not wish to see the Bishop of Norwich elevated to the primacy of the Church in England. He had neither the strength nor the courage to stand against the king at such times as it would be needful."

"You are concerned for tomorrow. I was thinking more about today."

"I do not see your meaning. It is true that King John has cast the monks out of Canterbury and seized the archepiscopal estates, but even if the Pope should condemn him roundly, even if he should punish him with interdict or excommunication—which I do not think he will until all hope of reconciliation is gone—that cannot be done today. All this must be matter for the future."

Something specific was in Sir Peter's mind, Ian knew, but the man did not seem to be able to come to the point.

"I meant that the king was much occupied with this matter. With his eyes fixed upon Rome, he may not see what is stirring under his nose."

Ian put down his goblet on the small table near his chair, and sat up. "What is stirring?" he asked sharply.

Sir Peter's eyes did not meet his. "Doubtless you know better than I, my lord," he said uneasily. "You are clan brother to Lord Llewelyn, are you not?"

"Llewelyn? I am his clan brother, yes, but Llewelyn does not tell any man all his secrets—especially me, when he knows I will argue against him. Anyway, I have not seen Llewelyn since my wedding. If you have heard rumors of trouble in Wales, you were ill-advised to keep silent. Why did you not send me word?"

"I have heard nothing," Sir Peter replied defensively. "I only thought that trouble in England spells trouble here."

That was false. The tone, the averted eyes, everything was wrong. Sir Peter had news, and definite news. But why should he keep it to himself? Ian's first reaction was to wonder whether it was news of more mischief the king was planning against him. In a moment he dismissed that notion. None of Alinor's men, whatever they felt about Ian, wanted their lady to fall into the king's hands. Even the few who had no concern for Alinor personally, preferred her management to John's. The news Sir Peter had heard must concern himself. Ian wondered if a report of the conversation he had had with Alinor about their suspicions of Sir Peter had somehow reached the man. If it had, no doubt it came in a distorted and exaggerated form, relayed from maid to maid, and then from man to man.

There was no doubt in Ian's mind that Sir Peter had friendly relations with Lord Gwenwynwyn. There was nothing wrong in that. It would be foolish to be at daggers drawn with the most powerful Welsh lord in the area. Certainly Gwenwynwyn had sent word from Powys that Ian was on his way to Clyro Hill. But if Sir Peter intended to defy Alinor and break his oath, surely he would have done it while Ian was engaged with Simon's rebellious castellans. He was not planning rebellion; he *had* been glad to see Ian come riding in, and he had been very sorry Alinor was not also on her way. A glimmering of an idea began to emerge, but Ian needed to work it over in peace, undistracted by small talk and verbal fencing. He stretched and yawned.

"So far," he assured Sir Peter, "there is no trouble— no more than usual, I mean—in England. Besides, any day there should be news that will settle the country more firmly. The queen should be lightened—God willing, of an heir—very soon." The last words were somewhat indistinct, lost in another yawn.

"You are more weary than you thought, my lord," Sir Peter remarked with poorly concealed relief. "Let me show you to your chamber."

"You must be right," Ian said, smiling and yawning still again, but a sudden cold had descended upon him.

It struck him with sharp warning that he had not seen any woman, except maidservants, in the keep, yet he knew Sir Peter had a wife and children. The absence of the lady and the children had not troubled him at first. He had ridden in after dark, and without thinking consciously about it, had assumed the children were abed and the wife busied with them or simply withdrawn into the women's quarters. Later, his mind had been on Sir Peter and their talk. Now, the lack of female attention was baldly apparent. A lady must offer her husband's overlord the normal courtesies—a bath if he wanted one, help in disrobing, an inspection of the chamber, bed and linen to be sure all was clean and proper, a pleasant word or two wishing him easy sleep. There were any number of innocent reasons why the lady of the keep would fail to appear, but her husband would have been quick to offer such explanations.

Unsure of whether or not his asking for Sir Peter's wife would arouse suspicion, Ian followed Sir Peter without comment, even when they turned into the stairwell. Normally, a guest, even an honored guest, would be housed in a chamber on the main floor. Women did not like strange men in the upper chambers where the maids and, if they were present, gently born maidens, were too available.

When they emerged from the stairwell, Sir Peter turned. "My wife is away," he said. "Her mother ails and she has taken the children to see their grandmother. I am no hand at housewifery, so I hope you will pardon me for making things easy for myself. I have given you our chamber. I know it is comfortable."

"I would have been comfortable anywhere, but I thank you."

The excuse was reasonable. Ian felt it would have had more of a ring of truth if it had been mentioned earlier, but altogether Sir Peter was so poor a liar that Ian grew more uncertain about his ill intentions the more lies he told. Sir Peter shepherded him solicitously through the doorway and into the bedchamber, gesturing toward the waiting maids and telling Ian to ask them for anything that was lacking.

"I did not know what to tell them to prepare. I suppose they know, but if there is more you need or want, tell them and they will fetch it for you." He paused a moment and looked away. "Do you want a woman?"

"No," Ian replied promptly, not because he was celibate when parted from his wife but because, more than ever, he needed privacy to think. It was an odd suggestion. His friends might make him such an offer, but it was a little unexpected from his wife's castellan.

"I will leave you to your rest then," Sir Peter said, and virtually scurried from the room.

Ian stood stock-still, staring after the man. He was torn between a horrible desire to laugh at the incredible ineptness of Sir Peter's attempts to conceal that he was planning some wrong, and the alarm bells that were ringing louder and louder in his brain. Only he could not see where the danger lay. True, he was unarmed and without weapons—he glanced around, noting a sturdy table that would make an excellent shield and the tall, wrought-iron candleholder that would make an excellent, if unwieldly, weapon. But it was insane. Surely the man would not bring him to his own bedchamber to murder him. Nor, Ian thought, as one of the maids came forward to undo his belt, would he leave two women in the room with him.

With his mind elsewhere, Ian permitted the women to undress him, and then washed sketchily in the bowl of warm water that was provided. He drew on a proffered bedrobe, shaking his head when they asked if he desired anything else. When a pitcher of watered wine had been set by the bed in case he grew thirsty in the night, the maids curtsied and withdrew. Ian sat down by the fire, drawing the table close on his left and the candleholder close on his right. Sure that he could reach both easily, he left the question of defending himself to his subconscious and concentrated on the real problem. In ultimate terms, it was far less important what Sir Peter intended to do than why he intended to do it.

Ian took out his glimmering of an idea and looked at it. He went back to his wedding time and put together his relationship with Llewelyn and Alinor's remark that she had spoken to Sir Peter several times without really attending to what he said because her attention was all for her husband. What had happened? Ian asked himself, his mind instantly diverted from the life-and-death questions of Clyro Hill. What had come between him and Alinor? Could Alinor so long hold a grudge because he had reproved her? That was not possible, but what could—He checked the bitter round of thoughts angrily. He had been over that matter ten thousand times already.

The conclusion he and Alinor had come to was that Sir Peter might be considering rebellion, but Sir Peter was an old and loyal servant. Besides, after the fall of the keep in Sussex, it was unlikely that any vassal not yet in rebellion would begin now. Turn the suspicion around and add in Ian's near surety that Llewelyn was casting eyes at Powys and looking for a reason to attack Gwenwynwyn. If Sir Peter had warned Alinor of Llewelyn's intentions, which he might have heard of through Gwenwynwyn, and Alinor would not attend to him— what must Sir Peter think? If Ian himself were an unimportant castellan and saw the upper millstone of Llewelyn above him and the nether millstone of Llewelyn's clan brother below him—saw also that the wedge that kept the two stones apart, that is, Lady Alinor, was withdrawn—he would expect to be ground to dust between them.

One matter was not clear. If Sir Peter was convinced and rebellious, why did he not act at once? Why had he welcomed Alinor on progress? Why was he so glad to see Ian? But rebellion had never been in question— only ridding himself of the baleful influence of the Llewelyn-bound husband. Murder was the logical answer. Presumably, when Ian was dead Alinor would return to her normal self. But surely that would be to fall off the spit into the fire. Alinor would scarcely be grateful for the murder of her husband if, as Sir Peter must assume to make the argument tenable, she was so enamored of him. Besides, murder was surely an excessive reaction. Why had Sir Peter not repeated his warnings when Alinor came on progress? Suddenly, Ian grinned. He probably had broached the topic, but from the wrong direction. Instead of warning Alinor of Llewelyn's or Gwenwynwyn's intentions, he had warned her against Ian. That would have set the fat in the fire, Ian thought. Whatever trouble there was between himself and Alinor, there was no distrust involved. She would have scorched Sir Peter's ears right off his head if he implied that her husband was about to betray her. Probably she would have lashed out even before she heard the whole tale—and that was why Alinor had never mentioned the matter.

Obviously, Sir Peter had not quite decided what to do. Possibly he had hoped that if Alinor came he could confront them both with his suspicions. Now he was in doubt. He had sent his wife and children away to safety, but the luxurious treatment Ian was receiving indicated that he had not brought himself to the sticking point. Ian seized a candle and stood up. Even if Sir Peter was innocent of evil intentions, was merely worried and distressed, it was unhealthy to have such ideas festering in his brain. The best thing was to lay it out in the open and try to put the man's fears, whatever they were, to rest.

The antechamber was empty. Ian looked at it blankly, wondering where Owain and Geoffrey were. His own surprise annoyed him. He should have realized he was alone. He had been listening for a step that presaged an attack. He would have heard the boys enter. Ian turned toward the door, but he did not move forward. Instead he stared at it with open-mouthed surprise. Slowly his skin darkened to an ugly mahogany, as the blood of rage filled his head.

Stupid! Stupid! Stupid! How could he have walked past that door and not seen it? How? Whatever Sir Peter's motives or intentions, they had been long thought upon and long planned. He had hung the door of a prison cell on the entrance to his bedchamber. There was the small barred opening through which a guard could speak to or observe a prisoner. There on the floor was the slot through which food could be pushed. Ian gritted his teeth to prevent himself from screaming with fury. Then, without hope, but because—too late—he would leave no small thing overlooked, he walked to the door, lifted the latch, and threw his weight against it. He might as well have put his shoulder to the 12-foot-thick castle walls. The door was not only locked but barred.

CHAPTER TWENTY-THREE

Alinor's messenger missed Ian by one day. The news he carried was happy and not urgent, so he stayed the night where he was and turned south again to follow his lord's track the next morning. In the afternoon, a terrific thunderstorm delayed him for several hours. He rode more quickly after that, fearing lest his lord arrive ahead of him at Monmouth. That would not please his lady in the least. It was near morning when he came to Caergwrle, but he waited only until his horse was rested and rode on again. He was still, they told him, a full day behind Lord Ian. He had asked anxiously whether his lord had turned east, and had been answered that Lord Ian had taken the road that ran south. If he turned east after that, they would not know, of course.

The messenger made the best time he could to Powys, and arrived some time before the sun set. The day had been hot, and neither he nor the horse could go further. He was very glad to hear that his lord had left only that morning, and had said definitely that he would stop at Clyro Hill. In the cool of the early evening, the messenger set out again. The moon was near full, and there would be light enough. He should come to Clyro Keep well before dawn and be able to deliver the letter he carried as soon as his lord woke.

That plan, all but the very last part, was fulfilled without difficulty. The track was easy enough to follow, and he had no other trouble until he came to the tight-shut castle. Energetic pounding upon the small postern gate brought a night guard. The first hint that all was not well came when the guard would not speak to him. He said no more than to stop his noise and that someone would come. It was a rather long wait, but at last a man of authoritative manner arrived. The messenger said at once that he came from Lady Alinor with letters for her lord. Instead of instantly opening the gate, as the messenger expected, the man spoke softly through the wicket. Lord Ian had not come, he said, nor was he expected, nor was the lord or lady of the manor at home. Try for his lordship at Bulith Wells, or perhaps he had taken the road east to Leominster or Worcester.

"He said at Powys he was coming here."

Even in the dim light, the messenger could see that the man's face was tense and troubled. Nonetheless, he only shook his head positively. "Perhaps he heard on the road that the keep was empty. He is not here, and I will allow no one to enter."

Before the messenger could protest that he needed rest and food and shelter, that any man from Lady Alinor had a right to so much in one of the lady's keeps, the wicket slammed shut. For a moment or two he stood staring at the blind door, with the realization creeping in on him that the whole thing stank to high heaven. Why should the guard not have said his lord was away? How could a messenger be denied a night's lodging even if only serfs lay in the keep—he was only one man, how could he endanger anyone? Wales was a mad place. Who knew what had happened at Clyro Hill? The messenger did not remount his horse. He tugged the animal's bridle and walked away toward the shelter of the woods, carefully keeping the beast between him and the wall. Probably no arrow would fly out after him. If they had wanted to kill him, it would have been easier to let him in and fall upon him there, but he would take no chances.

Once out of range, he did remount, but now he did not know where to go. Should he ride back to Monmouth in all haste and tell his lady this strange tale? But what if it was true? What if Lord Ian were at Bulith

Wells or at Worcester? No, he would not ride so far east as Worcester. And the messenger knew he could not go much further without rest. Back up the road was a track that might run east. There was a village of sorts there. It was nearly dawn. Perhaps he could get some refreshment and a place to rest. He could ask, too, if they had seen his lord's troop go by.

In Monmouth, Alinor was enjoying herself heartily. Isobel had had a quick and easy delivery; the child was large and lusty and gave every sign of doing well. It was sheer pleasure to talk to Isobel, sheer pleasure to hold the strong infant and play with the older children. Alinor made no attempt to understand her lightness of heart, but now and again a phrase that Ian had used, or a quirk of his brow that betokened some thought that did not please her, crossed her mind. Then her eyes grew bright, gold fires and green sparks lighting the dark hazel to brilliance, as her mind formed phrases that would prick him into a fury. No burden of guilt dulled the flashing ripostes that she imagined. When she felt any emotion besides anticipation, it was a flicker of shame that she had permitted her vision to become so clouded that Isobel needed to tell her how to manage her man.

Partly for that reason and partly because, no matter how well she loved Isobel, Alinor preferred to quarrel in the privacy of her own home, she had decided not to wait for Ian at Monmouth. That was what she had written to him, in addition to the news of Isobel's safe delivery, but she had also asked him to stop at Roselynde on his way back to the siege at Kemp. There was something of particular note that she wished to discuss with him that was better not written in a letter, she had said. Exactly what this particular matter was to be, Alinor had no idea. She trusted to the invention of the moment or to bedeviling Ian so much that he would not remember—at least until things were well enough be-

tween them for her to admit that the matter of particular
note had been no more than her desire to see him.

Thus, when Alinor was sure Isobel was well on her
way to recovery and would be leaving for Ireland in a
few weeks' time, she rode off with the men Ian had left
for her. Once on the road, she did not hurry. She
stopped for a day at Iford and came late in the evening
of the next day safely into Roselynde.

There were two days in which Alinor's delighted
children rediscovered the gay mother of whom they had
only seen flashes since January. Then Alinor's messenger
rode into Roselynde, fearful and exhausted. Alinor
needed no more than one look at his face when he came
into the hall.

"What is amiss?" she cried.

The man dropped to his knees. "I could not find him,
lady. I could not find him."

"What? What nonsense is this? What do you mean
you could not find him?"

"Lady, between Powys Castle and Clyro Hill, Lord
Ian and his men disappeared like smoke in the air."

Alinor's first impulse was to berate her man for a
fool of the worst kind, but she mastered that self-
deceptive desire. The man was not a fool. He had carried messages for her without failing many times. To
call him a fool was only to deny her own fears.

"Rise up, and tell me exactly what you did."

"From Monmouth, lady, I rode——"

"Begin from when you came to Lord Ian's vassal's
keep. What befell there?"

"Naught. I was welcomed in and told that Lord Ian
had ridden south the day before."

"What of the matter he went to settle there? Were
there signs of war? Of a truce?"

"A wedding, lady. The servants told me. The maiden's
father had been a little reluctant to make good his contract, but he thought better of it, and Lord Ian was in

time for the wedding. He stayed the full guesting period there."

"Very well, did he say to them where he would ride?"

"No, lady, but he took the south road—that was seen, and I followed. They rode quickly. I could not come up with them, but there was sufficient word of their passage, and Lord Ian stayed one night at Caergwrle in good spirits. I baited my horse there and followed again to Powys."

"Powys? Was Lord Gwenwynwyn at the keep?"

"Not when I came, lady, but he had left only that morning, just after Lord Ian rode out. The master-at-arms told me that Lord Ian had again taken the south road and that he had said openly he would go to Clyro Hill."

Alinor stared straight out across the hall while her frightened retainer described how he had been turned away from Clyro Keep.

"I did not know what to do, lady. I was of one mind to ride at once for Monmouth, but then I bethought me that Clyro is not a step, even from Monmouth, so I went round about asking for who had seen Lord Ian and his troop. Lady, lady, they are gone like smoke. From Powys to Clyro Hill they were seen. East, west, and south, no man had sight or sound of their passing."

"Then they are inside Clyro Keep," Alinor said in a hard voice. "Men do not fade into the air like smoke." For a moment she sat silent, mastering the turmoil of rage and terror and regret that tore her. If Ian was dead, she would never be able to mend the breach she had opened between them. He would have died believing she did not love him. She closed her eyes, but the image of the pain in his face when she would not answer to his rage could not be shut out. Dead? What would she do if Ian were dead? Alinor drew a deep breath. One thing was sure. She would not sit here and weep. First she would take Clyro Keep down, stone by stone, and take

Sir Peter apart, limb by limb, muscle by muscle, bone by bone. Alinor opened her eyes and looked at her messenger. The man whimpered and fell to his knees again.

"Go and summon Sir Guy to me," she said softly, and then, becoming aware of his fear, "It is not your fault, Bruse. You have done well enough."

As she dwelled lovingly on what she would do to Sir Peter, the man and her last visit to him flashed into Alinor's mind. Immediately, there was a strong smell of bad fish. Sir Peter might possibly have turned traitor, but he could not have turned idiot. If Ian was dead, the messenger would be dead also. There could be no difficulty in inviting Bruse in and slaying him if, as it seemed, the men-at-arms at Clyro had turned traitor with Sir Peter. Surely one more death on top of Ian's, his squires', and his troops' would be nothing—and it would have bought several weeks of time at a crucial time of the year. Soon would be the time for harvest, the time for fattening the cattle for winter. If Sir Peter had killed Ian, he would need that time to prepare for the retribution which he must know would follow. After all, Alinor would not have expected the messenger to return immediately, and even if she did, his disappearance would carry fewer tales than his living mouth. No, Sir Peter was not that kind of fool. Had he killed Ian, he would never have let the messenger go.

Then there must be a purpose for allowing the messenger to return to her, and that could only be to draw her out to her husband's rescue. Alinor examined that idea carefully, wondering whether it had been bred out of her desire to believe Ian was alive. After all, most women would not come themselves to pry a prisoner out. But Sir Peter knew her; he would know she would come herself. No matter how she turned it, however, the answer was still the same. Ian must still be alive. He must be both bait and hostage. Alinor began to laugh. It would be quite a fish that that bait would catch.

Sir Guy, entering the hall, stood stock-still and looked at her. He never thought he would fear a woman, but he feared this one. And the fear was worse because there was no outward reason for it. Lady Alinor was not large or overpowering; she was feminine in every way, beautiful, really; she was not vicious nor unreasonable. It was simply not possible for him to disobey her, and that was odd enough and fearful enough. A man did not obey a woman unless he loved her. Sir Guy looked at Alinor's exquisite face and shuddered. It would take a far stronger man than he to love her. Not the least of his admiration for Lord Ian was that the man was well able to stand up against his wife.

He remembered what Ian had said to him about the part he had played in the tourney. He had answered roundly enough. He did not fear Lord Ian, even though he freely acknowledged Ian could cut him to pieces in ten minutes' fighting. They had discussed the matter of his hatred against the king, and Ian had explained why it was necessary to remain faithful in spite of John's open and obvious attempts to harm them both. The logic had appealed to Guy, and a heavy burden had been lifted from him. He did not analyze it too carefully. It was enough that he was able to live with himself in peace. He did not need to know that Ian had provided him with a rationalization for ceasing to pursue a hopeless vendetta that could end only in his death. What Ian offered him permitted him to live a normal life, without guilt. There was a nobility about setting aside one's own right to vengeance for the good of the realm at large. It soothed the soul.

They had been in perfect agreement until Lord Ian asked for Guy's promise not to obey Alinor in ventures of that kind again. He had been forced to refuse and, when Ian had pressed him for a reason, had shrugged helplessly and said that he did not believe he was capable of keeping such a promise. To his surprise, Lord Ian had betrayed neither suspicion nor anger. He had been half irritated, half laughing, and had closed the discussion with an order that Sir Guy should at least do his best to turn his mistress from such purposes as he thought would be dangerous or dishonest.

So far, there had been no occasion to test his ability to obey that order. Lady Alinor had been little at Rose-lynde and, when she was, had given him no more than a passing glance and a smile. Now, however, listening to her laughter, Sir Guy realized that the time had come. Reluctantly, he got himself into motion again and presented himself to Alinor.

"Sit down," she said, waving him toward a chair. "I need advice on matters of war."

"My lady," he protested, "I am not fit to give such advice. Wait until Lord Ian returns home. He can far better——"

"If you do not give me what advice you can, Lord Ian will not come home at all," Alinor snapped. "He is held prisoner at Clyro Hill—for what reason I am not sure. We must go and crack that nut so I can have my meat out of it."

"We?" Guy gasped, so startled by the notion of a woman on a military expedition that he overlooked the crudity of the way Alinor referred to her husband. "Not you, my lady. Give me a letter to your vassals, and I will summon them for you, and——"

"Do not be a fool! Who is there to lead the vassals if Ian is inside Clyro Keep? Would they obey you? Sir John is scarce old enough to grow a beard, let alone direct a war. The others—one will say one thing, one another, and nothing will be accomplished. I know what to do, but there are things I do *not* know. Have you experience in taking keeps?"

"Experience? I know what any knight knows, but I am no great war lord, my lady. I am used to going where I am told and carrying out my orders."

"Well, I wish to hear whatever you know, no matter how little." Alinor then described most vividly the situation, construction, and defensive force of Clyro Keep. "How many men? What kind of war machines will I need?"

Sir Guy rubbed the back of his neck, and pulled his beard. "Men? Four or five hundred should do, but the machines are another matter. You see, because it is not a moated keep but stands on a hill, the force of your missiles is greatly spent only rising up the slope while theirs have that much greater force. Lady, I do not know how to explain such matters to you in words. From the wall, the trenchbut can cast——"

"You do not need to explain. I see that clearly enough. How large would our engines need to be?"

Sir Guy shook his head. "How can I say in words? Larger than any on Roselynde's walls except perhaps those that are made to throw stones out to ships on the sea."

"It is well wooded at Clyro. Will green timber do for construction?"

"For a while, perhaps. It warps, you see."

A nice young man, Alinor thought, but not too well taught. If he was to be useful, Ian would need to take him in hand. Ian— Her heart lurched. Alive, yes, but in what condition? Was he hurt? What did Sir Peter want? Would he hurt Ian if she came with an army? If he threatened to maim Ian in case of an attack, what should she do? What could she do? Perhaps she should go alone. She could promise anything. No, that would not do. If she were in Sir Peter's power, promises could be wrung from Ian—and he would keep his promises in spirit as well as in the letter, which Alinor, of course, had no intention of doing.

What could Sir Peter want? Only Clyro Hill and freedom from obligation. All that nonsense about Ian conspiring with Llewelyn, that must have been some kind of blind, but what? What? Let him have the land, Alinor thought—for as long as he lives, which would not be above a few days. Then her eyes narrowed. That would mean killing the sons also. Ian would not like that. He would be furious. Well, then, furious he must be. Ian was hers, and no one would be allowed to harm him. But the land was hers also, and she would not part with a rod of it. They were both hers! Neither Sir Peter nor any of his blood should have land or man.

Alinor sighed, and shook her head. There was more than one way of losing a man. She might achieve Sir Peter's death slyly enough to fool Ian—although he was sharper than Simon about seeing through her—but not the sons. And if she marched a small army halfway across England and into Wales, it was impossible that John would not hear of it. Of course, it was Alinor's right to deal with a disloyal castellan as she pleased, but God knew what interpretation John would twist the action to mean. Thought of the king brought Salisbury to mind. Dared she write to Ela and tell her? Could Salisbury keep the king from acting? Was Sir Peter's behavior somehow inspired by the king? No, that was not possible. He had been looking strange before John knew of her marriage.

Sir Guy had fallen silent when he realized that Alinor was no longer attending to what he said. He watched her expressionless face nervously. Her eyes looked right through him. Twice her lips moved slightly as though she was calculating, and both times she shook her head slightly as if what she had added was insufficient or unsatisfactory. Finally, she caught her breath as if an idea had occurred to her, and then she smiled.

"Please go and tell Father Francis that I desire parchment and pens to be readied. I will need to write seven letters. When you have done that, ride down into Roselynde town and tell the mayor that I will have need of twenty men armed and mounted. Ten will be the town's service to me, and ten I will hire at six pence a day, the extra two pence for the use of the horses. He will have my order for it tomorrow, and the men must be ready to ride tomorrow also. When you have returned, choose thirty of the men-at-arms and see that they are fitted and ready to ride."

"We are going to Clyro Hill with fifty men-at-arms, my lady?" Sir Guy breathed.

"No, we are going to Penrwyn or Llanrwst."

Sir Guy's mouth opened, and closed. It was not his business to question his lady. That the names meant nothing to him was not important. At least he had talked her out of going to war—maybe. More likely, she was going to gather men in Wales; the names sounded like Welsh. If so, there would be castellans or vassals there, men with more authority. Let them argue with her. Sir Guy went to do his mistress' bidding with a slightly lessened foreboding.

Alinor went to write her letters with such eyes that Father Francis began to remonstrate with her even though he did not know what to say. He counseled patience and forbearing, submission to God's will, at which point Alinor spat at him that she *was* submissive to God's will. She was, as was written, helping herself as best she could and thus was counting on God to fulfill his promise and help her. And a good priest would pray for her, instead of hindering her. At that point Father Francis did retire to pray, knowing that his lady was beyond remonstrance. His prayers were a little confused between the well-doing of her body and of her soul, but at the moment Alinor would not have cared if he was praying for her damnation, so long as he let her alone.

The first few letters were easy. She gave a brief explanation of what had happened and summoned those vassals who were near enough to meet her at Clifford, with those men they were obligated to bring to her defense, in two weeks' time. To Isobel she wrote a short note, containing the same information, and requesting her permission to use Clifford as a gathering point for her men. Isobel would certainly offer men also. Refusal or acceptance would depend upon the outcome of the rest of Alinor's plans. Only the last letter was difficult. Alinor trusted Ela well enough, and even Salisbury, insofar as his intentions went. What she did not trust was Salisbury's blindness to his brother's real viciousness. Therefore, the whole story of Alinor's intentions could not be told. She wrote as if she were in a furious hurry, dwelling largely on the treachery of her castellan. For the rest, she left all vague, beyond saying she was gathering men either to free her husband or to take vengeance for him. She named no names and no places. There might be some danger in that, but probably it was less than providing too definite information, which could give the king focal points for interference.

Bruse passed his letter into Lady Ela's hands just after Mass the following morning. He did not bow himself out of her presence at once. Seeing him stand waiting, Lady Ela broke the seal immediately. She had been about to put the letter away until after breakfast. She always enjoyed Alinor's letters and had intended to indulge herself with a relaxed half hour over it. However, if the messenger was waiting, Alinor must expect an immediate answer. Perhaps she intended to make a visit. Ela's eyes brightened.

"Your lady desires an answer?" she asked.

"I do not think so, madam," Bruse replied in crude and halting French. "The lady bid me wait to answer whatever questions you should ask of me."

Questions? Ela ripped open the scroll and began to read. What questions could she have to ask a servant? Unless it was trouble—and bad trouble at that. It was.

"How long did you seek your lord? How far did you go from Clyro? How do you know he did not go to visit Lord Llewelyn?"

"I beg you," Bruse faltered, "please, slower."

Ela repeated her questions more clearly, and Bruse told his story again, beginning with the suspicions raised in him by the odd manner in which he was turned away from Clyro and pointing out how impossible it would be for his lord's troop to pass absolutely unseen by everyone after having been well-noted on the road south. Yes, he had covered every road and track westward. After his first fright had abated, he also had thought Lord Ian might have gone to Llewelyn, and he spent some time searching.

"Was it a large troop?"

"No, madam, ten men and the two squires. It was all friendly land. All men he knew. He did not fear outlaws. They would never attack ten armed men who carried no goods."

"Where is Lady Alinor?"

"I do not know, madam. She has left Roselynde— that is all I know."

"Very well. You may go." Ela turned her head toward a maid. "See that he is fed and given a place to rest."

The words were a mechanical mouthing. Lady Ela's mind was essentially busy with how she should present this information to William, who was fortunately at home just now. Her immediate instinct was to accuse John obliquely of engineering whatever treachery had befallen Ian, but she soon thought better of the idea. William was a fool about his brother, but not such a fool that the suspicion would not occur to him on his own in this case. If John was innocent of this—and it was really possible that he was innocent of it because Ian's visit to Clyro seemed to have been totally unplanned—and if Ela implied it was John's doing, doubt might be cast on her future implications against the king.

No, let William come to his own conclusions. The best thing was simply to present the facts and transmit Alinor's plea that the king be warned, so that he would not take amiss her moving a large number of men around the country. She did not wish, Alinor had written, to be accused of treason or of starting a war when all she intended was to have her husband out of Clyro Keep or to punish her own castellan who had broken his oath of fealty. Having made her decision, Ela hurried down to the hall, clutching the letter without even putting the finishing touches to her toilet. She expected a reaction, but not quite as violent a one as she got.

"What did you say has happened to Ian?" Salisbury cried, leaping to his feet.

"He has disappeared. Well, Alinor thinks she knows——"

"From where? When? He is not a child or a maiden to be abducted without a struggle. How——"

"William, do not shout so. You make my head ring. I never said he had been abducted. I said he had disappeared. He spent a night in Powys Castle and told them there he was going on to the keep at Clyro Hill. At Clyro Keep, they said he had not come, but the messenger was not allowed in and Alinor believes——"

"Clyro? Powys? What the hell is Ian doing in Wales? The last I knew he was besieging a stubborn castellan at Kemp."

"I do not know what he was doing in Wales. Alinor did not take time to write the entire history of what happened, poor woman. Who cares for why he is there——"

"Ela, you are not silly, so do not talk silly. Why he is there might well have a bearing upon what happened."

"Well, I am not a witch, and Alinor did not tell me, so how could I know? And if you do not stop shouting at me, you will not only give me a headache but shake loose what few wits I have. Why do you not listen to what I say? Or, better yet, here, read Alinor's letter."

Lady Ela thrust the parchment into her husband's hands, sank limply into the chair he had vacated, and watched his unguarded expression as he read. It was just as well she had not tried to put it on the king, she thought, as she saw the concern mingled with relief painted on his face. William had had his own fears concerning Lord Ian, but obviously they had nothing to do with the keep at Clyro Hill. In another moment, however, Ela raised her hands defensively to her ears.

"What does she mean she is moving men around the country?" William roared. "Does she go with them to war?"

"I must suppose she does," Ela agreed faintly, cowering back in the chair. That aspect of the matter had not occurred to her before.

"That fool! How can Ian indulge her so much that he allows her to bring on his downfall and her own?"

"But William, if Ian is dead or imprisoned, how can he stop her? Be reasonable, do! Oh dear! Alinor is a very strong woman, stronger than you think, but this is out of all reason, I agree."

"That idiot woman!" Salisbury exclaimed, striding up and down. "I do not know whether to ride first to John and discover whether his spies in Wales know aught of this—which is what needs doing—or to ride to Roselynde and see if I can prevent this feminine folly."

"It is too late to ride to Roselynde. Alinor is already gone from there."

"Gone? Where? To Wales already?"

"I do not know. Her man said only that she had left the keep. Perhaps she meant to tell me where she was going, but you see that her letter is ill-writ. She must have been in haste and greatly disordered."

"Of a truth, she must be greatly disordered to conceive of such an idiocy," William growled. "Does she think men grown old in war will obey her? Does she intend to instruct them how to build catapults? How to storm a keep? Does she intend to lead them onto the walls?"

"Oh, not that, William."

"Are you sure?"

"Now William, you are allowing yourself to go too far. I do not really approve of what Alinor is doing, but there is some reason to it. Her chief vassal is John of Mersea, and he is little more than a score of years old. She does not really have a trustworthy man to control her men. You know what comes of that. What one suggests, the other says is too dangerous or not daring enough. Each wishes to be chief, and nothing but ill will ensues. Meanwhile, the real business lies languishing. I am sure Alinor goes to keep the peace, not to storm the walls."

The anger faded out of Salisbury's face, to be replaced by a kind of pitying concern. "Yes, it is true, and Pembroke, to whom she would have gone, is in Ireland. But why did she not come to me?" he cried.

"Because she did not wish to bring trouble upon you, William. John does not love Ian or Lady Alinor. She would never ask you to do what the king would disapprove."

Salisbury stood for a little while staring past his wife, pounding a fist into his open palm. Finally, he looked directly at Ela. "He saved my life, Ela, and—and I owe him a great debt for—for other favors."

The color had bleached from her husband's face suddenly. Ela had no time to be hurt by the oblique reference to the fact that Ian had taken Geoffrey after she refused him. She was struck at the same time with the realization that Geoffrey was with Ian and would doubtless suffer, or had suffered, the same fate as his master. She got slowly to her feet, clinging to the chair.

"Geoffrey is with him," she whispered. "Go! You must go at once, William. Oh God, if harm has befallen the child, I will never forgive myself, never. You will never be able to curse me worse than I will curse myself."

Two strides took Salisbury to his wife, and he gathered her into his arms. "Do not be a fool, Ela. Geoffrey would be in service now even if—if things had been different in the beginning. Whatever has happened, it is no fault of yours. And I could never curse you for any reason. Do not make yourself ill over this."

"Thank you, beloved," Ela whispered, "but go now.

Go. And send me word; as soon as you have any news about any of them, send me word."

Fortunately, the king was at Oxford rather than London, and Salisbury was in John's bedchamber by an hour after compline, catching him just before he got into bed.

"Where is Ian de Vipont?" Salisbury asked his brother, with no greeting and no introduction.

"In hell, I hope," John responded spitefully, and then seeing his brother's ghastly pallor, he frowned. "But if he is, it is not with my assistance. What ails you, William, to burst in on me and cry out for de Vipont without a word of greeting or explanation. I am not Ian's keeper."

"My son is with Ian. Where is he, John? Where?"

"How do I know? I swear to you, William, that the last I heard, de Vipont was besieging a castellan near Kemp. If he is gone from there— But I know the siege is being prosecuted with vigor. I heard— You mean he disappeared from the camp? When?"

"I am sure of nothing except that he was *not* in Sussex. Between Powys Castle, where he spent the night, and his wife's property at Clyro Hill, where they say he did not arrive, he disappeared. Have your people in Wales heard nothing?"

John stared right through his brother, slowly shaking his head. "Not a word of de Vipont, but I have no really recent news from Wales. All is quiet there. I am ready to swear on whatever you desire, William, that I have no part in de Vipont's trouble in Wales, whatever it is—I will go so far as to swear on the unborn fruit of my wife's womb, if that will content you."

Salisbury put an unsteady hand to his head. "Then what Lady Alinor believes must be true. It is the castellan at Clyro Hill that has taken Ian for some private reason. John, she is gathering men to take the keep. I am going to lead them for her."

"William——"

"Do not forbid me, brother. I beg you. My son is there. If Ian dies, Geoffrey dies."

"I was not going to forbid you," John said untruthfully.

He realized in time that forbidding William to go to his son's rescue would be useless. He would not obey—and there was little John could do, because he really loved his half-brother. William of Salisbury was the one man in the world John did not doubt or fear and could not hurt. This was an unfortunate complication to a clear and beautiful idea that had leaped into John's mind. He needed time, a little time alone, to work around William's presence.

"All I was going to say," John continued, "was that you should go to bed. Have you eaten anything this day? No? I thought not. No! I do forbid you to ride out again tonight. You will ride headlong for Wales, arriving before the lady or her troops. If you give me a little time to think, perhaps there is some help I can offer you—and you need not look at me that way. I would not lift a finger to assist Ian de Vipont. In fact, I will tell you plain that nothing could please me better than to hear of his death. However, Geoffrey is another matter entirely."

"I will eat, if you desire, but I cannot sleep," William protested.

"Oh yes you can," John insisted. He signaled to one of the squires of the body. "Go with him, William, and have a little sense. Eat and sleep, and tomorrow I will have something for you to make matters better. I cannot send troops with you. Royal troops in Wales can only mean trouble, but I will think of something."

Hardly had his brother left the room when another squire was running to bid a royal courier make ready to ride at once. John sat down and bit his fingers. If the castellan had taken his overlord prisoner, it must be to gain the estate for himself. There could be no other reason for such an act. If de Vipont had spent a night at Powys and intended to be at Clyro the next night, the estate must abut Gwenwynwyn's land. Probably the castellan and Gwenwynwyn were friendly enough, but if they were not it would make no difference. If both had the same enemy—de Vipont—that should ensure cooperation for long enough to suit John's purposes.

Another wave of the fingers brought a table, quills, parchment, and ink to the chair in which John sat. He began to write quickly, glancing up once to say that a second courier should be told to ready himself. One letter was very brief. It was addressed to a mercenary captain in a besieged castle in Sussex, and the words themselves were quite innocent. They announced the safe delivery of a son named Victor to the man's woman. The fact that the action that would be induced by those words would be a breach of faith that would open the keep to its enemies did not trouble John and would not trouble the captain. Wax flowed to hold the parchment roll closed, but no seal was pressed to it, and it was a woman's name that the king scrawled across the edges. A second letter, headed with the same name, bid the captain march his troops with all the speed he could get from them to Gloucester and wait there in the royal castle for further instruction. The messenger would not, of course, deliver both letters to the captain to whom they were addressed. Only the first would go to him. Once he received instructions to abandon the siege, the captain would know where to go to find his new orders.

John's eyes narrowed as he considered the time element and the chance that Alinor's troops, with William at their head, would arrive first. He chuckled softly. William doubtless would arrive, but it was very unlikely indeed that the troops would. She would need to argue and plead with her men, probably, and they would make one excuse after another. Very likely William would have to go and gather them after the woman had failed. By then—John drew a third sheet of parchment toward him and addressed it with rather fulsome compliments to Lord Gwenwynwyn, Prince of Wales.

"It has come to our ears," the king wrote, "that a man who wrongfully seized our servant, Lady Alinor of Roselynde, and married her against our will is seeking to make trouble for you, our well-beloved and obedient subject. Ian de Vipont has conspired with his clan brother, Lord Llewelyn, to seize the castle of Clyro Hill from his own wife's castellan and pass it into hands that will make it a lance pointed into the heart of your domain. We would not wish to have any quarrel erupt between you and our son-by-marriage, Lord Llewelyn, although in this case we will absolve you of any guilt in the matter if you must defend yourself against attack. Thus, it would be well to remove this troublemaker, de Vipont, before he accomplishes his purpose. If he should die by the hand of this outraged castellan, there would be no reason why the castellan should not become your vassal. We assure you that Lady Alinor, or her next husband, would cede the keep and lands to you, especially if they are already in your hands. We would have no objections to this. We would, in fact, urge that so just a reward for your effort to keep the peace be made."

John looked off into space for a few minutes, a faint frown creasing his brows. Then a beatific smile lit his whole face, and he bent forward to write again, the quill sputtering a little in his eagerness. He had remembered something quite wonderful.

"We must warn you that no harm should come to de Vipont's squires. The one is my own half-brother's bastard, and the other is a bastard cub of Lord Llewelyn's. If the castellan should slay or have slain the boys, no mercy may be shown him. *He must die!* In that case, of course, it would be only reasonable that you appoint such a man to hold the keep at Clyro Hill as would best suit your purposes. Because we fear some harm may come to our kin, Geoffrey FitzWilliam, we are sending Sir Fulk de Bréauté with four hundred men to Gloucester Castle. You may call upon them to assist you in any way you see fit—either to aid you in rescuing my brother's and my son's sons or to aid you in revenging their deaths. Sir Fulk should be at Gloucester in a week's time, after you receive this letter, or perhaps it will be a few days later."

A few more compliments and effusions on the esteem in which John held Gwenwynwyn closed the letter. John sealed it with his own seal, and the second courier was dispatched with orders not to stop, night or day, until that letter was in Lord Gwenwynwyn's own hands and in his hands only. The messenger had the right to buy or commandeer horses wherever he needed them, but he was to be in Wales before this time on the next day.

That done, John leaned back and sighed with pleasure. Everything had come right. At the very worst, de Vipont would be dead, Alinor would be in Salisbury's care (and William would be bidden to bring her to court). John would keep his promise to de Vipont not to give her in marriage—not at first. When he was ready, she would be glad to marry anyone he suggested. William would have his son back, and Llewelyn's bastard would be in Gwenwynwyn's hands. That would give John a lever to move Llewelyn with, because Gwenwynwyn, although he might be able to take Clyro Keep with what men he had, would not be able to do much more unless de Bréauté and his men helped. Thus John could make Gwenwynwyn jump by threatening to withdraw the mercenaries, and Gwenwynwyn could make Llewelyn jump for the safety of his son.

And that was only the *worst* that could happen. Thinking of the best, John licked his lips as if he could taste his satisfaction. At the best, Gwenwynwyn would read correctly between the lines of the letter. That would ensure that Ian and his squires would all die. A very neat way to rid the world of two people of whom William was entirely too fond—de Vipont and that damned bastard William was always brooding over.

William must love John and only John. It was intolerable that his heart should have room for others than his brother.

In addition, the castellan would be dead so no revelation about how de Vipont and the squires met their ends need be feared from him. Because it was her castellan, Alinor could be accused of treason, of the murder of her husband and his squires, of fomenting war in Wales. That would finish her. She could starve in prison, the boy could die—children died easily—the girl might be useful. The estate would come to the crown. And there would surely be war in Wales. Llewelyn would come raging out of his territories to avenge the death of his base-born cub for which, whatever he was told, he would blame Gwenwynwyn. The two Welsh cockrels would exhaust each other, and John would have no more trouble with either of them for many years—if either survived. In Wales, war for power was one thing, blood feuds were quite another. It was a pity de Cantelu and Cornhill were still at Canterbury making sure that all the archbishop's possessions were transferred to the king. He would have liked something extra special in the line of sexual pleasure tonight, but there was no one else he would trust for that kind of party. Then John's tongue flicked across his lips again. There was a new one among his wife's ladies, a 14-year-old bride. He crooked a finger at a body servant and whispered in his ear.

CHAPTER TWENTY-FOUR

Sir Guy straightened his back and glanced behind him at the column of weary men that followed. The horses plodded, elasticity worn from their muscles by hour after hour of movement, jarring the riders, who were nearly too tired to groan. He turned his eyes ahead, noting nervously that he could scarcely see the nearby curve in the road. It was beyond dusk, very nearly true night. His eyes shortened their focus. Just a horse length ahead, Lady Alinor's sturdy mare still moved steadily. Sir Guy set spurs to his stallion's side, then prodded a bit harder to encourage the horse's leaden response.

"My lady."

"Yes?"

Her head turned alertly. Sir Guy could not see her expression, and in the dark her white skin glimmered palely—at least, Guy assured himself, it should be pale with exhaustion.

"My lady, it is nigh dark. We must stop and make camp."

"Stop?" She put her hand to Pepper's neck as if to judge its resilience, then glanced around at the road. "Are the horses too weary to go on at all? Have any failed?"

"We are all weary, horses and men, but I am most concerned with you, my lady. You will be sick if you do not rest."

"I?" Alinor sounded stunned, and then laughed. "I rode with the queen—the great queen, I mean, not the painted puppet we have now. I crossed the Pyrenees on the wild goat trails, and I crossed the Alps in midwinter.

479

If tiredness could kill me, I would be long since dead."
Then she laughed again. "And do not say I was younger
then. It is true, but I was also tenderer of flesh. More
than that, the queen was over three score years—and
she laughed at *us* when we wept from weariness. The
body does not fail when the spirit drives."

"Well then, the horses are tired, and I fear the
men——"

"You need not fear *my* men. They will ride until they
die in the saddle if need be. It would be an easier death
than that which would come from failing me at such a
time. And they will not let the others fail. That is why
I bid you place the townsmen between two groups of
the Roselynde men-at-arms. The horses are another
matter. Ride back and see if any are in bad case. I wish
to continue until full dark if it be at all possible."

"It will be hard to set shelters in the dark, my lady.
I——"

"Shelters? What shelters? We will not camp. We must
bait the horses and rest them until the moon rises. Then
we will ride on. The men can eat if they wish also."

"We will ride in the dark? Into Wales?"

"Are you a child, to be afraid of the dark, Sir Guy?"
She watched him flush with chagrin—at least, she
assumed a flush because he turned his head a little
away. "The dark is God's time, the same as the light.
As for Wales, no band of robbers will attack fifty armed
men, and there is no war in these parts. I know because
I have just ridden through them."

"The Welsh bowmen, I have heard, are no respecters
of the peace."

"No, but they are not mad, either. They do not shoot
wantonly into a crowd just for pleasure. Ian has a good
name in North Wales, and we are openly displaying his
colors and carefully keeping to the road. We will have
no trouble."

Alinor was quite correct in her analysis of the situation. Sometimes it was true that there was a definite itch-

ing to the backs of the men's necks, as if eyes were gently touching them, but no arrows flew from the forests, which pressed closer and closer to the road as they traveled north and then west into Clwyd. Sir Guy made no further attempt to remonstrate with his mistress, merely thanking God when she permitted the troop to stop and wait for dawn before they climbed the mountain trails.

It must be true, he remarked to himself, that God helps those who help themselves. It was Lady Alinor's favorite saying, and it seemed to work every time for her. Not only had they come scatheless through the forest tracks and over the mountain passes but, when a large troop came galloping toward them in the near dark of the following evening, it was led by Lord Llewelyn himself. Guy remembered his momentary panic, but he was proud of the fact that he had not displayed it. He had shouted back a warning to the men, then spurred his tired horse forward so that his mailed body was between Lady Alinor and the oncoming riders.

Even as he went through the motions of making ready to fight, Sir Guy's panic had been subsiding. He was recalling another conversation with his mistress, when he pointed out that Wales was a large, wild place. How were they to find Lord Llewelyn? he had asked. Months could be wasted pursuing that will-o-the-wisp through the forests—as others had discovered. Alinor was not much in the mood for laughter, but she had smiled at her young escort.

"Do not be a fool. Lord Llewelyn will come to us. Have you not felt the eyes on your back? Do you think a troop of this size can move through Wales without news of it coming to him? Where he was, I do not know, but I will wager your years of service owed to me as to where he will be. He will be at Llanrwst when we come there—or he will meet us on the road."

An imperious voice called a question, and Lady Alinor replied, identifying herself. The leading rider dismounted at once and came forward on foot to peer into her face.

"Sister, what do you here?" Llewelyn asked.

"I come to seek succor."

Llewelyn's eyes flashed over the size of her following, took in the hanging head of her sweaty mare; his ears caught the husky fatigue of her voice. "Who follows you? How far behind? Where is Ian?"

She shook her head. "I am not threatened. Ian?" Her voice trembled. "It is upon his account and for your son that I seek aid."

"In Wales? Ian has come to grief in Wales?" There was incredulity in the question. Llewelyn was a power in Wales. If his clan brother could be taken in battle and he not hear of it, his defenses were worthless.

"Oh, no. It is not his Welsh who have betrayed him, but my English castellan. I——"

"So? Then do not tell me now. Come into Llanrwst, which is not far. Let your men and horses rest awhile. You can do no more tonight."

Sir Guy caught his breath, expecting a sharp reply that might breed trouble from Lady Alinor, but she merely allowed Llewelyn to kiss her hand and murmured, "Yes, my lord," most submissively. I am a fool, Sir Guy thought. She knows what she does. And, after they reached the castle, it was quite evident that that was no momentary weakness or accidental behavior. Lady Alinor knew exactly the right path to take to arrive at the end she desired. Sir Guy was coming to understand her very well. He saw the twitch of the fingers, the spread of the nostrils that betokened impatience, but no sign of it appeared in Alinor's voice or manner. She was, suddenly, a frail and distracted woman pleading for help.

Yet not a moment was wasted. When Llewelyn suggested she go to the women's quarters to wash and rest and eat, she sobbed softly that she could not rest or eat until her heart was unburdened. And so well and so

vividly did she unburden it, so cleverly play upon the
possibility that Ian's squires might be used as instruments to break Ian's affectionate spirit, that Llewelyn
saw his son being dismembered or stretched upon the
rack. As if blind to his fierce anxiety, Alinor told him
she did not know where to turn. She had summoned
her men, and they would be at Clifford by the end of
the week, but she could not draw an army around Clyro
Keep while Ian was inside.

"I thought Ian's Welsh vassals might know a better
way, but I fear they will not believe me nor be willing
to obey me. I thought, my lord, that if you came with me
to them—or if you cannot, perhaps you could give me
a letter that would———"

"I will not only bring Ian's vassals but my own also,"
Llewelyn broke in. "My brother and my son—" He cut
that off, moderated the rage in his voice to add gently,
"Do not fret yourself, Lady Alinor. Go now to your rest.
I will send my summonses out this very night."

Although he made no physical move, Sir Guy nodded
to himself. Lord Llewelyn was performing Lady Alinor's
will as if he were a puppet on a string. It was natural, of
course, that Llewelyn should go to his son's and brother's aid, but doubtless, if left to his own devices, he
would have gone a different way about it. The land, after
all, was not his. For him it would be cheaper to barter
the keep for Ian and Owain and leave to Alinor and Ian
the delicate problem of extracting Sir Peter from his ill-
gotten property, without infringing upon the sureties
Llewelyn had given that they would do no such thing.
Now he was, if anything, more anxious and enraged
than Alinor. It was plain to Sir Guy that Llewelyn believed no physical mistreatment could make Ian yield
and also that he could endure a great deal. But if torture
was applied to his squires, he would give anything to
save the boys. Llewelyn's one hope was that the idea
might not have occurred to the castellan at once. If

they came soon enough to Clyro Hill, Owain might be spared.

As he heard the next exchange, Sir Guy rose to his feet, following Lady Alinor. He was grateful for the movement, which permitted him to turn his face away. He desperately needed the relief of at least one grin as he listened to his mistress maneuver her way into accompanying Lord Llewelyn right to the battlefield. She must come with him to Ian's vassals, she pleaded, because they must know her in case of future need. And she must follow with the army to Clyro Hill because her own vassals were at Clifford just to the east. Would she not be safer traveling with Lord Llewelyn himself than making her own way through lands in which she might fall prey to "some enemy"? She did not name the enemy, but Llewelyn's eyes acknowledged the lever Gwenwynwyn would have if his clan brother's wife could be taken.

Llewelyn's counteroffer that she stay safe at Llanrwst Alinor refused with insincere regret. She pointed out that much time would be lost by Llewelyn's need to escort her back from Ian's vassals' keeps and that, not knowing where she would find Lord Llewelyn, she had not been able to leave word where her own vassals could reach her. Considering the news that had drawn them into action, she feared a letter from her would be insufficient. They would need to see her to be sure that she, too, had not been swallowed by an enemy. Sir Guy was not sure whether Lord Llewelyn finally agreed, whether he realized that she would find an answer to any argument he could put forward, whether he realized that she would go—with him or without him—no matter what he said, or whether he was simply so anxious to get to his son that he did not care if Alinor was safe or not. In any case, he argued no more and Alinor went sweetly and meekly to bed.

When Ian found the door locked, he did not bellow with rage or exhaust and bruise himself by a continued assault upon it. He had survived his father's handling and remained a reasonably whole person because he was able to retreat within himself and endure in the face of irresistible force. The total helplessness of his situation triggered that old mechanism into action, but instinctive response was soon backed by reason. No doubt rage would be the expected reaction. Quiet acceptance might make his captor very uneasy and throw him off balance. Moreover, sooner or later, someone must come into the room. When that happened, Ian intended to go out the door, dead or alive.

He racked his brains for some hours longer, trying to determine a reason for imprisoning someone in the most luxurious apartment in the castle. The only thing he could think of was that Sir Peter wished to starve him to death and imply that he had died of illness. This was so ridiculous that Ian could not forbear a laugh, and took himself off to bed. Morning brought instant refutation. A complete breakfast on the finest plate the castle held was shoved through the door slot. Ian, who had been wakened from his light sleep by the faint sounds of the dishes scraping along the floor, came to the door of the bedchamber and stared in blank incomprehension at the delicately arranged viands covered by a fine, clean napkin. Poison? That was as ridiculous as starvation.

Later in the day, a *Tristan* was pushed through under the door. Again, despite his anger and frustration, Ian was shaken with laughter. Apparently, Sir Peter did not wish him to be bored. He had furnished a book to while away the dull hours. Only Ian's hours were not particularly dull. He had first of all made a complete inventory of every object in both rooms. Then, in the inner chamber, safe from prying eyes, he was constructing some effective weapons from odds and ends. That was a very slow process, because the tools he was using had to be constructed from makeshifts, and also he wanted to make as little noise as possible.

His first hope for escape received a setback on the second day. Once it became clear that his detention—one could not call such gentle handling imprisonment—was to be as pleasant as possible, Ian had assumed that servants would enter to clean the rooms, empty the chamber pot, remove the soiled dishes, and perform other similar tasks. They would wait until he was asleep, Ian reasoned, or come with a strong guard. After a few visits their vigilance would relax. By then Ian was sure his weapons would be ready. He would take them by surprise and escape. However, no servant at all approached the door. It was Sir Peter's squire who brought the dinner and told Ian that he should pass out the pot through a larger opening which he unbolted for that purpose. The man—he was no longer a boy—gave Ian no opening for threat, pleading, or conversation. Having said his few words, he stood and waited, mouth firmly shut, until the pot came out. He took it, passed in a clean one, rebolted the opening, and hurried away.

That hope gone, Ian scoured his brain for another idea. What he came up with was to retreat to the inner chamber and refuse to come out for his food or any other purpose. He was quite certain that would bring someone, likely Sir Peter himself, to investigate. Several days were necessary to prepare for this plan. Ian had to stock food of the type that would not rot, and drink also, from the meals that were sent in. He had no intention of really weakening himself by thirst and starvation. Likely he would need to hold out for several days, because they would suspect a trick at first. Also, he had to finish his work on his weapons.

By the end of that week, Ian was ready. He was pleased with his plan, sure it would work. It had occurred to Ian that the reason no servant or man-at-arms was allowed near him was that Sir Peter did not trust his people. It also explained the luxurious confinement. As long as fine meals were carried up and served with ceremony, it would be easy to explain Ian's absence with a tale of sickness—at least for a week or two. Ian's own men-at-arms would be content for that long. They would assume that his squires were nursing him. That probably meant that Owain and Geoffrey were in another room on the same floor. More important, it meant that Ian only needed to win free and show himself to the men-at-arms of Clyro Hill.

The only drawback to having completed his arrangements was that it left Ian free to worry about whether he could escape before Alinor fell into the trap laid for her. An explanation of Sir Peter's pleasure at seeing him and disappointment over Alinor's absence had finally come to Ian. It must have been Gwenwynwyn who raised doubts of Ian's intentions in Sir Peter. And, if Sir Peter had assurance of Gwenwynwyn's support and his willingness to take Sir Peter's oath as a vassal, then Sir Peter would *not* fall into John's hands when Alinor and Ian died. The logic was good. The timing was right. After a few days of "sickness," Sir Peter would naturally send to inform Alinor that her husband was not well. Alinor would come, catch the "sickness," both would die of it, and the boys—Geoffrey and Owain —would be hostages to protect Sir Peter and Gwenwynwyn from Llewelyn and the king. Ian closed his eyes and tried to push the frightening thoughts away. Perhaps Alinor was so angry that she would not come. Perhaps she was sufficiently suspicious of Sir Peter——"

"My lord——"

Ian opened his eyes and turned his head slowly, but he did not move from the chair. He would not come closer to the door and allow Sir Peter to see how his complexion had changed, or lift his arms and display how his hands trembled. Sir Peter's voice at the door could only mean that his plan was useless. It was too late. If Alinor had come to harm— Madness curled in the black depths of Ian's mind.

"My lord, I am passing your arms and armor in to you. When you are ready, I will come in naked. I beg you to let me live long enough to explain what has happened. After that, you may do with me as you will."

Surprise held Ian frozen as he watched his hauberk being pushed in under the door through the opening that was large enough for a pot but not large enough for a man. Next came his swordbelt and his scabbarded weapons. When he made no move to seize them, a pole was used to push them further in and away to the side where Ian would be relatively safe from an arrow shot.

"It is no trick," Sir Peter said pleadingly. "I will tell you through the door if you do not wish me to come in. I only desire that you be less angry so that you will understand what I say."

"Where is Lady Alinor?" Ian asked.

"I do not know, my lord. I thought sure she would be here already. The first night, a messenger came for you, and I turned him away. I thought, since it was known you were here, that would bring her in haste without need for me to write any threats or lies."

It sounded like the truth. Ian should have felt relief, but he was swamped by pain. It seemed incredible that Alinor should hate him so much that she would not even send some men to discover what had happened to him. Two weeks, nearly two weeks, and not even a letter to Sir Peter to ask——

"Please, my lord," Sir Peter pleaded, "please listen. Because——"

"Where are my squires?"

"Here, my lord, well cared for. I would send them in to you, but I am afeared they will do themselves some hurt in their rage. My lord, you may come out, if only you will promise not to leave the keep until you listen to me. We are besieged."

"By whom?"

"Lord Gwenwynwyn. I am a fool! Doubly and triply duped!" Sir Peter cried. "I deserve whatever will befall me, for I have violated my whole life's beliefs to buy safety for my children, and instead I have purchased death and dishonor for myself and beggary for them."

Ian finally rose from his chair and walked over to pick up and draw his sword. He pulled his eating knife from its sheath and struck the sword blade sharply. It rang true—sweet, mellow, and sustained. No one had tampered with the temper of the steel. Ian turned toward the door.

"Come in and tell your tale, if you will."

"Will you pass your word that you will let me finish before you kill me?"

"I will not."

There was a little silence. Sir Peter's face disappeared from the barred window. Ian did not care. He was so confused, so torn between relief that Alinor was not in danger and hurt because she was indifferent to his life or death that he desired only to be alone to untangle his emotions. Solitude was not to be his, however. He heard a heavy sob, and then the sound of the bars being lifted from the door. It was pulled open, and Ian could see the room beyond was completely empty. Before he could wonder whether this was a trick in which he was to be "killed in battle," Sir Peter entered the room. True to his word, he was wearing no more than a house gown; even the sheath of his eating knife was empty.

At first he paused near the door, seemingly bracing his courage. Then he walked slowly toward Ian. "I pray you let me help you to arm," he said.

"Why?"

"Because I believe we will soon be assaulted. I was taken completely by surprise. I had barely enough time to close the gates, and they must know this. They will try to take us as soon as they can form and bring up their ladders and machines. I do not wish my keep to fall into the hands that have led me to my destruction. Someone must lead the men. If I am dead— But I am going backward about my tale."

"Where are my shield and helmet?"

"Just without the door. Listen——"

"Show me where my squires are."

"My lord, time is of the essence, and——"

Ian started to walk toward the door. Sir Peter uttered another sob and followed, pointing wordlessly to a second chamber with a closed door. A table stood outside, and on it lay a key. Ian unlocked the door and swung it open. Before he could step either inside or aside, both boys had launched themselves upon him. He staggered back and would have fallen had not Sir Peter caught him.

"Owain! Geoffrey!"

The sound of his voice froze them. They lowered the makeshift weapons they held and stared. Geoffrey burst into tears and embraced him. Owain stood panting. His hand half lifted the candlestick he bore, and his lips writhed back in a snarl when his eyes fell on Sir Peter.

"Not now, Owain," Ian warned. "Go below—cautiously— Do not go too far from the stair at first, so that you may come up again in haste if you are pursued. If you are greeted easily, go find your armor and Geoffrey's and bring it here. Also—" Ian turned toward Sir Peter. "Where are my men-at-arms?"

"Two nights ago I put them out of the keep. I did them no hurt. They had their arms and their horses."

Ian passed a hand across his face. "I do believe you are quite mad," he said amazedly.

"I do believe it also," Sir Peter muttered.

"They have been with me long," Ian pointed out. "Did you not realize they would fly either to my lady or to my vassals to seek succor for me?"

"Your vassals? I did not think of that. I was sure the Welshmen would run to Lord Llewelyn."

Ian's mouth opened to ask another question. Then he shook his head. "Go, Owain. Geoffrey, you come with me and help me arm. You also, Sir Peter. And I think you had better begin this tale of yours before *I* run mad."

"When Lady Alinor sent me word of her second marriage," Sir Peter began dully, "I was well pleased. I loved Sir Simon well, but his long illness left us with nowhere to turn for help. Lady Alinor would do what she could, but she was tied to her husband's side in his illness. Here on the borders of Wales it is often the knowledge that a strong man will come, rather than his actual coming, that keeps the peace. Soon upon that time, Lord Gwenwynwyn and I went for a hunt, and I asked him if he knew you. He was nowise pleased at my news—now I see it; then I did not. He spoke great praise of you, but he told me, too, that you were clan brother to Lord Llewelyn. I do not know how it came about, but he made it clear to me that you were a close party to Llewelyn's desire to eat all of Wales."

Ian's hauberk was on, and Geoffrey was buckling his sword belt. "No," he said shortly. "And not because I do not love Llewelyn or that I do not think Wales would do better under him as master. It is because I know the Angevins too well. If Llewelyn unifies Wales under his rule, John will fall upon him with all the strength of England—and I will be torn apart between my two liege lords. But that is beside the point. Why should you care if Llewelyn ruled Wales?"

"Because," replied Sir Peter, "I was given to understand that to rule Wales, the first step must be to draw Gwenwynwyn into battle, and what better way to do that than to set a man in Clyro Keep who would offend Gwenwynwyn?"

"You thought Lady Alinor would agree to this?"

"I believed she would obey you. At your wedding, she could look on no one else than you nor hear what any man other than you spoke. And when she came here, she near killed me when I barely——"

It was true, Alinor had come to him eagerly, Ian thought, Sir Peter's voice a meaningless mumble in the background. She had loved him eagerly. They had a month of nearly perfect joy. Quarrels, yes. It was impossible to live with Alinor without quarreling, but they had always ended laughing—or in making love. What had happened? Sir Peter's voice continued to drone on, and Ian caught enough of what he said to realize that his guesses about the man's intentions were close to right. He had been wrong only in believing Sir Peter disloyal to Alinor. Distracted as he was by wondering what was different in the quarrel after the tourney than in all the other quarrels, Ian could not make out the muddled reasoning by which Sir Peter decided he would prove to Alinor that her husband's plan of yielding Clyro Hill to Llewelyn's vassal was dangerous.

"And then," Sir Peter said, his voice wavering, "everything went wrong. Lady Alinor did not come. Instead Lord Gwenwynwyn has brought an army. He sent me a message—such a message as I never thought could be addressed to me. I——"

"Lord!" Owain hurried in carrying his and Geoffrey's armor and weapons. "Lord, no one in the keep knows aught of what has happened! When I came down, all the servants cried out to ask if you were well enough to join the battle. They thought you were confined with sickness and that we were nursing you. They were told not to come up for fear of contagion. They believe that Jamie and the men have gone to fetch your lady to you. The servants and the men-at-arms have no thought of this beast's treachery."

"Gently, Owain," Ian soothed. "Do not pass judgment before you know the whole. Arm yourself and Geoffrey and go out upon the walls to see the preparations there. Also see, if you can, what preparations the enemy makes. And tell me, how were you fed and kept in that room if the servants were ignorant of this?"

"Three men came once a day armed with pikes. They held us off, two of them, pinning us to the wall, while the third left the food and water and brought in clean chamber pots."

"That was why we fell upon you, my lord," Geoffrey

explained eagerly. "When we saw we could not fight them, Owain and I pretended fear. We clung together, making no attempt to escape or wrest the pikes from them. We thought, sooner or later, they would become incautious. When the door opened, and we saw two unarmed men——"

"Well thought and well done," Ian approved. "It was the only chance you had. Now hurry to make ready. This is like to be an ugly battle. Oh, be sure to look upon the walls for those who——"

"They are not here," Sir Peter interrupted. His tone was indifferent with hopelessness. "It was my own squires—grown men now but with nowhere to go but my service—and my wife's brother. I sent them out before I released you, my lord. I would not have them die also for my fault."

Ian said no more, but his eyes signaled Owain to look anyway. Although he believed Sir Peter, he would not dismiss the chance that this was all arranged so that he would "die in battle." He turned back to Sir Peter.

"What said this message from Gwenwynwyn?"

A faint color rose into Sir Peter's gray face, a small signal of the shame and wrath he would have felt if all emotion had not been deadened by despair. "It offered me three choices. The first was to kill you and send out your squires as prisoners into his hands. If I did this, I would not have to open my keep to him. He would take me as vassal, he promised, and protect me both from Llewelyn's wrath and the king's. If I did not like the idea that your squires would cry aloud of my treachery, I could have a second choice. I could kill you all three. If I made this choice, however, I must yield the keep to him, since for our own safety it must seem as if you died in battle."

"He did not explain how such seeming would be supported? And the third choice?"

"War——" Sir Peter's eyes, which had been steadfastly fixed upon his own lax hands or upon the floor, at last lifted to Ian's. "You never intended to drive me out, did you?"

"Of course not, you fool! What sort of idiot do you think I am to be the instrument of beginning a war in which Llewelyn had a right to summon me, which might rage for years, bringing in the king—who also has a right to summon me! To which would I go?"

Sir Peter shrugged. "Lord Gwenwynwyn has played me like a poor fish." He sighed, and his eyes dropped to the floor again. "My tale is done, and I am done also."

Clumsily, like a man whose muscles protest against what his mind forces upon them, Sir Peter knelt. Ian looked down at him. A single blow of the sword he carried bare in his hand would solve the problem of a disloyal castellan. But was the man disloyal? Stupid, yes, but death seemed an excessive punishment for stupidity, especially in this case. Lord Gwenwynwyn was by no means stupid; he was a very clever and devious man. He had known exactly how to play this poor fish.

Besides, Ian thought, how could he explain their leader's death to the men-at-arms who would, within hours probably, need to fight a much stronger force. They believed he had been sick. Their faith would be sorely shaken if Sir Peter suddenly disappeared, as well as his squires and brother-in-law. Had the man planned this? Was Sir Peter a clever archvillain rather than a poor fish? Ian looked down at him. He could not believe it. There was nothing, nothing even to hint at such brilliant deviousness. The chances Sir Peter had taken, was taking at this moment, were far too great. After all, had Ian been stupid, he would have killed him out of hand.

"I beg you, my lord, strike," Sir Peter pleaded, shaking with dry sobs. "I have done you a great wrong, but is my life not payment enough? Do not torture me."

"Oh, stand up, you ass," Ian exclaimed irritably, "and stop making me out as much of a fool as you. Do you think I would kill you now, just before a battle?

Every sword will be needed if we are to beat off this foe."

"What?"

"Get up, I say, and arm yourself," Ian repeated. "We are all like to die because of your stupidity, but I am not going to sell my life cheaper by even one fighter. You got us into this coil. Now do what you can to get us out of it."

"My lord, my lord," Sir Peter cried, seizing Ian's hand and kissing it fervently. "You will not regret your mercy, I promise you. I——"

"Do not praise my mercy too highly," Ian said with a wry twist to his mouth. "Nor do not think you will come out of this scot-free. I do but postpone your fate. Lady Alinor will have the judgment—if we come alive out of this."

Sir Peter's eyes widened. "She will have me torn to pieces with hot pincers. If I could have shown her——"

"I will not let her do that," Ian said drily. Then he began to laugh. "So much I will promise you, if we hold the keep."

CHAPTER TWENTY-FIVE

Once upon the walls, there was no reason to laugh. It was apparent that Lord Gwenwynwyn intended assault as soon as he could get his ladders fixed and his ram ready. He was making no effort to hide his preparations, nor even the size of his forces. Ian looked over the number of men laboring on scaling ladders and frowned. The force was not very large, but it was large enough to take the keep unless it was defended with very great determination. Worse, within the keep they were very few. Determination might withstand one assault, possibly two. After that they would be taken, because there would be no replacements for men wounded or killed.

As soon as Ian emerged from the keep, Geoffrey and Owain came across to him. Unless the men who kept them prisoner were deliberately being hidden, they reported, Sir Peter had told the truth. Those three were not on the walls. With his squires behind him, Ian went up through the tower near the gate and paced the walls, inspecting the preparations for defense and speaking a few words to each man. Owain had not been misled by the servants. The men-at-arms had believed he was sick. All asked anxiously after his health, and Ian reassured them. His appearance supported his statements. If his face was a little drawn and hollow-eyed, it was easy to see that he carried his weight of mail lightly and walked with a spring to his step. To each man his message was the same: Fight to live; yield and die. Gwenwynwyn would permit no tale of what happened in the keep to be carried abroad. Thus, each man, innocent as he might be, must die because Ian, his squires, and Sir Peter were all condemned to death.

The keep at Clyro sat on the crest of the hill. It had no moat, although there was a declivity at the base of the walls where the ancient ditch of a ditch-and-dike fortress had once been. No moat meant no drawbridge or portcullis. The walls were closed with great gates, foot-thick planks bound together with iron crossbars and sealed by triple tree-trunks that lay in great iron hoops. Opposite these gates, at the foot of the last rise, Ian watched the battering ram being readied. On either side of the gate, archers stood ready on the walls, but they would be of little use. Ian could see the framework that would support a shield of toughened hide that would protect the men working the ram. The archers might pick off a man or two who showed themselves incautiously, but on the whole they would be ineffective. The catapults could not be trained so close against the walls.

"Geoffrey, I want two winches and wheels, with a framework that will reach—oh, ten feet, beyond the walls. One this side of the gate, one that. We need also wood for fires and ten barrels of pitch—if the keep holds so much—five this side, five that. Set the fires at once. When there is a good bed of coals, the pitch is to be warmed over it until it begins to ooze. Have a care— tell the men to have a great care. The barrels must be turned, and they must not grow too hot or they will burst. Pitch is not lightly removed. Remember my back."

That would do for the ram and the men who worked it. Ian moved on. There were already fires burning on the wall, heating cauldrons of oil to be poured down on the attackers. Ian climbed up and craned over the battlement. Because of the declivity, the ladders could not be set close against the wall. That would make the climbers a little more open to arrow-shots, but not much. It was difficult to aim at any acute angle through an arrow slit. More important, it would save them from being inundated by the hot oil, which would run down the walls.

"Owain, lay your arm across the arrow slits and see the narrowest. Then run down and see if you çan find some troughs—you know, the kind they use for pouring grain—that will fit in the slits. The longer the better, and not too tight a fit, so the trough may be swung from side to side. If there are none, let the serving men wrench out every pipe and gutterspout they can find. Lay those some yards apart all round the walls—except not by the gates, they will have the pitch there—and bid the men-at-arms to thrust them through the slits when the attackers are halfway up the ladders—not sooner. Then the pipe or trough may be twisted so that it aims toward the climbers, and the hot oil must be poured through as quickly as possible."

Owain nodded and ran off, smiling grimly. That was a clever thought of his lord's. Owain remembered only two months ago how the oil had poured uselessly from the spouts made for it when they took the keep in Sussex. Then he had been surprised to see Lord Ian ride round and round the walls as close as he could get, daring death from arrowshafts, only to stare up at them. His lord had explained, of course. Lord Ian understood his duty to teach his squires all he knew of warcraft. Perhaps Lord Gwenwynwyn could be brave enough, clever enough, and thoughtful enough of his men to see where the oil spouts were and set the ladders well away from them, but it would not matter. With Lord Ian's arrangement, the oil would come to the ladder if the ladder would not come to the oil.

Every few yards around the wall, poles with hooks on the end lay ready to grasp the scaling ladders and push them outward. That might be possible, even when the ladder was weighted with men, because the angle would probably be more near the upright than Ian had set the ladders in Sussex. Even so— He beckoned a group of men-at-arms together and explained that there was another use to which the hook could be put. If it was impossible to topple the ladder backward, it could be pushed and pulled from side to side. With good luck some men would fall off, and all would be greatly impeded in their climb. With better luck, the ladder could be thrust off sideways, or one foot would break under the pressure and bring about the same result. When he was sure the men really understood what he had told them, he sent two off around the walls to explain the technique to other groups.

At the moment, it was all he could think of. He looked out once more at the preparations being made. They had still a little time before Gwenwynwyn's force would be ready to attack. From the spot he now stood on the walls, Ian looked down into Lady Peter's walled garden. It was smaller than the garden of Roselynde, but just as well kept. Ian, however, was not thinking of that nor of the pleasant hours he had spent in that garden with Alinor. "You," he said to the nearest man-at-arms, "go and find Sir Peter. Tell him to set the servingmen to tearing out the stones of the garden. Have them brought up to the walls, and the servingmen also. They are not trained in arms, but they will be put to the sword as much as we will. Let them fight as they can. They can cast down stones upon the attackers."

Lord Llewelyn did not wait at Llanrwst for his vassals. So well had Alinor worked upon his fears, that the men were summoned to meet him at a keep on the very borders of Powys. He did not, of course, write a summons to Ian's vassals. He had not that right. He would go with Alinor and lend his authority to her pleading. If the men refused to come, there was little that even Lord Llewelyn could do. It was not worth arguing about anyway. Ian's lands in Wales were not large. Perhaps 20 men might be had from each vassal. Because he did not wish to waste time, he rode with his own troop and Alinor's to Ian's keeps first.

To their surprise, they found there was no need to explain their case. In fact, they needed to ride very fast to overtake the first group, which had already left. When they caught up, they heard the story of the men-at-arms who had been put out in the night. Alinor and Llewelyn exchanged stunned glances. This was the maddest thing of all. It made no sense of any kind. It made no sense if Ian was to be pressured into ceding the keep into Sir Peter's hands; it made no sense if Ian was a hostage to entrap Alinor; it made no sense if Ian was dead. In the first two cases, the men should have been kept as prisoners; in the third case, the men should also be dead.

Alinor turned to her husband's clan brother. "Can this be some Welsh custom my man has picked up or misunderstood?"

"The Welsh may be different from Normans, Lady Alinor," Llewelyn replied drily, "but they are quite sane."

"Then, Lord Llewelyn, I begin to fear I have been the unwitting bait in a trap set for you. What else can this be but a means to draw you to Clyro Hill?"

There was a little silence, and then Llewelyn smiled. "If it is a trap, there can be only one man who set it. Do not trouble yourself, dear sister. I am willing, very willing, to spring this trap."

He sent men off to Ian's other strongholds with the information as to where they should meet his own forces, and he looked approvingly at the 47 men following Ian's vassal. The man must have stripped his keep of everyone except cripples and ancients. It was interesting that Ian was so well-beloved, and very helpful, too, in a case where, if this was a trap, every man would count. If every man counted, however, Alinor's vassals would have to come from Clifford as quickly as possible. How this was to be brought about suddenly became a greater problem.

It was reasonable that Alinor should be allowed to pass unmolested toward Gwynedd, if the purpose of the

trap was to catch Lord Llewelyn. It was equally reasonable that she would not be allowed to make the return
journey to bring reinforcements. The men discussed the
matter that evening in camp with considerable anxiety.
As soon as they passed the border of Powys, they would
be fair game for an attack. They were a strong enough
force not to fear that, but it made them uncomfortable
to have a woman in their midst. Yet they could not leave
her behind, since her men would not move from Clifford
without her command. Alinor, seeing the discussion
going in exactly the direction she desired, modestly held
her peace.

It was just as well for Alinor's purposes that none
knew that Lord Salisbury had started out for Clifford
that very night. He carried with him an order he had
wrung from the king, empowering him to command the
services of the vassals of Roselynde. His knowledge of
their place of meeting had come about simply enough.
Once Lady Ela was over the worst of her shock, she
remembered that Isobel of Clare was Alinor's closest
friend and that, in her husband's absence, she commanded a number of strongholds in Wales and on the
Welsh border. It was not impossible that Isobel knew
where Alinor was going or where her men were to
gather.

Lady Ela's messenger caught her husband soon after
Salisbury had left the king, and the hope of direction
her suggestion gave him contributed more to his ability
to eat and rest than all his brother's assurances. The next
day he asked for, and by evening obtained, the writ he
desired. When John asked where he would find them,
Salisbury did not really answer. He had no suspicion
John was playing him false; he was only trying to avoid
mention of the Countess of Pembroke. The less John
was reminded of what Pembroke was accomplishing in
Ireland, the more chance Pembroke would have to finish
the work.

Isobel did not have a devious mind. She knew her

husband liked Lord Salisbury and that Salisbury had spoken for William to the king many times. She knew also that Salisbury was Ian's friend and that Ian was fostering his son. It did not occur to her that Salisbury was also, and first, John's brother and might be playing a double game. She saw only the fear and pain in him when he spoke of Geoffrey. In any case, when he told her what Alinor was doing, she was so horrified that she probably would have told Satan where the men were, to prevent Alinor from leading them. Seeing how he had overset her, Salisbury spent a few hours calming Isobel and assuring her he would save Alinor from herself. It turned out to have been time well spent.

After evensong, Salisbury set out for Clifford, revolving expedients in his mind. He had learned from Isobel a piece of valuable information aside from where the men were to meet. That was that he would not be welcomed by them in the light of a savior from the whims of a silly woman.

"I am not sure what these men will do," Isobel had told him. "Old Sir Andre and Sir John would have tried to kill you outright if they thought your order conflicted with Alinor's good. I doubt Sir Giles, Sir Henry, or Sir Walter will go so far as that, but they may suddenly fall 'sick' or simply disappear so that you cannot give them orders they feel they cannot obey."

It was a valuable warning. Salisbury, who had been thinking he would need to urge the men to serve their mistress, turned his mind instead to ways of convincing them *he* wished to serve her. It was not so simple. Isobel might not associate him with the king, but these men, particularly Sir Walter and Sir Henry, who had fought in the tourney, would. He determined at last not to show the king's writ. Isobel's letter and seal opened Clifford to him without difficulty. Once within, he had reason to be grateful for Isobel's warning. Sir Giles of Iford, in bedrobe and slippers, came to greet him.

"How can we serve you, Lord Salisbury?" Sir Giles asked.

The tousled hair and sleep-heavy eyes gave evidence that the man had been roused from a sorely needed rest. The heavy lids, however, could not conceal the wary distrust in the tired eyes.

"By listening to what I have to say," Salisbury replied.

"Will you sit down? Can I offer you wine? Food?"

Salisbury sat, but to the other questions he shook his head. "I come to you as William Longespee, not as the king's brother," he began. "I come for two reasons. Ian de Vipont saved my life when we took Montauban castle in France. I owe him a life. More than that, my son is with him. Wherever Ian is, my Geoffrey is there also."

"I am sorry for that," Sir Giles said sincerely. "But I still ask, what do you desire from us?"

"To go with you. I have long experience of war, and I have broken open many keeps. I want my son out of there—if he is still alive."

"That is not unreasonable, but I can give you no answer."

"Why not?" Salisbury cried. "Is Geoffrey's danger not sufficient guarantee of my good will? If you do not command the men here, let me speak with Lady Alinor."

"I wish I could. Lady Alinor is not here. That was why I could give you no answer. We wait for her. I do not know what she intends. To break open a keep is not so hard, Lord Salisbury, but when the nutshell is cracked, sometimes the meat inside is crushed. I am not so ready to rush to attack when my lord—and your son also—are hostage within."

Salisbury rubbed his face and drew a shaken breath. "But what can we do?"

"I do not know, but Lady Alinor will have some plan, I am sure."

That remark left Salisbury speechless for a few minutes. Then he said, "You mean you will sit here and wait for a woman to decide whether or not to attack a keep while your lord is prisoner inside it?"

"I have no quarrel with Lord Ian," Sir Giles replied steadily. "So long as Lady Alinor is content, I am content. But she is my lady. My oath is to her—you heard me swear it—and to Lady Joanna after her. I do not say I would not have preferred Master Adam, but Roselynde and Lady Alinor's other honors are hers to do with as she wills, and her will is to pass it in the female line. Lady Alinor has done nobly by us in the sixteen years she has held the honors. I would be the worst kind of fool to disobey her. She bid me wait—I wait."

"But where is she?"

"I told you, I do not know. Perhaps something detained her at Roselynde——"

"No. The messenger who came to my wife from her said she had left the keep almost at the same moment that he did. She is not at Roselynde."

A spark of concern showed in Sir Giles' eyes. "That is not welcome news." Then suspicion clouded his face. "How did you know where to find us?"

"I told you. Lady Alinor wrote to my wife. I learned you were at Clifford from Lady Pembroke. Sir Giles, it is well enough to wish to obey your lady, but what if she herself be taken prisoner? What if some accident or illness has befallen her."

"She is never ill—at least, no illness could stop her from coming here, I am sure," Sir Giles said, but his voice was absent. Plainly, his mind was elsewhere and his thoughts were making him uneasy.

"Listen, this Clyro Hill, it is not far from here, is it?" Salisbury asked.

"Some five to eight miles only, but over rough country."

"Let us go tomorrow," Salisbury urged, "not to attack the keep," he added hastily as he saw Sir Giles' face harden. "We can leave the men hid, but at least we can spy out the land, and perhaps we can hear some news of Ian and the boys."

"Not tomorrow," Sir Giles said hesitantly. "We only came today—I suppose it is yesterday by now—ourselves, and we came early only by riding through the night." He hesitated again, then added, "Of a truth, I was surprised my lady was not here before us. The summons said, 'with all haste.' But if she had some business we are not aware of— One day more we will wait. Perhaps I will ride out myself to look at the keep, but—"

In the midafternoon, Ian leaned against the breastwork, his whole body heaving with his breathing. For a short while he was aware of little beyond his gratitude for the respite, gratitude that he did not need to push his overdriven muscles to further effort. Soon other concerns touched him. He turned his head. Geoffrey was squatting limply just behind him, breathing as hard as he was. Ian's eye raked the boy, saw some blood but not much. Geoffrey had done a man's work this day and had come well out of it—thus far.

That thought brought another more urgent. How long would they have before the attack was renewed. Ian found an arrowslit and looked out. He smiled with satisfaction. They would need to construct a new ram before setting to work on the gates again. The pitch had not only burnt through the oxhide shield, but the ram itself was burning. Ian looked at the black-coated, burning forms sprawled under, around, and a little way from the ram. Most were very quiet; a few still writhed and made noise. He grinned again, wolfishly. It would not be so easy to find men to work the next ram, nor would their work be effective as they looked above and strained to hear whether another barrel of burning pitch was being dropped.

He looked to the other side along the wall and then farther out. There were not quite so many still bodies as he had hoped, but there seemed to be rather more limping and crawling away than he expected. Some of those would not fight again. Unfortunately, that was a nothing. They were still badly outnumbered. And that thought turned his ear to the groans and sobs that drifted to him along the wall.

"Geoffrey." He watched the boy struggle upright, supporting himself against the wall. As soon as he was sure the effort would not topple his squire unconscious, he said, "Go and see how Owain does. On your way, count the dead and the wounded who will not be able to fight again. If Owain is whole, bid him from me to send up the women with water and bandages—food and ale for the men also. If he is hurt, go yourself, but return to where you went down and, when you come up again, finish your count of the dead and wounded. As you pass, order the servingmen to carry down the bodies of the dead. They are to put them out of sight—in the storeroom of the keep would be best. The enemy also."

Geoffrey started to sheath his sword, which was still in his hand.

"Wipe it first," Ian said sharply. "Any dead man's shirt will do. If you sheath it bloodied, it is like to rust or, worse, to stick to the sheath so that you cannot draw again in haste when needful."

"Sorry, lord," Geoffrey muttered.

He knew that rule, of course. It was one of the earliest things he had been taught about the use and care of his weapon, but this was the first time he had practical need of the lesson. The mixture of pride, horror, excitement, fatigue, fear, and sickness had driven it—and everything else—out of his mind. As he started off around the wall, Geoffrey could only hope he would remember how to count. He was not sure, if Lord Ian had asked him his name instead of addressing him by it, that he would have remembered that.

Now, adding to his confusion, came anxiety. He was worried about Owain. What if Sir Peter had turned on him or deliberately failed to turn aside a blow from him? There had been no gratitude in Sir Peter's face when Lord Ian told him Owain would serve as his squire, since his own were gone. It had been clear enough, from Owain's lack of protest and his expression of grim satisfaction, that his real business was to make sure Sir Peter did not weaken his section of the wall by a half-hearted defense or premature yielding.

Owain was safe enough, however, even somewhat less exhausted than Geoffrey, because the attack on the rear had been lighter. That section was well away from the easy entrance of the great gates at which the ram had been battering. Scaling ladders had been used, but only enough men climbed them to ensure that no help could be sent to those who defended the forepart of the walls. Owain nodded at Geoffrey's message and walked a little way with him.

"Tell our lord that Sir Peter is firm enough in defense —or has been so far. He has not tried to rid himself of me, and he has done his best to shield me as I have done to shield him. Of course, I do not know whether this is a feint to convince us that he is true—but I think not. I do not think he is clever enough for such an idea. The only thing I do not like is that he is not trying to shield *himself*. I think—I think he would be well pleased to catch his death upon these walls."

They parted, and Geoffrey continued his round and his sad count. Ian was still standing when he returned, breathing much more easily, but staring anxiously toward the enemy camp.

"Pass the word," he said to Geoffrey as soon as he saw him, "no man save the sore wounded may leave the walls for any reason. Even if he must piss or shit, he must do it here. I think they will come on us again while they are still hot and eager and while they think we are disordered."

Geoffrey walked the few yards to the first knot of men-at-arms and repeated his message. He did not fear it would become garbled in transmission from one group to another. Men who cannot read and write have excellent memories for the spoken word and could repeat much longer and more complex orders word perfect. One of the men nodded, repeated the order, and set off to pass it further along. Geoffrey returned to Ian, to whom he gave Owain's comment on Sir Peter and then the count.

"Nine are dead, two of them only serving men, so we may count seven. Three more are like to die shortly and may be dead already. I think you must count ten dead, my lord."

Ian nodded. That was somewhat worse than he hoped, but not so bad as it might have been. His eyes, however, remained fixed upon the scurrying groups of enemy below. Geoffrey expected that and went on without urging.

"The wounded are even harder for me to judge, my lord. I would say fifteen cannot—or should not—fight again. Two that claimed to be sore hurt I think are malingerers. I spoke them softly in the ear and reminded them that if the keep were taken, everyone in it, even the women, would be slain. But the kind that will cry out 'death' for a scratch cannot, I think, be counted upon for much."

"Mayhap not, but you spoke the right words to draw from them the best of whatever is in them," Ian approved, glancing around for a moment to look at Geoffrey's face.

To expect the best of a man often brought just that from him. So had Simon reclaimed him from hell; and Geoffrey had also answered well to that method. Geoffrey's mind worked well and swiftly, even fuddled with pain and tiredness; and he had suffered no sickness in this fighting. Perhaps he will never match me in inches, Ian thought, but he may well match me in fighting skill—and not long from now.

"On the other hand," Geoffrey continued, smiling a little at the praise but intent on transmitting the necessary information, "there are three that insisted to me they were little hurt and could fight again, but I judge either that they do not yet feel their hurts or are of such spirit that they do not wish to yield. I counted them in with the sore hurt, my lord. I did not order that they be carried down, but those three will die, I judge, if they strive again."

Ian shook his head. "There you judged wrong. You should have sent them down. I will tell you why. It is true that if we lose, we all die, but I have some hope of succor. If we can hold the walls for a few days only, my Welsh vassals may come or Lady Alinor may come, or my northerners may come. Remember, Sir Peter set free my men-at-arms, and they will fly for help. Thus, those men might live if we live. Nor do we lose all if we lose the walls. If we are beaten back from them, we will fight in the bailey, and then we will close ourselves into the keep itself and fight. That would be time enough for those three to die, if needful."

"I see. I will remember. If there is time, I will go send them down."

There was no resentment in the voice, merely thoughtfulness. In this, Ian thought, Geoffrey was a shade better than Owain. The older squire always bristled a little under criticism, even when he knew that his master was offering instruction through that path. Ian knew Geoffrey could be resentful enough; he did not lack spirit. But he was not resentful about such things. Geoffrey would be a fine man. Then he passed his hand over his face tiredly. Geoffrey might never have the chance to be a man at all. There could be no doubt now. Lord Gwenwynwyn's men were forming for another attack.

By midmorning, before the assault had been launched against Clyro, Salisbury had managed to make Alinor's men thoroughly unhappy. They all admitted that it was not like their lady to summon them and not be waiting to give them orders, or at least send a messenger to explain her delay. An hour before dinner the word went out to the men to make ready. They would move to Clyro Hill after they had fed. One party, under Sir Walter, would wait at Clifford to explain if Lady Alinor came there. Then she would be free to join them at Clyro, send orders as to what she wanted done, or recall them to Clifford. Meanwhile, the bulk of the men, plus Salisbury's own household retainers, would lie in hiding to discover what they could and be ready to attack.

Due west of Clifford, in the woods a little south of Painscastle, the Welsh force was taking a much-needed rest and a hasty meal while Lord Llewelyn's scouts tried to determine whether they could safely take the track that ran past Painscastle to Clyro. They could move much more swiftly over that than through the woods, but Llewelyn and Ian's vassals were uneasy and suspicious. It seemed impossible to them that they had traveled diagonally almost across Powys and had not been challenged once. Of course, they had carefully skirted each stronghold, but it was not their secrecy of movement that had kept them safe. Scouts had ranged outward cautiously and had reported many keeps closed and silent, as if braced against attack while they were denuded of defenders.

The only answer to that puzzle was that Lord Gwenwynwyn had summoned his men. If so, an army lay in wait for them. The question was—where? One said that Painscastle was the obvious place. They would be allowed to pass, and then attacked from the rear. Another suggested that the force might be split in two. They would, indeed, be attacked from the rear at Painscastle, but the purpose would be to drive them forward into the arms of the waiting party, which would cut them to pieces while they were disordered with trying to run or to reverse themselves and fight.

Alinor listened to the arguments in silence for a time, her expression growing more and more dissatisfied. In talking of tactics, these idiot men had forgotten what had started this affair. "My lords," she said at last, "I know little of Wales and nothing of war, but what you say puzzles me greatly. Unless spies have reported our movements—which you tell me you do not think likely —why should Lord Gwenwynwyn think we came this way at all. How could he have known our route, which we did not know ourselves, enough days in advance to summon his army to Painscastle? Why should he even bother to set spies? If I was the bait for this trap, there is one place he knows we *must* go."

"Do you think we will find him openly encamped around Clyro?" Llewelyn asked a trifle sarcastically.

"Perhaps not openly, I do not know, but it is at Clyro you will find him. He would be a fool to split his force when he does not know how many come with you, and he would be a worse fool to try to guess which road you would take. You will find him at Clyro, perhaps hid in the woods, but what I fear is that you may find him inside the keep. Where else could Sir Peter seek protection from me and where else could he better lay a trap for you?"

It was a thought they had not considered, and Llewelyn ground his teeth at the idea of Owain being a hostage in his enemy's hands. Alinor's suggestion did not still the argument, but it was given strong support by the scouts, who reported that Painscastle was as still as the other keeps and, more important, there was no sign on the road or in the nearby woods of horses or men converging upon the place. What they had seen of animal droppings was on the road and, they judged, two days old.

"Let me be bait," Alinor then offered. "My men and I will ride out along the track. The scouts can follow alongside. If we are attacked, you can come to our rescue."

That brought a unified howl of protest. Sir Guy held his mouth, as if he were considering the problems that would be his lot, but really it was a useful device to smother his laughter. His lady wished to make all speed. She had decided there was no danger from Painscastle. No doubts of her ability to judge such matters troubled her. Having decided, she called the men "coward"—not in plain words, which would arouse anger and stubbornness, but by indirection. To her subtle insinuation there could be but one reply. When the rest period was over, they moved out and, half a mile west of Painscastle, out of sight of the keep, they moved onto the well-marked track to Clyro.

From opposite directions but only a few minutes apart, the English and Welsh approached Clyro Hill with the greatest caution. Long before they were in sight of the keep, however, both groups realized their stealth was a total waste. Crashes and screams and, thinly, the clang of metal against metal came to them. Quite obviously, no one at Clyro Hill was going to pay much attention to new arrivals if they did not make an effort to be noticed. At present they—whoever they were—were fully occupied.

"Who? Who?" Lord Llewelyn asked of no one, merely voicing his shock and frustration.

From the edge of the woods beyond the border of arable land at the foot of Clyro Hill, they could now see that a violent assault on the keep was in progress. Tiny figures climbed ladders that wavered and swayed, as men on the battlements tried to push them off. Once they saw the toy men at the bottom of one of the ladders throw up their hands, scream, fall, crawl away. They could not see the cause of the action, but most could guess. From the keep, burning oil or hot sand had been poured down upon the attackers.

The gentlemen were puzzled. Plainly, this was not the first assault. The smoking ruins of the battering ram told of at least one previous attempt. The positions of the oil spouts should have been noted and the ladders moved away or, if that was too dangerous, new ladders set up. But that was not their concern—unless the failure to move the ladders was really evidence of the stupidity of the attacking battle leader. If it was, the attacker was not Lord Gwenwynwyn. Incautious and spendthrift of his men's lives he might be, but not stupid.

To Llewelyn's "Who?" there could be no answer from where they stood, yet they could not come closer without knowing whether they wished to attack or join the forces assaulting the keep. Applied to, Alinor was for once at a loss. No banners showed; it was not the kind of battle in which banners could be of any use. The distance was too great to permit the reading of devices on the shields. One of her castellans, she was forced to admit, was brave enough, bull-headed enough, and stupid enough to urge his men to remount assault ladders from which they had once been driven by hot oil.

"But," she added desperately, "I do not believe Sir Giles would let Sir Henry do anything *that* foolish, and, besides—look, Lord Llewelyn, some ladders have been moved or abandoned. See where those dead men lie?"

"We must decide and decide full soon," was Llewelyn's only reply. "The defense is failing."

CHAPTER TWENTY-SIX

Stooping and dodging, Owain paused briefly to thrust his sword through a man's back as he slid over the battlement. He did not wait to finish the work, if it needed finishing. He ran when he could, fought when he had to, wove and sidled when the press of battling men blocked his path. They were either saved or dead, but Owain did not know which, and he could only carry word of what he had seen.

"Lord Ian," he called at the top of his voice.

He could not see his master. Here near the gate and the stair down into the bailey, the attack was heaviest. A moment of panic choked him. If he could not see Lord Ian, who stood a head taller than most other men, perhaps his lord was already sore wounded or even dead.

"My lord! My lord!" Owain shrieked, striking with the flat of his blade at a man he knew to be their own, in an effort to make him move so he could struggle past.

Greater violence erupted at the center of the group. One man fell, another jerked back. The red and silver of Ian's shield flashed briefly; a third man toppled sideways. The man-at-arms blocking Owain struck and then shifted to the side so that Owain could slide through. His eagerness almost undid him, for he set his foot upon a body that was not dead. A hand grasped his ankle. Owain swung his sword downward in a vicious blow, no longer caring whether it was friend or enemy he struck. More than one man's life hung upon his message.

His frantic effort seemed to spur the men around him. For a few minutes the battle raged with such violence that Owain could not have found breath to speak even if he had been beside Ian. Then, there came a little pause. Men were still pouring up the ladders—three had been set close together at this vulnerable spot so that the oil and throwing stones were exhausted—but they were grouping to attack rather than running singly into combat.

Ordinarily, Ian would not have permitted that. It was far more dangerous to fight a coherent group than individual men. However, two factors held him back from urging his men to attack. The defenders were so exhausted, that the few moments' respite might be of greater benefit to them than the increased danger from a concerted attack. The narrow space on the wall prevented too large a group from being effective in any case. More important than that to Ian was the sound of Owain's voice. Only a matter of crucial importance could have brought Owain from his post.

"My lord," Owain gasped, "an army comes. We saw them from the back. They come from the east. Many men, and steel armed."

Rigid, with muscles tensed to combat exhaustion, Ian's expression did not change. His dark eyes were fixed upon the men grouping for attack. This news was either salvation or death—but there was no way to determine which. Then through the dull glazing of pain and fatigue, fire lit Ian's eyes. Since death was sure no matter what they did, if this was a reinforcement for their enemy, there was no reason to hold the walls. They could ride out and meet their fate—and the fate might be salvation. It was very unlikely that support for Gwenwynwyn would come from the east—unless this was part of the king's work, and the army was his mercenaries. An army from the east should be either Alinor's men or his own northerners.

"We live or we die," Ian said and smiled. "It is hard

upon us now. Owain, go down, taking with you any grooms you can find, and saddle horses for as many men as you think can ride."

"We go out, my lord?"

"We must go out. My men left believing me a prisoner. If those who come, come to save us, how will they know that those who attack are not also striving to save us?"

"But if we open the gates———"

"We will lose the walls and bailey—but we will do so anyway. And if we are not within to be slain, Gwenwynwyn will do no hurt to the wounded or the servingmen and womenfolk. They would be killed only to silence them on the how and why of our deaths."

"Lord—" Geoffrey's voice was muzzy.

Ian turned his head sharply, relief lending even more animation to his face. Owain had not seen his lord because Ian had been stooped over, dragging his younger squire to safety, or what safety he could provide for him. "Lie there," Ian said. "Do not stir. Look and see if you can find where you are worst hurt."

"My head," Geoffrey mumbled. "I am not hurt. From the wall one struck me on the head with his shield."

"Can you stand?"

Geoffrey began to struggle upright, and Ian turned to Owain again. "Take him with you. If he can help—good. If not, he may rest until we ride out, and then he must be bound to a horse and guarded as best as may be. When the beasts are ready, return to Sir Peter and tell him. Then let blow the trumpets for retreat into the bailey. When the men come down, we can tell them to mount. It can do no hurt to say help comes. Go! Now! They come at us again. Go, I say!"

The paralysis of surprise and the discussion that followed did not hold Lord Llewelyn long, but unfortunately, it was long enough for some of the servants in Gwenwynwyn's camp to notice them. Word spread quickly. A few started cautiously toward the fighting to carry word to their master, if they could find him. Most fled to seek hiding places. Thus, by the time Llewelyn's common sense reasserted itself so that he thought to look for a camp and send a few men to seize a servant from whom they could quickly learn whose force was attacking the keep, it was no longer so easy a thing to do. It was necessary to scour the woods to catch a bird that could be induced to sing.

Even when they had heard the song, willingly sung, they were none the wiser. Although they now knew for certain that Lord Gwenwynwyn had summoned his men and attacked the keep, they could not guess why, and the servant, of course, could not tell them. It was highly unlikely that Gwenwynwyn would move on his own to interfere between Ian and Ian's castellan. If he had been outraged by the rebellion, he might have sent word of it either to Alinor or to Llewelyn—thereby profiting by their gratitude—but he would scarcely attack. If he favored Sir Peter, all he need do was look the other way. Suddenly, before they had any real chance to discuss the matter, it became apparent that something important was about to happen. Horns began to sound, and men broke from the groups at the base of the ladders to run toward other groups.

Lord Llewelyn's face hardened. His son was his son, and he loved him. If he had known what was best to do for Owain, he would have done it. There was no way he could discover that. It was as likely that inaction would harm Owain as that action would, and here was a chance he had sought for years. Gwenwynwyn was attacking a keep in which his clan brother lay. That brother's wife had sought his help. He had cause enough to absolve him of any guilt for attacking Gwenwynwyn.

"Lady Alinor, you and your men bide here. Whatever caused this assault on Clyro Keep, I know one thing surely. Ian is safer in my hands than in any others.

We go forward. We will take your banner, and we will cry Ian's name and fighting call. If they are his friends, they will not attack us. If they are his enemies, we will fall upon them."

"Go," Alinor agreed instantly, "but take my men also. You will need every sword."

"Do not be a fool. How dare I leave you unprotected? In any case, although they are more than we, they are weary already." He saw she was about to argue, and he saw from the stubborn set of her jaw that she would order the men out after him if he did not pacify her in some way. "I see you are determined," he said. "Very well, I will agree with you so far as this. Hold your men back for now. If you see that we are worsted, keep four or five of the best and fly for Clifford where you say your men lie. Send the others to our support. It will soon be dark. With their help, we should be able to make do until night falls. If God is willing, your men from Clifford may be here before the dawn."

"Done," Alinor agreed. "Go then. God go with you."

When she spoke, Alinor fully intended to keep her word, since Lord Llewelyn's plan seemed wise. She did not bother to silence the protests of some of her men, who felt that they were playing too passive a role in the rescue of their own lord. They might growl but they would obey her. There was no long time of doubting whether Llewelyn rode to meet friend or foe either. Hardly were his men clear of the trees and Ian's banner well visible, than the attackers began to turn from the walls.

What Lord Gwenwynwyn would have done had he had a free choice would never be known. Lord Llewelyn had no intention of allowing his rival to decide whether he would stand and fight or retreat. Gwenwynwyn, his rival for power in Wales, would not be allowed to slip through his fingers. So excellent a chance for blamelessly ruining Gwenwynwyn might never arise again. Even if truce had been cried. Llewelyn might have suddenly suffered a disorder of the ears and not heard. As it was, his honor did not demand deafness. Archers, who had been shooting at the men who strove to push away the scaling ladders, turned their bows on the oncoming forces.

The battle was soon joined in earnest, but, before anyone could guess which way it would go, a new and totally unexpected factor was introduced. The gates of the keep opened, and men began to ride out from behind the walls they had so lately defended. Into Alinor's mind leaped the conviction that the battle had been a ruse to cover Ian's death. It seemed to her that a man so lost to honor and faith as Sir Peter would not care how many died to hide his sin. To give strength to her conviction, the gates were not shut after the men came out.

Alinor did not stop to think that shutting the gates would be a useless and dangerous gesture when enemies who could reopen them were already on the undefended walls. Neither did she wait to see with which party those who came from the keep would side.

"That is my keep," she cried furiously. "Mine! The gates are open. Come, let us go to defend it."

Desperately, Sir Guy reached for her reins. If she killed him, it would only be another kind of death, but to allow a woman to ride out onto a battlefield was against everything he had ever believed or been taught. He was, however, too late. The sturdy mare had leapt forward, driven by whip and urgent heels. The men did not even look at him. They charged right after their lady, only too eager to act. Swept into the rout, Sir Guy followed, spurring his destrier viciously to overtake Alinor. It was too late to turn her back. To struggle or delay on the field would draw attackers as a corpse drew crows. He could only hope to protect her.

On the field a tight-knit group of men, riding hard, was actually in little danger except from a chance arrow. Llewelyn's and Gwenwynwyn's forces were too much engaged with each other to trouble anyone who did not launch a blow at them. Perhaps if Gwenwynwyn had known that Lady Alinor was among the riders, an effort would have been made to take her. But Alinor was dressed for hard riding in the Welsh forests, and there was little to mark her as a great lady in her home-spun dress and dark, undecorated wimple. Besides, the idea of a woman in the midst of battle was so foreign to all men's minds, that even if one had caught sight of her delicate features, he would have dismissed what he saw as the face of a boy.

The danger lay inside the gates, and Alinor was well aware of that. She slowed her mare's pace sufficiently as they approached, so that Sir Guy and some of the men could precede her. There were, indeed, enemies in the bailey, but those men had fought hard already. Some were wounded; all were tired. Her fresh troop made short work of them, and Alinor called imperious orders for the men to dismount and clear the walls. Her voice rang high and clear, the tones carrying well above the muted sounds of the battle that raged outside the walls. It carried also to the open windows of the keep itself, where frightened servants clustered, watching the progress of the battle below.

They were all familiar with that imperious voice. They had heard it only a few months past when Lady Alinor had visited Sir Peter. To them, now, that voice meant salvation. The lady had brought an army to save them, but even the servants knew that the bailey was no safe or proper place for her. A few of the bolder men, carrying weapons discarded by the dead or wounded, hurried to unbar the door, to run out and beg the lady to come in to safety.

However impulsive, Alinor was no fool. She had achieved her purpose, and her presence was now more a danger than a help to her men. Sir Guy was competent enough in so clear a matter as taking prisoner or driving away the remnant of the enemy on the walls and guarding them from further attack. She delayed no longer than to make sure Sir Guy and the men knew where she was going, and followed the servants inside. There was more than enough for her to do there. Her firm authority brought order out of chaos very quickly. The wounded were separated from the dead; water was set to heating; salves and ointments and silk for sewing wounds were gathered.

Alinor's one act of cowardice was to avoid asking for Ian, but for once good news came swiftly. As Alinor bound up the wounds of one man-at-arms, he whispered thanks to God for her and for her good lord.

"My lord?" she asked, barely louder than the wounded man's exhausted sigh.

"Without him we would have been overwhelmed on the first assault. He showed us—" Then the eyes rolled up, and the man was unconscious. Alinor sat back on her heels for a moment to steady her breath.

"Where is Lord Ian?" she asked the man who lay on the right.

"Ridden out with Sir Peter and those who could ride," was the reply.

With Sir Peter? Alinor bent to look at the next wounded man with her mind in a whirl. If Ian had ridden out with Sir Peter, all her deductions had been false. Her hands tensed, and the man she was working over groaned. Alinor murmured an apology, a promise of greater care. The man gasped his own apology for the protest. At her worst, he assured Alinor, she did not wrench them about like the ham-handed leech.

"And where is he, this leech?" Alinor asked sharply. She had already inquired why the castle leech was not attending the wounded and had been told he was not in the keep. She had not pursued the matter at the time, but now her curiosity was aroused.

"I do not know. He has been gone more than a week, near two. First we thought he was gone to gather herbs to treat Lord Ian's sickness, but——"

"Lord Ian has been ill?" That question was even sharper.

"None said so to me, but he did not come from his chamber for nigh two weeks, nor did his squires. But he is well again, lady," the man assured her earnestly. "No man who is sick can fight like Lord Ian fought this day."

A momentary panic induced by the news soon subsided. Alinor was not soothed by the man-at-arm's conviction that a sick man could not fight. She had seen what Ian's will could enforce on his body, but no matter how sick he had been, there could be no reason to turn a messenger away and say that Ian had never arrived at Clyro Keep. Was it she or Ian who first suggested that Sir Peter was inclining to rebellion? Alinor wondered suddenly. She moved to the next man and looked down at him. She remembered that it was Ian who had mentioned Llewelyn's desire to come to grips with his rival. Had he been sounding her out to judge her willingness to be a party to such a thing? When she disapproved so strongly, had he decided to circumvent her? Was this all some mad plot on the part of Lord Llewelyn, Ian, and Sir Peter all together to entrap Lord Gwenwynwyn into war?

"Pardon lady," the man-at-arms she was staring at quavered. "Lady, what have I done? Be not so wroth."

Hastily Alinor smoothed her features and produced a smile. "I am not wroth with you, good man, but with those who caused you to be handled so roughly."

The phrasing was peculiar, but a man in pain who is listening to a language not native to him makes nothing of such niceties. To him it was sufficient that Alinor absolved him of any fault. Although she was careful to guard her expression, Alinor tended the remainder of the wounded seething. If her men had been so mauled to satisfy some political purpose of Ian's clan brother, she would have a bone to pick with her husband that he would be sorry he ever presented to her.

Outside the keep, the battle was rapidly drawing to a conclusion. There had been a period when the outcome hung in doubt, but that doubt had been eliminated when Salisbury and Alinor's English contingent rode onto the field. When they had come up behind the keep and seen the attack, they had been prey to the same doubts as Llewelyn's party. Decision had come more slowly to them because Salisbury could not enforce his will upon Alinor's men. Sir Henry wished to rush out and join the attackers, sure that they too were bent upon rescuing Alinor's husband. Sir Giles wanted to wait upon the outcome of the battle. Salisbury had convinced them, at last, to move through the woods around to the forepart of the keep, so that they would at least have a chance to determine who was engaged with whom and for what purpose.

By the time they had worked their way around, there was no longer need for doubt. Llewelyn's men, waving Ian's banner and shouting his name and fighting motto, were clearly allies. Swords were drawn, lances set, and Salisbury and Alinor's men thundered out to join the fray. At that point, the battle was over. Those of Gwenwynwyn's men who could, tried to flee, but the party opposing them was now so large that few succeeded. Finally, Lord Gwenwynwyn himself was taken, and the last core of real resistance died away.

There was then the immediate business of the battlefield to see to: prisoners to be collected, stripped, and guarded; the wounded to be gathered up; the dead to be laid out decently so that they could be protected against the carrion feeders who were already gathering in the woods and trees, to descend with the coming of dark. In a great battle, the dead were often left to their fate, the living being fewer than they and sufficiently busy with those for whom hope remained. In this brief action, however, there were not so many dead, and, friend and enemy alike, orders were given that they should be reverently, if hastily, gathered up.

Next, most immediate was both fathers' need for their sons. This need, Ian thanked God, was easily satisfied because Owain and Geoffrey were close beside him. Geoffrey then caused some anxious moments by fainting in Salisbury's arms, but he soon revived and, having been stripped and examined over his protests, was seen to have no serious injury. Ian, still uneasy, told of the blow on the head. Careful probing by the leech, which made Geoffrey wince and curse, could determine no soft spot that would be a token of a dangerous hurt to the skull. Still, the doubt in Ian's and Salisbury's eyes that remained—leeches did not always tell the truth to great men—reminded Llewelyn of Lady Alinor, who would be as knowledgeable as any leech and much more reliable. He cursed himself aloud for having forgotten her.

"Alinor!' Ian cried, abandoning his questioning of Geoffrey, "what do you mean, you forgot Alinor?"

"How did you think I came here?" Llewelyn asked, hurrying out of Gwenwynwyn's tent, which the victors had appropriated to their own use. "Your lady came to summon me to your aid."

"And you brought her to a battlefield?" Ian gasped.

Llewelyn paused for a moment to glance irritably at his clan brother. "If you could have stopped her— short of throwing her into a dungeon—you are a better man than I. She said she would remain down there in the wood, unless the battle went ill——"

Obviously, it was pointless to explain further. Ian was already shouting for a horse, anxiety lending new strength to a body on the borders of collapse. Llewelyn shrugged and returned to the tent. He might as well have his own slight hurts dressed, and then, he smiled with satisfaction, he would have a word or two with the captive Gwenwynwyn. He was deeply immersed in this, for him, delightful conversation when a raving lunatic burst into the tent, seized Gwenwynwyn by the throat, and began to choke the life out of him while beating his head against anything solid he could reach.

Llewelyn leapt upon Ian, struggling to tear him loose before he killed his half-stunned victim, and began bellowing for help. Half a dozen men rushed in. It took all their combined efforts to pull Ian off and restrain him.

"Where is my wife?" he screamed, when he at last realized he could not free himself.

The expression on Gwenwynwyn's face convinced Llewelyn that the man knew nothing of Alinor's whereabouts. "Ian," Llewelyn cried, interposing his body between Ian and Gwenwynwyn and taking his clan brother's face in his hands, so that he could force him to meet his eyes. "Ian, she is a woman. Doubtless she was affrighted by the battle and fled toward Clifford. Calm yourself. Calm yourself. I will send men after her. She will soon——"

"I do not believe it. Alinor fled affrighted? She would be more like to join a battle than flee it."

"What would I want with your wife?" Gwenwynwyn growled. "I do not prey upon women. The king wanted *you* dead, and I was very willing to accommodate him. You are not beloved, de Vipont. The king was willing to pay high for you—a captain and four hundred mercenaries for an indefinite term of service."

It was on these words that Salisbury hurried into the tent. He stopped in the entrance, doubly appalled by what he heard and what he saw. It seemed he had led Alinor's men into a trap and Ian was a prisoner—and John had lied to him again.

"I doubt you will have use of them," Ian replied, and then, irritably, "Tell your men to let me be, Llewelyn. I will not fly at him again."

Llewelyn's nod came on the words, and the men-at-arms released Ian. Another gesture sent them from the tent, Salisbury stepping aside to clear the entrance. He would have spoken then, but Ian had continued bitter-

ly, "My quarrel with the king is my affair. I wish only
to hear you swear on your honor that no party of yours
lay in the woods to take my wife prisoner."

"I will swear to that readily enough, on my honor or
what else you will," Gwenwynwyn replied, and laughed
harshly. "You are addlewitted even to ask for such
assurance. If I knew your wife was on her way with
enough surety to hold out a troop of men from a desperate struggle, would I have been so ill-prepared to
meet Llewelyn when he fell upon me?"

"Ian," Salisbury interrupted—Gwenwynwyn's words
had brought conviction to him, whether or not Ian was
in a state to recognize truth when he heard it, "the keep
is closed."

"What? Where is Sir Peter?"

"It is no fault of his. He is sitting quietly near the
prisoners' tent, as if he cannot decide whether he
should join them. And I have not tried to enter—I only
saw the gates were now closed and there are men on the
walls. Do you think we——"

His voice cut off as, with a strangled oath, Ian
rushed past him, again shouting for a horse. Salisbury
started after him, but Lord Llewelyn caught at his arm.

"Let him go, in God's name. I think he has just discovered the whereabouts of this precious wife of his."

"But what if someone else——"

Salisbury left that unfinished. There simply was no
one else, except perhaps some of the more enterprising
servants of the keep or a few of Gwenwynwyn's men.
Ian was in no danger from either of those groups.
Gwenwynwyn's people would quickly barter the keep
for their own freedom—they had no other hope—and
the servants would be delighted to see Ian. He looked
at Llewelyn.

"Would a woman——"

Llewelyn shrugged. "There are women and women.
For all I said before that Lady Alinor was affrighted
by the battle, that was said to stop Ian from trying to

kill Gwenwynwyn here. It was the first thing that came to my mind. I say to you now, having time to think on it, that *she* would."

Dismissing the problem of Lady Alinor for one nearer his heart, Salisbury next asked, "Have I your leave, Lord Llewelyn, to put some questions regarding these four hundred men?"

"By all means!"

"You will know what I know in two minutes if you seek in my tent. You will find there the king's letter which brought me here." Gwenwynwyn grinned wolfishly at Llewelyn and Salisbury. "You have won this battle, my lords, but you may have lost the war. The king will *not* be pleased at what has happened."

Before Salisbury and Llewelyn were engaged in reading John's letter, Ian was at the castle gates. He did not need to demand admittance. His horse and shield had been recognized by Alinor's men who patrolled the walls now, and the gate swung open for him. Scarcely checking his pace, he rode through, across the bailey, flung himself from his mount, and entered the keep. In the doorway of the great hall, he stopped, breathing scarcely less hard than when he had been fighting on the walls.

"Madwoman!" he bellowed, "crazy bitch! How dared you ride out on a battlefield. What do you here?"

From the chair in which she had been sitting beside the fire, Alinor leapt to her feet. "Traitor! Sneaking dog! Thief!" she shrieked in reply. "I thought I came to save you. I find instead that I am barely in time to save my lands."

Ian was struck dumb, not so much by what Alinor had said—he had not had time for the meaning of her words to sink through the roiling mixture of weariness, rage, and relief into his understanding—but by the fact that she had raised her voice to him. It was the first time in seven months that she had done anything except offer silence, sweet reason, or meek apologies. He strode down the hall, completely undecided whether he would take her in his arms to kiss or to strangle, but sure that the place for this flaming virago was in his arms.

"What do *you* here?" Alinor continued furiously as he came forward. "For very shame, I should think you would flee my eyes."

"What the devil are you talking about?" Ian asked, reaching for her.

"You call me a liar by indirection. Are you so innocent of that?" Alinor spat, holding him off. "Did you not connive with your beloved clan brother and my treacherous castellan to use me as bait to draw Lord Gwenwynwyn into war?"

Ian caught her hands and captured them. The rage of relief, an emotion very similar to that of a mother who embraces a child with one hand while beating it for engaging in dangerous mischief with the other, had gone out of him. He was too tired now to be roused to fury by anything else, and too relieved that Alinor seemed to have been restored to her normal, unreasonable self, to be angry at anything she said. Despite her struggles, he drew her against him.

"Do not be such a fool. The last thing I want is any war in Wales of sufficient import to interest the king. Do you think I wish to be summoned by *both* my overlords to fight on each side? On my honor, I have not acted in concert with Llewelyn on any matter of any kind since before I left for France last year. As for Sir Peter, I do not wish to tell you his tale now. You are too cross and would act in haste."

It was a most unsatisfactory embrace. Ian's armor was filthy and he stank. The rings of his mail bruised Alinor's arms and back. Nonetheless, she grew quiet. Ian might refuse to speak, might act without speaking, but he would not lie, and what he said about the situation he would be in if real war came to Wales was true. She raised her face to him.

"Why did you turn my messenger away, then, and say you were not here?"

"I did not turn him away. That was Sir Peter. At that time, I was imprisoned. No! Hush!" He tightened his grip again as he saw her wrath rekindle. "I said I would not tell you that tale now lest you act in haste. And, in truth, Alinor, I have sorer needs than the need of revenge on Sir Peter. I am hurt, a little, and I cannot say how tired."

"Curse me for a stupid, ill-natured witch," Alinor cried remorsefully. "Can you come up to the chamber above, or shall I bid them make up a bed for you here."

"Here," Ian replied immediately, surprised at the unease he felt when the room he had been held prisoner in was mentioned. He then smiled and shook his head at the intensified anxiety in Alinor's face. "Not because I am too weak to mount the stairs, Alinor. That was where I was locked in."

"In the main bedchamber?" Alinor asked with surprise.

Still she did not respond directly to Ian's nod of agreement. Instead, she pressed him into the seat she had risen from and went away briefly to make arrangements for a bath and bed for him. She did not return to the subject again until Ian had been bathed, had his wounds cared for, and was stretched on the bed.

"Whatever can the fool have been thinking of to lock you in there?" she muttered more to herself than to Ian, who was half asleep.

"Later," he said wearily, but a frown creased his brow. "That is the only false note in his tale. To hang a prison cell door in the entryway of the antechamber was not the work of an hour, nor was it done the day I arrived. A door must be built to fit the frame, and the very frame of the door needed to be built, and that was no brief hour's work. Thus, the plan had brewed in his mind for some time."

"Oh, no," Alinor replied. "You may acquit Sir Peter of hanging that door. It has been there since my grandfather's time. One of the castellans had fits of madness in which he tried to kill anyone who came near."

"And your grandfather kept him as castellan?" Ian laughed, waking up a little in his amusement.

"The castellan was very old then. His sons held the keep and did well by it and the lands, and by their father also. What should my grandfather have done? You cannot cast an old servant out just because he becomes useless."

"You are right about that." Ian sighed, and his eyes started to close. Suddenly he opened them wide again. "Is Sir Peter by any chance of that brood?" he enquired. "It would mayhap explain what—to speak the truth—seems to me ever and ever more mad than vicious."

"No. That is not the explanation. The younger son also became crazed and killed himself. The elder died in battle. There were no children—wisely so, I think— and my grandfather appointed Sir Peter. Sleep now, love. I think I hear the others coming in, and I must tend to them also."

Ian's eyes drooped shut, but he forced them open once more. "Alinor." She returned quickly to bend over him. "See to Geoffrey's head," he mumbled. "The leech says it is safe, but you look at it."

He slept through the next hours, while Alinor attended to the very slight damages suffered by Llewelyn, Salisbury, and Gwenwynwyn and examined Geoffrey and Owain to be sure they had been properly treated. After Gwenwynwyn had been settled into the locked chamber—exactly suited to both his status and his situation—she came at last to Sir Peter, who shied away and would not meet her eyes.

"I have done a great wrong," he said at last with considerable effort, "but I meant well to you, my lady. I thought I would be a more faithful servant than one appointed by your husband through Lord Llewelyn's favor. My wrong was in misjudging Lord Ian, not in my intent."

"Did I not tell you Lord Ian would have no part in anything not to my benefit?" The question was sharp, but the reprimand might have been much harsher and the manner colder had not Alinor fallen prey to the same suspicion herself. "He loves his clan brother well," she added more gently, softened by the gray face, the bloodstained armor, the eyes dull with despair, "but he and I are one flesh, one blood, and one bone. You must never doubt him again. As for yourself—we are all weary now. Tomorrow will be soon enough." She softened still further, remembering suddenly, as she looked into Sir Peter's hopeless face, that the pain was gone from Ian's eyes. Isobel had been right. "Go to. Rest well. Since things have come out not at all ill, you need not fear me. We will come to terms easily enough."

Unfortunately, far from silencing Sir Peter, Alinor's obvious sympathy unlocked his tongue. She had the whole story from him, but it was midnight before she was able to return to the chamber in which Ian slept. She entered softly, signaling the man and maid who accompanied her to lay the pallet and blankets they carried on the floor near the bed. Then, without speaking, she waved them out. Since Ian was still asleep, she would not wake him. She set down the platter of cold meat and bread she had brought with her and covered it with a cloth. Probably he had missed a meal, but sleep, she judged, was more necessary now. In the dim light of the single night candle, she undid her belt and pulled off her cotte and tunic. At the moment she had no idea where the scanty baggage she had brought had been placed. She did not remove her shift. Normally, of course, Alinor slept naked, as did everyone who did not sleep in the clothing worn all day, but the floor would be colder than a bed, and her bedrobe was in her baggage. If she had to attend Ian in the night she did not wish to be stumbling about naked or seeking for something to wear. Fatigue made her clumsy, and she bumped against a stool.

Almost on the instant, Ian's hand pulled back the bedcurtain. He relaxed as soon as his eyes fell on Alinor, but as she moved toward him he saw the pallet and blankets on the floor.

"Are you hungry?" Alinor asked. "I have food——"

He did not answer that, but asked sharply, "Do you not share my bed any longer?"

"Of course," Alinor soothed, "but you are cut about and bruised. I did not wish to hurt you. Will you eat, Ian?"

A slow smile, part mischievous, part sensuous, touched his lips. "Later, perhaps. Take that off."

"For heaven's sake, Ian," Alinor protested reasonably, "I am tired to death, and you have done enough this day also. Eat if you will, and go back to sleep."

He froze, then turned his head away. "Thank you, but I do not wish to eat."

Obviously, this was no time for reason. Alinor caught her husband's averted face and turned it toward her. "I was not refusing you, my love," she said softly. "At least, if I was, it was for your sake, not of my own will."

"Yes— Well——"

She could turn his head, but his eyes looked away past her into some unpleasant distance. He was so sore from her previous rejections that no words would soothe him. Alinor bent lower and put her lips to his. For a little while he lay quiet, accepting the caress passively, then raised an arm to encircle Alinor. Oddly, both passion and nervousness swept her together. She knew she would have no trouble responding to Ian tonight, but if her orgasm terminated in tears again, she would undo all the good her burst of temper had accomplished. Perhaps if the pattern of their lovemaking were different, that dreadful, senseless grief would not come upon her. Lately she had been a completely passive partner; this time she would reverse the roles, as she had on their wedding night.

Ian was drawing her down beside him. Alinor resisted, and the pressure on her relaxed at once. She freed her mouth. He was staring at her now, face tense, eyes wary. Alinor smiled and pulled off her shift. Then he reached out eagerly, but she shook her head and lifted away the light blanket she had pulled over him.

"I said you had done enough this day," she whispered. "Lie still and let me work."

CHAPTER TWENTY-SEVEN

"I have a great doubt," Ian sighed when Alinor finally lifted herself off him and lay at his side, "that I have done less in this manner than if you had let me mount you." He laughed softly. "If fact, I know the contrary. You have more ways of raising a fever, Alinor— As God is my witness, I did not sweat in this day's battle as I did tonight abed."

"Perhaps that is true," Alinor giggled, "but at least you did not tear loose any stitches, as you would have done had you played your usual part. Sleep is a quick and easy mending for weariness."

Ian glanced down at her, but he could see only the glossy black hair on the top of her head. He did not like her insistence on sleep. Her voice was not revealing, either. The low tone and slight breathlessness might be a natural result of their coupling, but they also might be produced by a struggle with tears.

"But I am now very hungry," Ian said rather plaintively. "You offered me food before. Now I need it worse."

Alinor chuckled again and rolled out of the bed. Ian pushed himself upright and watched her, but he could see nothing in her expression that conflicted with her laughter. When she handed him the wooden platter of bread and meat, however, she raised her brows.

"Why do you stare so?"

"Have I not reason enough? You are a sight to delight the eyes, clothed as you are in nothing but your hair."

"Liar," Alinor exclaimed, but smilingly, and seated herself on the bed beside him.

Ian took a bite of the meat and chewed reflectively. Alinor saw too much. He could not ignore what she said, nor could he come to the question he really wished to ask. "To call it a lie is too much," he said when he had swallowed, "but I did have another matter in my mind while my eyes took their pleasure. I wondered where you came by the idea that I had conspired with Sir Peter against your will."

Bright sparks of anger immediately lit Alinor's eyes. "Why should I not think you desired Gwenwynwyn to take the keep when you rode out, leaving his men on the walls and the gates wide open. And one of the wounded men you left behind said you rode out with Sir Peter. What should I think but that the whole thing was planned between you."

That made Ian grin. Alinor obviously knew by now that he had not been in collusion with Sir Peter. It was leaving the keep unprotected that was enraging her. "You will have to take my word as a soldier that it was a better thing to do for the safety of all—and of the keep also. Sometimes it is better to take a risk and act quickly than to try to hold everything tight. You are a greedy little devil," he added affectionately.

It was so innocent a remark, so obviously meant to tease lovingly, yet it struck straight on the one sore spot that remained in Alinor's heart. "Greedy, am I?" she hissed. "Perhaps I am. Yet I am not so greedy as to take your jewels to give to a lover as you took mine to give to your 'fair lady.' "

"What?" Ian said, pushing the food hastily out of the way. "When did I ever take a thing of yours? Even the jewels you pressed upon me when we married, I returned to your chests. I never——"

"How easily you forget—or do you lie? I did not think you would lie, but upon so sacred a subject—" Venom dripped in Alinor's voice, a venom made more virulent from being distilled through tears for seven months.

"I do not lie upon any subject, for any reason," Ian blazed. "Who told you such a tale of me?"

"Told me a tale? Would I believe such a thing of you for a telling? You did it before my very eyes! On the morning of the melee, when I was cold and wet with sweat for fear of what would befall you— And you did not even deign to bid me farewell! You took my sapphire necklet, so that some woman who does not care a pin for you——"

"On the morning of the melee!" Ian went white. "It is true, I remember now. I did take your necklet. In the name of God, is that what has lain on your heart all these months—the price of a necklet? Name it! Name the price! I will pay you in gold—or if that will not content you, I will buy it back from the whore I gave it to, even if I give double the worth. I thought my life cheap at the price—but plainly I am not worth a sapphire necklet to you."

Alinor was staring with wide, starting eyes. "To whom did you give it?" she whispered.

"What does that matter? I told you——"

"Ian, answer me! It is all in all to me. Answer me!"

Even the intense grief Ian felt at the crumbling of his goddess was pierced by Alinor's intensity. "I gave it to buy information from a highborn whore—Lady Mary Gaillon, if you need the name—because she is known to bed de Quincy, and he is known to have a loose mouth in drink." Bitterness overcame him. "Shall I tell you where she lives so that you can buy it back at the best bargain? Do you fear I will pay too much? I assure you it will be my gold that——"

"Ian! Oh, Ian!" Alinor cried, and flung her arms around his neck.

He pushed her away brutally, nearly weeping, so that she fell from the bed to the floor. "Oh God! I called you greedy in jest, but to see you cast into transports over one necklet— I cannot bear it!"

"Who cares for the necklet," Alinor laughed, picking herself up and wiping her eyes. "You may give them all to whores for all I care! You do not love anyone but me? You do not, do you? Ian, do you love me? Tell me! You have never said it—never once. Do you?"

"Do I love you? Madwoman! I have loved you all my life, since I first laid eyes upon you on the road when you knelt to Queen Alinor. What has this to do with that accursed necklet or to whom I gave it?"

"Why did you never tell me you loved me?"

"Why did I never tell my best friend's wife that I loved her?" Ian's voice rose incredulously.

"Not then, you fool. When you came to propose marriage to me. Why did you speak as if——"

"How would you have me speak? Simon was not dead four months. I knew what had been between you. Was that false? Were you ready to speak of love?"

Alinor tried to think back. "It was not false. Oh no! But because it was so good, so very real, I was the more empty, the more ready— Oh, I do not know. Perhaps you are right. Perhaps talk of love then would have been too soon, but later——"

"I tried, more than once. You would not listen. You turned away, or turned to ice, or spoke of other things. And what of you? You blame me, but did you offer me a word of love?"

"I thought the same, that you did not wish to hear of love from me."

"Why?" Ian asked, really amazed. "What did I do or say to make you think that?"

"For one thing, you would not come next or nigh me all those weeks before our wedding," Alinor said petulantly.

That broke the tension. Ian whooped with laughter. "And, wise woman that you are, you did not see the cause for that? Was it not plain enough that I was ripe for rape?"

"I saw that clear enough, but—but that is not love, Ian."

"How right you are—which was why I spent all those weeks sleeping on the cold ground, eaten alive by lice, and bored to death. But I still do not see why, if you were angry about the necklet, you did not speak of it. I took it in haste, Alinor, because there was no time to buy anything, and I knew we did not have gold or silver sufficient in the house to content Lady Mary. If you had reminded me, I would have given you its worth, or bought you another, or redeemed that one."

"You know I do not care for that. It was not even something Simon had given me. I do not want it back. If it bought knowledge that saved you one bruise, I have its value a thousand thousand times over, beloved."

"Then why?" Ian burst out, unwilling to ask, but driven. "Why did I become a stranger to you? Why did you freeze when I touched you, as if I were a ravisher? Why did you weep thereafter, as if I had soiled you?"

Instead of showing signs of anger, hauteur, or renewed coldness, Alinor blushed fiery red and hung her head. Ian watched her, enchanted by an aspect of his wife he had never seen before.

"I was jealous," she whispered.

"Jealous?" Ian asked gently. "How? Of whom? I had not been out from under your eye for a moment—at least, not a moment that you did not know where I was and what I was doing. And, in truth, Alinor, you leave me no strength for such sly games."

"I was not jealous of your body. I knew you were content with what I gave you, and for when I was not by—I do not care. A man must eat and drink and piss and shit and couple—that is nature. I was not even jealous of your heart. I suppose I knew you loved me as men love earthly women. You will laugh at me."

"I swear I will not."

"I thought you held some dream of love, some woman more precious, more perfect than I—and that is not hard to find—in some inner place that I could never reach. I was *not* angry, Ian. I was ashamed that I could let some soft dream of the past change me. I strove to be a better wife, more what a man desires, not so quarrelsome or headstrong——"

"Good God! You were my dream, Alinor. Always you and only you—just as you are."

Alinor put out her hand, and Ian took it. He drew her gently, but she put her other hand on his shoulder to resist without resisting him. "I have something more to say, something for which it is even harder to find words that will carry the true meaning. Ian, I loved Simon as much as a woman can love a man. I would not have you think I forget him or that I am disloyal to him. But there was, between Simon and me, thirty years. There was as much of father and daughter between us as of husband and wife. I did not see it then. I see it now only because what is between you and me is —is so very different. I love you, Ian, as a young woman loves a young man—and for me it is the first time of such loving."

Ian did not reply to that. There was nothing to say, fortunately, because he could not have spoken anyway. He took her face between his hands and gently and carefully, as gently and carefully as one would handle a fragile glass object, rare and precious, he kissed her and drew her down beside him. For a long time neither slept; their content was too great to need a sweetening of dreams. At last the body would not be denied, however, and sleep came.

Morning came also. Alinor was aware, after a time, of restless movement in the antechamber. She turned and tried to burrow her head into Ian's shoulder to shut out the demand on her conscience. The device did not succeed. Her nuzzling rubbed on a sore spot on Ian's shoulder and woke him instead.

"Yes?" he called. "What is it?"

"Ian, this is Salisbury. I am sorry to break your rest, but I must speak to you."

"Geoffrey!" Ian cried, leaping out of bed and running into the next room.

Alinor was not two steps behind him, holding a hastily snatched up blanket around her. "What ails him?" she asked. "Can he not be wakened? Is he blind? Dizzy?"

"Geoffrey is very well," Salisbury assured them, looking from one worried face to the other. "God has been good to me, to place him in such loving hands."

From time to time in the past, Salisbury had tried to circumvent his brother's spite against one man or another. When he could not succeed, he had shrugged and put the matter out of his mind. John was more dear to him than other men. If he did not know his brother's true character, he at least knew enough of it to understand that he must accept what he could not change—or abandon his brother completely. Now, for the first time since they were small children, Salisbury considered applying active pressure to John. He owed Ian a debt; he loved the man for himself; moreover, having seen Geoffrey again after a parting of some months, he was determined that his son would grow to manhood under Ian's tutelage and no other. Geoffrey was becoming what a man dreams a son will be—and seldom are such dreams realized.

The letter Salisbury had read had made one thing clear. John intended Ian should die—and he did not really care if Geoffrey died with him. The far uglier purpose underlying the words in the letter, Salisbury did not see. That was partly because he could not yet permit himself to believe John's real intentions. In addition, the kind of jealousy that motivated them was so foreign to Salisbury's nature that he could not conceive of any motive John could have for harming his son. There remained to him only two paths—remove Geoffrey from Ian's care and abandon Ian to his fate or protect Ian from John.

"I did not come to speak of Geoffrey but—but about —about the king."

Alinor opened her mouth, clamped it shut again with determination. Salisbury had come in person to save Ian, and, if he had not brought her men, the battle might easily have gone the other way. She had not expected even so much from him, but he was still John's brother. It was wiser to keep a still tongue in her head. She went back into the bedchamber and brought out Ian's bed-robe and a pair of slippers. Then she stepped out and found a servant whom she sent to look for her baggage. In broken pieces she heard them discussing the letter that Salisbury had brought for Ian's perusal. When she had set in motion what needed to be done, she held out a hand for the letter. Ian passed it over without really thinking what he was doing. It was fortunate that the men were deeply involved in thrashing out the political consequences of Llewelyn's capture of Gwenwynwyn and did not look at her. To Alinor the intentions were sickeningly apparent. John had obviously hoped Gwen-wynwyn would be stupid enough to execute all three— Ian and the two boys—and depend upon John's favor to make him supreme in Wales. To her, having so recently emerged from a bout with destructive jealousy, the double motive was clear enough. It did not occur to Alinor to abandon Geoffrey, because that could not save Ian. In any case she would not have entertained the idea. Geoffrey was a part of Ian, and Ian was hers! Her attention was drawn by the rising tone of Salisbury's voice.

"I will do it in any case, Ian. You can make it harder for me or easier for me—that is all."

"But William, I cannot abandon my life. The siege at Kemp must be brought to some conclusion——"

"I think you will find that matter finished," Salisbury interrupted bitterly. "I think the keep is in your men's hands by now. Where do you think the four hundred mercenaries that were promised to Gwenwynwyn came from?"

A little silence fell. Ian had been reasonably sure that it was the king's men who held Kemp against him. He had guessed that the castellan had refused to resist unless the mercenaries were sent inside the castle. The first castellan had depended upon the king's promise to send men to attack Ian's force from behind. Why John had failed, Ian was not sure. The men may have been engaged elsewhere; the king might have been in one of his slothful periods when it was simply too much trouble to write a letter. The reason was not important. The second castellan had learned a lesson from the taking of the first keep and had yielded. He had been put out, of course, but had suffered no other harm. Obviously, the third wanted better assurance from John than a promise. Ian hoped the mercenaries had told the castellan they were leaving and had given him a chance to yield. He hoped they had not merely turned on the garrison of the keep and slaughtered them.

"I did not think you in any real danger," Salisbury said softly, looking aside. "I would have sent you word if I thought——"

"You were quite right, William," Ian said quickly.

"What is it you wish us to do, Lord Salisbury?" Alinor asked.

"I would like Ian to go where the king's power does not run or is not strong. Not for long, Lady Alinor. I have some influence with my brother, but I need time. I am sorry to say it, but John will be— He will not be pleased by Ian's escape or Llewelyn's easy victory over Gwenwynwyn. I believe, and Ian agrees with me, that John hoped for a war in Wales that would weaken both Llewelyn and Gwenwynwyn so that——"

"Yes, I see that, and I see that he would blame Ian for the failure of that plan also."

"Alinor," Ian warned sharply.

She shook her head at him. "I do not blame the king

for that. It is reasonable enough to wish to see those you think may become a danger to you weakened, and it is only a human thing to set the fault where already you do not love. He cannot blame you, my lord," she said to Salisbury, "because he loves you. Llewelyn is his daughter's husband, and is necessary to him, although he would prefer Llewelyn to have less power and to be more obedient."

She stopped speaking abruptly as a servant came in with the basket that had her clothing, and gestured for it to be carried into the bedchamber. Salisbury looked at her with gratitude. He had not expected her to take so tolerant a view, but she did not smile. She met his eyes purposefully and then, as purposefully, glanced toward the doorway. Thus, the earl was not particularly surprised when, instead of continuing the discussion, Alinor suggested that she and Ian dress so that they could all go to Mass and then break their fast. Salisbury did not hesitate but went at once. Alinor's glance had not been lost. He believed she wished to be alone with her husband to convince him to seek safety.

Ian made no protest at the abrupt termination of the conversation either. He had far less reason than Salisbury to expect such sweet reasonableness from his wife on the subject of King John. Thus, Alinor's desire for privacy was quite apparent to him also. He followed her quickly into the bedchamber, noting she still had John's letter clutched in her hand.

"We will go to Ireland," Alinor said abruptly. "It has long been planned for you to go there, that is well known."

"So that my face may be saved and all men will not know that, cowardlike, I flee an unjust anger," Ian rejoined hotly. "I will know. Why should I flee? I have done no wrong."

"I was not thinking of you, Ian. You have rated me harshly enough for trying to protect you that I would not urge safety on you now," Alinor said most untruthfully. "You have said also that you are a man grown, and it is true, and when there is danger you will know how to protect yourself. But Geoffrey is not a man grown. It is him I fear for. Ian, look again at this letter. Look at the meaning under the words. Think what that —that venomous worm was hoping, nay, urging Lord Gwenwynwyn to do. Think of the terms Gwenwynwyn offered Sir Peter—yes, I have spoken to him already, and he has confessed the whole. Never mind that now, except that I do not think Sir Peter was lying to save himself."

Ian did not need to reread the letter, nor had he forgotten the terms Sir Peter described. Gwenwynwyn had understood the king. Of course, he was no fool. His purposes would be better served by keeping Owain and Geoffrey alive, and he had tried to arrange that, but John's intention was nonetheless clear. Ian followed the track of Alinor's mind easily enough also—except for not seeing that she was using Geoffrey as a lever to move him. Even if he had seen it, that would have made no difference. Wherever they were in England, John's hate would follow Ian and Geoffrey would die with him.

"But why?" he breathed sickly.

Alinor understood the question. "Because Salisbury loves the boy, and the love grows. And John is such a man that he cannot bear for Salisbury to love another." Color rose in her face. "As you know, my lord, I, too, have a jealous nature."

Ian dismissed that. Alinor might be jealous, but she was not foul. It was herself she had torn apart. She had not meant to hurt him, nor had she sought to find out who "the woman" was so that she could hurt her.

"Can it really benefit Geoffrey, to run with him?" Ian mused, as much to himself as to Alinor.

"Yes," she replied. "In two ways. The first you know —Geoffrey would be out of reach. The second is that Salisbury will not say his name with praise every other moment."

"Nonsense," Ian exclaimed, almost laughing. "That is a woman's way with infants. Salisbury has other interests and other children."

"They are too young. Mark my words, he will return to the king, meaning to speak well of you and will rave of Geoffrey's perfections—how strong in arms he has grown, how tall, as if you had pulled him up by the hair——"

"If he does so, John *will* have both of us executed only to save himself from death by boredom—and I will not blame him."

Although he was laughing, Ian was also thinking over past idle-hour conversations with Salisbury, which certainly did seem to center on Geoffrey. Of course, the topic was of absorbing interest to Ian also, and much of it was frankly practical—how much Salisbury was willing to pay for clothing, arms, horses, and the like. Yet there, too, was a hint Alinor was right. Salisbury was willing to give far more than Geoffrey needed and far more than Ian thought it healthy for a boy to have.

Ofttimes extra gifts came from the father—a second, exquisite lute, even though Geoffrey had professed himself delighted with the one Alinor had given him on Twelfth Night, a fine horse, a purse of gold "to buy such little comforts as others might not think of." Ian had removed that from Geoffrey's hands and written Salisbury a sharp note of reprimand for sending gold to a boy just on the ripening side of manhood when he was on a battlefield where he could spend it on nothing but whores—and unclean ones at that.

Ian remembered begging Salisbury to be more reasonable and not destroy Geoffrey's sense of values, and he remembered the answer he had had. Geoffrey would not need to worry about such things. His grandfather's estates had already been secured to him through a special charter from the king—not only the daughter's portion, but the whole—and much of Salisbury's own property, since Ela's enormous estates would be more than sufficient for his legitimate children. Another reason in that why John might wish to be rid of Geoffrey. Because Geoffrey was illegitimate, Salisbury was not his son's heir. The property would revert to the crown if Geoffrey died.

"All jesting aside," Ian said after his thoughts had run their course, "I begin to agree with you. But distance will not mend matters if Salisbury does not mend his ways."

"You may leave that to me," Alinor suggested. "And do not fear. I will say nothing of the king." She paused, studying Ian's face. "My lord, my love, what troubles you?" she asked after a moment.

"A curse on this life and on him who makes it impossible for me to taste a moment's joy without tears to follow," Ian said bitterly. "I have found you only to lose you again."

"How lose me?" Alinor asked fearfully.

"Perhaps lose is too strong a word," Ian corrected himself, "but I am tired of sweet letters instead of a sweet woman abed."

"But I am going with you!" she exclaimed. "And do not begin to argue with me about taking a woman to a land all at war. Isobel will be going to William. I can stay with her. We can all even go together. If you do not take me, Ian, I will follow you—and that will be more dangerous to me. In this, I will not obey you."

"I thought you feared Ireland."

"I do, but not for myself. I told you that before. I swear I am not a witch, Ian. I do not have foreseeings, but when I think of you alone going to Ireland, such a black terror comes over me as I cannot describe. Yet when I think we will go together—that is different."

"Is it, Alinor?" He studied her face, which was lifted to him, and the eyes were clear, the complexion healthy. "And Adam and Joanna?" he asked.

Then she paled. "Not the children! You and I—that

will come to a good end. There will be trouble, but not such as courage and caution cannot mend."

"But Alinor, we cannot leave Adam and Joanna unprotected. Ireland is not far, but it is not a day's ride, either."

"While you and I are together, alive, out of reach, and young enough to breed, the children are safe. There is no profit in harming them when more seeds may be planted and come to fruition. Adam, moreover, can go to Robert of Leicester, who is well able to protect him. Robert has written to ask for him, his oldest squire being knighted and having left. Adam is a little young—eight, but Robert is the right man to understand Adam's wild humors and still teach him to control them—and Adam is very willing to go. At first he did not wish to go. He thought you would be more at home, and he wished to be with you."

"And I, too, wish——"

"Yes, but it is not good for either of you. You love him too much, Ian. I have seen you sweat with fear when you knocked him down—and even I could see he was not hurt. Robert is right for Adam, and Robert's wife also is right. She is like Isobel, not stupid, but very gentle. I am too strong. It is not good for a boy to have a masterful mother as he grows older."

"But Joanna——" Ian began hastily.

He agreed too much with what Alinor had said about herself and her son to make any remark that would not hurt her. Since she saw it herself, he need never tread on that delicate ground. To his surprise, Alinor suddenly smiled broadly.

"I shall send Joanna to Lady Ela."

"No!" Ian roared. "She is your daughter, but I love her. I will not have it! I would sooner have her spout prayers and repentance and resignation at me than have her another Ela. She will return fluttering her hands and holding her head and her side and——"

Alinor shook with laughter. "Oh no, she will not. You do not value Ela as I have come to value her. She is too wise to teach a healthy mare like Joanna the tricks of a frail bird. And she is clever, Ian. You do not know how clever, and I will not tell you. She does not tend her men and her flock and her fields as I tend mine, but that Joanna knows already and, God willing, I will have some years more to teach her. Ela can teach Joanna what I never could because, of a truth, I dare not go near King John. She can teach the child the ways of the court, and with Ela there and right under Salisbury's eye, Joanna will be safe enough."

"Safe for now," Ian said uneasily. "Yet I am not over-happy that she should go to court. She will attract the king's eye and, even now, all unripe as she is, Joanna is beautiful."

"There may be a little to fear in that, but not more than in her going to court as, say, Geoffrey's bride and striking that lecher's gaze in the full beauty of her womanhood."

Ian shifted from one foot to the other. Alinor watched him as, without speaking, he pulled off his bedrobe and reached for the shirt she had laid out. He shook his head at Alinor when she moved to help him, even though she could see some of his motions pulled at the new set of stitches and caused him pain. Hurriedly, Alinor dressed also, distastefully aware that her clothes were dirty and stained and not particularly becoming. She fastened the veil of her wimple and turned to see Ian, his face very still and quite expressionless, start toward the door.

"Ian," she cried softly, "beloved, what is your discontent? I have hurt us both through unadvised silence. Do not you now fall into the same error."

He looked at her blankly for a moment, then lifted his eyes and looked over her head. "My discontent is in myself, Alinor, not in you—except that you have offered me something I desire so much that I cannot trust my judgment on whether it is a good thing or a bad thing. Are you really willing to come to Ireland with me—after all you have said against going? Is what you propose really safe for the children?"

"Yes, of that I am certain. I swear all will be well with Adam and Joanna, barring plague or some accident that is truly in God's hands," Alinor assured him fervently.

"And the other?"

"I am perhaps a little afraid," she replied slowly, "but——"

"Then why do you insist upon coming? As you said yourself, it is a country all at war. Why——"

"I can give you many reasons," Alinor interrupted. "I can tell you how it is less safe for me to be here where John might take me by stealth. I can explain that it would be wise for me to show myself on my Irish estates. I can suggest that if we were more together I might conceive an heir to your lands, which would add to the safety of Adam and Joanna as well as to our joy."

She paused, and Ian saw with considerable surprise that she was blushing hotly.

"Do you want the truth?" Alinor asked.

"Yes, I do," Ian insisted.

Alinor bit her lip. "I am coming because I am jealous," she said passionately. "Simon told me that Irish women are very beautiful. I am not going to let loose a face like yours among them. To couple a whore to satisfy a need is one thing, but I know you do not like whores. To woo an Irish lady is something else again. In Ireland I intend to be by you, to abate your lust and to watch what you do."

For a moment Ian was laughing too hard to answer, but finally he swept Alinor into his arms. "Madwoman," he gasped, kissing her again and again. "Madwoman, there can be no woman more beautiful than you." Then he laughed again for a while. "Thus are great decisions made. Not on right or wrong or deep necessity, but on the whim of jealousy of one headstrong woman. So be it. If the keep at Kemp is ours and if Salisbury and Leicester agree about the children, I will take you to Ireland."

AUTHOR'S NOTE

Although scholarship in the past 30 years has redeemed King John as a king, not even Alan Lloyd in his *Maligned Monarch* (Doubleday: Garden City, N.Y., 1972)—who makes a strong effort—can really explain away the evidence concerning John's unpleasant character. The fact that John was not a bad king in modern terms (in modern terms he was a far better king than Richard) is irrelevant. In terms of the period in which he lived, John was a despicable person, and Richard was a hero. It is hard for us now to understand because, by and large, the difference between the brothers turned upon the word "honor," a term which is not only obsolete at present but very nearly laughable.

Richard was a bad king. He was not only disinclined to the "business" of kingship but also extravagant in everything. He was far too generous in giving away crown property, thus impoverishing the throne and making it dependent upon taxation; he made extravagant vows, like taking the Cross, and fulfilled them to the political and financial detriment of his subjects; he was profligate in war, fighting everyone and anyone who would give him the opportunity. John was none of these things. He was efficient and attentive to the "business" of being a king; he reformed the courts, being very much interested in the law; he was more careful than ungenerous in rewarding those who served him; he fought only when war was forced upon him or when he could foresee a quick and easy victory.

In medieval terms, however, the characteristics we see as failings in Richard were considered virtues; although damaging to those he ruled, the extravagance in war and in giving were "honorable." That John lacked these characteristics was not seen as an advantage. Worse yet, John inherited the fiscal and political disaster Richard left when he died. John was unlucky. He reaped the whirlwind that Richard had sowed, and he did not have the personality for riding whirlwinds.

Modern historians ameliorate John's military incompetence by pointing out that he did win battles and that he often lost them or was forced into retreat by the defection of his supporters. This is true. It is also probably the strongest indictment that can be brought against John's military ability or personality, or both. Never did Richard's nobles refuse to fight or desert him. They believed in him, trusted him, and died for him when he was wrong. Obviously John's did not believe in him, did not trust him, and were not willing to die for him. This behavior was relatively consistent over a period of more than 15 years and must be meaningful. There can be no avoiding the fact that John's subjects did not like him or respect him.

The distaste for King John cannot be traced to political causes, and this seems to induce surprise in modern historians. But the people John reigned over were not historians looking back at the development of a nation. They were concerned with their own codes and mores. The contemporary hatred for John was based not in faults in the king but in "faults" in the man himself. John murdered subjects from time to time—but so did Richard. The difference in the reactions to the act brings us back to the word "honor." Richard murdered his subjects in fits of rage or after open challenge. He did it in person, confessed, and grieved loudly after the act. John murdered by stealth, by the hand of an assassin, and denied complicity. This was "dishonorable."

Moreover, John preyed upon women. In the late 12th and through the 13th century, the status of women was rising; Queen Eleanor (John's mother) had brought the conventions of *amour courtois,* which venerated women and set them up as goddesses, into fashion; this was also the time of the cult of Mary, when the Mother came close to surpassing the Son in religious significance. This does not mean in hard fact that women were really venerated and well treated, but a conscience about them was developing. John did not even pay lip service to this conscience. He starved the wife and young son of William de Braose to death; he seduced and sometimes raped (by political if not physical force) the wives and daughters of his noblemen.

Lloyd points out that John did not have more illegitimate children than other preceding English kings (except Richard, who had none) and therefore claims that his reputation for lechery was unjust. This is nonsense. No one (except possibly a religious fanatic) expected a king, or any other man for that matter, to be chaste. Some were, and were praised for it, but those who were not were criticized very tepidly, if at all. Despite religious fervor, sins of the flesh were not important in medieval times; they were confessed and absolved as a matter of course. There was nothing Victorian in the medieval view of the body and its needs. The number of bastards a man fathered and acknowledged was irrelevant. What gave John a reputation for lechery was the fact that he dishonored "honorable" women, using his power to force compliance.

Worst of all, John did not keep his word. He reneged on promises. Often these were unwise promises, and he was right, in modern terms, to go back upon them. In his own times his behavior was, again, "dishonorable." To the medieval mind an "honorable" disaster was preferable to a "dishonorable" happy outcome. Of course, every man probably sidled around strict honor from time to time. John was simply unlucky or not astute enough to get away with his defections from the code.

In any case, in his own time King John was accused of horror upon horror. It is unlikely he was guilty of all;

it is equally unlikely that there was *no* real cause for the way his people and noblemen felt about him. John was the "evil king" of legend (Robin Hood and others) and the legends began in, or very shortly after, John's reign. These legends were not generated by political considerations (as the legends about "evil" King Richard III were generated by the conquering Tudors), because John's own son reigned after him.

Under the circumstances, I have felt free to make John the "villain" of this book, although I have tried to express the duality of his personality. Because the central characters are fictional, all the machinations against them are, of course, constructed for the purposes of the story and are not real. However, the rumors about the death of John's nephew Arthur (although not the story told by Sir Guy, who is also fictional), of his treatment of William, Earl of Pembroke, and his conflict with the Church and his barons are historical fact. The "evil" characters of Fulk de Cantelu and Henry of Cornhill are, again, contemporary judgments and come from a prejudiced source (Roger of Wendover's *Flowers of History*). These men did the bidding of the king. Fulk disappears from history, but two other de Cantelus and Henry of Cornhill served John's son with honor and distinction. Perhaps Roger of Wendover was unfair to these gentlemen, or perhaps it is true that a "dishonest master makes dishonest servants." All in all, although I may have maligned the latter gentlemen, I do not believe there is any serious inaccuracy in my portrayal of King John.

Certain words, however, have been used anachronistically as a convenience. The word "English," as in English lords, English vassals, and so on, is the most important inaccuracy. These men were, of course, not English at all. Some had English blood, owing to intermarriage of the Anglo-Saxon nobility with the Normans who came with William the Bastard, but each successive king had brought followers from his own provinces. By the time of King John, there were Normans, Angevins, Poitevins, and many others. The mixture was complex, but, by and large, the entire nobility of England in the early 13th century was French. Thus, when the word "English" is used in this book, it means those noblemen whose major estates were in England and who spent most of their time in that country.

The word "fewter" is another convenient inaccuracy. The fewter was a rest for a lance attached to the saddle, which had not been invented in the early 13th century. However the verb form of the word has been used to obviate the necessity for a long, involved phrase describing how a spear was held. A few other similar anachronisms appear, but I ask the reader to remember that styles in clothing and furnishings, in the wording of oaths and challenges, and so on, did not begin or change according to strict dates.

The spelling of names is the final problem I must mention. There were no rules for spelling in medieval times, and when names had to be transliterated from one language to another, difficulties were merely multiplied. For example, the name of the Welsh Prince is Leolin in Roger of Wendover, Llywelyn in the *Oxford History* series, and Llewelyn in the *Encyclopaedia Britannica;* de Cantelu in Roger of Wendover becomes de Canteloupe in the *Dictionary of National Biography;* Alberic in Wendover is Aubery in the *Oxford History* and in the *Encyclopaedia.* Under the circumstances, I have felt free to be arbitrary, choosing the name I preferred for aesthetic reasons.

If more serious errors appear, I would be most grateful to have them called to my attention. Although the "story" is a fiction, a real effort has been made to keep accurate the history that impinges upon it and into which it is set.

R.G.

GLOSSARY OF MEDIEVAL TERMS

BAILEY
: any open area surrounded by the walls of a castle

BAILIFF
: a person charged with administration duties of an estate; the agent who collects and manages an estate or farm for the landlord

CASTELLAN
: the governor or constable of a castle, assigned at the will of the "holder" of the castle and liable to removal at that "holder's" will

DEMESNE
: the land held and possessed by the owner and not rented or controlled by any subordinate, such as a vassal or castellan

DESTRIER
: a war horse, a highly bred and highly trained animal

DISSEISE
: to put out of possession; to dispossess a person so that his legal heirs were also disqualified from inheriting; the term was usually used when the dispossession was wrongful

HAUBERK
: armor; the mail shirt made up of linked rings or chains of metal

INTERDICT
: a sentence issued by a high ecclesiastical officer (bishop, archbishop or pope) who debarred a place or person from church functions

JUSTICIAR
: technically a judge, but one with considerable power

KEEP   innermost, strongest structure or central tower of a castle, the place that served as a last defense; in general used to mean the whole castle

LEECH   a person who treated injuries and sometimes illness, sometimes combining this with the profession of barber; not a learned physician but a doctor of sorts

LEVY   a calling up of men for war or other purposes, the men being those who were required to do military service to "hold" their lands

OFFAL   garbage, refuse

PROVENDER   food, especially dried or preserved, like corn or salt meat and fish

REAVERS   technically those who tear, split and cleave; thus, robbers who use great violence

SQUIRE   a young man in training to be a knight; he attended upon a knight, exchanging personal service (combined valet, secretary, messenger, and bodyguard) in exchange for lessons in manners, fighting techniques and military tactics

TRENCHBUT   a machine of war used for throwing stones; it could be mounted on ships or castle walls or carried

TUN   a large barrel in which wine, ale or beer is stored

VASSAL   a nobleman who held his lands on conditions of homage and allegiance, which included military service, from an overlord

    Vassals might be very great lords who held many large estates from the king or could be minor knights who held one small estate from another nobleman. In any case the tenure of a vassal was permanent and heritable by his children. The property could not be taken away from them legally except for high crimes, such as treason.

VILLEIN   one step above the serf; equivalent to the sharecropper of the early twentieth century
    The villein was a free man (not bound to the land like the serf), but he did not usually own his land.

WIMPLE   a veil of linen or silk worn by women and so folded as to envelop the head, hair, chin, sides of the face and neck

OTHER SELECTIONS
BY —
ROBERTA GELLIS

ROSELYNDE $1.95
(First book of the four-volume saga, THE ROSELYNDE
CHRONICLES) In an era made for men, Alinor is at no
man's mercy. Beautiful, proud and strong-willed, she is
mistress of Roselynde and of her own heart as well—until
she meets Simon, the battle-scarred knight appointed to be
her warden, a man whose passion and wit match her own.
Boldly Alinor defies lionhearted King Richard's command
to marry one of the land-greedy nobles swarming around
her and shrewdly maneuvers through Court intrigues and
alliances to be near the man who has awakened her to
tender yet volatile love. Their struggle to be united against
all obstacles sweeps them from the pageantry of the Royal
Court to a daring Crusade through exotic Byzantium and
into the Holy Land. As they plunge into the events of a
turbulent age, they endure bloody battles, political treach-
eries and heart-rending separations before their love con-
quers time and destiny to live forever.

THE DRAGON AND THE ROSE $1.95
Henry had been hunted, betrayed and attacked by his
political enemies since the day he was born. He had con-
quered his fear of the constant danger surrounding him,
but could he conquer the woman he had agreed to wed—
the woman who represented all he had learned to despise,
the one who would profit most from his death? Fair, beautiful, passionate and clever, Elizabeth had been born of
royal blood and possessed the arrogance and self-control
of a queen. Forced by her mother to marry a man she
abhorred, she went to her marriage bed with head held
high and a heart filled with fear.